Alexander Fullerton, bo
in France, spent the yea
Dartmouth, and the res
under it. His first no
experiences as gunnery and torpedo officer of HM
Submarine *Seadog* in the Far East, 1944–5, in which
capacity he was mentioned in despatches for distinguished service – was published in 1953. It became an
immediate bestseller with five reprints in six weeks. He
has lived solely on his writing since 1967, and he likes
to recall that, working for a Swedish shipping company
at the time, he wrote it in office hours, on the backs of
cargo manifests.

Praise for Alexander Fullerton:

'The prose has a real sense of urgency, and so has the
theme. The tension rarely slackens and the setting is
completely convincing'
Times Literary Supplement

'Impeccable in detail and gripping in impact'
Irish Independent

'Has the ring of truth and the integrity proper to a work
of art'
Daily Telegraph

By Alexander Fullerton

WESTBOUND, WARBOUND

Alexander Fullerton

A *Time Warner* Paperback

First published in Great Britain in 2003 by Little, Brown
This edition published in 2004 by Time Warner Paperbacks

Copyright © Alexander Fullerton 2003

The moral right of the author has been asserted.

A CIP catalogue record for this book
is available from the British Library.

ISBN 0 7515 3480 3

Typeset by Palimpsest Book Production Limited,
Polmont, Stirlingshire
Printed and bound in Great Britain by
Mackays of Chatham plc, Chatham, Kent

Time Warner Paperbacks
An imprint of
Time Warner Book Group UK
Brettenham House,
Lancaster Place
London WC2E 7EN

www.twbg.co.uk

WESTBOUND, WARBOUND

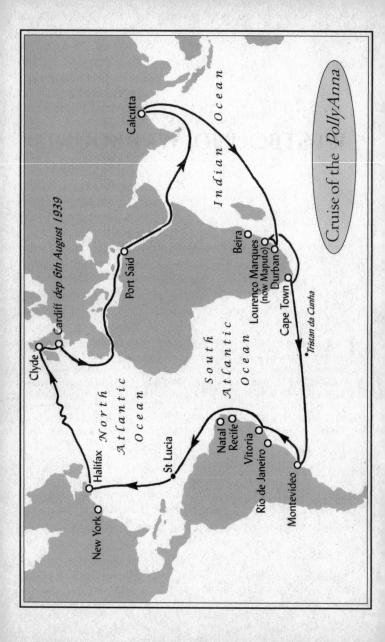

Cruise of the *PollyAnna*

New York · Halifax · Clyde · Cardiff *dep 6th August 1939* · Port Said · Calcutta · Beira · Lourenço Marques (now Maputo) · Durban · Cape Town · Tristan da Cunha · Montevideo · Rio de Janeiro · Vitoria · Recife · Natal · St Lucia

North Atlantic Ocean · *South Atlantic Ocean* · *Indian Ocean*

1

The SS *PollyAnna*, 6,200 gross registered tons and known to her crew more familiarly as the *Anna*, was five days out of Cape Town, bound for Montevideo – best part of 1,500 miles out from the Cape, nearest land Tristan da Cunha – when in the morning watch a lookout spotted a ship's boat appearing and disappearing on the long Atlantic swells a few cables' lengths on the bow to starboard. Dave Halloran, first mate, had this watch, the 0400 to 0800, and after studying the object with binoculars he whistled down the tube to the Old Man, who within seconds came stumping up. Meanwhile, Third Mate Andy Holt, who was due to take over from Halloran at eight and had been in the saloon wolfing down ham and eggs – wolfing because it was seven minutes to the hour and Halloran wasn't a man to be kept waiting for his relief, *his* breakfast – heard from the second wireless officer who'd just blown in that something was going on 'up top', gulped the last of his coffee and shot up there too.

Sun well up, *PollyAnna* under helm, turning her stern out of that already warming orange glow. Rolling harder as she swung beam-on to the blue-black swell. Tending to roll briskly in any case, the 9,000 tons of coal she'd loaded in Lourenço Marques having lowered her centre of gravity to the extent that she was decidedly 'stiff', her holds being nowhere near full, in terms of space. Halloran had sent down for a boat's crew to muster on the starboard side and for the foremost of the two boats that side, the one with the motor, to be turned out ready for lowering. Also for extra lookouts to be sent up. There was after all a war on – and although they hadn't seen anything of it yet in this ship, they were all well aware that German surface raiders were operating here in the South Atlantic. The Old Man had been briefed on this not only in communications from home over the past weeks, but more recently and specifically by the Sea Transport Officer in Cape Town, where they'd called for bunkers and fresh water, and during the past few days the Marconi boys had picked up several distress calls as well as other less easily compre-hensible transmissions: could have been from raiders conversing with their support vessels; could have been Royal Navy ships hunting *them*.

Would hardly have been Germans, anyway. If they'd any gumption at all they'd be keeping their mouths shut. Receiving orders and intelligence, no doubt, from Berlin or wherever, but staying off the air themselves. While the *Anna*'s lookouts would be scanning the horizon primarily for funnel smoke.

Any funnel smoke. At sight of it, turn stern-on and run, had been the Capetonian advice. No especial kudos in braving it out, likely as not being caught and sunk – really none at all. As to one's own smoke – unavoidable to some extent in a coal-burning ship – the engineers had been told that if she showed more than a wisp at her funnel-top between dawn and dusk they'd be bloody keel-hauled.

The ship's boat, though. Upper strakes on its near side had been splintered and holed, most likely by machine-gun fire, and its stern – counter, rudder-post and rudder – was mostly gone too. Half-swamped, rolling sluggishly on the rise and fall of blue-black ocean, kept afloat only by unpunctured flotation tanks, Andy guessed. He'd seen all that within seconds of focusing the old telescope which Don Fisher, second mate, kept in a drawer of the chart table; now it was the boat's contents one gawped at – mentally gagged at. The bodies weren't all intact, not by any means. Explosive shells – pom-poms, Bofors, Oerlikons; whatever raiders used on helpless men in boats – had done that to them. Target practice was what sprang to mind. What else? *Sport?* What other purpose in slaughtering unarmed, defenceless seafarers whose only endeavour by that time could have been to stay alive? The main bulk of the carnage seemed to be in one cohesive waterlogged heap, while looser elements on the fringes, washing heavily to and fro but as of now more or less tethered as well as enclosed by the splintered timber, would as like as not be washed clear out before much longer. Some, and definitely a whole lot of blood, would probably have been washed out already.

No sign of sharks. You'd have thought there would have been. And they were close enough not to need the telescope now. Snapping it shut, with his eyes still on that horror, Andy heard his name spoken, Halloran suggesting to his captain, 'Send Holt, sir?' Holt jerking round and meeting his captain's brief glance. Captain shortish, stocky, approaching sixty years of age, not given to idle chatter or unnecessarily speaking his thoughts aloud; having considered the first mate's suggestion he nodded – might have gone so far as to grunt – reaching a short, thick arm to the binnacle for support against a heavier roll. Another nod, then – 'See if there's life in any of 'em, Holt. And what ship.'

He'd rung down to stop engines by this time, and had port rudder on to turn her starboard side to the boat, forty to sixty yards clear. Grunting to the man at the wheel – Parlance, Able Seaman, red hair and a squint – 'Midships the helm.' Halloran had his glasses on the boat again where it slumped with the seas washing through and over it: not *his* glasses, but the pair that was kept up here for use by the officer of the watch. The Old Man had his own, but that was as far as it went, except for the battered old telescope for which Fisher had paid a few shillings in some pawn shop on Merseyside. The SS *PollyAnna*'s (and several other ocean-going tramp steamers') owners, Messrs

3

Dundas Gore of Glasgow – known in the trade, because of the name Gore, as the Blood Line – were careful men, not addicted to lavish expenditure, especially on gear of a kind that was notoriously liable to disappear.

Andy was on his way down now, hearing Halloran call, 'You too, Janner!' Janner was one of the ship's two cadets – the taller, dusky one who didn't drink, not even when ashore with his fellow cadet, a hairy little ape by name of Gorst. They'd both come from the training ship *Worcester*, on the Thames at Greenhithe – which, as it happened, had been Andy's father's alma mater too, shortly before the '14–'18 war. Despite that personal link to the *Worcester*, the old man had sent Andy to do *his* cadet's time in *Conway*, on the Mersey, from 1932 (when he'd been fourteen) to '34, then on to Blood Line ships, circling the globe one and a half times as a cadet before sitting for his second mate's certificate and getting it at the age of twenty, which was the earliest they'd let you sit for that first one. He was still twenty now, would be twenty-one in three weeks' time, but had been around, knew his onions – most of them anyhow – only until now had never been given any such job as sorting through a mess of dismembered corpses.

Please God, let them all be corpses; not bodies still in the process of becoming such. Wouldn't any live man among that lot be raving mad by now?

War. One's first sight of it. Of its actual detritus – and at close quarters. Just get a grip, boy.

'All right, Bosun.'

Batt Collins was the boatswain. Jockey-like even to the detail of bow legs, and as tough as weathered oak, an ugly little sod with a sheath-knife and a marlin-spike on his belt. Thoroughly decent fellow too. The motorboat was already turned out but held by webbing gripes (or 'bowsings') against the padded griping-spar rigged horizontally between the davits, and a five-man crew standing ready, now at a curt order from the bosun swarming up into it: ABs Martin, Crown, Timms and Shuttleworth, and Hart, a greaser, who'd see to the motor. Andy sent Janner up, then followed; the gripes were knocked off, Senhouse slips allowing instant release, and control against the ship's motion now being by fending off from her grey side with stretchers while checking fore-and-aft swing by crewmen's weight on crossed lifelines. Inboard, three lowerers had moved to each fall and taken turns on the staghead cleats for lowering.

'Lower away!'

Andy's call, echoed by the bosun's snarl: they all knew their business. For'ard and aft in the boat the disengaging gear was in hand: pins out, and at the bosun's order 'Slip!', Collins having judged his moment, she thumped in more or less even-keeled on the rounded crest of a swell and in a sheet of upflying salt. Engine spluttering into life, two of the hands ready with oars in case it hadn't, and the other two fending off, Janner at the helm. At a seemingly immense height above them, Halloran leaning over the bridge rail, watching. Lifting his glasses now, settling them on the other boat again. Andy, like the rest of them, bracing himself against the violent battering motion as the boat sheered away, and yelling to Janner, 'Put her alongside bow to bow – other side, eh?'

Lee side, and for'ard, where the damage was less, where he'd be able to get aboard among them – if he had to.

As it turned out, there'd been no life in any of them – no question of it; couldn't have been for quite some time. There'd been no ship's name or port of registry on the boat either, where you'd have expected one. Not even a part of one single letter where timbers had been smashed. No clues by which to identify either the ship or these former inhabitants of her; no personal gear at all, not even the haversacks you were advised to keep ready-packed with private and personal items – papers, valuables, etc. There might have been some such stuff washing around at some earlier stage, but now there was not. He'd made as thorough an inspection as was possible, from around the lifeboat's sides and over its wrecked stern, had for a short time been in among them, before giving up and telling Janner, 'Nothing.' A jerk of the head towards the ship, then: 'Back . . .' Actually relieved at not having to return with even one still technically 'living' cadaver, assuaging any stirrings of guilt in that relief with the truth that it was also – retrospectively speaking – in these men's own best interests that they'd got it over, known the worst and finished with it.

Three or four days ago, he'd guessed. There'd been gulls around in fair numbers – Arctic terns no doubt among them in these latitudes – but the blood had all been leaked and washed away, so that to a shark the surrounding water might by now be odourless. Which was something the air was *not*, downwind of that boat.

He said to Second Mate Don Fisher a few hours later, Fisher being then in the process of taking over for his own afternoon watch, the noon to 1600 stint, 'Not necessarily the *Admiral Scheer, Deutschland* or *Graf Spee.*' Those were the monster raiders that were reputed to be out here on the loose. 'Could just as well have been one of their so-called armed merchant raiders. More likely, in fact – wouldn't you say?'

'Don't much like the notion, but you could be right.'

Fisher was about twenty-five, a standard-sized, sandy-haired, quiet man, who'd been third mate in the Blood Line's *Burntisland* when Andy had been a cadet in her, so they knew each other well. Not that they wouldn't have in any case, with *PolyAnna* now more than four months out from the Clyde and then Cardiff, where they'd filled her up with coal destined for Port Said. They'd sailed from Cardiff on 6 August; there'd been a lot of war talk, obviously, and frantic preparations for it, despite hopes in some quarters of averting it, but in the meantime ships couldn't be left idle or valuable freights passed up, so it was Cardiff coal to Egypt, then in ballast to Calcutta to load manganese ore for Durban. But having been shipmates before did make a difference: Andy certainly knew Fisher a great deal better than he knew Halloran, a cold-eyed bastard who'd as it were sprung from nowhere, performing what was known colloquially as a 'pierhead jump' into *PollyAnna* a day before she'd left Gourock; he hadn't set foot on any Blood Line ship before, only at the last minute replaced the old first mate (Harve Brown, with whom Andy and Fisher *had* sailed before) when he'd keeled over with a heart ailment and been carted off to a Glasgow hospital. Old Harve had survived, so the skipper had heard from the owners when they were in Calcutta, but might never get to sea again.

Fisher had felt uneasy around Halloran from the start. More so than Andy had. Oil and water, those two – Fisher quiet and thoughtful, one might even say 'reserved', while the first mate was surly, overbearing and reputedly over-ready with his fists. That had been no more than hearsay – he *looked* it, and had that snarling, raw-edged manner, but this could have been about as much as there was to it – until an incident ashore in Calcutta ten weeks ago, since when one had known it for a fact. At any rate he, Andy Holt, knew it. Wished he didn't – all the more so for the victim having been a girl. A puzzling angle there being that the man had an absolute stunner of a wife. There was a portrait of her in his cabin: knockout, absolutely. A good ten years younger than him: Halloran was thirty-one, by his looks could have been nearer forty, and had confided – boasted, more or less – that she was ten years his junior, which made her pretty well the same age as Andy. He'd found himself becoming more than somewhat attracted to her, catching himself sneaking looks at her picture until caught in the act – by Halloran, of course, who'd seemed more than anything amused – or contemptuous? – and he'd realised it was something he'd better watch. Not only in relation to the distant and of course totally inaccessible Mrs Halloran – which in the circumstances hadn't been *too* difficult – but also in general terms, renewal of resolutions made on one or two previous occasions in the light of (a) what he knew by now of his own propensities, and (b) advice received from time to time from his father –

who was a Master Mariner and a commander in the Royal Naval Reserve, had been running or helping to run defence course for Merchant Navy men since 1937, and who had very recently landed himself a seagoing job as second in command of an armed merchant cruiser. That news had come in a gloomy letter from Andy's mother, when *PollyAnna* had been in Calcutta. An overlong stay, the Calcutta call had turned out to be.

Anyway, the old man's advice on the subject of girls and so forth had been delivered in instalments over the years, varying from 'Get your boozing and whoring done before you're thirty, boy' to '*Never* play around with another man's wife. *Never*, Andy! You're getting to be a big, good-looking fellow, they'll be after you – lots of 'em will – but do yourself a favour, lad, tie a bloody knot in it if you have to!' He'd obviously been talking from experience, going by his adamance, the note of urgency in that warning, and as it happened Andy did know for sure that when the old man – his father, Charlie Holt – had married his mother, Amanda, she'd already been pregnant with him – *him*, Andy. He'd come to suspect it a long time ago, and at the age of about fifteen had been able to research it in the family archives, namely a locked tin trunk in which such things as marriage and birth certificates were stashed away. The old man's mates' and master's certificates too, and Admiralty notifications of the two Distinguished Service Crosses he'd won in '14–'18. As to the other business, though, that discovery – or confirmation – had intrigued him more than bothered him, largely because another thing he'd had no doubt of was that at the time of their marriage and his birth his parents had been wildly, recklessly in love. They were proud of it, boasted of it, revelled in the memory – especially after a few drinks, at times of celebration such as anniversaries – and he, Andy, unquestioningly accepted it as justifying the fact that only by a whisker had he avoided being born a bastard.

1918 had been the year, June the marriage, and 20 December Andy's birthday. From later stages he also remembered domestic flurries, periods of tension at intervals during the course of his own childhood, which he guessed in his father's own hindsight must have provoked the advice about giving other men's wives a wide berth; the old man not having done so, one might assume. This too was therefore genuine and relevant, to be accepted and paid heed to, coming as it did from a man whom one both loved and respected. Would keep it in mind, therefore, and as far as Mrs Halloran was concerned, in the last month or two when visiting the first mate in his cabin – with a message or a report to make, or for an answer to some query – he'd managed not to glance too often at the girl's portrait in its leather frame.

She *was* a stunner, though. Knowing now what sort of man Halloran was, it was astonishing that any girl with her looks should ever have let him within a mile of her – or stayed within a mile of him.

Didn't have to now, of course. Already four months apart, and bound to be for several more. Having herself a good time, perhaps? Did look as if she might. The thought had begun to take hold, rather – lubriciously, and involving *him*. Halloran here, himself *there*.

Fisher was saying – on that other subject, whether the Huns responsible for that floating butcher's shop might have been in a *merchant* raider – 'Perhaps more likely. If you're thinking on the lines that that'd make 'em a crowd of roughnecks? Blokes like us?'

'Not at all like us, thank you very much. Who's a roughneck anyhow? I'm not, you're not' – a jerk of the head, then – 'and *he's* not.' Meaning the seaman who'd taken over as helmsman a few minutes ago. Ingram, by name. Thick greying hair, craggy features. Admittedly, some of them did look rough – some to a fairly high degree – but by and large they were as right as rain, or as the master, Josh Thornhill, had more than once observed, 'Every inch as good as God made 'em,' Andy went on, 'Whereas Germans – coming back to that – well, Nazis, and merchant raiders with hidden guns sailing under false colours, aren't

9

they. Predators, and on the sly at that. And look here – they'd have a crew of say forty or fifty, might be, what, thirty hands on deck to see a thing like that boatload being murdered? But then a battleship like *Graf Spee* – Christ, there'd be a couple of hundred witnesses!'

'Secondary puzzle, to me' – Fisher pondering this in his quiet voice – 'why they'd leave the evidence floating around for all to see.'

'Reckoning on it sinking by this time. And on sharks maybe. But evidence – the kind *I* was looking for – must have been deliberately destroyed. Else there'd have been *some* damn thing!'

'They'd have a biggish problem what else to do. Weight each body so it'd sink? Time'd be a factor, wouldn't it. After a sinking, no raider'd want to hang around. Especially if the victim had got a distress call out. But just sugar off and leave that lot to mark the spot?'

'Some special circumstance. Look, not the ship that did the sinking – another one, say – if it had found 'em adrift and –'

'Christ.' A shake of the head. 'If you'd seen it close up –'

'Glad I didn't.' Fisher had the glasses up, scanning the horizon ahead and down the starboard side. Glancing at Andy again, then: 'Hadn't you better go down and eat?'

'I suppose I had.' He checked the time and nodded. 'Then a one-to-three.' Meaning a couple of hours with his head down. 'Lucky bugger, ain't I?' Asking as he moved away, 'What's on the menu? Still on the Cape Town beef, are we?'

Fisher would have had his own meal at about half-eleven. As second mate he was the navigator, and having to take over the watch at twelve he'd been in one of the bridge-wings in good time to take a meridian altitude of the sun. A matter of routine – and a sweat for young Gorst, the chimp-like cadet who was at the chart table now, wrestling with calculations. He wasn't good at it, and Fisher was giving him every chance of becoming so by keeping his snout to the grindstone. Navigational expertise of a high order was the norm for all deck officers – it had to be. The skipper took his own sights – morning stars, as often as not – and Fisher having taken his noon altitude would also be taking evening stars at twilight – as would Andy, although it wasn't actually his job, only normal practice in the Merchant Navy, a matter of keeping one's hand in. He usually came up for morning stars as well. Routine – up at dawn, then below to shave and breakfast, back up again for the eight to twelve. Life might not be such plain sailing for much longer, he realised. That boat, for one thing – he'd have *that* in his mind's eye as long as he lived, he guessed. Except maybe there'd be worse to come, sights and experiences to put that one in the shade. In fact there probably would . . . The Old Man had expressed it well enough, when they'd been steadying on a course of 270 degrees due west out of Table Bay five days ago; he'd said to Hibbert – *PollyAnna*'s outsize chief engineer, who'd come up to report on the maintenance job they'd been working on while in Cape Town, and had stayed up there at the skipper's invitation to smoke a pipe and watch the sun go down in a sky-filling flush of scarlet – 'Our back-door entrance to the war, you might call it, Chief. Where it starts for us, this time around.' Putting it like that because those two had both been in the last war – the Old Man with his master's ticket even then.

2

Cardiff to Port Said had taken sixteen days, *PollyAnna* arriving there on the forenoon of 22 August. Discharging her coal had occupied another ten days, during which time the approach of war had been swift and sure. Virtually as she secured alongside on the coaling wharf the BBC was reporting Neville Chamberlain's warning to Hitler that Britain would stand by Poland, and on the day she entered the canal – in ballast, late on 1 September – Germany invaded Poland. Due to congestion in the canal's lower reaches it was necessary to spend a night at anchor off Ismailia in Lake Timsah, and getting underway again in the early hours of 2 September, the BBC was announcing the call-up of all males aged from nineteen to forty-one. And children were being evacuated from London and other cities, in expectation of bombing and perhaps the use of poison gas. Then on the 3rd – a Sunday, when *PollyAnna* had left the canal and Port Tewfik astern, and was ploughing south through a dead-flat calm in the Gulf of Suez – Chamberlain's broadcast to the nation at 1100 GMT had told them that Britain and Germany were at war.

By way of confirmation, a U-boat sank the Glasgow liner *Athenia* off the Irish coast that same evening, with the loss of more than a hundred lives, including those of a number of Americans. Shaw, third engineer, commented in the saloon next day, 'Bring the Yanks in, sure as eggs'; and the Old Man, who had a lot of friends in New York and other

US ports had growled, 'Nothing sure about it. There's a lot don't want in at any price.' Sure enough, before they were out of the Red Sea, President Roosevelt had made a declaration of neutrality.

The Red Sea, as always, was as hot as hell, but the job of sluicing the coal dust out of the ship's holds couldn't be postponed. Gulf of Aden then, out of it between Cape Guardafui and Socotra, and from there a reach of about 1,600 miles to pass around Ceylon into the Bay of Bengal. Another thousand miles, that stretch; they'd met and spoken to a dozen or more other Red Ensign ships, and war news had been coming in continually. At such a distance from it, and getting further away at every turn of the ship's big single screw, and still in pursuit of her normal trade, one had an uneasy feeling of having turned one's back on it; and the BBC, one knew, wouldn't necessarily be mentioning the worst. Ships other than the *Athenia* would have been sunk by this time and some proportion of their crews would have drowned; you could bet that wouldn't have been the only U-boat on its war station in the Atlantic before the balloon went up. Which brought to Andy's mind the one bone of contention that existed between him and his father. From *Conway* or *Worcester*, or for that matter Pangbourne, one could have gone to sea with the RN as a junior officer of the Royal Naval Reserve. It was what his father had done in 1914 and what most of his own *Conway* friends had opted for this time. Whereas Andy had made his mind up to stick to what he'd gone in for in the first place and been trained for, at *Conway* and then at sea.

His father had challenged him with, 'What's wrong with serving in a *fighting* ship, for God's sake?'

'Nothing at all. Happens I'm a *Merchant* Navy officer, that's all!'

'When it's all over you could go back to that if you wanted to. Or switch to a permanent commission maybe – if they'd have you. Meanwhile, the RN needs all the sea-trained men it can get. Chaps like you, Andy!'

'To man escorts protecting Atlantic convoys.'

'Not only Atlantic – *all* the ocean routes.'

'So who'll man – officer – the merchant ships?'

'Chaps who're doing it already, lad!'

He'd stuck to his guns. 'I happen to think it's a job worth doing. Why I wanted to do it in the first place. I like it – *enjoy* it – and it feels – well, worthwhile. In a lot of ways it's what I already am – and want to be. Basically, I suppose, a seaman.'

His mother had come into the room, heard that bit and put *her* oar in.

'It's the fighting men who get the respect, Andy.'

He'd looked at her, thinking, *You'd like to be able to say your son's an officer in a destroyer or a battleship. You'd never want to admit he's in a tramp steamer. That's all it is with you, Mama . . .*

Always had been, he realised. Not that one could blame her for it: it was simply how she was. She'd gone along with his entry to *Conway* because cadets from there didn't *have* to graduate into the Merchant Navy: there was a stage at which you could transfer to the RN college at Dartmouth, if you were up to it and wanted to; there was also an entry scheme to the Royal Air Force. And the old man could hardly have objected, having been a *Worcester* cadet himself, pre-1914. Although he still might have – with maybe some slight interest in social climbing under his own salt-stained skin, however furiously he'd have denied it. But he hadn't, and there hadn't therefore been a damn thing *she* could have done about it, not without insulting her husband, *his* background – which she must have accepted wholeheartedly – or blindly – when she'd married him. The old man must have assumed that when it came to war, or as close to war as it had come by that time, Andy would follow in his footsteps, Dad having been a war hero in '14–'18. He'd flown airships, for God's sake. Had started off in a minesweeper or some such, seen the navy's dirigibles hunting U-boats in the Channel, and got himself transferred into the Royal Naval Air Service to fly those

14

contraptions. One DSC had been for sinking a U-boat –
which he'd said had been pure luck and as easy as falling
off a log – and the bar to it for an operation behind enemy
lines, bringing out some female spy, a Belgian girl; he'd
described that as 'the dickens of a lark'.

It was no small matter, though, this difference between
them. Andy was close to his father, always had been; he
looked quite like him and, generally speaking, *thought* like
him, but on this issue he wasn't giving way. No question
of it. Couldn't understand why the old man felt as strongly
as he seemed to – unless, as with his wife, it *was* the social
thing, the *class* thing. Or, to give him the benefit of the
doubt, it might have been in respect of *her* feelings – to
keep her happy and family relationships on an even keel.
Which in fact Andy himself would have liked to have been
able to do, but simply couldn't. His sister Annabel, three
years his junior and now training as a nurse, understood
and applauded. But another exchange he and his father
had had on the subject had stuck in his mind, and he
often thought about it, although he wouldn't have dreamt
of mentioning it to anyone else. It was the last time they'd
discussed the matter, in fact. Newly-qualified Third Mate
Andy Holt face to face with Commander Charlie Holt
DSC* RNR, and both as it so happened in uniform –
reason for this being that it had been 11 November 1938,
not only Armistice Day but the twentieth anniversary of
that first war's end, and there'd been a big turnout and
parades on Clydeside as well as everywhere else. And after
it, at home in Helensburgh, there they were – one rather
grand, the other distinctly less so. (His mother had told
him he looked like a bus conductor.) But Charlie Holt's
hands grasping Andy Holt's shoulders – close, face to face,
and a slight up-angle in the contact; Andy did bear a
distinct resemblance to his father, but stood a couple of
inches over six feet while Charlie was only five-eleven.
Charlie demanding quietly in his low, growly voice,
'Imagine how it'll be in the Atlantic convoys? How it was
last time – when, as I've told you, the country damn near

starved?' A shrug of his heavy shoulders: 'Told you often enough, I dare say. Doesn't seem so damn long ago either. But this time it'll be worse – most likely a lot more U-boats, bigger and faster at that, and God knows what in the way of weaponry!'

'But convoy escorts will be more numerous and effective, too – better anti-submarine weaponry as well?'

'Wouldn't count on it, boy. At least not in the early stages. We haven't a fraction of what we need. I wouldn't go around saying this, and don't quote me, but the plain truth is we're going to be well and truly up against it, your lot probably worse than any. We'll get the better of them in the end – bloody *have* to – that or starve, be starved into surrender, that'll be their aim . . .'

'Saying I'll be more of an Aunt Sally on a freighter's bridge than I would be on a destroyer's?'

The old man let go of him. 'Saying nothing of the sort.' He'd turned away. 'But it's going to be tough all round – and if you had any damn sense at all—'

He'd cut himself short. Glancing back briefly, then away again. And to Andy's mother as she joined them, 'Old for his years, is this lad's trouble. Doesn't look it, but he is. Cat that walks by itself, uh?' At which she'd snorted and asked them both, 'And where does he get *that* from, would you say?'

That *was* what he'd been saying, though, and they'd both known it. Effectively he'd been telling his son that he'd have a better chance of survival in a fighting ship than he would in a merchantman. And when you thought about it, it made a kind of sense, merchant ships – or to be precise their cargoes – being the enemy's prime targets.

PollyAnna had docked in Calcutta on 16 September. There was more awaiting them than the cargo of manganese ore; the ship was to be painted battleship-grey, obliterating her hitherto black hull and white upperworks and the blue bands on her funnel, and she was to have a twelve-pounder gun mounted on her poop, the poop itself needing to be strengthened for this and a steel gun-deck built on it. Similar things were happening to half a dozen other steamers in the port, while an Ellerman passenger-liner was being converted for service as an AMC – armed merchant cruiser. In *PollyAnna*'s case, painting-ship would be the first job, while she was high in the water: her deep-tanks (ballast) would be pumped out, scaling, chipping and painting would start at the waterline and be done by her own crew simultaneously with the loading of the ore, and by the time it was finished she'd be pretty well at the head of the queue for the engineering job aft – another week's work, at least.

Andy's father, his mother had written, had been appointed second in command of the armed merchant cruiser HMS *Andalusia*, 14,000 tons . . .

Of course he's overjoyed. She has a four-stripe Royal Navy captain, and a team of gunnery experts, and flies the White Ensign, but most of her officers and crew are the same Merchant Navy men who were serving in her under the red one. They sign on under some special form of agreement. Does Voluntary Emergency Agreement mean anything to you? Anyway, fifty or sixty liners are being converted in this way, he tells me, in about a dozen different ports all over the world, but the *Andalusia* was one of the first to be taken over and it seems will be off quite soon now. I and Annabel are the only ones who are <u>not</u> cheering. Off <u>where</u>, you ask, and although I shouldn't put it in a letter, I will, and you can tear it up when you've read it – better still, when you've answered it. Anyway, they'll be joining something called the Northern Patrol, patrolling between the Faeroes (spelling?) and Iceland and in the Denmark Strait – wherever that is. You'd know, I'm sure. I made a few notes when he told me about it, so I could tell you when I wrote, although like everything else now it's hush-hush. So not only tear this up, remember you don't know anything about it until HE tells you – when you write, I mean, which I hope and pray you will do, some time in the next fifty years?

17

Annabel, let me tell you – also in strict confidence – has a new boyfriend. I might add, in the <u>real</u> navy – or something like it. She's at home at the moment, sends her love . . .

During *PollyAnna*'s three-week stay in the heat and bedlam of Calcutta – temperature often higher than eighty in the shade, and extremely humid – Russia invaded Poland from the east while the Germans were blitzkrieging in from the west, and before the end of the month – September, still – the Germans were in Warsaw (as much as might be left of it) and they and the Soviets had formally agreed to split the country between them. And on the 17th, the aircraft-carrier *Courageous* was sunk by a U-boat in the Western Approaches – with the loss of more than 500 men, as well as one of the navy's most valuable ships; and a British Expeditionary Force of something like 160,000 men had been deployed in France.

Among the things that were *not* known at that time – not even to the Admiralty – was that the German pocket-battleship *Admiral Graf Spee* had sailed from Wilhelmshaven on 21 August, slipping away into the Atlantic under cover of darkness. Her support-ship *Altmark* had preceded her, and the pocket-battleship *Deutschland* and her support-ship the *Westerwald* had followed a few days later.

On 20 September the loading of manganese was completed and the *Anna* was shifted to an inner dockyard berth for the gun-deck to be built on to her poop, and that evening First Mate Halloran invited Andy and Don Fisher to a sundowner in his cabin, then maybe a run ashore – which could apply only to Andy, since Fisher was duty officer that night. A whisky called King's Legend was the drink; Andy had wondered often enough how Halloran could afford it – and especially the frequency of his shore-going – a mate's pay not being all that terrific – three or four hundred a year maybe, plus war bonus, if and when that began coming through – and guessed he must have money of his own somewhere, somehow. You wouldn't have thought he had – from his style, and so forth – but – well, his business, no one else's, and he was a strange character in a lot of ways. Anyway, he'd given his reasons for celebrating on this particular evening as (a) completion of loading, and (b) having had a letter that day from his wife, Leila, which had bucked him up no end.

'Don't hear from her all that often.' A shift of black eyes towards her portrait. Andy and Fisher looked at it too: it would have seemed churlish not to. Halloran adding, 'Fuck it, I don't write *her* all that frequent. I wasn't looking for a pen-pal, was I?' A wink at Andy. 'Get my drift?'

He'd let that go; only asked – for something to say – 'OK, is she?'

One eyebrow cocked; 'Doesn't she look OK to you?'

'Looks – fantastic. Only –'

'Only what, then?'

'I meant her letter – well and happy, or missing you, no doubt –'

'Want to read what she says about missing me – *what* she misses?'

'Well – no – Christ's sake –'

'You wouldn't believe it. Doesn't hold much back, that kid, calls a spade a bloody spade. What's *more*—'

Fisher cut in – flatly, expressionlessly – 'What a lucky man you are.' Making it plain he didn't want to hear 'what was *more*'. Glancing at Andy; getting a hostile stare from Halloran and ignoring it, draining his glass and putting it down close to the lovely Leila's portrait. A nod: 'Thanks for that. Enough for me, though. Good Scotch though it is.' Checking the time: 'Fact is, I'll be getting to grips with a wad of chart corrections – which I might have left to young Gorst, but –'

'Whisky wouldn't help with that, you're right. However . . .' Reaching to replenish Andy's glass and his own. 'Next item on the agenda then – you game for a run ashore, Holt?'

What he'd planned on, obviously; they couldn't all three have gone ashore, and he wouldn't have wanted Fisher's company in any case. He added, 'Happens I know an address or two – one in particular, if it's still there. Up to it, are you?'

'Well.' Andy had shrugged. 'Why not. About time I streched my legs.'

'Stretch more 'n *them*, lad!'

Halloran must have had a tot or two before they'd joined him, Andy thought, and down-town he insisted on having a few more in a bar where they were joined by two of the ship's wireless officers and the second mate of an Anchor Line steamer. Those three had been on beer all evening, and Andy was taking it as easily as he could – for reasons of economy as well as not much wanting to get drunk, especially in view of the evening as planned – but Halloran was well on his way, had been buying himself doubles while giving them a tedious account of how he'd come to be available for the mate's job in *PollyAnna*. He'd worked mostly on tankers in earlier years – the depression years, in which there'd been twice as many merchant seamen thronging dockyard streets as treading ships' decks – but all right, he'd been lucky, maybe hadn't realised *how* lucky; he'd got his first mate's certificate – which you needed before you could be taken on as a second mate – and then after the statutory period of sea service, his master's ticket, which after another couple of years at sea would have qualified him for a first mate's job if there'd been one going, but which in the tanker line when that time came there hadn't been.

'Case of dead men's shoes, I suppose.'

'You'd suppose damn right . . .'

The others were at most half-listening by this time, but Andy had some interest in it – having thought about tankers, off and on, and anyway he didn't want to offend the man. He prompted, 'So you pulled out, eh?'

'Not just like that. Want to know where the next meal's coming from, don't you? The way it was then, you did. By God, you did . . . No, I hung on a while. I'm thirty-one years of age – you know that?'

He nodded. 'You mentioned.'

'So then, late twenties . . . But I tell you – tankers – not all beer an' skittles. Quick turn-rounds is the worst – load and unload so quick, hardly time to dip your wick and you're away again. What's more, the tanker berth is bloody miles out of town, often as not – go ashore, where are you? So I'm thinking, *might* make a change, and so happens I get to know the marine super of Grant Shipping – Glasgow. You'd know, the tartan funnels, cargo liners? Seemed there was a future there – first mate's berth at that, tailor-made. I go for it – *wham*, I got it – two-year contract. *And* run into a bit of good luck financially – for a bloody change . . . Well – cut this short, there's a young lady I'm taken with.' He nodded to Andy: 'Yeah. *Her*. So a year back, we made it legal – she being over twenty-one –'

'Thought she was twenty-one now.'

'She is – end of this month she's—'

'Year older than me, that makes her.'

'And I'm counting on regular employment with Grant Shipping, so seven, eight months back I moved her up to Clydeside. Greenock. *She* found the semi we got now – renting, mind, and it's still an arm and a leg, but there we are – home of our own, steady job, prospects of command – looked to be, and *should*'ve been – and all Clyde-based. Well – steady job, my arse! Renewal of contract time, fuckers don't want to know. Marine super's retired, new sod don't give a damn. I'm out, *finish* – rent to pay, wife to keep –'

'Hard cheese.' Dewar, the chief wireless officer. Pasty-faced and flabby-looking, but all right, quite a decent sort. Scotsman, bachelor, came from Crieff in Perthshire. Halloran telling him, 'So happens by this time I'm not stuck for a bob or two, thank my stars things aren't as they were – which I can tell you –'

'Lucky feller, then.' Dewar sucking at his beer, others nodding, Halloran insisting, 'Point is, if I *had* still been on my uppers' – the forefinger jabbing, black stones of eyes malevolent, tone condemnatory – 'been finished, wouldn't

21

I. And what *that* amounts to is never trust fucking owners. *Never!*' Tossing his whisky back: he'd sworn it was raw spirit but had still managed to down a few. He was blinking at Andy now: 'On our way, then?'

They drifted out. No great surprise that none of the others wanted to tag along: Dewar catching Andy's glance, raising his eyebrows, Andy shrugging . . . Halloran then starting again on how badly Grants of Glasgow had treated him; Andy cut in with, 'Food now, eh?'

'Bugger *food*!'

'I want some anyway. Sorry, but—'

'You bloody piking, Holt?'

'Something to eat, that's all,' he added, into the mate's glare of contempt, black eyes half hidden in narrowed sockets but still gleaming, snake-like, their darkness matching the short crinkly black hair and blue-black jaw: he never looked as if he'd shaved since yesterday. Andy telling him relaxedly – aiming for that effect at any rate – '*First*, eat. All right?'

'If you want to duck out, sonny boy –'

'I said, I don't. Hungry, that's all.' The mate had been facing him with his fists clenched and shoulders bunched during this exchange, and he'd remembered again that someone had said – in Cardiff, it must have been – that he was a sight too ready to lash out. Even more so when stinking of whisky? Unless it was bluff and bullshit when it didn't look to him like a walkover? He was calming now, anyway; Andy assuring himself that this was nothing to back away from. He was a stone lighter, maybe, but also younger, taller by three or four inches, had the reach and knew how to use it, had boxed for *Conway* against various other institutions – he'd acquired a bit of a reputation, even. Could risk insisting on satisfying his hunger therefore – hunger *first* . . . 'How about curry? Speciality in these parts, isn't it?'

They had beer with it. Andy had thought this might have finished Halloran off, but if anything it seemed to sober him a little. And he – Andy – paid the bill, since the mate was making no move to and it had been at his own insistence they'd come here anyway – but it left him distinctly short, and in the gharry, clopping though the dark to wherever Halloran had told the man to take them, he asked how much the rest of it was going to cost them.

It did actually matter. As a Blood Line third mate his pay was £120 a year. On top of which there was now to be this much talked-about war bonus of £10 a month – doubling that income, which would be really *something* – but it hadn't actually manifested itself yet, and until it did he wasn't spending it.

Halloran muzzily and belatedly caught on to what he'd asked.

'You mean Queeny's?'

'If that's what it's called.'

'Cost *you* fuck-all, old son. My shout – eh?'

'No – thanks, very generous, but –'

'You paid for the curry, *I* pay for the –'

The alliteration made him explode with laughter. Andy trying to quieten him down, embarrassed by the bawling of obscenities into the sweaty, odorous night, and telling him all right, but strictly as a loan, he'd repay him when they got back on board; Halloran shaking his head, guffawing intermittently and repeating that line over and over until the gharry driver pulled his scrawny old horse down from a trot to a walk and stopped at the entrance to a stucco'd building in what looked like a business section of the town. There was a sliding metal security gate and a turbanned guard who clashed it open and salaamed to them, and had clashed it shut again by the time they reached Queeny's mahogany front door.

Queeny wasn't Indian, she told them, she was Iranian. She wore a strikingly decorative as well as revealing sari and sat at an ornate desk in a large reception room strewn with carpets and furnished with sofas and armchairs. As Halloran and Andy entered from a curving flight of stone stairs under coloured-glass chandeliers, two male attendants who might also have been Iranian – or Indian – rose and bowed, then leant against the wall on each side of double doors at that far end, while Queeny came slinkily from behind the desk and squeezed Halloran's and then Andy's hands, managing somehow to stroke as well as squeeze, telling them that they were fortunate, this was so far an exceptionally quiet night; in what way might she have the pleasure of being of service? Halloran muttering, with an elbow into Andy's ribs, that they hadn't come to have their teeth pulled; then, having raised no laugh, staring at her down his nose and adding, 'Two prettiest girls you got. Prettiest for me, runner-up for this sahib.' Andy looking around and taking it all in: the decor, furnishings, the woman's purring voice and opulent, silk-wrapped figure, and the two men leaning with their arms folded and eyes almost as dark as Halloran's – as hooded, too. The woman murmuring meanwhile that she'd been assured – oh, many, many times – that *she* was by far the prettiest, while as for the skills born of experience and artistry as well as passionate nature and womanly inclination—

'*Young* girls is more to my liking.' She'd shrugged. *His* loss, not hers. She called some instruction in God only knew what language to the attendants, one of whom slid out of the room. Andy came back from studying a picture of naked Persian girls with a sex-crazed satyr to find that the subject under discussion now was money; Halloran had counted some out but was keeping it in his hand until he saw what he'd be offered. Queeny glancing at Andy: 'You are paying for this gentleman also?'

'Sure.' A wide grin. 'He paid for the curry, I pay for—'

He'd checked himself – open-mouthed, gazing at the girl they'd brought to him. Indian – probably – and no more than fifteen. Sweet-faced, small and tiny-waisted, with surprisingly large breasts, all of her visible through the diaphanous material of her garment. Halloran finding his voice again, grating, 'Oh, yes. *Hell,* yes!' and dropping the handful of rupee notes on Queeny's desk. Andy had a girl beside him too, smiling up at him. Slanted eyes, skin the colour of oiled teak, full lips . . . 'You come, big boy?' She wasn't as young as the other – which was just as well: despite that little one's provocative physical endowment it would have felt like copulating with a child – and this one was extremely attractive – actually, more so – and there he was, slightly but not at all obviously drunk, with an arm around her now and one of hers around his waist, moving towards the double doors Halloran and *his* girl had gone out of.

She was heaven, this one. Truly was. All right, so he'd been very much taken with her at first sight, but it had never occurred to him that a whore in a brothel would be – could be – as she was. As – well, no other word for it – as *loving*. Then it was over, his time up too damn soon – his fault, mostly – and reality, the plain commercialism as clear as a bell in her bright 'Come see me again, big boy?' He was trying to delay it a little, telling her how terrific she was and that he really *liked* her, when a colossal shindy broke out in the next room or the corridor or both: a female shriek, door crashing open, Halloran roaring obscenities over the girl's screams, then other voices too, as well as thumps and glass or china shattering. Andy's own girl wide-eyed, rigid, seemingly in shock, wrapping herself up while pointing at his discarded clothes and squealing, 'Hurry, hurry!' and 'Your friend, your *friend*!' Halloran had gone for that child with his fists, allegedly; this one screaming, 'He *striking* her!' – having heard it in all that yelling, Andy assumed – not doubting the truth of it either. She – the little one – was still inside her room, although its door had been flung open and slammed a couple of times, Queeny out of it again now, wailing, Andy's girl staying put like the other – standing orders presumably for any such emergency situation – but sending Andy out half-clothed and with his shoes in his hands, head buzzing, trousers on and pulled up, shirt flapping loose – finding himself then face to face with Halloran who had a male attendant clinging to each of his arms and his trousers around his ankles. The girl must have sounded an alarm of some kind to bring them all running, and Queeny must have left Halloran to be hauled out by these two while she'd been seeing to the kid; howling now over Halloran's bellows of protest – indignation? – 'I call police! You *filthy* man!'

Andy began, 'Hey, Dave –' and Halloran'd swung round, getting one arm free at that moment and stooping sideways to drag his trousers up, shouting, 'Bitch pulled a bloody knife on me!' The attendants had got him moving anyway – or the mention of police had – and Queeny was now out in the corridor, preceding them mostly backwards towards the reception room, counter-claiming – to Andy – that his friend had puked over the girl and when she'd tried to get away from him he'd begun hitting her; if she'd as much as touched a knife it would have been only in self-defence. Fingers to her own cheekbones, wailing, '*Here*, skin broken, so hard he strike her!' Andy didn't doubt this was the truth, because it was in character: Halloran *looked* like it, *was* like it. Shouting as those two quite skilfully forced him through into the reception room, 'Who pays the fucking piper calls the fucking tune – right? Take your fucking hands off me, Sambo!' He'd flung that one off him again and near-missed with a back-hander at the other, Andy managing to get past them then, to urge the woman, 'Please, no police. I'll take him. He's just drunk, he—'

'Yes, you take! Not come back, not *ever*!' Addressing the attendants then in rapid Iranian or Bengali, Hindi, whatever it was they spoke, while Andy urged Halloran to calm down and come on, get the hell out before she changed her mind. Didn't want to end up in police cells, did they . . .

'We could take these two, easy. You and me, make fucking *mincement* –'

'And end up in cells. Not on your life. Come on . . .'

Halloran panting like a dog, staring at him: getting his brain to work, maybe. He'd ceased to struggle and those two were cautiously disengaging themselves from him. You could smell vomit on his breath. So that bit of it was true. But it was a reasonable guess that Queeny wouldn't want the police in here, especially as the kid was almost certainly under age; if in Calcutta there was such a thing as under age. She was saying something now about compensating the young lady for her injuries; Andy told her firmly – sure that he was right, that the last thing she'd want was a police doctor examining the girl-child – 'No money. He gave you about all he had, we need some for a gharry and I've none at all. I'm sorry she was hurt, but –'

Halloran growled, 'Shouldn't't've pulled a knife, should she. Had it under the donkey's breakfast.' Donkey's breakfast being foc'sl slang for mattress. They were on the stairway by this time, lurching down with the attendants following, panting from their exertions and keeping out of range of Halloran's fists. The mahogany door then – Andy pulled it open and one of them called through to the man on the gates to open up. This time, no salaams. Andy asked Halloran, outside, 'She pull the knife before or after you hit her?'

3

This now was 2 December. Andy had taken morning stars and had a good fix from them; Don Fisher as navigating officer had been up there too, of course, and Halloran, who as always had that morning watch, the four to eight. The Old Man had arrived on the bridge while they were busy with their sextants on the wing; he'd only turned in at about three or half-past, Fisher said, would have come up again in the first light of dawn because in that half-hour or so as the stars faded and the horizon cleared was a time you might see smoke or even a warship's fighting-top. Might, but please God would not. There was a surface raider about though, for sure. One indication being the boat with the bodies in it five days ago, and another, several distress calls the wireless officers had picked up since then. None of them seemingly very close, as far as they – Messrs Dewar, Starkadder and Clowes – had been able to tell. You didn't always get a position with the call for help, and without it could only estimate very roughly how near or far it had been by the strength of the signal, the operators' judgement of that. The raider invariably ordered his victim: *Do not use your wireless,* and had his own operators listening out, so that at the first Morse peep, the start of the 'RRR' that meant *Attacked by surface raider,* and the sender's four-letter identification, the enemy's guns would open up. In the *Graf Spee*'s case, one of her secondary armament – five-point-nines, if that was what

28

they were – would be more than adequate. Then, abrupt end of message.

Might as well say, abrupt end of everything.

Andy was on the bridge again before eight, to take over the watch from Halloran. Who, in the interval of something like eight weeks since Calcutta, had been glum-faced and uncommunicative, discussing (with Andy, anyway) nothing but ship's business, almost as if he thought *he'd* been in some way wronged. Maybe, Andy reflected, one's revulsion had shown through more plainly than one had realised. Maybe still did – or might seem so to Halloran. Ludicrous, if so, that anyone who could behave as he had should display such sensitivity on his own account. But quite possibly one's disgust *had* shown. As had some scratches on Halloran's right cheek – the nails of the girl's left hand, one might guess, either through her being left-handed, or unable immediately to free the other, Halloran having presumably been on top of her when he'd vomited. It was a mental picture that recurred frequently and in itself was sickening, while another guess was that with her right hand she might have been groping for the knife – if there'd been one; if that hadn't simply been an attempt at justifying his attack on her. Anyway, at breakfast in the saloon next morning, with the din of the engineering work back aft already clanging and clattering, drilling through their skulls, the Old Man had obviously seen and wondered about those claw-marks; Halloran offering no comment or explanation, skipper glancing quizzically at Andy, no doubt aware they'd gone ashore together. But getting nothing out of either of them, had let it go, switched to discussing with the chief the fitting of the gun and gun-deck – which was being done of course by dockyard engineers but on whose work a sharpish eye needed to be kept.

Andy had repaid the twenty-five shillings he'd owed, as soon as they got back on board that night; he'd got it from a locked drawer in his own cabin and taken it along to the mate's, finding him stooped at the mirror over his hand-basin, bathing those wounds and dabbing Milton on them.

Andy recalled noticing the mildly astringent odour of it as he put two ten-shilling notes and two half-crowns on the desk, muttered 'Goodnight', and left him.

Halloran told him now – on the bridge, 0800 2 December, a Saturday – 'Same course, same revs, lookouts as before. You know where we are, huh?'

'Well enough.'

The Old Man had left the bridge by this time, gone down to his own breakfast. Horizon being clear, no smoke or warship's upperworks in sight. If you'd been close enough to see that, of course, there'd have been nothing to do except send up prayers; with a much greater height of eye from say the *Spee*'s fighting-top, she'd have seen you long before you saw her. For the moment, though, all was well. A matter of luck entirely: you ran into the bastard or you didn't. The *Anna*'s grey hull plunging westward – actually west by south – with spray from the smashed crests of the swells flying in regular bursts over her foc'sl and for'ard welldeck, the tarpaulin-topped hatch-covers of numbers one, two and three holds agleam with it. There'd been porpoises escorting her all day yesterday, but no sign of them this morning. Late-risers, maybe, in these latitudes. He pivoted slowly with the binoculars Halloran had surrendered to him, searching the northern and western horizon; then moved around checking the lookout positions – bridge-wings, monkey island – meaning the compass platform above the bridge – and the gun platform aft. All were manned by lookouts who seemed to be alert – *would* be: they all knew of the menace out there, and weren't idiots.

He came back to the mate. 'All right, I've got her.'

'Make Monte day after tomorrow, will we?'

Apparently wanting to chat. It was a question for Fisher, if anybody; the mate was perfectly capable of checking it for himself, in any case. Feeling isolated by this time, perhaps. He and Fisher hadn't ever got on well, and the Old Man, who mostly kept his own counsel, seemed wary of him. Halloran did have the bosun to talk to, but Batt Collins wasn't much of a conversationalist, except on matters connected directly with the working of the ship, especially the employment of the hands, a subject on which mate and bosun needed to confer at least once a day. Or the cadets – he could have conversed with them, if he'd made a point of it. One of them – Janner – had been up here with him throughout the four-hour watch; he'd just sent him down.

Andy said, answering his question about arrival at Montevideo: 'Should do, I'd say. Barring diversions. Or a Pampero . . .'

Pamperos were storms that blew up suddenly, roaring seaward out of the River Plate and Argentina. Halloran shook his head: 'Late in the year for those.'

'Dare say you're right. Yes – sure . . .'

'Barring only Huns, then.'

Barring them – *please* . . . But it was one hundred per cent good luck or bad luck – steaming blind, hoping for the best, or at least to avoid the worst. Retrospectively, one knew now how close *PollyAnna* had come to disaster in the southern approaches to the Moçambique Channel a month ago – although there and then they'd known damn-all about it. Unless maybe the Old Man *had* known; ships' masters were kept as fully informed as they needed to be – had the owners' private code kept under lock and key – but weren't obliged to pass anything on to their officers or crews unless they wanted to or there was sound reason to, and Josh Thornhill did tend to play his cards close to his chest. Anyway, the Moçambique business – the *Anna* had left Calcutta on 5 October, carrying out frequent gun-drills under Don Fisher's direction, gunnery as well as navigation being a second mate's responsibility now, and passing not through that channel but to the east of Madagascar, reaching Durban on the 25th. Eight days then discharging the manganese ore into lighters, using the ship's own gear, derricks and steam winches, the port must have been unusually congested for that to have been necessary – hard, hot work, performed as always by dockside labour while the ship's crew got on with maintenance both on deck and below. After which, instead of the hoped-for on-routeing homeward, maybe via some other South African port where you might have picked up cargo for West Africa or Britain or both, orders came via Messrs Dundas Gore's Durban agents to turn back northward to Lourenço Marques – a three-day trip in ballast – and load coal for Montevideo, Uruguay.

Not homebound yet, therefore, none of that feeling of being over the hump; nor by any means, although they hadn't realised this at the time, in anything like safe waters. They'd arrived in Portuguese East – Lourenço Marques – on Guy Fawkes' Day, 5 November, loading had taken nine days, and on the day of departure southbound the *Graf Spee* sank a small tanker right there in the Moçambique Channel, and next day – the 16th – stopped and examined some neutral steamer in the same area, thus establishing her own identity beyond question. For *PollyAnna* it must have been about as near a squeak as one could imagine; and in Cape Town then – on 20 November, that brief call to replenish bunkers, water and fresh stores before the long haul westward – the STO (Sea Transport Officer, a bearded RNR commander) had told the Old Man, who'd afterwards relayed most of this to his officers, that the Royal Navy had *thought* the *Graf Spee* had been in the South Atlantic, until she'd shown up in the Indian Ocean. Now a cruiser force was patrolling south of Good Hope to intercept her if or when she tried to head back west, which it was thought she would do, having drawn attention to herself off Moçambique as a ploy to confuse and divert the naval forces who were searching for her. Having achieved that much, it was expected that she'd sneak back to the South Atlantic's richer hunting grounds, catching both prey and hunters off guard.

Josh Thornhill had commented – at the window of the STO's office, putting a match to his pipe – 'Could be back already.'

'In which case you could have him on your tail again.'

The temporary and somewhat ramshackle office was on

the town side of the Duncan dock. *PollyAnna* was along-side in a fuelling berth in the Victoria dock, and her master had plodded all the way round on foot. It was hot enough too: but it had been hotter in LM and Durban, and would be more so, also more humid again, on the coast of Uruguay. This, however, was a fine Cape summer, hot enough but with none of the Indian Ocean swelter they'd been through recently; here, Table Mountain, Devil's Peak and Lion's Head were clear-cut, dramatic against a sky that didn't have a wisp of cloud in it. It would be a fine place to live, Josh had thought, to retire to. Most of his seafaring life he'd thought it – although a rider to that now, which he hadn't found in his thoughts before, was *if* one lived long enough to retire anywhere at all.

Touching wood that could have done with a lick of paint, turning from the window, removing the pipe from between his teeth . . . 'Do what I can to stay clear of the bastard.' And a rider to *that*, as he sat down: 'Toss-up, though, isn't it. Hit or bloody miss!'

Darkening ship would be one thing: from here on, *PollyAnna* would show no lights. Restrictions on dumping gash and stoke-hold ash he'd already discussed with Halloran and the chief engineer respectively. Watch-keeping officers would be told that if they saw any other ship that *was* showing lights – navigation lights, steaming lights, or just leaks through uncovered portholes – they were to turn stern-on to it at the same time as calling him.

He'd asked the STO, 'South of here, you say, some cruisers. Any other friendly forces along my route?'

'Right at this moment, I couldn't say. There was a hunting group off Freetown when I last heard, another in the West Indies. Could be anywhere by this time. Where you're headed, as of three or four days ago there were two cruisers in Port Stanley, two others somewhere off Rio and the Plate. We don't get that kind of intelligence on any regular basis, only when it affects us or they reckon it might do. For instance, one piece of bad news – all right, long way off, Northern Patrol – some elderly cruisers and AMCs patrolling Faeroes-Iceland and the Denmark Strait –'

'Far enough off *my* beat.'

'Yes, but – sadly, seems we've lost an AMC. Can't tell you which, no name supplied, I got this about an hour ago from a leatherneck on the staff at Simonstown, but whoever she was, seems she took on the *Deutschland* single-handed. Result – foregone conclusion, obviously. As her captain would have known before he started. Christ, some old liner dished-up with a few six-inch guns, no armour, comparatively slow – put her up against a socking great Hun battleship – huh?'

'Wouldn't've been there to take on battlewagons, would she.'

'Of course not. Northern Patrol's job is enforcement of a blockade of German trade – the right of "visit and search". Stopping and searching neutrals, so forth. But as you say, when anything like that colossus shows up – no more chance than your *PollyAnna*'d have. Or *Anna*, as you call her. And flying the White Ensign she can't turn and run as *you're* advised to.' The STO shook his head. 'Wouldn't catch me in the queue for that job, I tell you. Anyway – what interests us here is that if it was the *Deutschland,* who *was* in the South Atlantic not long ago, odds are she was on her way home to Germany. If so, three cheers!'

'Not the *Andalusia*, was it, this AMC?'

'No idea. Why?'

'Happens my third mate's father is her second-in-command. RNR, same rank as yourself. No reason it should have been that ship, but –'

'I'll get on to my chum in Simonstown again. Let you know as soon as there's an answer.'

Next afternoon at about four, *PollyAnna* had been on the point of departure, pilot on board and a tug on its way to pull her off the wall, when the STO arrived at her berth on a bicycle, propped it against a bollard and hurried up the gangway, barking at deckhands who'd been about to swing it up and inboard to hang on, he had to see the master on urgent business. He was with him in his cabin for about two minutes, then left, and the Old Man stalked up to the bridge, told the pilot all right, let's get the show on the road. And later, when they were out in the bay and had stopped for the pilot boat to get in alongside and take him off, he'd beckoned to Andy to join him in the port wing of the bridge.

'Word in your ear, Holt.'

Andy waited for it.

'Forty-eight hours ago, an armed merchant cruiser, the *Rawalpindi* – former P&O, right?' Andy had nodded; the skipper went on, 'On the Northern Patrol, which you mentioned the other day – I was asking you about your father? Seems *Rawalpindi* fell foul of a German warship they think but still aren't certain was the *Deutschland*. And of course, goodbye *Rawalpindi*. Well, I heard this yesterday, but my informant didn't know the AMC's name, and – see, there was a possibility it might turn out to be the worst possible news for you. Just could have been – eh? Not too nice for me if I'd had to break it to you, either. So there you are – pleasure to tell you that to the best of my knowledge, your father's alive and kicking; don't let anything you hear suggest he might not be.'

It was perhaps the longest speech Andy had ever heard from Josh Thornhill. He didn't just respect him now, he liked him. As it happened, he'd had a letter from his father the day they'd arrived in Durban – addressed, as the form was now, to SS *PollyAnna* c/o GPO London, and giving his own address as HMS *Andalusia*, similarly c/o GPO. His main purpose in writing had been to say he was likely to be out of touch for a while, '*doing what comes naturally*'; with any luck, he'd added, some of their leave periods *might* coincide – '*meanwhile, God bless you, old lad.*'

Andy had replied at once, improperly – contrary to all the principles of security – letting the old man know where he was at that stage by mentioning the racket kicked up by mynah birds, which proliferated at that port, as his father would well know.

* * *

35

At midday Andy was waiting to hand over the watch to Don Fisher, who was out in the wing getting his noon meridian altitude. He had young Gorst with him, and came back into the wheelhouse at a few minutes past the hour, sending Gorst to the chart alcove to complete the figure-work. Fisher telling Andy quietly, 'He may be getting the hang of it. Half his problem is he *thinks* he's not up to snuff – which is nonsense.'

'He's better than Janner at signals, anyway. I had Starkadder give 'em a Morse test the other day, and he wasn't at all bad.' As third mate, Andy was responsible for signals other than wireless. He glanced at his watch: 'Anyway – want to take over now? Course and revs the same, lookouts changed over at the half-hour. You've got Edmonds on the wheel here – if he looks older suddenly, it's because it's his thirtieth birthday.'

'Well!' A hand out to shake the helmsman's. 'Many happy—'

'Smoke!'

A lookout had yelled that from monkey island, above their heads. Three points on the starboard bow, sir – *smoke!*'

'Port wheel, Edmonds.' Andy added, 'Steer due south.' He still had the watch, and was at the voice-tube to the Old Man's cabin now. You blew into it, and it whistled at the other end – same as with the tube to the engine room. He heard the answering bark of 'Yup?' or 'What?' and shouted, 'Smoke starboard bow, sir, I'm altering away to port.' Edmonds was still winding-on port rudder, the lookout in that bridge-wing was shouting and gesticulating, Fisher had shot out and up to monkey island – access to it was external, vertical ladders port and starboard – and now the Old Man came pounding up. Andy told him, 'Was three points on the bow, sir, lookout on the island reported it. Bearing would have been about three-one-oh. I'm altering to steer south.'

'South?'

'Well –'

'Steer southeast.'

'Southeast, sir.' Edmonds kept the rudder on her. The skipper's orders *had* been to turn stern-on to any such sighting; Andy's intention had been to compromise on that, reckoning that from the position they were in now, steering south and watching to see which way that smoke 'grew' –

'Who's that – McAlan?'

The Old Man had whistled down to the engineer officer of the watch: the answer came thinly through the tube, 'Howie, sir.' Howie was fourth engineer – from Ardrossan; McAlan was the second, a Glaswegian. The master shouted, 'I'm turning away from an unidentified vessel's smoke, Howie. I don't want to see any, not a damn smidgin, coming out of the *Anna*'s stack.'

'Do our best, sir.'

He'd left it. Edmonds was letting the wheel's spokes slam through his palms as the rudder came off her: Andy leaning that way to check on her heading as the rate of turning slowed. She was rolling more than pitching, now – beam-on to the swell, rolling quite hard. On southeast she'd be more comfortable than on due south, though. Coming to her ordered course now. This was a repeater of the gyro compass – which was down below, well protected from the weather – and there was another on monkey island, as well as the standard (magnetic) compass, which was sited up there so as to be as far as possible from other magnetic influences. The Old Man, Andy saw, was out in the wing now, checking on *PollyAnna*'s funnel-top, which he himself had just had a peek at from the other side and seen hardly any smoke, no more than a haze. Old Man back inside again, Fisher too, Old Man telling him to take over the watch from Holt, Holt to find the chief engineer and ask him to make damn sure no more smoke was emitted than was visible now. Andy shot down there: it was vital, he knew it – very little smoke at one moment could become a gush with a long tail to it a minute later; depending on the quality of the coal, it wasn't always easy or even possible to control. It was South African coal they were burning now – at the rate of about twenty-five tons a day. He found Hibbert, chief engineer, in his cabin, and gave him the skipper's message; the big man nodded, tapped his pipe out and got to his feet. 'Wondered why we was turning circles . . .'

Within half an hour they'd lost sight of the smoke. Gorst and others watching it from the island after *PollyAnna*'s turn to the southeast, which had put the dark stain of it directly astern, had seen that it was drawing right – eastward, at no great speed and not in sufficient volume to leave a trail; only a smudge like a thumbprint on the horizon. Could have been a raider on the hunt, or a cruiser on patrol, or an enemy armed merchant raider or support-ship; any of those seemed more likely, from a study of the chart – the big one covering the whole South Atlantic – than its being another steamer, British or neutral, on a course only slightly divergent from the reciprocal of *PollyAnna*'s Cape Town–Montevideo track. The point being that it didn't seem to be leading from A to any recognisable B, and the alternative was to be simply on the prowl – hunting or patrolling, or in the case of a raider's support-vessel, perhaps waiting for a pre-arranged rendezvous.

If the Old Man had made any guesses, he wasn't airing them. Only when visual contact was lost did he tell Fisher to hold this southeasterly course for another half-hour, and at one-fifteen bring her round on to a corrected course for Montevideo. Then went down to his lunch – sausage and mash – in the saloon, which was most unusual for him when they were at sea, let alone in present circumstances. A deliberate display of calm, maybe? Andy and others were already at it when he came down, were masking their surprise, or trying to, but were somewhat silenced. The Old Man's eye roamed over them and settled on the chief engineer.

'Your lads been doing a good job, Chief.'

'Thank you, Skipper.' A nod and a half-smile. 'I'll pass it on.'

Old Man to Andy, then: 'Why'd you have steered one-eighty, Holt?'

'I guessed he'd be steaming either east to west or west to east, sir, reckoned due south'd be the quickest way to lose him.'

'Wouldn't have if he'd been steering for the Falklands, would it?'

'No. I – I'm sorry. I just sort of assumed –'

'Sort of know better next time, won't you.' The steward had put a plate in front of him. 'Thank you, Jackson.' Stabbing at a sausage with his fork. 'Who incinerated these, Bloom or Hughes?'

'Assistant Cook Hughes today, Captain.'

'Might've known. Might've known.' Reaching for the mustard. 'I was going to ask you, Holt – how come you fetched up in the Blood Line? If I ever knew, I've forgotten. Your father with us at some time, was that it?'

Andy swallowed and shook his head. 'I took the first job I was offered, after *Conway*. My father was mostly with the Baron Line – from 1921 when he left the airship business – or it left him –'

'Captain, sir . . .'

Mervyn Clowes, junior wireless officer. He was eighteen, looked fifteen, came from Carmarthen and spent most of his off-watch time playing cribbage. Wireless officers were not technically-speaking Merchant Navy officers; although they wore uniform they were employees of Marconi International, who contracted them out to shipping lines. Clowes was offering the skipper a folded sheet of signal-pad, murmuring, 'Just took this in, sir. Distress call.' The skipper, peering at it with his eyes narrowed under the grey, jutting brows, would have found it easier if he'd put his glasses on, but for some reason was doing without them.

'Damn it.' Blinking. Addressing Halloran then: '*Doric Star*. Six-sixty miles east by south of St Helena. That must be – oh, heck . . .'

Andy thinking to himself, *couple of thousand miles away,*

must be . . . No – more than that. Visualising the chart and guessing that that distance east of St Helena would put the ship about halfway between the island and the coast of German Southwest. Two and a half thousand miles, say. And *Doric Star* was Blue Star Line, of course: 10,000 tons or so, her refrigerated holds doubtless packed with meat and other foodstuffs that now would *not* reach Britain. From Australia round the Cape, he guessed. The skipper had handed the signal back to Clowes: 'Ask Mr Fisher to put it on the chart, tell him I'll be up shortly.' To the rest of them then: 'It was the *Graf Spee* was at her. So the bugger *is* back this side of Africa.'

The southeastward diversion had lost them about three and a half hours, but if there was no further interruption *PollyAnna* should still make Montevideo by late afternoon on the 4th. Could in fact have ensured it by squeezing an extra half-knot out of her, but that would almost certainly have led to excessive smoke emission, and Hibbert wouldn't have wanted to overstrain her anyway.

The *Doric Star*'s RRR position, which Fisher had marked on the big chart, was in fact 2,750 nautical miles from the River Plate. So that guess hadn't been far out, and seemed to indicate that the *Spee* was far enough away for the *Anna* to feel reasonably secure – at least, as far as that particularly feared predator was concerned. He said as much to Halloran, in the course of taking over the watch from him at eight that evening. They were studying the chart – Fisher's marked EP – Estimated Position – which would be confirmed (or corrected) shortly by evening stars – and measuring the distance yet to be covered. Andy had made that comment about the *Graf Spee* presenting no threat to them in the immediate or near future, qualifying it with, 'But since we don't have a clue yet where we'll be going *after* Montevideo –'

'No need to look that far ahead, neither.' Halloran stubbed out a cigarette. The chart table was at the after end of the wheelhouse, in a recess now fitted with a canvas curtain to keep light from spilling out. 'Tell me this, for a start – what's the *Graf Spee*'s best speed?'

'About thirty knots?'

'So she can make seven hundred miles a day when she needs to. Right?'

He did the mental arithmetic and nodded. 'Seven-twenty, at a pinch.'

'So she could be off Monte in two shakes – eh?'

'Well –'

'When they've made a sinking, they shift as far and as fast as they bloody can. Plain sense – eh?'

'I suppose they would. But –'

'No buts, lad. What they *do*. Don't sit there waiting for the Royal Navy to come calling, do they. So tell me this. You're the *Graf Spee*'s skipper – you just sank the *Doric Star*, you need to move a good long way, smartish. Best economical speed – what, fifteen, eighteen knots? So you're looking at this chart same as we are now, asking yourself – well, got to leg it anyway, may as well go some place where there'll be targets. Where'll you make for?'

'The Cape, maybe.'

'Where you'd meet warships coming north out of Simonstown? St Helena to the Cape's not much of a change of area, neither. Likely patrolled, what's more. Coming down *here*, though – where there's more than a few of us fetching ore and that . . . Look – we're in Monte day after tomorrow. December fourth. Discharging'll take say a week. Nine days, even. Takes us to the eleventh or thirteenth – right?' Black eyes intent, stubby hands spread: 'She could be on the doorstep waiting for us – uh?'

'Better pray she's making for the Cape, then.'

He took over the watch, and an hour later when Fisher was out there taking star-sights, Gorst noting down the chronometer times, he sent down orders for the ditching of stoke-hold ash and galley refuse. It had become a first watch routine by this time. Ashes were normally put overboard at the end of each watch, but in order not to leave floating trails for any raider to follow they were now dumped on deck and shovelled over after sundown; while gash during the day was tipped into forty-gallon drums suspended over the stern with permanently rigged tackle for up-ending them. During the dark hours the muck would sink or at any rate be widely enough dispersed by wave-action. These measures had been outlined in Trade Division (Admiralty) literature received when they'd been in Durban; they were intended primarily for application in the North Atlantic, U-boat waters, but the skipper had decided to implement them after the bunkering call at Cape Town.

Fisher came back in with the figures from his sights, sextant cradled under his arm, and Andy heard him telling Gorst that he'd attend to this lot: he – Gorst – could go down and turn in; he'd be back up here as assistant watch-keeper/general dogsbody in less than three hours' time in any case.

Andy asked quietly, 'Getting a soft heart, are we?'

'Not all *that* soft. Worked him hard today. Poor sod's got to get *some* kip.'

The sights he'd taken were good and resulted in an adjustment of course from 268 degrees to 266. Distance to Montevideo 530 miles: at twelve and a half knots, ETA 1600 on the fourth.

4

They were meeting and crossing the paths of other steamers that night and on the third, had consequently given up the practice of turning stern-on to all newly sighted ships. Whatever came into sight you examined carefully, and at anything like close quarters played safe by switching on navigation lights and following the Rule of the Road. After midnight there'd been a good moon, in any case; its loom had been silvering the horizon when Andy had been turning over the watch to Fisher, and it had been well up, competing with the sun's first efforts, when they'd met up here again for morning stars. There'd been a few ships in sight then, and were again during Andy's forenoon watch – as one might have expected, with vessels of all nations using Montevideo and Buenos Aires, Mar del Plata, Bahia Blanca, Rio Grande, Porto Allegre, Santos, Rio de Janeiro, Vitoria, Salvador, Natal, Recife; or, southbound, the Magellan Strait en route to Chilean and Peruvian ports.

Some playground for a pocket-battleship, he thought. With at least half of all this traffic flying the Red Ensign.

The Old Man came back into the wheelhouse from the bridge-wing, where he'd been taking a look at a Spanish passenger-steamer to which Andy had perforce given way, passing two or three cables' lengths under her stern, just minutes ago. Skipper wearing his reefer jacket unbuttoned over an open-necked shirt and a pair of old grey flannels;

Andy remembering that when he'd first met him – on Clydeside for the formal signing of articles – his rig had been a brown serge suit and a bowler hat. Coming to a halt in the wheelhouse doorway now and mumbling – holding a match to the bowl of his pipe – 'Wouldn't trust *that* crowd not to let their Hun friends know where the pickings are.'

'Think Spain'll come in against us, sir?'

'Your guess is as good as mine. No secret where Franco's sympathies lie though, is it.'

She was back on course after that brief alteration, the helmsman intoning, 'Two-six-six, sir.' The Old Man said, 'You were telling me, Holt – about your father, how he came out of airships, back where he belonged, you might say?'

Andy nodded. 'End of that war and afterwards he was with Vickers – lieutenant-commander in the RN Air Service, but in an Admiralty team working with them – Vickers – on rigid airships. Meaning Zeppelin type as distinct from the old blimps, dirigibles. Metal airships – one of 'em crossed the Atlantic and back in 1919. The old man was in on that – at the time he said they were all cock-a-hoop about it.'

'Old man? Your father? How old is he?'

'He's – forty-six, or –'

'If forty-six is old, Holt, I'm Methuselah.'

'Well – manner of speaking . . . No, not old at all . . . But what sent him back to sea was the R38 disaster in 1921. She broke up in mid-air, on her trials. My father would've been on board her but he'd cried off because of – well, family crisis, my mother nearly dying giving birth to my sister Annabel. August 1921 – her birthday, how I can put the date to it – the crash, I mean. He's always credited my sister with having saved his life. But it put an end to all that military development, and he chucked his hand in.'

'Mother pulled through all right, eh?'

'Oh, yes –'

'And he was taken on by Hogarths – Baron Line, you said – as what?'

'Junior officer, uncertificated. But with his record he

had a head start, sat for all his certificates, put in the necessary sea-time and – well, caught up pretty quick.'

'Would've needed to, with a wife and two children to support.'

'Well – just family stuff, this, don't want to bore you, sir – happened he'd sold his inherited share of my grandfather's farms in Herefordshire to his sister and her husband. So he had a bit behind him – bought the house we have now at Helensburgh, for instance.'

'Lucky blighter. Lucky it was 1921, too, not later when we hit rock-bottom. Must've kept up his annual RNR sea training, too – accounting for the defence courses, eh?'

Andy nodded. 'Since 1937 it's been pretty well a full-time job. You'd have heard of him through that, I suppose.'

'And Blood Line offered you a cadetship when you passed out of *Conway*.'

'I was lucky too. Wasn't the best of times, was it, thirty-four, thirty-five?'

'It was a bloody awful time, Holt. And there were owners took full advantage of it. Most of 'em, you might say – kept their own bellies and pockets full while there were officers with masters' tickets signing on as deckhands sooner than rot on shore, sell matches on street corners. But – low pay, foc's'l conditions not fit for pigs – a man could like it or lump it, there'd be a dozen trained seamen on any dockyard street corner only too ready to sign on in his place. Wouldn't call it exactly ritzy now, but my God, compared to how it *was* . . .'

Becoming talkative, *this* Old Man. Initially he'd hardly opened his mouth despite spending a lot of time on and around the bridge when he, Andy, had been on watch. In days gone by the 0800 to 1200 and the 2000 to midnight watches had been kept by ships' masters; and a third mate being new to it customarily stood under his captain's eye. In fact, *PollyAnna* had been halfway through the Mediterranean when he'd realised he was being left entirely on his own, had evidently passed muster.

* * *

During the forenoon, Don Fisher mustered his seven-man gun-crew and drilled them with a dummy projectile, while the bosun made a target out of vegetable crates lashed together. That was put over the side, and with Fisher spotting and correcting, they fired six rounds at it, bracketing it with the fourth and fifth shots and dropping the sixth so close that the splash obscured it. This was at a final range of 5,600 yards, measured by the Chernikeef log, distance covered from the moment of dropping the target overboard; he'd had young Gorst singing out the ranges. The skipper had authorised the expenditure of six rounds maximum, since they had only a couple of dozen and no certainty of where or when they'd get more.

Cadet Janner had exclaimed, in the mate's hearing, on the bridge-wing from where they'd been watching the show with plugs of cotton-waste in their ears, 'That wasn't at all bad, by golly!' and Halloran asked him cuttingly, 'Know much about it, do you?'

'Not much, sir, no. But we did a gunnery course.'

'Tell me this – why do we have it mounted aft, why not on the foc'sl-head?'

'I'd say because' – Janner screwing his eyes up, applying either memory or logic – 'well, seeing as we're civilians and the gun's only for self-defence – on the poop because in any action we'd be trying to run for it?'

'That's the theory.' A shrug. 'If you can imagine us with our twelve knots running from the *Graf Spee* with her thirty?'

Andy wrote to his father that afternoon, before getting his head down for a couple of hours.

We're new at all this, of course, complete beginners – at whatever there is ahead of us, I mean. All guesses and theory – not having experienced anything of the sort as yet, I just hope we'll find we're up to it. I suppose that's what most men worry about, at such times. My skipper was at sea in the last one, so was the chief engineer – and the bosun, as it happens – but apart from those we're greenhorns. You knew it very well, of course, and knowing where you are and what you're in I guess you'll already have seen quite a bit of this one. My captain, I may say without breaking too many rules about security, had wind just recently of the loss of an AMC but not her name, made a point of finding out before I heard of it, because it occurred to him that it might have been your ship; he is, I may say, a very decent sort. I think I mentioned before, he recognised your name, knew all about the defence courses you were running. He's 59, by the way, been at sea near enough half a century.

Now I'm going to grab some kip, finish this later or perhaps tomorrow – when we'll be within reach of a post box. Touch wood, we will!

Odd, he thought, his mind drifting as he transferred from desk to bunk, it felt as if he'd been writing to an older brother, rather than to his father.

Soon after four he doused his head in cold water and went up a deck and outside, leant on the now grey-painted rail that ran around this midships superstructure, looking down on to the fore-deck where the bosun had men at work overhauling and greasing winches and five-ton derricks – and on the foc's'l-head, the steam windlass and other anchor gear – prior to arrival in Montevideo and as likely as not having to use the ship's own gear for discharging her coal. They'd evidently passed through more rain while he'd been sleeping; decks and hatch-covers were steaming, raising a mist that drifted astern over the sizzling, spreading wake. The swell was lower, as she approached the shelter of the land, the ocean not ridged, just heaving, like some great beast sleeping one off; there was very little movement on the ship, only this steady, rhythmic lunging, so regular you barely noticed it. Current would still be westerly, he guessed, but by sunset would need watching; even now, still 300 miles offshore, you might be getting into the southerly flowing Brazil Current, which complicated matters just off the Plate by coming head to head with what was known as the Falklands Current – an offshoot of the Cape Horn one.

Don Fisher's concern, of course, not one's own. Although next time – or in a year or two, say – it might be. He went inside, paused to light a cigarette then continued aft and down again on his way to the saloon. It was a substantial block of accommodation, this bridge 'island', including two two-berth passenger cabins intended originally for use by the ship's owners or their more important customers – shippers, charterers. They were on the same level as the master's quarters, i.e. one level below the bridge. One of them had been allocated to the chief engineer and the other to Halloran, freeing what would have been their cabins for use by Don Fisher and the second engineer, McAlan. Those were on that same level, as was a cramped three-berther used by the wireless officers, whose W/T office was immediately abaft it. Andy's small cabin, and the third and fourth engineers' and one shared by the cadets were on the next level down, which was also the saloon deck.

This one. Those four cabins, and the washplace, then the saloon, and abaft it the pantry and galley. He pushed into the saloon to get himself a mug of tea, and Fisher looked up from one he'd had *his* nose in.

'Good grief. Bestirring ourselves, at last . . .'

He passed around the long table, en route to the pantry hatch. It wasn't much past four; Fisher couldn't have been down from the bridge for more than a few minutes. There were several others at the table – not that this was any sort of mealtime. 'Tea' – or supper – was normally laid on at five, although in harbour it could be as late as seven. Andy nodded to the assistant steward through the sliding hatch: 'Tea please, Watkins.' Then to Fisher, 'Are we in the Brazil Current yet, d'you reckon?'

'Time will tell. Should be, though, I'm allowing for it. Stars tonight will put us right. But listen – the bugger's done it again.'

'Which bugger's done what?'

Shaw, third engineer – whose particular responsibility was the ship's electrics – cut in with a supposedly German-intonated scream of 'The Herr *Admiral Graf Spee*, no less!'

Fisher winced, shaking his head, and told Andy, 'Distress call from a ship by name *Taroa*. Furness Withy, eight thousand tons, the Old Man knew of her. Six hundred miles west of where the *Doric Star* was caught – and the interval was thirty hours, so the *Spee*'s been on west-southwest at twenty knots.'

'Coming *this* way.'

'This coast, maybe. If she holds on.'

'Not at twenty knots, she wouldn't.'

'Is that somehow relevant?'

'The mate and I were pondering her likely movements, that's all. Economical speed about fifteen, we reckoned.'

'Might well be. Or could be twenty. Either way, by the time we're ready to leave Monte—'

Shaw cut in again: 'Sit tight and keep our knees together until she's pissed off again, is what *I'd* propose.'

By dawn on the 4th, still with about twelve hours to go, the wind had veered northeast, same direction as the Brazil Current. Andy and Fisher took their morning stars and the results, in close accord, suggested a small alteration of course, which was conveyed to Halloran. Fisher noted the time and log reading, and laid the new track off on the chart.

'Sets us back a bit. ETA at the dredged channel seventeen hundred, more like.'

'Dredged channel?'

'Here.' He spread a new chart – 2001 – on top of the other. 'See. Bahia de Montevideo. Channel's here – five miles of it, leading due north. Our approach'll be here, between English Bank and Rouen Bank, then hard a-starboard. Giving ETA at the channel's outer end because that's where the pilot meets us. Channel's dredged periodically to thirty feet – soft mud, silts up like mad. Only good thing about it is you can't seriously damage yourself on soft mud. But once in the estuary there's not a hell of a lot of water anywhere . . . Your first visit here, is this?'

'To Monte.' He nodded. 'Passed close by in the old *Burntisland*, though – when we came down from Rio and visited BA, remember?'

Buenos Aires being a hundred miles up-river and on its other bank. Argentina on your left, Uruguay on your right. From BA in the *Burntisland* they'd steamed on down to the Magellan Strait and up the Chilean coast to Santiago; himself a cadet, Fisher third mate. The Spanish war had been at its height: the bombing of Guernica, all that. Couple of years ago, but it felt more like last month – because, he guessed, he'd enjoyed what he'd been doing. *So far*, anyway, had enjoyed it. As he'd tried to explain to his father that day – he'd found himself in what felt like his own element, a role that suited him – seaman, *working* seaman with no frills, no bullshit, or at any rate very little – and definitely preferring the cargo business – tramping – which gave you the whole world as your stamping-ground, no port on earth you wouldn't eventually get to know.

And no bloody passengers . . .

Fisher was telling him about Montevideo – 'Likely thing, with coal, is they'll want us to anchor in what's called the Antepuerto and discharge into lighters. Agents may tell us when they answer the Old Man's message, otherwise the pilot will.'

The Old Man had wirelessed last night to Messrs Todhunter and Rodriguez, Dundas Gore's agents in Monte, giving an ETA of 1630. He might have amended that now, but had decided to let it wait, and in mid-forenoon received Todhunter's reply. As foretold by Fisher, *PollyAnna* was to anchor in the Antepuerto. Todhunter looked forward to seeing Captain Thornhill, and would come out to the ship as soon as Port Health had cleared her; he'd meanwhile arranged for lighters to be alongside by 0830 local time on Tuesday.

He and the skipper were old friends, apparently. But not a word about the ship's future movements. Could be a matter of discretion – no need to broadcast what could be discussed face to face in a few hours' time. The Old Man acknowledged Todhunter's message and gave him an amended ETA, main purpose being not to ruffle local feathers or incur extra costs by keeping the pilot boat waiting; and in the event he did not: the boat was coming down the dredged channel as they made their own approach – a splash of colour that resolved itself into a red-painted cutter under a red-and-white pilot flag. *Polly-Anna* going dead slow at that stage, her master then stopping engines and finally putting her astern for half a minute, kicking up what might have been cocoa flooding for'ard along her grey sides, and stopping her half a cable's length from a light-buoy that was named on the chart as the Whistle Buoy, marking the entrance to the channel. You could smell that mud. Meanwhile, Batt Collins down there on the fore-deck was putting a Jacob's ladder over, then watching as the boat chugged in alongside; the pilot transferred himself to the ladder and old Batt leaned over to haul him up. Halloran there now too, touching his cap to the pilot before shaking his hand; pilot glancing aloft, checking that the blue-and-white-striped Uruguayan flag was up there – mark of respect, the ship being now in Uruguayan waters and jurisdiction. She was also flying the Dundas Gore house flag – a blue pendant with D/G in white – the yellow international code flag 'Q' for Quarantine, and on her stern of course the one that mattered, the Red Duster. In addition, her four-letter identification was bent on ready for hoisting – if the Old Man decided it should be hoisted at a later stage. Factors in this were that while there'd almost certainly be other British ships in the port, in which case identification might be appropriate – they could look her up, see who she was – there might also be Germans, and why provide *them* with information they weren't entitled to? Although they could get it easily enough if they wanted to by looking it up in the Customs register; or even more simply by focusing a telescope on the name painted in black capitals on her bows and counter. The concern behind this was the possibility of German freighters going on the air on raiders' frequencies with messages such as British freighter *PollyAnna* sailed for this or that port at – time and date, plus maybe cargo details. And *wouldn't* they, if they could get away with it? The skipper had agreed, said he'd ask Todhunter what the form was when he came aboard.

The Old Man nodding down towards the pilot now, muttering to himself or Fisher, 'Think he was a bloody admiral, wouldn't you?' Referring to the Uruguayan – smart white uniform, cap aslant rather as Admiral Beatty had worn his, and that jaunty manner. He was out of their sight then, following Halloran in through the screen door on his way up to the bridge. Pilot cutter meanwhile sheering off; sounds from below of those two clumping up. Andy joined Fisher at the chart, out of the others' way. If they'd been going into the port itself and berthing alongside, Fisher, as second mate, wouldn't have been up here, he'd have been down aft, in charge of the stern ropes and wires. Halloran's station was on the foc'sl-head – would have been if they'd been berthing on a quay, still would be now, anchoring. Time – five-ten: should be dropping the hook by six, maybe – and with any luck the agent, Todhunter, would be bringing mail with him . . . Pilot now arriving in the bridge, looking, as he approached the Old Man, like some comic-opera sea-captain – as if he might start singing and dancing at any moment. Beaming smile exposing gleaming white teeth under a black moustache with up-curling ends, shiny black hair curling out around the edges of his cap, odour of Brylcreem or something worse redolent even from this distance of about fifteen feet.

Clasping the Old Man's hand: 'Captain Thorn-eel, we have been meeting before, I sink – vairy nice, vairy nice!'

Andy murmured, 'Christ.'

Fisher said even more quietly, 'I couldn't have said that in Spanish, though.'

'No. Nor could I.' Wouldn't have wanted to, either. But

that was how Fisher was – prone to give everyone his due. Making it easy to see why he and Halloran didn't hit it off. They were opposites in that and other ways as well. While he himself, he guessed, came somewhere in between – neither 'proper', as Fisher was, nor sour-minded like the mate. At least, one *hoped* . . .

The anchor splashed in at six-fifteen and was secured with seven shackles out by half-past; Port Health officials had visited and given pratique by seven, which allowed for the gangway to be rigged, starboard side aft, in place of the Jacob's ladder, and for the motorboat to be lowered and moved back to that quarter. The Port Health men's tug returning to the dockyard passed the agent's launch on its way out; a small man in the launch's sternsheets wearing a striped blazer and Panama hat would, Andy guessed, be Todhunter: and plainly was – the Old Man having seen him from a cabin window came down aft to welcome him.

There were half a dozen other ships in this Antepuerto: three British, two Dutch, one French. No Germans – although Andy heard Todhunter telling the skipper that a Hun was due in next day; he added that the port authorities would surely berth it well away from any of the others.

'They've got *that* much sense.'

'Glad to hear it. Though mind you, the lads running into 'em ashore –'

'We've an answer of sorts to that, too. In any case, neutral port –'

'Until we've sunk 'em all – or the bloody *Graf Spee*'s sunk all of us . . . Any news of that damn thing?'

'Nothing certain. Rumours, of course. Believe me, we all keep our ears pinned back. My word, Josh, you're looking extremely fit!'

'Virtuous life, Mick, that's the secret. Never too late, why not try it? That our mail you've got there?'

It was: the Old Man took it from him and passed it to Cadet Janner – one of those nearby keeping *their* ears pinned back – to sort and distribute. The Old Man's own private mail, as well as official bumf from the owners, Admiralty and Ministry of Shipping, was in an attaché case that the agent was hanging on to as they went in through the weather door and up to the day cabin. There was always a lot of paperwork to be got through. Details of cargo, for instance, on bills of lading and the manifest – simple enough with a single bulk cargo, for sure, but by no means invariably so. Todhunter or his clerks would have to 'enter' ship and cargo at the Customs House – first thing in the morning, one might suppose. He'd also see to the ordering of fresh provisions and any other requirements – mechanical, electrical, medical, legal or financial; he'd have cash with him in that bag, local currency for advances against men's wages, and so forth.

Andy had a letter from a girl by the name of Liza Sharp, who lived in Helensburgh and when he'd last seen her had been attending a secretarial college in Glasgow. He hadn't read it yet, hadn't even opened it. It surprised him that she'd have written – correspondence was something they hadn't indulged in before, and he wouldn't have recognised her handwriting – but there it was under 'Sender': Miss E Sharp, Helensburgh. There'd been some exciting moments with her last summer, and touch wood might be more; an intriguing thing was that she looked – or *could* look, when she wanted to – as if butter wouldn't melt, whereas in fact she was pleasantly on the wild side. Another factor – *not* all that advantageous – was that his parents and hers knew each other and lived within a stone's throw of each other; her father was a lawyer of some kind, with a practice in Glasgow.

Anyway, he'd read this later, when things had settled down. Another letter he'd noticed with interest was addressed to Halloran in a back-sloping hand which he'd recognised as the lovely Leila's – whose last communication (or the last he knew of) he'd been invited to read – oddly enough – that evening in Calcutta. It had been one of three or four remaining unclaimed on the table in the saloon, where Janner had sorted them then taken the crew's to their mess room below the poop. Anyway, the mate finally dashed in, spotted it instantly – not difficult, that same violet-coloured stationery – and snatched it up only seconds before Mervyn Clowes, third wireless officer, arrived with a message that the captain wanted him – Halloran – to join him and the agent up top.

'Does, does he . . . ?'

He was up there about twenty minutes; would probably have had a tot with them, while discussing aspects of ship's business. It was close on eight o'clock when he came down and sent Gorst to the bosun with a message for all hands to muster on the fore-deck, where the master would address them.

Fisher asked him quietly, 'Know where we go from here, do we?'

A nod. 'Vitoria, for iron ore. From here to there in ballast.'

Andy looked at Fisher: 'Vitoria – that's –'

'North of Rio. Say four day's steaming.'

'*Graf Spee* permitting.' McAlan, second engineer, stubbing out a cigarette. 'Where do we take the ore? Home?'

'Old Man'll tell you – if he wants to. Let's get up there.'

The hands were milling around on deck, quite a few of them dressed as if they thought they might be going ashore. Which might be possible, if the skipper authorised it and boat transport in both directions was made available, and as long as the agent *had* brought cash with him. In the last day or two the skipper would have been working out, as he always did before making port, how much was owing to each individual – accrued wages less advances and deductions, including any fines for indiscipline or breaches of the terms of engagement.

You could hear car horns and music floating on the warm evening air, see lights all along the shore and around the bay. On the town side, this eastern part above and behind the port, neon lights blazed multi-coloured over cinemas, dance-halls, restaurants.

The Old Man, with a megaphone in his hand and the stout little Todhunter at his side, was on the railed walkway fronting his own quarters, two decks up. Halloran called to the bosun, 'All hands, is it?' and getting an affirmative, turned to look up towards the bridge. The last of the officers were still filtering out around him, and a wireless or gramophone from the nearest other ship – 300 yards away, but the sound came loud and clear across the water – belting out 'Is You Is Or Is You Ain't My Baby?'. Halloran shouted up through cupped hands, 'All hands present, sir!'

'So listen here.' Old Man's voice raised, trumpeted through the megaphone over the ship's own familiar creaking, straining noises and the distant motor-horns, music and voices. The gramophone had gone silent for a moment, started up again now with 'Alexander's Ragtime Band'. 'Won't take long, this.' He certainly did need the megaphone. 'First thing you'll want to know is when we've discharged our coal – commencing 0830 and taking maybe a week – we'll be sailing light ship up-coast to a Brazilian port to load ore for Britain. That's as much as you need know about it for now – and it's for your private information, no one else's. This place like most others has its share of Nazi spies, and we don't want 'em tipped off when or where we're going next – huh? Remember – answer no questions, and don't be overheard talking about ports, routes, cargoes – it's your lives at stake, uh? *And* mine . . . Well – this connects to point two, and should reduce that risk, and save you money. British residents here in Monte – businessmen, among them Mr Todhunter here, our Line's agent – have set up a place of recreation for use by British crews. Calling it the Liberty Inn. Cut-price drinks and snacks, billiards, darts and table tennis, staffed by British residents who'll give advice and local information. Regular bars and restaurants aren't cheap, d'you see; what's more, although Uruguayans are mainly on our side, there's some as aren't, and in the wrong place at the wrong time a man could find himself up against it. There's local Nazis for one thing – and a Hun steamer of some kind due in tomorrow for another. We don't want trouble if we can avoid it, and as for the local police – well, they're neutrals, can't take sides: get into a fight you could end up in quod as easy as a German could.'

He'd broken off, listening to Todhunter. Nodding then and raising the megaphone again: 'Should've said. Liberty Inn run their own launch, collect and return between shore and ship, costs you nothing. That's the launch there, lying off . . .'

Liza's letter was warm but also pointless. She told him she'd recently met his sister Annabel at some dance in Glasgow and this had put it in her mind to write to him. She – Liza – was still at the secretarial college and intended to join the Wrens when she finished in a few months' time, but with any luck she'd still be around when he got back. Annabel had said she was sure he'd be home long before that. She – Annabel – had been at the dance with a rather nice-looking RNVR sub-lieutenant – they'd been mostly naval people at the dance, to which Liza had been taken by her cousin Charles – and Annabel's sub-lieutenant had told her he was 'standing by' a submarine then building in one of the Clyde yards. She'd had the impression that Annnabel and this submariner were quite heavily involved . . .

Anyway that's only gossip. Excuse to write and let you know I'm still around and looking forward to your return – hoping it may be soon, and that I have such lovely memories of last summer, Andy. Please do make it soon.

He pushed the letter into his pocket. Thinking, *nice of her to have bothered* . . . She had something in mind for him, obviously. Otherwise *why* bother? Give her a run for her money in any case. Why not? Man should not live by bread alone . . . Thinking of which, there was also – in and around Glasgow – another chum of Annabel's, Sheila Gilchrist –

oh, and one he'd met when he'd been out with – well, girl called Susan, Susan Shea – a girl by name of Paula – Paula West – who was *really* hot stuff . . . Thinking of her more than of the others as he headed for the bridge; he was duty officer on board tonight, one of whose duties was to check anchor-bearings every hour. With the wind as light as it was and in its present direction there was very little chance of the anchor dragging, but you still had to make sure it didn't.

The German SS *Eisleben* dropped her hook on the afternoon of the 5th at the western end of the Antepuerto, with the German merchant ensign – red with a black swastika in a white circle in its centre – drooping damply over her stern. She was riding high, obviously in ballast. It felt unreal, unnatural to be sharing an anchorage with the bastard, and having to tolerate the sight of that foul emblem day after day. 'Bloody insult,' was Batt Collins' view of it. There'd been rainstorms during the day – a day stinking of coal dust and loud with the clatter of winches and steel grabs thudding into the holds then swinging up and over to drop half-ton loads thundering into the lighters. In the heavier downpours Batt would blow his whistle for the stevedores to knock off and ship's crew to cover hatches, some of them having done so choosing to stand there in the rain, have themselves as well as the decks washed down. In the evening, strains of Nazi anthems – brass-band martial music, anyway – carried thumping across the anchorage from the German, and other ships turned up the volume on their own loudspeakers to drown it out.

Andy went ashore in the Liberty Inn launch at about seven with a crowd of others, including the two cadets and Halloran. They were all in civilian clothes, as was *de rigeur* in a neutral port; identifying themselves only by wearing on their jackets the new Merchant Navy lapel badge – silvered letters MN under a crown – which had been issued to them during the ship's stay in Durban. At the Inn, which had formerly been some kind of warehouse, the four of them had beers and Janner's customary soft drink together, Halloran paying for the first round and Andy for the second; Halloran holding forth on the fact he'd never had the kind of start *they* were getting, had never been a cadet, only a poor bloody apprentice, thirteen years old and five foot fuck-all, given all the filthiest jobs and no damned instruction, no help of any kind, whatever you'd wanted to know you'd had to find out for yourself. Interrupting this by jerking a thumb towards a grey-haired English-woman at a desk with a notice on it reading ENQUIRIES AND LOCAL INFORMATION, and challenging the cadets with a muttered, 'Half a crown to the man who asks her where's the red-light district.' Neither of them was keen to take him up on it. He jeered, 'I'd tell *her*. In the old town – Ciudad Vieja they call it – vicinity of Piedras y Juan Carlos Gomez. If you can get your tongue round that.' Soon after this he announced that he was off; had wanted to give this place the once over, was all, and as church halls went, he supposed it wasn't bad. To Andy then: 'Don't care to tag along?'

'No. Thanks all the same.'

'Once a year's your lot, eh?'

Andy gave him time to get clear, then told the cadets he'd see them later and went for a look round on his own. Spent no money, enjoyed the bright lights and carnival atmosphere, politely declined a couple of invitations and got an idea of the layout of the town – this end of it at any rate. Then back to where the beer was cheap and not too bad – it was American, came in screw-top cans not unlike Brasso tins – and food came in such forms as baked beans with sausages, fish and chips, sardines on toast, apple pie and ice-cream. This time he joined Batt Collins, who had the carpenter – Postlethwaite – with him, and trotted out the old chestnut about beer being sent for analysis and the report coming back: 'this horse is not fit for work'.

*   *   *

Wireless reception was erratic, in the Antepuerto anyway, and no listening watches were being kept. It was Todhunter who brought the news, on 7 December, of yet another sinking by the *Graf Spee*. Andy saw the agent's launch coming out to them, and the diminutive, now familiar figure in its pork-pie hat in the sternsheets; he sent a man up to warn the Old Man that he had a visitor, and was at the gangway himself to meet him and take him up.

'Well, Mick?' The Old Man, buttoning his shirt, emerging from his cabin doorway. He'd dined ashore with the Todhunters last night, and had obviously been enjoying a 'one-to-three'.

Todhunter said, 'Came to tell you the *Graf Spee*'s been at it again. Here, see this.'

Transcription of a distress call. 'RRR – SS *Streonshalh* – under guns of *Graf Spee* in 25 degrees 1 minute south, 27 50 west. Abandoning—'

'Cut off at that point. Want to see it on your chart?'

'Yes. Yes . . .'

Up to the bridge and to the table, where Andy spread out the appropriate Admiralty chart – number 4007 – and marked that position on it. The Old Man muttering, sliding steel-framed glasses on, 'Martin Vas islands, vicinity of. Still making for this coast, not a doubt of it.'

'*And*' – Andy, pointing at the mainland – 'due east of Vitoria, our next port of call?' He checked it with dividers against the latitude scale. 'Six hundred miles east.'

'December seventh today. If we finish here on the twelfth – then four days' steaming – sixteenth. But (a) the bugger won't hang around twenty-five south for ever, and (b) we might have the Royal Navy with us by then – please God.' A glance at Todhunter. 'Know anything about this *Streonshalh*, Mick?'

'She was up-river here at Rosario ten days ago. Took on five thousand tons of Argentinian wheat for London. She's – *was* – three-eight-nine-five gross, owners Marwood of Whitby, and they'd routed her to Freetown to join a home-bound convoy.'

'Did your homework, then.' Old Man patting his pockets, then giving up – pipe left in cabin. Gesturing towards the chart: 'Freetown, though. *I* wouldn't've routed her that way, knowing what was out there in the middle.'

'Well,' Todhunter protested, 'no one could have *known*, Josh –'

'After the *Doric Star* and the *Taroa*?'

'*Doric Star* sinking was December second, *Taroa* on the third. As I said, she started out ten days ago, so –'

'All right. Point taken. Thick-headed this afternoon. Something I had to eat last night, maybe. Any road, we know *now*, don't we. Hope and pray the Royal Navy does, too. Thanks for coming out, Mick.'

5

On 12 December the last of the coal was out of her by noon, and within a half-hour a tug had come for that half-filled lighter. Deckhands were casting it off now, frayed old ropes flopping over, and the tug's tall, slim funnel belching smoke as it dragged the barge off the ship's side. Hoses had been running for some time, sluicing down decks; the next day or day and a half on the way up-coast would be spent washing and scrubbing out the holds, preparing for the load of iron ore they'd be embarking at Vitoria.

Graf Spee permitting. There'd been no distress calls and no reports of her since her destruction (presumably, destruction) of the *Streonshalh* five days ago, and there was intense speculation, afloat and ashore, as to where she might be by this time. In five days, shifting her ground at, say, twenty knots, covering something like 500 miles a day, by now she could be almost anywhere. The Old Man's theory – in discussion mainly with Chief Engineer Hibbert in the saloon on Sunday – had been that as the *Streonshalh* had managed to put out that distress call including her position, and the *Graf Spee*'s captain would have been very much aware of it, might well have retreated into mid-ocean, be dwelling a further pause out there before starting back in again to these rich hunting grounds.

'Could have reckoned on the Andrew being hereabouts by the time *he*'d've been. So he'd sheer off . . .'

'The Andrew' was a colloquial term for the Royal Navy. Of whose likely movements, presence or absence, there'd been rumours galore. Most of them concerned a cruiser force which the STO in Cape Town had told the Old Man had been deployed at some earlier stage between Port Stanley, Rio and the Plate. This would have been the South American squadron, which Todhunter too had known about but had no idea of its disposition now. Another rumour was one Todhunter had picked in the English Club, where he'd overheard a visiting nabob from the USA asking Mr Eugene Millington-Drake, British Minister at the Legation in Monte, whether it was true that the battle-cruiser *Renown* and aircraft-carrier *Ark Royal* were due here shortly. The Minister had shown considerable surprise, then exclaimed, 'If they are, my dear fellow, by Jove *won't* we have a party!'

You could interpret that in half a dozen different ways. Millington-Drake was, Todhunter said, by no means as light-headed as that might have indicated – might have been *intended* to indicate. In fact he was an astute and well-liked diplomat, and as it happened a personal friend of long standing of the Uruguayan Minister for Foreign Affairs, Dr Alberto Guani. While the men he'd been entertaining in the club that lunchtime, Todhunter had discovered afterwards, were a Royal Navy captain by name of McCall, naval attaché at the embassy in Buenos Aires, and a man by name of Ray Martin who was generally believed to be 'some kind of cloak-and-dagger merchant' also linked to that embassy. Between the three of them, Todhunter had surmised, they might well have had an answer to the Yank's question; on the other hand, maybe they hadn't – this argument being advanced by Hibbert, the engineer, who as well as being exceptionally large, was a slow-spoken man who read a lot and Andy thought was cleverer than he looked. He'd queried why diplomats, spies or even naval attachés ashore should be provided with information about ships or squadrons at sea, intelligence that would surely be closely guarded and which no one in the Legation, let alone the English Club, could really need. Mightn't that get-together have been more or less routine hobnobbing, a mainly social business? If they'd had secrets to discuss, wouldn't they have done it in the Legation – or on private premises?

Todhunter had shrugged – maybe, maybe . . . As a ships' agent, he admitted, while he had frequent dealings with the Consulate, he had no business at all with the Legation, was not either functionally or socially in that league.

On Sunday, though, in that debate in the saloon, the Old Man had elaborated on his own suggestion that the *Graf Spee* might have turned back into the deep blue yonder; what if she'd done so not only to evade hunters who might have picked up her trail by then – in fact surely *would* have – but also turned on to what had been the SS *Streonshalh*'s route from the Plate to Freetown. Since he might well not have known that British tonnage was being routed that way, but having by chance come across the *Streonshalh*, could have reckoned on there being other potential victims on the same route. If his boarding party had found the *Streonshalh*'s papers, for instance – in other words, if her skipper hadn't got rid of them before a boarding party reached her. Several British steamers had left this place homebound during the week *PollyAnna* had been here; one had sailed only that forenoon. And if the battleship *was* out there – staying well out of sight from shore, of course, on the great-circle route from the Plate to Freetown, and doing his damnedest to ensure that his victims did *not* get out any calls for help . . .

'Like a bloody great shark waiting for its dinner!'

Shaw, third engineer, had said that, and for a moment it had hung in the air somewhat chillingly – until the Old Man defused the notion, pointing out that the *Anna* would not be shaping course for West Africa. Far from it – he intended hugging the coast all the way up to Vitoria.

That German freighter, incidentally, had shifted yesterday from the Antepuerto to a quayside berth in a section of the docks called Darsena 1, allegedly to embark general cargo. Whether she'd been waiting for the berth or for the cargo to arrive wasn't clear. But Halloran had queried whether she mightn't be a supply ship for the *Graf Spee*. She'd arrived in ballast after all, which suggested she'd have discharged a full cargo elsewhere on this coast, but mightn't she have discharged it into the raider? And now come in for replenishment which would no doubt be manifested to some German port but might actually get no further than a rendezvous in mid-ocean?

A tug brought a water barge alongside during the lunch hour, and Tom McAlan went to ensure that pumping it into *PollyAnna*'s fresh-water tanks commenced immediately. Fresh provisions had already been embarked, bunkers filled, and the deep tanks forward and aft flooded: standard practice, when the holds were empty, trimming her down both to reduce the tendency to roll and ensure the propeller was at least submerged.

Sailing time was set for six p.m.

Andy wrote to Liza,

> When I have reason to believe I may be home in the reasonably near future I'll write again. I won't be able to say anything in the letter about getting back – there's a lot one isn't allowed to say, for obvious reasons – but simply getting a second letter from me will signal that with any luck, crossed fingers etc, it may not be many weeks before I'll be home. What I'd suggest is that when you next hear from me, *if* you're being shipped off to some wrennery, you might let my mother know where you are or will be. Tell her I've suggested you might do this. Otherwise I wouldn't know where to find you, and if it took very long to get together – heck, I might be gone again. As people keep saying, there *is* a war on. But listen – after you've had that next letter, if some time goes by and you don't hear from me, don't imagine I'm up there learning to play the harp. I might have guessed wrong, been too optimistic – or some higher authority changed its mind and sent us off somewhere

else. It was sweet of you to write – lovely surprise, when I'd been thinking about you so much in any case . . .

Another piece of advice his father had given him – never admit to anything on paper. No harm in telling her he'd thought about her – that was simply paying her a compliment – but better to stay clear of 'lovely memories of last summer' that she'd mentioned, for instance.

Todhunter came on board with the ship's Customs clearance and other business documents at about four p.m., spent some time with the Old Man, then said goodbye and good luck to the rest of them. No, no news of the *Spee*, not a whisper. 'Shouldn't meet her on the route you'll be taking anyway. Sure you won't. Give my love to Blighty when you get there, eh?' The sack of last-minute mails that he was taking ashore with him was already in the launch; by what route it might be sent that would be quicker than *PollyAnna* in getting home was anyone's guess, but you could be sure it would. By air via the USA was probably the answer.

The motorboat had been hoisted and secured – and provisioned, its essential contents as a lifeboat checked, as had been those of the three other boats – but the gangway was left in place for the convenience of the pilot, who was late, finally arriving at about six-twenty, by which time the cable had been shortened-in and the Old Man was muttering about not needing any bloody pilot anyway, another five minutes and he'd leave without the bugger. In fact it was compulsory to employ one, and the fine for not doing so would certainly have cost Dundas Gore more than the standard pilot's fee; what was more, the diminutive 'cruiser' *Uruguay* was lying at anchor just off the naval harbour on Punta Lobos, 3,000 yards distant across the neck of the bay; if the port authorities and/or the Uruguayan navy had opted to stand on their dignity, it might have led to considerably greater delay. In any case, the red pilot boat was coming now: Andy saw it come into sight around the end of the stone jetty called Muella A, reported, 'Pilot's coming out, sir!' and the Old Man signalled to Halloran to weigh anchor.

It wasn't the same pilot – not 'Flash Harry', as that one had been nicknamed. Similar white uniform but less immaculate, and an older, heavier man inside it. As soon as he was on board – the Old Man had sent Andy down to meet him, Halloran being busy on the foc's'l and Fisher *looking* busy at the chart – Batt's men were slinging the gangway up and inboard, dropping a Jacob's ladder over in its place. *PollyAnna* on the move by then, southward at dead-slow towards the gap between the two stretches of breakwater, men on the decks of other merchantmen waving goodbye and good luck as she slid past them. In all their minds, Andy realised, at each departure, was the question of whether *this* one might fall in with the German lurking out there.

Very *much* like a damn great shark.

The entrance/exit between the ends of the breakwaters was about 300 yards wide, with light-structures on both, and on the one to port, marked on the chart as Escollera Sarandi, half a dozen men were fishing over its seaward side. Some of them stood up and waved their hats, and the Old Man moved out into that wing, waved back to them. Sea dead calm, sky a milky haze; at this point you were still in full shelter of the land. Pilot directing the helmsman to take her straight on down the channel now – the channel being marked at approximately half-mile intervals by pairs of light-buoys set well back from its dredged centre. He also rang down for slow speed ahead – as distinct from *dead*-slow speed – so she'd be coming up to four or five knots, with the red cutter following astern. Four knots was the maximum permitted in the channel, although Flash Harry had brought her up it a week ago at nearer ten. It took about fifty minutes anyway, to the Whistle Buoy, was seven-twenty when they stopped to drop the pilot, seven-thirty when they got under way again, with Halloran as officer of the watch, course east by south and revs for twelve and a half knots. Halloran asking the skipper, 'Steaming and navigation lights, sir?'

'No.' Old Josh was hunched in the forefront with binoculars at his eyes, scanning the estuary and its outer approaches while there was still some light to see by, rose-tinted light with the colour deepening as evening faded into dusk. Lowering his glasses, glancing round at Halloran: 'No, Mister – no lights. Double-up lookouts, end of this watch.'

So much for that assurance of immunity in inshore waters. Might have given it further thought, Andy guessed, decided that during the hours of darkness the raider *might* chance his arm and dash in 'on spec', as it were – as sharks had been known to do. Navigationally there'd be no problems, since coastal lights were all functioning. One on Isla de Flores, for instance, which would be coming up to port soon after Andy took over the watch at eight, then a couple of hours later Punta Negra, and Punta del Este after that. In Fisher's watch, Punta del Este would be. But the *Graf Spee* had RDF – radar – so one had heard.

He went down to the saloon for supper – a bit late to be called 'tea' – which was hake caught on handlines off Montevideo early that same morning, bought directly from the boat on its way back in, and in the past half-hour or so fried in batter. Perfection, absolutely. He was back up top shortly before eight, by which time there was even less light left – a rust-red smear of afterglow astern, and ahead no clear horizon. A white light just discernible to the naked eye and giving two flashes four times a minute on the bow to port had to be Isla de Flores; he went to the chart to check on this, and while he was there freshened his memory of the track and DR positions laid off by Fisher; then he took over the ship from Halloran, who'd smelt the fried fish and was keen to get down to it. The Old Man had already gone down for his – in his day cabin – extra lookouts were closing-up at their stations, and Crown had taken over the helm from Edmonds. *PollyAnna* merging into the night now: from a distance of even a cable's length she'd be visible only as an interruption to the dark gleam of the sea's surface – the stars applying that polish to it – and by the swirling phosphorescence of her passage through it. With the propeller as close under the surface as it was, you could hear it, a regular thrashing beat clearly audible over the engine's thrum.

When he handed over to Fisher at midnight – 13 December now – Punta del Este bore 045 degrees at about three miles. In another twenty minutes, when it would be safely abaft the beam, Fisher would alter 27 degrees to port for the next stage of forty miles – three hours, roughly – to Cape Santa Maria. And when Andy came up again at five-thirty – making this customary dawn pilgrimage despite being well aware that with land fixes all the way, star-sights weren't essential – Cape Polonio was abaft the beam at a range of about *ten* miles. From here on, in point of fact, distance offshore would be steadily increasing.

Halloran asked him what he was doing up here – who wanted bloody star-sights? Andy could only tell him vaguely, 'Habit, I suppose. Wide awake anyway, no point *not*.' There'd have been a better answer, but what the hell, it had been a stupid question. Something to do, maybe, with Halloran himself only very rarely getting his own sextant out of its box. He had at the start of this voyage – had taken his own star-sights every evening, as was normal practice.

Andy was at the chart now, checking the Cape Polonio light's characteristics – as if it was his job to do so, which it was not – hearing Fisher and Gorst out there and deciding to leave it to them; he went out into the other wing just as the skipper hauled himself up into the wheel-house, exchanging gruff good mornings with the mate and helmsman. Ingram, that was. The sky broad on this beam was getting lighter, with a colour-wash of mauve above an increasingly well-defined horizon – which Fisher would welcome, for his stars. Wind east or southeast, he reck-oned, but very little of it. No white water, except around her forefoot and along her sides, ripples reflecting that peculiar colour. He'd come up, he admitted to himself, to see this growth of first light and maybe a pocket-battleship in black silhouette against it: had had that image in his mind in half-sleep, and if he'd stayed below probably wouldn't have shaken it off, therefore might not have got back to sleep. What you *wanted* to see, of course, was that it was *not* there: hardly surprising, considering that for several days they'd all had such visions in and out of mind.

Light was spreading laterally as well as brightening and reaching upward, and there was definitely no other ship in sight. Hell, why should there have been? Answer: because the bastard was out there somewhere – near or far, and could as well be near *as* far – and it was for ships like the *PollyAnna* that it would be hunting. Nothing either far-fetched or pusillanimous in recognising this: you'd got away with it, was all.

So far, you had. Or thinking back to events in the Moçambique Channel, might say got away with it *again*.

'Looks like we're on our own, sir.'

The bridge-wing lookout – Brooks, ordinary seaman. Lanky, flaxen-haired, he'd been a 'lumper' – baggage-handler – in Southampton, signed on as a galley-boy in some coaster, signed *off* – and on again as an OS in *PollyAnna* – in the Clyde in August. Pleasant fellow, played a mouth-organ quite well. Andy said, 'We weren't expecting company, this close inshore.'

'Not in daylight, bosun was saying.'

'Bosun's right. Glad you chose this way of life, Brooks?'

'Been called up by now if I hadn't. Left-right, left-right on the barrack square, like. But – yeah, suits me well enough. Sir.'

That was a lot of it, he'd noticed, in most cases – a dislike, even horror of regimentation. On top of that, in some cases – whether recognised or not – love of the sea and the attraction of 'foreign parts'. All of which boiled down to the sense of independence – being one's own man.

Andy suggested, 'By the time we get home you might be thinking of getting yourself certificated.'

'Well – dunno, but –'

'Earn a few bob more. Just about double your pay, in fact.'

'Readin' an' writin''s no great shakes, see.'

'Don't need all that much. Except to know what goes down in your own papers. But if you wanted – must be chaps who'd help?'

'Yeah. Reckon . . .'

'Why not break the back of that first, *then* have a stab at certification?'

'Certification' meaning qualifying as Able Seaman. Which was no sinecure, certainly couldn't be achieved in a dog watch, but could be the making of a man like Brooks.

Getting towards six – 0559, to be precise – and much lighter than it had been. *PollyAnna*'s own greyness noticeable, whereas ten minutes ago you might have forgotten it, assumed she was as black as she'd been before all the scraping and painting in Calcutta. Salt-stained grey now, ploughing sea already glinting blueish in the first flush of the new day, which had of course to be brighter still sixty miles to the east, where although you hadn't a notion of it at this stage, three other grey ships were steering in company for the Plate – cruisers *Ajax*, *Achilles* and *Exeter*. Todhunter might have mentioned them as comprising the South American Squadron, but you hadn't been memorising any of that or taking notes, had none of those warships' names in mind, no way of guessing that those three names would soon be ringing around the world and in such a context that you'd be more than ready to say, 'Oh, we were there!' Aware as you would be by then that Commodore Henry Harwood, flying his broad pennant in *Ajax*, had calculated from as long ago as the *Doric Star*'s sinking on 2 December that the *Graf Spee* might be expected to show up off the Plate by about the 12th, and that six minutes ago, at 0608/13th, *Achilles* having reported smoke in the northwest, he'd sent *Exeter* to investigate it and received at 0614 her signal: *I think it is a pocket-battleship.*

Fisher joined Andy in the bridge-wing.

'Not a sausage, eh?'

'Short on sausages, this morning. Shot any good stars?'

'Gorst has. Can't have him resting on his oars when we were just beginning to make progress.' Waving a hand eastward and upward: 'Light comes quick around these parts, doesn't it?'

He nodded. 'Lovely morning. Virtually damn-all wind.'

'Precisely as forecast – for once.'

'Yeah. Hey, what's . . . ?'

Thunder, in the east?

And again – like distant, rolling echoes . . .

'*Can't* be bloody thunder!'

'Harder edge to it, isn't there.'

'Gunfire?'

'I'd say so. Sainted aunt . . . Hellish long way off, mind you . . .'

More of it then. Big ships' guns in action – God only knew how far away. Or how big. But you could guess. He'd fairly leapt to the wheelhouse doorway: 'Captain, sir . . .'

Those opening salvoes had been heard at six-fifteen and gunfire continued with varying intensity and intervals of never more than a few seconds through six-thirty, six forty-five, 7 o'clock, seven-thirty. The *Anna*'s off-watch crew all over her upper deck, foc's'l and gun-deck listening to it with their eyes glued to an horizon that stayed empty. Clean-edged horizon too, visibility exceptionally good, the land on the other side, a dozen or fifteen miles away, clear-cut even to the inland hills – a visibility range of twenty-five miles at least – but out there to starboard not a wisp of funnel smoke. So the battle – *Graf Spee* versus whom? – had to be a long way beyond that horizon; ships in action, needing full power, would surely be emitting smoke. Might be the cruisers Todhunter and the man in Cape Town had spoken of, Andy guessed; and by now, an hour and a half since it had started, men in them would have been killed and maimed, ships' armour-plating blown away, hulls punctured, gear smashed, guns knocked out. *Graf Spee*'s guns, please God; but that might not be the case, one knew only too damn well it might not be. The rate of fire, he realised, *was* slackening, thunder storm petering out. He found himself face to face with the Old Man at this moment – had stood aside to make way for him coming back out into the bridge-wing – asking him, 'D'you think cruisers *could* stand up to a battleship with eleven-inch, sir?' The answer came over his shoulder as he pushed on out: 'Don't know they *are* cruisers, do we. As I recall it, there was talk of bigger ships. But' – pausing, glancing round with a blunt hand raised, two thick fingers crossed – '*could*, I reckon. Well enough handled, could, I'd say.' Shake of the head: 'Bugger's got the reach as well as the weight, though, hasn't he . . .'

There'd been no thunderclaps now for several minutes. Time – seven forty-five. And he, Andy, had to take over the watch at eight, before which it would be as well to cram in *some* sustenance – a bucket of coffee and whatever else came to hand quickly and in quantity. No time to shave, or—

'Plain language signal, sir – to all British merchant vessels from cruiser HMS *Achilles*!'

Young Clowes, looking excited; the skipper snatched the flimsy sheet from him. Muttering it aloud to himself jerkily, as if having trouble reading Dewar's or Starkadder's scrawl: 'German battleship – *Graf Spee* in position – *that* – steering to enter Plate estuary – speed twenty-two knots. Shipping advised stand clear . . .'

Staring round as if bewildered – at Andy, Fisher, Brooks and Clowes – swivelling then to bawl to Halloran, '*Graf Spee*'s running for the Plate! They got her on the bloody *run*!'

6

The warning message to merchant shipping was put out again an hour later and repeated hourly throughout the day, but it was coming then from the *Ajax* instead of the *Achilles*. *PollyAnna* was well clear in any case by this time, plugging steadily up-coast on a northeasterly course with normal lookouts posted and all hands employed cleaning decks and holds – steam-powered saltwater hoses backed by men with buckets and brooms sluicing coal dust from decks, gear and superstructure into the scuppers, and from her holds into the bilges, pumps running to clean *them* out, initially staining the ocean in her wake. In the wireless room, meanwhile, the operators were shifting constantly between frequencies in search of intelligible reports of the recent battle, or at any rate of the phase of it that seemed to have ended at about seven-forty. The one clear picture you had at this stage, derived from that warning message, was of the *Graf Spee* pounding south-westward at twenty-two knots and British cruisers shadowing; to an extent it was almost all you needed, would be weeks or maybe longer before you'd have it explained that that signal had been made by the *Achilles* the first time because *Ajax*, Commodore Harwood's flagship, who *would* have made it, had been dismasted, and was thus unable to use her wireless until she'd rigged a jury mast and aerials. Or that the *Exeter* had been ordered back to the Falklands for repairs. As the best-armed of the three – 8-inch guns, the other two having 6-inch – she'd been the *Graf Spee*'s primary target, in consequence of which at quite an early stage she'd had only one gun left in use – one of the pair in her after turret – and no internal communications, no gun-control circuits either; she'd been holed, had a heavy list, flooding in her forepart and internal fires. By the end of the engagement the one remaining 8-inch gun had been locally controlled by her gunnery officer who'd moved down aft from the smashed fighting-top to give his spotting directions via a small armoured hatch in the turret itself; he, the gunnery lieutenant, crouched at it on his knees with one eardrum burst and the other ear pouring blood.

Not that the other two had got off lightly. *Ajax*, for instance, before her dismasting had been hit twice in her bridge and had had two of her four 6-inch turrets knocked out in a single direct hit from one of the Germans' 11-inch. She and *Achilles* had been shooting fast and accurately while manoeuvring like destroyers to dodge their heavyweight opponent's very much more powerful and very well directed armament, a crucial stage coming then at 0710 when Harwood had ordered them to close the range as rapidly as possible so as to take more of the heat off *Exeter*. You acquired bits and pieces of all this gradually: sparse facts embroidered with conjecture, backed maybe by logic, otherwise only probability. The upshot in any case being that they *had* 'got her on the run'; and whatever the detail of it, the ultimate truth and glory was of Nelsonian spirit and tactics at their simplest and utmost having led to victory by a small, heavily out-gunned force against one of the most powerful ships afloat – well, in comparison to *their* capabilities anyway – and one who'd had no problems at all in handling herself against unarmed, defenceless *civilian* ships.

This was the picture that had taken root and grown in his own mind, and others' too, Andy thought, in the course of the long day, although it wasn't easy to differentiate later between what you'd actually known of it or had partly guessed at, in some areas maybe adding two and two and making five. But there *had* been a lot of bits and pieces, especially later, sunset-time for instance, in the brilliance of its afterglow – a series of plain-language transmissions in English from a French passenger ship, the *Formose*: inbound to Montevideo, she was being overhauled by the *Graf Spee* on that same track, and therefore quite reasonably calling for help – in English – to the British cruisers which she had in more distant sight, black miniatures a long way astern but holding on doggedly, from time to time dashing in terrier-like to keep their giant adversary on the run. The French-accented broadcast rattling on, 'Captain giving order for passengers put on lifebelts. Mamas taking children in arms with coverings of wraps. Now shells falling around *Graf Spee* – we *see* zem!' The cry for help had become an excited commentary as the battleship rushed on by, the Frenchman's outpouring ending with, 'Oh, most heartfelt thanks to our British allies!' While very much more formal, even stilted bulletins were coming out of London at about that same time and throughout the evening – typically one they'd taken in shortly after Andy had come on watch at eight, for instance, to the effect that the German pocket-battleship *Graf Spee*, having been brought to action at first light this morning off the mouth of the Plate by cruisers of the Royal Navy, had turned away under cover of smoke, apparently with the intention of taking shelter in Uruguayan or Argentinian waters; this was repeated at nine p.m. with the additional information that the *Spee* and her pursuers, reportedly now inside the Plate estuary although her captain's intentions were still far from clear, were again exchanging broadsides.

PollyAnna had left Rio Grande abaft the beam by this stage. Fifty-five miles offshore, course unchanged, showing no lights, her big propeller thrash-thrash-thrashing through black water glittering with stars. ETA Vitoria first light 17 December. Get the full facts of it all then, Andy thought, moving out into the port wing of the bridge to check that the lookout was on his toes. Then back in, through the wheelhouse and out the other side, exchanging a word or two with the lookout in that wing while using binoculars to look for movement on the gundeck. Which – all right, there *was* . . . Back in the wheelhouse, he found that during his brief absence the Old Man had come up, was at that moment agreeing with some comment the helmsman – Harkness – must have made. Harkness was older than most of his shipmates, a widower who'd left the sea at the time of his marriage and now come back to it. Old Man nodding: 'Was, lad. Truly was. Make a good yarn for the kids and grandkids, won't it. You've kids, haven't you – yeah, two boys, I remember – living with your sister-in-law, right?' Turning to Andy then: 'All right, Holt?'

'Losing just over a knot to the current now, sir.' He gestured towards the land. 'Not done badly though – Cape Santa Marta's near abeam. Saw it a couple of times, ten minutes back. Pure fluke, of course.' Had seen its light, he meant, the double flash every fifteen seconds which should not have been visible at anything like its present distance. Phenomenal visibility wasn't unheard of on this coast – and at this time of year, presumably – but he hadn't realised it could apply at night as well as by day. Almost 2330 now. Checking that in a side-glance as he cleaned the front lenses of the glasses, then put them up, resuming his own contribution to the looking out. Old Man meanwhile crouching below the level of the surrounding windows while holding a storm-lighter to his pipe.

'Captain, sir?'

Starkadder – second wireless officer – stepping off the ladder, hadn't seen him until the skipper had turned, still at the crouch and clicking the lighter again, sucking its flame down . . . 'Uh?'

'Private to you, sir. Plain-language message via the Cerro station.'

The Cerro was the wireless station at Montevideo. Actually a hill with the remains of an old fort on top and the signal station built on that, on the bay's western side.

The conical hill was invaluable as a leading mark when making landfall. Andy was continuing his search of the horizon on the seaward bow while the skipper straightened himself and took the message over to the chart where he could read it inside the canvas light-screen. It could hardly be a change in their orders, Andy guessed; anything of that sort would have been sent in the owners' code, not plain-language. Maybe it was his birthday or something, and Todhunter knew it . . . Starkadder muttering, however, in his fluid Welsh lilt, 'Bloody amazing, is this. If it means what I'm guessing it does. You'd never have dreamt, not in a million years –'

'Man's pulling my leg.' The skipper was on his way back to them. 'Pulling my damn leg, *must* be!'

'Would ye say so, sir?'

'No. Since you ask. I would *not*.' Slapping the signal sheet with the back of his other hand. 'Because the man's not that much of an idiot, and – the way she was heading, last thing we heard . . .'

PollyAnna lurching slightly in her sensitive, light-ship condition, feeling the movement of the sea under the growing influence of a moderate northeasterly. The breeze had backed that way and had strengthened during the past hour, might even qualify as a wind now. The Old Man said, 'It's from Todhunter. Inviting me to guess what ship's just dropped her hook in the Antepuerto. *You* want to guess?'

'Christ . . .'

'Right. He's telling us the bloody *Spee*'s in there!'

Three days and nights plugging northeastward then, with confusion on the airwaves as to precisely what was happening, but in all their minds a mental picture of the raider lying at her ease in that anchorage within a few cables' lengths of British merchant ships whom in the normal course of things she'd have sent to the bottom with their cargoes and as like as not their crews. There'd no doubt be a lot of diplomatic wrangling going on, and it would be up to the Uruguyans to sort it out, basing decisions on international law – the Hague Convention – and German pleas, maybe threats. Those were enormous guns to have trained on the centre of a smallish city – if that was how it went. The British cruisers, meanwhile, maintaining a blockade in or just outside the estuary; but it was in a lot of seamen's minds that if the *Graf Spee* wanted to blast her way out past them, they'd have a hell of a job to stop her.

Presumably she did *not* have such intentions. Or guts. Astonishing. Had suffered greater damage in the action than any of the scanty bulletins had indicated, maybe; this seemed to be the general view. But she'd still had twenty-two knots at her disposal and had been using her guns until long after sunset. Anyway, the Uruguyans shouldn't allow her to stay longer than twenty-four hours, was the skipper's opinion: twenty-four hours to effect whatever repairs were necessary to make herself seaworthy – but without increasing her capacity to fight, that was a clear proviso in international law – then clear out, take her chances. With a choice of several routes open to her, at that, as far as getting out of the Plate estuary was concerned, as well as the distinct advantage of 11-inch guns and as likely as not *thirty* knots. But she was still there on the night of the 14th, and apparently – according to the BBC – she'd asked for *ten days* . . . Another item was that the Uruguyan dockyard authorities having refused to help, Argentinian technicians were being sent down-river from Buenos Aires. Meanwhile, a British merchantman, the SS *Ashworth*, had sailed on the 15th, and under the terms of the Hague Convention had to be given a twenty-four hour start before a hostile man of war could be allowed to set out after her. Chief Engineer Hibbert suggested in the saloon that evening, 'Might suit us to have her stuck there a while. If it's still only cruisers we got outside. Sail a steamer so she can't leave – and if we got any pull with the Uruguays, that too – hold her while we get a couple of *big* ships up?' He could have been right, since on the 16th another merchantman, SS *Dunster Grange*, was sailed

– and the world told about it, one of the commentators pointing out that this should hold the *Spee* in Monte another twenty-four hours . . . Shortly after this, however, it was announced in a multi-language broadcast that following a technical inspection of the battleship ordered by the Uruguyan government, the President of the Republic had decreed that she might stay a total of seventy-two hours, time limit expiring 8 p.m. on 17 December.

Sunday, in other words.

'Hardly seventy-two hours, is that!'

'From the time the decree was signed, maybe?'

'So what'll they do if she still hangs on?'

'Intern her.' Halloran, authoritatively to Shaw. 'Presidential decree's a presidential decree, they'd bloody have to.'

PollyAnna would be tied up in Vitoria by then. She'd be there Sunday morning, in fact. The Old Man had cabled the Dundas Gore agent, a Dane by name of Martensen, on Friday: *ETA Vitoria first light December 17th, ready to commence loading on arrival*, and had his reply this Saturday noon: *You should anchor to the south of Baixia Grande on arrival and await pilot*. The Old Man's comment on this being, 'He should teach his granny to suck eggs too, shouldn't he.' Arrival procedures at this port or that, pilotage and berthing arrangements were all in the Admiralty Sailing Directions, in this case the *South America Pilot Vol. I*. He didn't need bloody neutrals telling him what he should or shouldn't do: the bugger was probably only worried that their early arrival might spoil his Sunday lie-in. Relationships with this agent, Andy guessed, weren't going to be as sunny as they'd been with Todhunter.

Sunday's first light, then; the approach and entrance to Vitoria looked somewhat tricky. Approaching on a course of north by west with a scattering of low, hump-backed islands four or five cables' lengths to port, sea calm and glittering with dawn; dead ahead in that slightly confusing mix of haze and darkness the entrance to Baia do Espirito

Santo, which wasn't easy to define visually on account of its encircling low-lying foreshore. Not easy while this light (or lack of it) lasted, anyway. Which as a matter of fact shouldn't be for long now: the flush of dawn that was creeping inland over that western curve would put paid to it pretty soon – was in fact already high-lighting the Ponta de Santa Luzia, hardening its edges out of what only minutes ago had been so wishy-washy as to be indistinguishable. That there was a mile-long hidden reef diagonally across the bay's centre was one of the first things he'd noticed in a preliminary study of the chart; then seen that it was a hazard one didn't need even to approach, thank God: you'd be making a sharp turn to port before getting anywhere near it – and in fact anchoring before *that*, in the anchorage stipulated by the Danish agent. *Baixio* was Portuguese for a shoal, Fisher had mentioned – having looked it up – and Baixio Grande was this one right in the entrance to the bay. It did at least have a light-buoy on its southwestern edge – if it was lit, and hadn't drifted, as some of the marker buoys in the Plate estuary did tend to do, their last pilot down there had mentioned – and seemed glad of, maybe because it justified *his* employment. Anyway, you'd anchor say half a mile south of that shoal, and on the present line of approach – course 345 degrees – well, daylight *was* coming fast now, but even if you'd been making the approach in total darkness you'd have had Ponta de Santa Luzia coming up to port at a distance of about three quarters of a mile with a light on a tower there group-flashing four every twelve seconds, and for a cross-bearing if you needed it, another on Ponto do Tubarao a mile and a half on the other bow.

Not so bad, therefore. And you'd know it next time. If there *was* a next time.

Half-five now. Had been up early not only for this landfall but because late last evening there'd been a report from Montevideo (an American broadcaster who'd been on the air before, giving his name as Mike Fowler) to the effect that although the *Graf Spee* had been given until

81

Sunday 8 p.m., rumours had been circulating that she was secretly intending to break out during this last night. It would have made sense from the German point of view, they'd all agreed. Take the blockading cruisers by surprise, smash out past them – with several more hours of darkness ahead in which to disappear. In fact – Hibbert had pointed out – the cruisers would *not* be taken by surprise; unlikely they would have been anyway, but that Yank's broadcasts would be as receivable on board those ships as they were here: the Huns might well be cursing Mr Fowler. And anyway, there'd been no break-out; the airwaves were still busy but nothing sensational was coming through. Five thirty-five: Fisher had rejoined him at the chart – briefly, leaving again now, commuting between here and the Old Man, watching those bearings and the distance run by log; you wouldn't much want to run on over the Baixio Grande, which the chart showed as having only six feet of water over it. If that buoy *had* been out of position for instance – which it might have been; no navigator worth his salt would have taken its reliability for granted. It was in sight now, in fact, a small black lozenge in the old telescope's lens, its light no more than a flicker as the sea around it reflected these early stages of the dawn.

There were no other ships in the anchorage. They'd passed several southbound steamers during the night, and some of them might have come out of Vitoria. According to the pilot – *Sailing Directions* – the channel they'd be using – river actually, estuary of the Rio Santa Maria, the town and wharves of Vitoria being four miles upstream – could be used by night as well as by day. It was surprising because at some points the channel itself wasn't even a hundred yards wide. Anyway, out here in the first light of day *PollyAnna* was at anchor just before six in fourteen fathoms, a cable's length southwest of the buoy, the charted position of which had by then been verified. The bottom was soft mud again; very soft, just dropping the hook into it left her rolling gently in what might have been mushroom soup, despite that depth of water. Andy saw to the hoisting of the yellow flag then – since this was their first Brazilian port of call, they'd need pratique again – and also four-flag identification; it could be read from the pilot station, which was on an island less than a mile from where she was lying: Ilha dos Practicos, around which one had as yet seen no movement, not even a light.

Breakfast, therefore. This would have been Halloran's watch, but he was shirking it, leaving only Janner with one lookout/bridge messenger; Gorst would relieve Janner when he'd had his breakfast.

The pilot boarded them at eight-fifteen, coming out from the island in a red motorboat with a black 'P' on each bow. Halloran was on the foc's'l by then and the Old Man sent Andy down to receive the man as he hauled himself up the Jacob's ladder. He was dressed in what was virtually a Merchant Navy officer's uniform – summer whites like theirs – with a master's four stripes on the shoulder-boards and scrambled eggs on the cap's peak. A little man of about forty with a limp; could have been a cousin of Batt Collins – the same sharp, foxy look. Andy shook his hand: 'Holt. Third mate. Speak English, Captain?'

A side-to-side wagging of the head. Glancing up to where the Old Man was peering down at him from the bridge-wing. 'Little English, sure.' A thumb to his chest then: 'Mendoza, me.'

On the bridge, Andy introduced him: 'Captain Mendoza, sir – talks English.'

'Good for him.' Skipper with his hand out. 'Welcome aboard. Josh Thornhill.' Jerk of the head towards the estuary: 'Up-river now, eh?' He'd signalled to Halloran to weigh anchor, asked the Brazilian as he turned back, 'What news of *Graf Spee*?'

'Ah. *Ah*!' That was a *good* subject; you could see he liked it. 'Sail from Montevideo tonight, eh?'

'You reckon?'

'Go Buenos Aires maybe.'

'You think *that*?'

A shrug: 'More bigger English ships come, eh?'

'That a fact?'

'So is Germans saying.'

'D'you mean on the wireless, or Germans here?'

'Here. Motor vessel *Glauchau*. For engine repair, is here. Wait for spare part coming maybe from Rio. Been already three day.' A glance for'ard: they had a hose playing over the side, sending mud streaming off the cable as it came clanking up. And a yell from Halloran then – anchor aweigh. Mendoza pointed, telling the helmsman, Shuttleworth, 'Thisaway – slow ahead.' Checking the compass, adding, 'Two-nine-zero degree.' A glance round at the skipper: 'Maybe tonight a battle?'

'On course two-nine-oh . . .'

Shuttleworth's Adam's apple wobbled as he reported it. Tallish, balding, slightly stooped; as good a helmsman as they had.

They stayed on 290 until the light-structure on what the chart called Ponta de Santa Luzia bore due south, then altered to 245. Mendoza pointing out for the Old Man's benefit, 'Ponta do Tagano. *This* side, Ilha do Boi. You like I tell you, Captain? Not come Vitoria before?'

'Never. Fifty years at sea – darn near – and never was.'

'Is a port we make now, you see. City old, port little but soon make very good. For the mines, huh?'

Fisher had brought the chart from the table, folded appropriately. *PollyAnna* holding this course for about ten minutes at six knots – one mile covered – leaving on their right a starboard-hand marker-buoy flashing red. The buoyage wasn't as in British waters, where a starboard-hand buoy was green and can-shaped, port-hand buoy red and conical. Starboard-hand meaning a buoy you left to starboard when entering with the flood tide, or up-river: *that* wasn't any different, only you had to be on your toes to remember which was which.

Mendoza was waving an arm like a vertical pendulum or metronome, pointing from bank to bank: 'Here is for build a bridge. When there is moneys for it.'

Old Man reaching for the chart: 'Long bridge, eh? Cost plenty?'

Something like a mile of bridge. Mendoza looking serious, nodding. 'Plenty. Plenty.' To Shuttleworth then, 'Starboard – two-six-seven.' Pointing again: you could see the next mark, a port-hand buoy half a mile ahead, the light on it sparking green. Old Man asking, 'Berth alongside, will we?'

'Sure. Berth where is chute for loading. See where is number three berth?'

'Here.' Fisher displaying the chart, skipper then asking was the place crowded, ships at berths four and five, for instance? Not bothering to ask about numbers one or two because it was plain from the chart that there wouldn't be enough water alongside at that point for any ship of ocean-going size. Presumably berths were to be constructed and dredged there, otherwise why put numbers on them? Mendoza was telling the skipper, 'At berth four is Brazil ship. Coming tomorrow also a French – berth this side, south, new berth only for ore – no cranes, no chute – not yet. But number three is good – has chute and cranes, not use ship's gear, uh?'

Halloran muttered behind them, 'Five days instead of ten, then?'

'Be nice, wouldn't it. Oh – First Mate Halloran.' Performing introductions. 'Captain Mendoza.' They'd shaken hands, Mendoza continuing his explanation, that berth five although marked didn't yet exist, had no quay and wasn't dredged. The Old Man asking, 'So where've you put the German?' Andy didn't hear the answer, he'd moved out into the bridge-wing to see whether the pilot boat was following – and it wasn't. Mendoza would no doubt get other transport back to the pilot station, or wait until some other ship needed taking out. They'd passed the green-flashing buoy; the next green light wasn't on any buoy but on a point of land, a light tower. The channel would be at about its widest here, he guessed. The swapping of green for red and red for green was still confusing, but in daylight you could at least see from the buoys' positions on which side you had to pass them. On a dark night, though, seeing only the actual light flashing and having no shoreline for guidance, if you forgot for a moment that it was all back to front – well, could be somewhat dangerous. Back in the wheelhouse then, borrowing the chart from Fisher he saw that the river opposite the town was marked as an anchorage – half a mile of it roughly, width about a cable's length – having an anchor symbol in the middle of it. Confined-enough water for a ship of any size to swing in, he thought. Shuttleworth at the pilot's order was edging her further over to starboard; pilot leaving him to it then, drawing the skipper's attention to other features – islands and so forth, and up ahead what looked like a very sharp narrowing of the waterway. And some mention of the fact that the tide was flooding, adding maybe two knots to her speed. But a further course adjustment suddenly – to get out of the way of a tug with a string of barges. The tug-master had for some reason taken them on what was surely the wrong side of an island: well, you could see what he'd done – cut a corner through shallows which he'd have known were all right for him, but had now to cross back into the main channel, at serious risk of a collision if this ship which presumably he hadn't seen at an earlier stage had *not* put her helm over. As it was, the barges were going to be tossed around in the *Anna*'s wash. In fact it was happening to the tug already. Serve him right if it broke some lines, lost him his tow. Mendoza had shot out into the wing to scream and shake his fists at him; was returning now, muttering angrily in Portuguese and gesturing to Shuttleworth to bring her back on course.

The narrows were now only a few hundred yards ahead. Half a mile, maybe. And between here and there, two islands to starboard and one to port; there was plenty of room between them, but despite this, after another minute, Mendoza was ringing down for dead slow. Wondering why – and borrowing the chart again – Andy realised (a) that with the tide running as it was you could have *stopped* engines and still be carried on through, and (b) that beyond the bottleneck you'd be coming up to the wharves that fronted the town, where there'd be other ships alongside and/or at anchor, so that busting through there at any speed, dragging a wash through those narrows with you, wouldn't be popular at all. Although you did need some engine-power on her, simply to maintain steerageway; and another factor was that the wharves didn't start immediately after that constriction: there was a stretch of, say, a couple of hundred yards of natural shoreline, *then* the straight-edged quays.

He gave Fisher back his chart. Hearing Mendoza ask Halloran whether all the holds were empty.

Affirmative grunt. 'Except for essentials. Ore'll be waiting for us, will it?'

'In trucks – rail trucks – is coming. I don't know they work today. Some time work Sunday, some time work not.' A shrug. 'Senhor Martensen telling you what's fix up, eh?'

The Old Man came in on that. 'D'you know Martensen well, Pilot?'

A shrug. 'Know him, sure. Is not such big place you know, Vitoria. Not *yet*. See, now . . .'

Entering the narrows, she was making about three knots – one by her own efforts, two by the tide's. Effectively therefore making no wash at all. Marker-buoys on both sides indicating that the channel was even narrower than it looked. But once through this squeeze you'd be in comparatively open water. Rough foreshore to start with, as expected – both sides – and on the town side – starboard – a small warship. Patrol boat, they might call it – in view suddenly, moored in there with an anchor out for'ard and a floating brow plus wire-rope moorings connecting stern to shore. Until this moment the little ship had been hidden by the bulge of land on that side. Brazilian ensign at its masthead and a gun on the foc's'l, sailors in white caps pausing to stare as *PollyAnna* passed within thirty yards of them. Mendoza telling the Old Man, '*Cabedelo*. Is minelayer. Building the last year, in Rio – six like this one. Pretty, huh?'

'Hm.' He had his glasses on her. 'What'd she be – five or six hundred tons?' Training the glasses left then: 'And there's your German . . .'

At anchor in mid-stream, her bows this way of course, stemming the tide. Lying as she was you couldn't see much of her but you'd guess at roughly *PollyAnna*'s tonnage. Black hull, grey upperworks, here and there patches of red lead, and that red, white and black thing – Nazi merchant ensign – sluggish above her counter. Mendoza had taken the chart from Fisher, was jabbing a forefinger at it under the skipper's nose: 'See. The *Glauchau* here. Brazil vessel *Volcao* here. *There.*' Pointing at the ships themselves then, in the stream and alongside in berth four. 'Pass *Glauchau*, also *Volcao* – for turning here, and' – fingernail tapping the chart again – 'in berth three. OK?'

'Port side to, then. Suits me. Right way for when we leave, eh?'

'Stop engine, please.'

Shuttleworth reached to the telegraph, jerking it over and back again. Mendoza answering the Old Man, 'Depart on flood tide only, Captain. Ebb tide, ships this side not move, tide holding them against the quay – eh?' Demonstrating it – his hands up and pushing an imaginary ship's hull against a wall. *PollyAnna*'s single screw was now effectively at rest but the tide still carrying her up-river; Andy thinking of the single screw because turning the ship in such a confined tideway would have been a darned sight easier if she'd had two of them. No doubt the Old Man would show them all how to do it – or out of respect for the pilot's local knowledge might leave it to him. Telling Halloran now, 'I'll have an anchor ready for letting go, Mister.' Which *was* of course the answer. Drop the hook, have the tide swing her around it, then go slow ahead *against* the tide while weighing and then manoeuvring into the berth. He yelled after Halloran, 'Less than a shackle'll do it. Eight and a half fathom we'll be in.'

'Starboard . . .' Mendoza to Shuttleworth. Pointing – that he should take her midway between the anchored

German and the Brazilian steamer alongside in berth four. Brown hull, yellow upperworks, twin yellow funnels with brown badges on them. Five thousand tons, Andy guessed. While the German, of which one could now see more, might be more like 7,000. Men were moving on its decks, a drift towards the port-side rails. With a Red Ensign flapping in their faces, he guessed, they'd be wondering what might be happening or about to happen around the *Graf Spee*. Well, who *wasn't* – or at any rate wouldn't be once this ship was berthed? Meanwhile, of course, the Huns would love to see them make a mess of the berthing operation: the Old Man would be conscious of that, too. Most likely leave it to the pilot – who after all was being paid for it, and must have executed the same manoeuvre a thousand times – but be ready to shove *his* oar in if said pilot showed signs of screwing up.

Asking Mendoza now, referring to the chart, 'This a shoal here – this Pedras What'sit?'

'Pedras das Argolas. *Si* – four fathom. Don't be scare, Captain, we not touch!'

'Who's bloody scared?'

'Four fathom where is the buoy, you see?'

She'd be OK in four fathoms, empty as she was. You wouldn't chance it, though, because it could turn out to have become, say, three and a half fathoms overnight. As was stated often enough on charts and plans: *Depths in the dredged areas may be considerably less than indicated.* Passing the Brazilian ship now: and a clattering from for'ard as Halloran's foc'sl party walked the anchor back with the windlass until it was clear of the pipe, then screwed on the brake. They'd take the windlass out of gear now, and have only to release the brake to send the anchor plunging down.

Passing the Hun. Not a soul on the *Anna* so much as giving it a glance. Not even when a Hun shouted something that was probably abusive and his shipmates around him laughed. Mendoza did glance in that direction, though – and looked sour about it. He asked the skipper now, 'I do this, or you?'

'Go ahead. Holt – in the wing, pass orders for'ard.'

'Aye aye, sir.' Scooping up the megaphone as he went, Fisher leaning in the doorway to hold it open. Mendoza telling Shuttleworth, 'Engine slow astern.' Because while she was still making two or even three knots in relation to the shore and that anchored ship, in a tide that was running at the same rate she'd have no steerage-way, would take not a blind bit of notice of her rudder whichever way you put it. She was well enough clear of both the Brazilian and the German, was getting into the eight, eight and a half fathoms which the chart showed as the depth of water opposite the centre and eastern end of berth three, and if one wasn't going to risk grounding on that allegedly four-fathom patch – which would make the bloody Germans' day for them –

Mendoza called, 'Drop anchor!' and Andy howled, 'Let go!' Brake off, anchor splashing down, cable rattling out. Mendoza telling Shuttleworth, 'Hard port!' and himself ringing down for *half* astern. The anchor had to take hold, that was all – snub her round, put her on the swing.

7

The tug that had made a nuisance of itself in the vicinity of Urubu Island, Mendoza had admitted, should have been here to assist in *PollyAnna*'s berthing. Sure, there was another tug, he'd said, but it was laid-up for boiler cleaning: as that guy knew perfectly well, had simply been chancing his arm, wanting to complete some job he should have finished yesterday.

'You handled it damn well, though.' The Old Man was trying to say goodbye to Mendoza at the open doorway of his cabin. Port Health were on board, Halloran looking after them, and as soon as they'd cleared her and cleared off you'd have the agent, Martensen, with his paperwork and problems – and please God, mail and local currency. At the moment the connection between ship and shore was a narrow plank over which the Health team had come teetering ten minutes earlier; and the agent had to be that long stick of a man in a grey suit and a Homberg, who a few minutes ago had arrived abreast the ship in an open-topped motorcar, got out and then seen flag Q still flying, dumped his bag back in the car and begun pacing up and down like Felix the bloody cat. Mendoza wasn't thinking of leaving yet, though; replying to that 'handled it damn well' with 'Show *them* – huh?' – pointing in the direction of the German ship, repeating, 'Show *them* how can be done – huh?'

A nod. 'Wouldn't've done to have cocked it up.' They

were at the rail outside the day cabin now – port side, skipper looking aft at the ore chute which was positioned abreast number five hold. In fact it was a matter of having positioned the ship, as that old chute contraption wasn't moveable; he'd be moving her a fair number of times in the next few days, shifting her this way and that along the quay for each hold gradually to receive its quota. This had been Mendoza's main reason for berthing her with her bows pointing downstream; the other way round, she'd eventually have had to come out almost stern-first from berth number two, having nosed further and further into the narrowing slot between the quay and that buoyed shoal, Pedras das Argolas, and *then* turn – again on an incoming tide, and by that time of course deep-laden.

He *had* done a good job, in fact. And the Old Man liked him. Only wished he'd bugger off. Well – he'd have to now. Port Health had finished, had just appeared out on deck there with Halloran. Yellow flag fluttering down, and the gangway already swinging over, under the direction of the bosun, two deckhands guiding it with steadying-lines. The Health people would be gone and Martensen on his way up here in a minute – but Mendoza was still in no hurry: waving towards empty wharves and commenting, 'Nobody work today, huh?'

'Except a few of us, including me. You got a home to go to, have you?'

'Ah, *si*. Home, wife, children –'

'Lucky man.'

'You not?'

'No. Not now.'

'In England – no home, no wife?'

'Home, of sorts, but no wife.' Pointing: 'Is that Martensen?'

'Hm.' Disinterested glance: more interested in this English skipper's wifelessness. 'Martensen, sure. But, Captain – hearing what happen with *Graf Spee* now, eh?' A sweeping gesture towards the town: '*Everyone* listen this!' A narrowing of the eyes: 'Germans, too – Germans in

Glauchau? Is not good, *Glauchau*. I tell you, Captain –'

'You don't have to. I know it. No German's any bloody good.' A glance down towards the gangway: Port Health were ashore and Halloran was waiting to greet the Dane. The skipper clamped a friendly but compelling hand on Mendoza's arm, turning him towards the ladder. 'She's here for engine repairs, you said. I'd have thought they'd have put her alongside. Anyhow –'

'To anchor is what her captain is *wanting*, and why I am saying—'

'I'd be keen to hear it, but I *must* see this damned agent, then fifty other things – paying the hands and – see, I'm *sorry*, but –'

Andy and others drinking coffee in the saloon heard the buzz of the loudspeaker as it came on, and the American voice from Montevideo telling them in the cheery tone of a wakey-wakey call, 'Sunday seventeenth September, day the *Graf Spee*'s time runs out! Her luck may be running out too, who knows! Anyway, by eight o'clock this evening, Uruguayan time, she has either to get the heck out or be interned here. It's being said there could be as many as five or seven British warships waiting for her to put her nose outside the three-mile limit, but like a lot else that's being said, it's nothing more than rumour. For all I know or anyone has been able to tell me authoritatively, the blockading force is still just three cruisers, same ones that drove her in here. There's been mention of bigger Royal Navy ships, an aircraft-carrier and a battlecruiser, but only that they were expected at Rio to refuel – to 'bunker' as seamen call it – and Rio's a thousand miles from here. Maybe the German captain – Langsdorff – knows for sure what odds he'll be facing, maybe he doesn't, but as of now his ship is still right here in the anchorage, along with a German steamer, the *Tacoma*, which has moved out from the inner harbour and anchored close to her – for what purpose is something else we don't know. From this café on the waterfront – a café in which I may say I'm standing on a table, to see over the heads of the crowd outside – well, I have a view of both ships, and when I know what's going on you can bet you'll get to know it too. A transfer of stores is I guess the most likely thing. I might add that a lot of folk here in Monte believed the *Spee* would make a break for it *last* night: that seemed credible enough, might even have been their best bet, but it emerges now that Captain Langsdorff was not even on board, went out to her by launch no more than an hour ago, having spent the night in the German embassy. But incidentally, when I referred a minute ago to *a lot of folk* here in Monte – let me tell you there truly *are* a lot – *thousands*! And of course this waterfront in particular is jammed solid . . .'

You could visualise it, those quays – the *muelles* – and the streets behind them jam-packed with people. But nothing might happen for hours yet, most likely wouldn't, and one didn't have the patience to sit around listening to what was still no more than speculation and a certain amount of 'local colour' – the commentary continuing, as Andy swallowed the last of his coffee: 'Folk packing the waterfront, on roofs even and in every window, agog to see whether that mighty ship will make a run for it, face the near-certainty of battle – in which case it might be asked why did she run away from battle in the first place?' Perfectly sound question, might well be asked, but only Langsdorff and company could have answered it. He shut the saloon door behind him; he was as eager as any of them to hear of those bastards getting their come-uppance, especially having in mind the ships like this one that she'd preyed on – ships sunk, crews drowned or otherwise slaughtered, *PollyAnna* herself having come close enough to that same treatment.

Didn't bear thinking about. No *point* thinking about it.

Mail, in any case, was the thought in mind. A hope that the agent might be bringing some.

No packed waterfront *here*. A van just driving off, and – with perfect timing – a man who could only have been the agent just starting up the gangway. Grey lightweight suit, grey Homberg, Gladstone bag; and Halloran at the ship's side waiting for him. He was replying to some question from Halloran: 'No – no work today. Sunday, for one thing, but also this *Graf Spee* business, all ears are pressed to wireless sets. Tomorrow 0800, loading is to start.' Adding as he got up there and put his hand out: 'If you'll be ready for it – as I presumed you would be. How d'you do? I'm Martensen.'

Grave-faced, with a rather formal manner and perfectly enunciated English. *Too* perfect – Germanic, rather. And that excessively loud music, Andy realised, was coming from the German ship, not from the Brazilian along there. Wagner? He was only guessing, knew damn-all about it, but that was how it sounded, the name that sprang to mind. Leaving those two, he moved over to the starboard side for a look at the German. Tide on the turn, he realised, *Glauchau* on the swing, within minutes would be lying with her stem up-river. Time now being nine-fifty. Crossing back to the shore side he heard Halloran say, 'I'll take you up, then. But d'you have mail for us?'

'No private mail. Only ship's business.' Cold blue eyes, weak mouth. 'You'll have had some in Montevideo, I imagine?'

'Some, but—'

Anxious to hear from Leila that she still loves him?

'Could get some tomorrow. If we do I'll send it straight along. You'll be here – what, six or seven days?'

'Skipper'll aim for six or less, since Sundays are a washout. Depends how they handle that chute – eh?'

'Oh, they are efficient enough. The equipment is antiquated, sure, but – you might be surprised. Do you have all the dunnage you require?'

A nod. 'Took on a whole lot in Calcutta not long ago.' Dunnage in the form of heavy burlap mats, the holds needing cushioning against the ore's weight and other characteristics, rock being heavier and harder than coal, for instance, as well as having cutting edges. Martensen had glanced at Andy, taking in his rank, such as it was, and deciding not to bother. Halloran similarly – only inviting the agent, 'This way, then . . .' Andy having hoped for mail because Wednesday – the twentieth – would be his twenty-first; there'd been no reference to it in recent letters from home and he'd told himself they must be holding their fire: closer to the great day there'd be a rush of it. Still, could be tomorrow or Tuesday, even the day itself. And if there wasn't any – which was a possibility one had to face now – hell, couldn't blame *them* for it. Might have written in what would have seemed to them good time, and the GPO sent the lot to Sydney or Mombasa.

His father would most certainly have written. Mama too. *And* Annabel.

But what the hell – one might well have been at sea, pure chance that one wasn't. *Is* a bloody war on, mate . . .

'Ah – so sorry!' The pilot, Mendoza – Andy had almost knocked him down in the screen doorway. He tried French: '*Pardon, senhor . . .*'

'*Pas de quoi.*' Smiling, and now back to his brand of English, with a glance at the thin, single stripe on Andy's sleeve: 'Third mate, uh?'

He nodded. 'Name's Holt, sir.'

'Not in Vitoria before?'

'No.' Backing out, letting Mendoza out, and glancing townward – stone-coloured buildings, slate-grey roofs, near-vertical slicks of chimney-smoke, a cathedral spire against pale-blue sky, backdrop of green hills. He pointed: 'Nice to walk, up there?'

'*Very* nice.' Nodding emphatically. 'After sea is good, such place.' Squinting up at the hillsides . . . Then abruptly, 'But also I tell you – *that* way' – to the right, the start of a road slanting northeastward like a gully through the close-packed buildings – 'that way, then turning to the' – working it out, slapping his own left forearm – 'to port, eh?'

'Left.'

'So – left. Café-bar, Manolo's. Is good fellow, not cheating you. Also girls very nice.'

'How far?'

'Ah.' Screwing his face up. 'Three, four hundred metre. Tell him you friend of mine. Mario Mendoza, huh?'

Except for some RCs, including Fisher, who'd been given leave to visit the cathedral for mass, the hands were being allowed shore-leave from midday, could more or less please themselves in the interim, except for cleaning up their own quarters, especially the mess-hall, in which once the skipper had got shot of Martensen he'd lay on his usual Sunday business, reading a few prayers and suggesting a hymn or two to sing. It was mid-forenoon by the end of this, and he had still to make and record pay advances in cruzeiros to those who'd applied for them; these as it happened included Andy, whose intention was to make a bit of a reconnaissance of Manolo's – in advance of Wednesday, when he thought he might treat himself to a birthday binge.

News from Montevideo was that the German steamer *Tacoma* had shifted berth, re-anchoring between *Graf Spee* and the shore, interrupting the watchers' view of whatever they were doing. Crowds were even thicker along the waterfront than they had been earlier, and the café from which the broadcast was being made had sold out of practically everything.

Music booming across the water from the *Glauchau* now was brass-band stuff – reminiscent of the emissions of that other one, at Monte. And if they were listening to that, Andy thought, they were *not* listening to broadcasts from Monte or elsewhere. From Berlin, for instance; or even, if they had a competent interpreter of English on board, to that Yank. Unless – well, might be listening to news broadcasts down below, maybe? *That* noise only on deck – camouflage, persiflage anyway – or call it Teutonic bullshit – plainly for the ears of outsiders only, since there was only one Hun on deck. No – two: another had just emerged from the midships superstructure, joining one who had a chair – of sorts, was sitting on something anyway – close to the ship's side, starboard side amidships, abaft number three hatch. Those two were presumably the watch on deck. Or the one on the chair was – the newcomer taking over from him. Which rather bore out the concept of the rest of the crew congregating elsewhere, listening to the wireless. To the Yank, even – they'd only need one man capable of acting as interpreter. Both of those still there, though: seated Hun still seated, the other leaning against the rail and in the process of lighting a cigarette.

No gangway rigged. A Jacob's ladder was all, and not where those two men were, but much further aft – abreast the mainmast, i.e. between hatches four and five. There was a boat close to the ladder's foot, too. Black-painted, not all that easy to see against the ship's black hull: motor-boat with a shelter for'ard and its engine amidships, engine about the size of a cabin trunk.

You'd have thought that the quartermaster, or watch on deck, would be stationed at the point of entry to the ship, namely the Jacob's ladder. It made no sense *not* to be.

For a better view, and a possible solution to the puzzle, he went up to monkey island, stopping en route at the chart table to borrow Fisher's telescope. Up top then he found cadets Gorst and Janner doing bookwork, 'hearing' each other on the subject of *Regulations for the Prevention of Collisions at Sea*, and on the spur of the moment asked them if they'd like to go ashore with him after lunch, climb those hills – maybe have a look at the cathedral on the way. They both said they'd like to, then continued with their studies while he crouched in the starboard for'ard corner and focused on the German.

Only one man there now – the one on the chair. He was smoking; maybe they *had* changed round. Blue trousers, paler blue shirt, a round, fat face. Brass band still pumping out martial music: where he was sitting it had to be *deafeningly* loud.

The loudspeaker – or *a* loudspeaker – was fixed to the bulkhead, that for'ard corner of the superstructure, virtu-ally within his reach. *Would* be, if he tilted the chair over a bit and stretched a long arm. It was the usual box-shaped thing, shiny brown wood showing up clearly against grey paintwork. Nobody in his senses would voluntarily remain that close to such a volume of sound. *Had* to, obviously. And there'd been music of sorts playing at about that same pitch since early morning – certainly since *PollyAnna* had slid in past them a couple of hours ago.

Think about it. Because it didn't make any sense, and things *should* make sense. At sea, anyway. Scanning the rest of her now. All five hatches covered and secured. Only that one boat in the water: you could see the davits it had come out of, also two lifeboats secured in theirs. One derrick, the closest to the empty davits, was the only one not lashed down on its chocks. For the purpose of – well, when the boat was hoisted it would surely be brought up on its own falls, so the derrick had been left ready for use for some other purpose.

For hauling up the engine-spare or spares Mendoza had said they were waiting for?

Boat collects spares from shore, brings them (or it) to where it can be hoisted on that derrick. Boat itself then to be hoisted. Sounded like sense: but such a state of readiness rather suggested *imminent* arrival of the spares – and equally imminent departure of the ship? Whereas surely her engineers would fit the spares before departure – if they needed them at all – taking at least an hour or two, possibly a *day* or two.

But all right, if they didn't want contact with the shore – as presumably they didn't, having chosen to lie at anchor – they'd bring the spares off in the boat, hoist them on that derrick, fit them in however long the job might take, and push off – having paid their dues and got clearance, needing the boat for at least *that* much shore-going.

It still looked like a ship just waiting for the 'off'. The look, the feel of it. Even though there was no discernible heat-haze at the funnel-top. And the band playing on. The guy on the chair lighting another cigarette. Might well need it too, Andy thought, glancing round as Gorst answered Janner, who had the book open in front of him,

Gorst with his eyes shut in an effort of concentration: 'Where by any of these Rules one of two vessels is to keep out of the way, the other shall keep her course and speed. When, from any cause, the latter vessel finds herself so close that collision cannot be avoided by the action of the giving-way vessel alone, she also shall take such action as will best aid to avert collision.'

'Spot on!'

Andy commented, 'Common sense, isn't it.'

Gorst shrugged. 'But why couldn't they have put it in plain English. I ask you – *as will best aid to avert . . .*'

They landed soon after lunch – Andy, the cadets, and Howie, fourth engineer – in shirtsleeves and flannels, starting off eastward along the quay for a look at the Brazilian, *Volcao*, in her smart yellow and brown livery. A heavy-built quartermaster in white ducks came to the gangway's head and stared down at them as they passed; Andy raised a hand in greeting and the man called something first in Portuguese, then English: '*Graf Spee* – feex her wagon, hunh?' Showing the right spirit, anyway. Howie called back, 'Feex it good an' proper, chum!' Then they were abreast the *Glauchau*, Andy seeing that the watch-keeper – *a* watchkeeper – was still there, same place and still seated, but wearing a hat; the speaker was thumping out a marching tune that he'd heard before but couldn't have named. She was about a cable's length out into the stream, with her bow still pointing upstream of course; you could see the strength of the still ebbing tide where it fizzed dirty-white around her cable and sheer stem. Nearer three knots than two, he guessed.

Janner queried, 'Particular interest in the Hun?'

'Well.' Stopping, staring. 'There's certainly one peculiarity to my mind. Spot it?'

Oddly, none of them did.

'See the character in the boater?'

They'd all noticed him. So what?

'The boat and the Jacob's ladder? Wouldn't you expect

your gangway watch to be less than two hundred feet from it?'

'I'd say he's sitting there for the shade he's got.' Howie again. 'If a boat were coming he'd see it, gi'e 'em a shout below an' nip aft – eh?'

'See the loudspeaker that racket's coming out of?'

'Aye.' Double-take then: 'Crikey. If yon *is* a –'

'Drive anyone nuts, wouldn't you have thought?'

'Could be it's a wireless playin' inside – not that thing at all. Screen door there's open – uh?'

'Then anyone inside there would be *really* deafened – and we wouldn't be hearing it this loud. I'll bet they're cursing it all over town.'

'Aye.' Howie nodded. 'Siesta time, an' all.'

'Surprised someone doesn't shut 'em up. Port Captain or police, whatever.'

Andy agreed with Gorst. 'That *is* another peculiar thing. Here's where we start inland, though.'

Some boys on bicycles flashed past, yelling to each other, the bikes juddering over the quayside's cobbles: they'd come out of the straight, narrow street Mendoza had pointed out to him. To the left up here, then left again. There were a few perambulating couples and families; would be more later in the afternoon or evening, he guessed. Mendoza's turn to port came after only about fifty yards. He told them, 'Left here, then I reckon we head for the cathedral spire. But did you check out the hills?'

They had, and Janner, who'd made a pencil sketch of them, proposed starting on Morro Sao Francisco – charted height about 300 feet – then pushing on about a mile further inland, down through a valley and up to Morro Frade Leopado.

'Then, return route over this one – Morro do Avezedo. None of 'em's exactly Snowdon, is it.'

'Still hear that Hun's racket . . .'

Could see Manolo's, too. White-painted brick frontage with a glass door in it, the name Manolo on that in flowery script, and some iron tables and benches each side of it.

No light showed from inside, and with the narrowness of the street it was dark in there: not open for business at this hour, therefore. Well, as someone had mentioned, it was siesta time. There were notices displayed inside the glass of the door which might have been menus and/or given opening and closing times, but he didn't pause or go close enough to read them, because (a) they'd have been in Portuguese, and (b) he didn't want to draw attention to the place, risk having Halloran hear about it and queer the pitch. He'd thought of this when Mendoza had mentioned girls.

They were back on board by five-twenty, and Andy was in the saloon by half-past, drinking tea and hearing the American telling his audience, '. . . "skeleton crew" is what we keep hearing about now. Reflecting what I caught on to a little while ago – that it's men, not stores, that are being transferred, and not out of the *Tacoma* into the *Graf Spee* but the other way about, boatload after boatload of *Graf Spee* crew being shunted over and disappearing below decks in that steamer the minute they get on board. They have their kit with them too, which suggests they're staying – leaving behind only that aforementioned "skeleton crew". What's being asked now of course is *what for*? For instance, a suicidal battle against tremendous odds, Langsdorff taking no more to their deaths than he has to? Or is he putting his ship into internment in Buenos Aires, leaving as many free as possible? That, I'm told, is as good a bet as any – to get her up-river to BA he might only need, say, a couple of dozen men. And he couldn't *fight* the ship, man all her guns and control positions, so forth, without a full compliment. So what other choices does he have?'

Halloran growled, 'Sneak away. Flat out. Man one turret – and torpedo tubes maybe – crack on thirty knots or more – and she has radar, in other words can see in the bloody dark . . .'

The chief engineer was shaking his head, with one hand over his eyes, but not bothering to comment. McAlan murmuring, 'I'd've thought you'd man all your guns. Apart from speed, fire-power's her big advantage.'

The broadcaster was saying, 'Consensus here is that scuttling would not be an option – that the implication of unwillingness to fight, well, wouldn't be acceptable. On the other hand . . .'

Fisher cut in quietly while the Yank continued, 'Man's already made it clear he doesn't want to fight by running for Monte in the first place, hasn't he. I think he *will* scuttle.'

'And be shot for cowardice when he gets back?' Halloran shrugged contemptuously. 'Want to bet, Fisher?'

'No. But then –'

Shutting his mouth as the Yank told them, 'Fresh news now – Langsdorff has expressed the intention of sailing at six-fifteen. Gave this assurance to the Uruguayan authorities, apparently. So in fifteen minutes, ladies and gentlemen . . .'

'Twelve and a half minutes.' Fisher asked Andy then – both with one ear to the continuing waffle – 'Good run ashore, was it?'

'Terrific. Did literally run – *down* the hills, mind you.'

'. . . another piece of news is that some tugs have arrived out there in the bay from Buenos Aires. They're German-owned – a German company in BA. But what part they'll be playing in this . . . Yeah, what was that? Ah – something I missed, but I see it now – *Graf Spee* has hoisted two very large German ensigns, one at each masthead, and – sure, she's weighing her anchor. To folk outside that's audible, the chain clanking in. So here's what we've been waiting around for all day – the answers to our questions, climax of this historic naval drama. Yeah, it's begun, *Graf Spee* is on the move; and so incidentally is the *Tacoma* . . .'

Steward Jackson meanwhile setting the table. Knives, forks, and side-plates for bread and cheese. Now the pantry hatch was open, there was an aroma of frying fish. Andy guessing that his father might be listening to this commentary; Dewar had told him it was being picked up by the

BBC and simultaneously retransmitted in their world-coverage. You could bet the old man would be getting it. So would the cruisers outside there, waiting – as likely as not still only the three of them, awaiting battle, even praying for it. Well – why not? Moving round to his usual place at the table he whispered to himself, 'God, be with them.'

'Folk – hear this now – the *Graf Spee* has up-anchored and is on her way out of the anchorage, with the *Tacoma* following. In fact the *Spee* is already outside. From where she was berthed, didn't have far to go, and I guess I was a little slow on it. She's hauling round to starboard now – that's to say, turning into the sun which is on its way down, shadows already lengthening, and a fine, still evening. Well, I know there's a dredged channel out there that leads due south, but Langsdorff seems to be ignoring it. Maybe with three-quarters of the crew out of her – could be light in other respects as well – he's reckoning to pass clear over the mud shoals. What's being said now is maybe he's cutting a corner on his way up the estuary to Buenos Aires – *maybe* – because if those Royal Navy ships were aware of any such intention you can bet they'd try to catch him between here and there, and I guess they *could*, if—'

He'd checked the flow. Background voices intervening, and Jackson with the first plates of fried fish in his large, allegedly heatproof hands, assuring Hibbert, 'Skipper's having his up top, sir. Watkins took it up couple o' secs ago.' Skipper would have his own speaker on, naturally. This one now blurping back into life with, 'The *Graf Spee* has stopped. *Tacoma* too. Less easy to see now . . .'

'Spuds this way, Janner?'

'Ah – sorry . . .'

'Wouldn't mind being back in that Antepuerto this minute. Grandstand view from monkey island, uh?'

'Hake, is this?'

'Hake it is, sir. Brought in this morning.' Back to the hatch: 'Two more 'll do it . . .'

But neither *Graf Spee* nor *Tacoma had* stopped, apparently.

Error of observation, that last report: but as mentioned, rather tricky light . . . Nothing else of much interest was coming over now: if the *Spee* was still underway she'd have to be moving pretty damn slowly, Andy thought, to be still in sight. And still nothing happening, as far as the broadcaster knew . . . Until seven, anyway – or just after, four minutes past – when a small Uruguayan warship stopped the *Tacoma*. Probably that little so-called 'cruiser' which he remembered seeing in a naval anchorage close to Punta Lobos – from where she'd have been in an ideal position to intercept or overhaul the Germans. Sprat pursuing whale, one might think: but *Tacoma* having sailed without obtaining clearance, maybe.

And now the tugs from BA had come into it, or been brought into it: were alongside the *Tacoma*, embarking *Graf Spee* crewmen from her.

'Can't guess why, but that's what they're at . . .'

It took a while, too. The hake was finished, cheese and fruit in circulation. Then, at about seven-thirty: 'The *Graf Spee* has stopped. Definitely has, this time. She's on her own . . . No, there's one tug with her, and boats in the water. Kind folk here are telling me she's outside the three-mile limit. I'll take their word for that. She's lying stopped anyway – black against a reddening sunset, and' – a two-second pause, then louder, tones of growing excitement – 'She's hauled down her ensign! Should've said ensigns, plural – she had two flying. Hauled 'em down, which surely means—'

They all knew what hauling down an ensign meant. Jackson had put coffee on the table, no one was speaking, but cigarettes were being lit. Seconds, minutes ticking by: you could have been in church, if it hadn't been for the drifts of smoke and the coffee jug going round. Then, drowning out a mutter from Halloran of 'Come on chum, what *are* the buggers—'

'Oh now, see *that*! A great shoot of flame – and another – lighting a sky that's already lit by the kind of sunset you only see in pictures! The heck – *another* flame – that one must've shot up a hundred feet or more – and the sound's reaching us now – cracking, thunderous explosions! The *Graf Spee*, ladies and gentlemen, is burning from stem to stern, the sunset's fiery red beyond her, but believe me her fires are brighter!'

And that was that. *Graf Spee finito*. No more RRR calls on *her* account. She'd founder there where she was burning – if there was enough water under her to founder in. It wasn't deep, out that way. Andy asked Fisher, 'Feel like fresh air? Stroll along the quay?'

'Good idea.' Fisher glanced at Halloran. 'All right?'

That was Fisher being tactful: Halloran had the duty anyway. He'd shrugged: 'Why not?' To Andy then: 'Doubt you'll find a boozer open, Sunday.'

8

Sounded like a party going on aboard the *Volcao*. Dance-band music and female as well as male voices – loud enough to be hearing it on the quayside despite the noise still blaring from the *Glauchau* in midstream. Fisher solved the puzzle of such goings-on on a Sunday evening: 'This ship's wireless, Andy. A play or something. Up loud to drown out the Germans.'

'Of course.' They'd stopped, on hearing it, now moved on again. 'Thought it might be the *Spee*'s demise they were celebrating.'

'One thing's for sure, *they* aren't celebrating.' The Germans – *Glauchau* – of which having passed the Brazilian they now had a beam-on view, as well as the full blast of her noise: the riding lights at her mastheads were halo'd by sweaty-damp night air and reflected in quivery streaks on dark, fast-moving water, the glow from uncovered scuttles here and there yellowish, less distinct. Having swung with the flood tide it was her port side she was displaying; and there *was* a source of light from where the watch on deck had been – a floodlight effect across the forefront of the midships superstructure. From this level and angle of sight the watchkeeper wasn't visible; conclusion being that if he was there at all he'd stayed where he'd been before, star-board side, whereas one would have expected him to have moved to this side, facing the town. Same with the Jacob's ladder, which any watch on deck would want to have in view.

The loudspeaker too. Wouldn't they have wanted *that* on the town side if they were so keen on annoying the local populace? And this gave rise to yet another question, which had occurred to him earlier on – why some port or civic authority hadn't asked them to shut up.

He told Fisher, 'They had a quartermaster of sorts sitting there all day – starboard side, close to the island's fore corner. Starboard after corner of number three hatch, right? And the speaker from either wireless or gramophone within a yard or two of his head, blasting his eardrums out. As like as not still there – they'd have *a* watch on deck, wouldn't they. What caught my eye earlier on was his being stationed there amidships, and a Jacob's ladder – just that, no gangway – back aft near the mainmast. Hey, there *are* Huns moving around there – just this moment – see, passed across the light?'

'I saw. Pacing the deck. Mourning the *Graf Spee*, no doubt.' Fisher added, 'Knowing the Andrew's on this coast might have 'em a touch nervous, too. Like we felt leaving Monte.' They'd resumed their stroll along the quay. Fisher said, 'Old Man might put the word out, in fact. May have done already. Can't sit here for ever, after all.'

'If transmitting from inside the port's allowed – d'you know? Or if he reckoned he'd get away with it. Neutral port, so forth. Bastards are safe as long as they stay put, but whether *that*'s allowed, or for how long . . . Awaiting engine spares – could be that they are, but who knows?' He'd stumbled over something – dead cat, maybe: they were diverting around a heap of chain cable. The light was good enough where there *were* lights, but there were dark areas in between. 'The German's well down to her marks, incidentally – did you notice?'

'Don't think I did. Take your word for it . . .'

'Well, listen – what if she'd been heading for a rendezvous with the *Spee*? All right, I know, *Spee* was said to have a support-ship with some other name – forget it, but – may have had more than one? Big ship, big crew, longish time at sea, must need all she can get. And this one's full of *something*. With the *Spee* gone west, what'd she do?'

'Ask for fresh orders.'

'Might've done that and been told "sit tight". This is as good a hidey-hole as any, isn't it. And look here, Mendoza said she'd been here three days – means she arrived on the fourteenth. *Spee* took refuge in Monte on the thirteenth. It'd fit, wouldn't it – they've arranged a rendezvous, *Glauchau* finds herself as it were stood up, with whatever she may be carrying – stores, food, ammunition – huh?'

'Not bad as a theory. Certainly not implausible. But look – have we come far enough, d'you think?'

'Well – as you like, but, so happens, up that street here and then to the left – three or four minutes, no more – there's a café-bar called Manolo's. I'd thought I might take a gander, see what it's like – if it's open. Ten minutes from here, I'd guess. May *not* be open – Halloran could be right. Thing is, I have a birthday coming up –'

'We all know about your birthday.'

'*Do* you . . . ?'

'Wednesday – right? Gives you Monday and Tuesday to prospect this joint – or others, must be dozens, uh?'

'Tomorrow I'm duty on board. OK, still leaves Tuesday. But this place was recommended by our pilot, Mendoza. I wasn't asking, he just came out with it. Anyway – as you like. The town does seem fairly dead. Although *they* don't know it . . .'

They being Brazilian sailors, arm-in-arm and singing. Andy had put on a tweed jacket and Fisher a sweater – having been in uniform 'whites' all day – but apparently were still recognisable as Merchant Navy men: there was some clapping and a shout of '*Graf Spee* kaput, huh?' from the Brazilians, and some cheering. A few other passers-by, civilians, were then smiling and raising their hats, offering what might have been Portuguese congratulations. Fisher protesting, 'Cheers for the RN – fine. *We* didn't have a darned thing to—'

'It's our side winning they're happy about. Don't like

Germans – and what's wrong with that? Look, there *are* a few people about – up that way more than here, and that's where Manolo's is. D'you mind, Don – quick look-see?'

Off the cobbles, across the dockside road and into the one the sailors had come out of – the way he'd gone this afternoon with the cadets. Narrow pavement here now, Fisher in the lead, and as they progressed there were actually quite a few people around. Andy telling Fisher, 'Forty or fifty yards up here, no distance at all, really. Convenient for the likes of us, eh?' Ahead of them some well-dressed people were coming out of a house in which music played. Loud voices, major spillage of light, party breaking up or moving on. A fat man in a fedora pointed his cigar at them as they passed, called in a high-pitched tone, 'Victorious British Navy come to Vitoria, huh?' The women began clapping and another man called, 'Bravo, Bravo!'

'Crazy. Or pissed. British *Navy* –'

'We *are* British Navy. British *Merchant* Navy.' He was walking backwards, acknowledging the applause and waving goodnight to them, but a motorcar with huge headlights and high, sweeping mudguards was drawing in to pick them up, and they forgot about the British Navy. Andy shouted to Fisher, who was by now some distance ahead, 'Left at the next corner. *Left*, Don!' Putting a spurt on then to catch up – Fisher having heard him after all and swung left as instructed – and rounding the corner after him at fair speed Andy almost collided with a dapper little Brazilian commander or lieutenant-commander – a lot of gold braid on his sleeves, anyway – and a tall, dark girl who just about took his breath away. Long dark hair over bare brown shoulders, big slanted eyes, wide red mouth that happened to be open, laughing, and a figure no artist or male imagination could have improved on. She seemed to be laughing at his reaction to her – and maybe not actually repulsed by the look of him. The commander wasn't much enjoying the situation, going by the snarl on his face, only talking fast and urging her along – away. In the last half-minute that street corner had become quite busy, was so at this moment anyway, and the girl, while allowing herself to be hauled along was looking back at Andy over one lovely shoulder: was then gone, less spirited away than dragged. Andy stock-still and semi-stunned, telling Fisher, 'I'd ask *her* to my party! Oh, sainted *aunt!*'

'Are we going to find this pub?'

'Didn't you *see* her?'

'Also saw the guy she was with – who looked distinctly riled –'

'Must have either rotten eyesight or ice-water in your veins, Don!'

'Neither – but I have a steady girlfriend, as I've mentioned a couple of times, and – all right, being no sex-maniac –'

'Saying I *am?*'

'Saying one should be able to pass a pretty girl in the street without getting the bloody staggers!'

'That one wasn't – isn't – just a "pretty girl", she's—'

'This the place?'

They'd stopped. Andy insisting, 'That girl – Don, you must admit . . .'

Although maybe Don wouldn't. While *he* – Andy – most certainly would. Old for his age maybe, or maybe not, but in this department he *was* susceptible: had a notion you couldn't be too old for it. Or too young, even. And when they looked anything like *that* one – well, words failed. Were fading anyway as he on the light and noise emanating from Manolo's, and began coming back to earth. 'Came by this afternoon and it was shut, all dark inside. So, quick look inside – since we're here – OK?'

There were some people at the outside tables, but the jollity was all inside, and the glass door was standing open. Background guitar music, Spanish, pushing other sound to higher levels, men and girls at the bar and at tables, and one couple trying to rhumba on a dance-floor about three feet in diameter; other heads were turning as Fisher and Andy came in, meeting more of that instant recognition and applause. Two uniformed Brazilian merchant

111

officers – from the *Volcao*, might be – stood up and bowed, and a table of what looked like petty officers – naval, from the minelayer perhaps, and they had women with them – made a show of clapping. Others, all kinds, welcoming them as they pushed through towards the back of the room – Andy in the lead now, Fisher bleating, 'It's ridiculous, really quite embarrassing . . .'

'Manolo?' There were two men behind the bar; Andy had picked on the nearer of them, who'd called simultaneously – in English – 'Welcome, senhors!' Sounding as if he might be English. Dark, about thirty, could have done with a shave. Andy tried again: 'Are you Manolo?'

'Tonio!' The British-sounding one beckoning the other, who on closer inspection was obviously the boss: older, fatter, more of a Brazilian look about him. Moving closer: 'I can be of service, senhor?'

'Are you Manolo?'

'For my many sins, why yes, I—'

'Captain Mendoza said this was the place to come. He piloted us in this morning. My name's Andy Holt, this is Don Fisher.' Shaking hands across the bar – then with the other one, who said his name was Frank Cluny but that most of them called him Franco.

'British?'

Shake of the head: 'South African.' A nod towards Manolo. 'Tonio's a Spaniard. What'll it be, fellers?' Glancing away then at a smallish man – grey hair, grey suit, a hard-faced blonde and another, younger man with him. They were crowding in on Andy's left, the grey-headed one putting some question, addressing it either to him or Fisher, sharp brown eyes flickering between them; Andy meanwhile telling Franco, 'Two beers,' and the small man asking 'Sheep *Pooley-Anna*, you?'

Looking down at him for a moment: deciding it wasn't as rude as it had sounded, only that he wasn't anywhere near at home in English. He nodded: 'How'd you guess?'

The younger one cut in with, 'This Senhor Mario Caetano, he is Acting Port Captain. Is correct how I say it, "acting"?'

Caetano took over again. 'How I know that is here now *Pooley-Anna.* You asking how I guess – uh?'

The blonde aired *her* English then with, 'Port Captain go Montevideo, so is mine hosband become—'

'Most *everybody* go Montevideo!'

A waitress said it, giggling as she squeezed almost lovingly – certainly very closely – past Fisher and then Andy. Closer than ever when up against Andy. Little dark girl, very shapely. Frank Cluny, getting their beers, wagged a finger at her and then beckoned with it to Andy, who'd been gazing after her, to move in nearer. He said into his ear, 'Caetano speaks more German than English. Wouldn't say anything you'd sooner *they* didn't know. Have a word later, man, OK?' Voice up loud again: 'Two beers it is, gents, and' – querying glance at Manolo, who nodded – 'on the house, this round.'

He hadn't always been a barman. In his home town of Durban and then in Beira he'd been a shipping clerk, moving up to Beira when the company he worked for offered him promotion to assistant manager at that branch. But they'd ratted on him – he'd been there three years, picked up the language and done well for the firm, yet when the manager retired, and it had been taken for granted that Frank would step into his shoes, buggers sent up a new bloke – a Capetonian who happened to have married a daughter of one of the directors. As a sop to Frank when he made a fuss about it, they offered him a trip as supercargo in a steamer that was routed more or less round the world and had Vitoria as one of her ports of call, and – cut a long story short – he'd spent a few days and nights ashore, got tied up with this popsie, and – hell, bloody ship sailed without him. His own fault, sure – the *really* awkward bit coming when it turned out the girl had a husband. One of those things, man – damn-foolery compounded by the fact he'd never before drunk much cachaca.

'*That*'s what it is. I'd forgotten, I was thinking it must

be gin.' Andy looked at Fisher: 'Remember – in the old *Burntisland*?'

Caetano, who'd still been hanging around although his wife seemed to have departed, raised his glass of the colourless liquor. '*Prosit!*'

'What's that mean?'

Fisher said, 'German for cheers.'

Acting Port Captain Caetano shaking his head: 'Cheer. I mistake me.' Then: 'Cachaca too much, uh?'

'Meaning he's had a few too many?'

'Paint-stripper, isn't it. Rum of a sort, but –'

The other man said, 'Cane spirit, high proof.'

'Homemade?'

'Not here, man.' Cluny looked offended. 'Tonio 'd never *dream* of –'

'You a partner in the business, Franco?'

'Well. Working my way in, sort of.'

'What you were saying – about the hole you were in when you got stuck here then found she had a husband –'

'Very emotional, while it lasted. Would you believe it, the bugger went off again, and before I could blink – hell, you wouldn't believe it, man –'

'She came calling?'

'*Didn't* she just. After all that. Anyway, far as making a living's concerned, I did tally-clerking for a while, and a couple of other things, and to make the ends half meet, worked nights for Tonio as well. *And* got shacked up again. No, Christ, not the same one. Two kids now, so –'

'All's well that ends well.'

'Might say so. Yeah. Make a living. Tonio and I get on – good friends all over, too. Did think of shipping back, joining up, but then what about Maris and the brats? Look, I better vamoose, man . . .'

He'd only joined them 'for a moment', when they'd shifted to this table, leaving Manolo – Tonio – presiding at the bar. The rush had been ending by then, was definitely over now, they'd closed the kitchen and the girls were washing up. Cluny said into Andy's ear as he left them, 'Talk later, eh?'

'Not *much* later. Starting work at eight.' Checking the time: 'Oh, *no* . . .'

'I did suggest' – Fisher, primly – 'some time ago –'

'Work loading sheep, huh?'

Caetano's man, asking it of either of them. He'd been listening intently to everything they'd said. Wanting to improve his English, maybe. But from time to time interpreting some remark or other to his boss. Fisher was answering that rather pointless question: 'We're at the ore chute. As you'd know, surely – if you have anything to do with the running of the port.'

Andy liked that. Fisher showing his teeth for once. Justifiably too – there'd been no explanation of that one's function, or of his relationship to Caetano. He – Andy – backed it up by asking Caetano, 'D'you speak German?'

Blank stare. He'd heard, and by the look of him might have understood, only wasn't keen to admit it. The other one – name Ferras, something like that – was providing a translation, and Andy supplied him with an unnecessary explanation of the question: 'He said "*prosit*" a minute ago.'

'Mistake. Few word he learn, get mix up. In English, "Cheer", hunh?'

'Speak other languages?'

'Ozzer?'

'French, for instance. Speak French?'

'Coming tomorrow French sheep, yes.'

'*Moutons*, you might say?'

'Well.' Fisher scraped his chair back. 'Let's be on our way?'

'Why not. Before it gets any worse.' Andy reached to shake Caetano's hand. 'Goodnight, sir.' For good measure he shook the other one's as well. In for a penny . . .

At the bar then, Cluny told him, 'Goodnight is *Boa noite*.'

'You wanted a word?'

'Not in earshot of that skunk. Any rate, there's a guy I'd

want with us, fill in on detail. Usually drops in, course of an evening, tonight of course he hasn't. Wouldn't want Caetano or Ferras seeing the three of us chewing the fat, either. Come back tomorrow, man?'

'If it's something that really matters.'

'Matter to *you*, damn sure.'

Manolo proposed to Cluny, 'Why not see them out, see they turn the correct direction?'

Andy shook his hand. '*Boa noite*, senhor. Thanks for those beers.'

'My pleasure. Come again?'

'Will do. And on Wednesday, may bring some friends. My birthday.' To Cluny: 'That's what we could have been talking about, anyone asks. OK?'

'Great.' He looked pleased with this. 'About a table, and the menu. Sure . . . Show you out now, eh?'

Caetano and Ferras were leaving too, though, would be neck and neck with them. The South African gave up, went and held the door open for all of them – Andy and Fisher exiting and turning right, Andy looking back before they reached the corner and seeing those three still in conversation on the pavement.

Back on the quayside, heading west, the *Glauchau*'s music maybe softer than it had been earlier, more like a Salvation Army rendering than the massed bands of the Brigade of Guards, Fisher broke a longish silence with, 'Still waters running deep, eh?'

Andy nodded. '*Something* stinks.'

'I'd have thought a Port Captain would've worn some kind of uniform. Merchant marine with four stripes, most likely. All right, in his civvies, Sunday evening, but he didn't even call himself "Captain" – I mean the others didn't, not even that stooge, Ferrars . . .'

'Could be that Caetano's a pen-pusher. Office-wallah, knows the ropes and routines well enough to stand in for the boss when he wants time off. If there's no one else. He's a chum of *theirs*, anyway.' Gesturing towards the

Glauchau. 'Cluny said he was – you wouldn't've heard, he was making sure Caetano didn't – told me he spoke more German than he does English.'

'Didn't like it when you picked him up on the "*prosit*", did he?'

'No, he didn't. Interesting slip-up, though, wouldn't you agree – suggests he has German or Germans on his mind? I should have said – Cluny also told me not to say anything in Caetano's hearing that I wouldn't want Germans hearing. Why I didn't say anything about the bloody music. Should have, maybe – if anyone was going to tell the bastards to cut the volume, Port Captain would, wouldn't he. We'll see tomorrow what Cluny has to tell us, anyway.'

'What he has to tell *you*, Andy. I'll have to take your duty for you, won't I. We might swap, Monday for Tuesday?'

'Yes. Christ, yes.' They were passing the *Volcao*. She'd fallen silent now, and there was no sign of life at the gangway head. 'Hadn't thought. But if that's OK with you –'

'Prospect doesn't disturb me in the least. Doubt if I'd want to land either night.'

'And Halloran has the duty Wednesday. Works out nicely. Next point, though – think we should tell the Old Man there's something going on?'

'Tell him *what*'s going on?'

'After I see Cluny again, then.'

'But before that, maybe. Hang on a mo.' Pausing in their approach to the *PollyAnna*'s gangway. 'Your theory about *Glauchau* maybe having linkage to the *Spee*. Dates and so on – *may* be just coincidence; on the other hand it does seem to add up – begins to seem more likely than *un*likely, even. I was thinking about it when we were in Manolo's –'

'I'd have sworn you were too busy trying to see down that blond hag's dress. In fact –'

'I'm talking seriously, Andy.'

'– could have been why she scarpered when she did.'

'What I'm saying is it might be as well to let the Old Man know about it.'

'Then you, as second mate –'
'Your brainwave, Andy, you tell him.'

He woke with the tall, dark girl in his mind – the one with the long hair and lovely shoulders. Lovely *everything*. Kicking himself that he hadn't asked Frank Cluny who she was or what the form might be, whether for instance that little commander had any kind of lien on her – as husband, for instance, or established lover. She hadn't looked or acted as if *she* thought he had.

Get it out of Cluny this evening. He'd surely know. Those two might well have been in Manolo's, coming from there when he'd run into them. Nodding to himself, thinking that if he did get to see her again it might rate as their second meeting, he could act as if they already knew each other.

Loading started not at eight but before half-past, which for a place like this wasn't bad. There was a steam-powered elevator that lifted ore from the railway trucks into the main body of the chute, and an outlet trunking trained out over the hold – aftermost hold, number five – with a semi-flexible tubular spout made of jointed steel that hung down into the ship's guts and convulsed when the ore was crashing through it. The speed of loading was governed by the rate at which a gang of eight or ten dock labourers could shovel the ore from the trucks on to the elevator: the racket was tremendous. Halloran had the bosun and half a dozen hands standing by, and when the flow was stopped, as it periodically was, getting down inside and trimming – levelling, squaring the stuff away between pre-rigged fore-and-aft partitions of heavy timber that split it up, would prevent the whole immense weight of it shifting in one mass, which in foul weather with the rolling of the ship it would otherwise be inclined to do, and which would be extremely dangerous.

As a wartime cargo, ore was dangerous enough in any case – or would be in U-boat waters, which they had to reckon on being in at some later stage. The Old Man had pointed this out when they'd been loading manganese ore in Calcutta, Andy remembered: Old Man having had experience of Atlantic convoys in the '14–'18 war, and given them a talk about precautions they'd be taking when the grimmer times arrived. Having lifeboats permanently turned-out in their davits, for instance, ready for speedy lowering; he'd spelt this out to Andy, Fisher and the cadets, some of the engineers and the wireless officers too, Halloran also present, although feigning prior knowledge – didn't need telling, knew it all, as first mate having a master's ticket after all, only nodding agreement as the skipper explained, 'Such a weight of it, see, that when she's right down to her marks there's most of all the holds still empty. Each ton deadweight fills no more 'n fifteen to twenty cubic feet, that's the nub of it. So, punch a hole in her then – as a torpedo does, that being the nature of the beast – sea bursts in, fills that big empty space in, say, two and a half seconds, down she goes like a stone. I've known of a ship near enough *PollyAnna*'s size taking fifty seconds – *fifty seconds* – from being hit to going under.'

Gorst had murmured, 'Got to be darned nippy!'

'Damn right, lad. If you're going to have any chance at all. But I'll tell you all another thing, while on that subject. Any ship I command, officers see their men into the boats before *they* get into 'em . . .'

Andy sought out the Old Man in mid-forenoon, asked if he could have a word, and gave him his *Glauchau* theory.

The noise of the loading was excruciating; even up here in the day cabin with its door and scuttles shut you had to shout to be heard. There'd been a blissful fifteen-minute break, but the chute was back in action now: the ore-dust cloud had taken that long to settle, was now again poisoning the air you breathed. The rest of the hands were being employed chipping and scraping – preliminary to red-leading and then repainting – and out on deck you couldn't even hear *that* cacophony.

Or breathe. Or hear the *Glauchau*'s brass band, either.

Skipper gazing at him, blue eyes blinking slowly.

'May be codswallop, sir, but the dates coinciding as they do – and the fact she's still doing damn-all, just lying there . . . I thought, no harm mentioning it.'

'No harm at all.' Blink, blink. 'No harm at all, Holt.'

'But there's something else, sir. Funny set-up ashore here.'

He told him about Manolo's, and what Cluny had said; about Caetano, the so-called acting port captain, allegedly pro-German and in front of whom Cluny hadn't wanted to talk, had therefore asked Andy to go back tonight. 'I said I would if it's something that really matters, and he said, "It'll matter to *you*, all right!"'

'To do with the *Glauchau*, you think.'

'Seemed so, sir. And definitely with Caetano. I got the feeling that in his hearing I'd better not show interest in the *Glauchau*. As it happened, second mate and I'd been discussing her – that theory about the *Spee* – and then Cluny warned me not long after we got there, "Don't say anything you wouldn't want the Germans to hear about".'

'Cluny being a South African barman, you say.'

'Decent sort of fellow, sir. Rolling stone, all that – has been – but I'd say he's straight enough.'

'You'll go back and get whatever it is he's offering, then.'

'Was planning to, sir.'

'Let me know how it goes. I'm glad you told me. Anyone besides you and Fisher know about it?'

'No, sir. Thought until we knew what we were talking about –'

'Wise man, Holt. Wise man. Be a full-blown man Wednesday – eh?'

There was no mail – none was delivered on board, anyway. News on the wireless was that last night after the *Graf Spee* had blown herself up, the cruisers *Ajax, Achilles* and *Cumberland* had steamed up the Plate estuary, passed close to the still-burning and smoking wreck – she'd settled on a mud-bank and remained clearly visible – and entered

120

Montevideo, to the vociferous delight of many thousands of spectators. Commodore Harwood had been promoted to rear-admiral overnight, and the captains of *Ajax*, *Achilles* and *Exeter* had received decorations. *Cumberland* was the replacement for the badly damaged *Exeter*; Harwood had whistled her up from Port Stanley on the 13th. There was no mention of *Renown* or *Ark Royal*; *Spee* would have faced only those three cruisers. Now her remains were lying with oily black smoke still drifting from her while Uruguyan and Argentinian fishermen were doing good business ferrying tourists out to snap her with their Kodaks. Langsdorff and his crew were said to have been landed in Buenos Aires – from those tugs, presumably.

Halloran asked Andy, over supper in the saloon, 'Shore-going again, Holt? Found yourself a woman – that it?'

'Not exactly found. Ran into, sort of. Got an idea where I might run into her again.'

'And that'll be it, eh? Gets an eyeful of our third mate and bingo, she's in the sack?'

Derisive . . . Andy looked back at him – at the blue-black jaw, eyes like fat, black currants in a bun, nose like a trodden-on potato. He shrugged. 'Never know your luck.'

'Oh, I know mine!'

Fisher gazing po-faced into his scrambled eggs, Halloran throwing his fork down and telling Andy, 'Place for girls here is the Casa Colorada. If you was after a birthday treat, for instance . . .'

9

The tall girl wasn't here. On his way through to the bar he told himself by way of encouragement, 'Not here *yet*.' In any case, no reason she should have been – girls didn't *live* in bars. On a Saturday nght he might have stood an odds-on chance, but this was bloody Monday: she'd as likely as not be at home, washing her smalls or all that long hair. Glancing round again, seeing no familiar faces – except Manolo's. Guitar music again: they had a radiogram at the back with an automatic record-changer, Cluny had told him – you could put eight records on it at each reload. Cluny must be at the back somewhere now. Doing that or – whatever . . .

Manolo, pouring drinks, smiled and called, 'Welcome back, senhor!', and Andy asked him – casual tone, as if it didn't matter – 'No Franco?'

Slow shake of the head, while keeping his eyes on what he was doing; Andy's eye taken then by the little waitress with the hour-glass figure who'd rubbed herself against him last night. She gave him one of her smiles as she wiggled by with a tray of glasses. If it hadn't been for the existence of that other one, might well have gone for her. Certainly no lack of encouragement – if encouragement had been needed, which as yet it never had been. And one wasn't thirty yet: nine years and two days to go . . .

Manolo, having collected cash – *dinheiro*, one of a few words Andy had learnt last night – from those customers,

122

was sliding this way: 'Tonight senhor, no – no Franco. To my regret. Wanna beer?'

A reminder that what you were certain you could count on often didn't happen: another of Andy's father's dicta. Not easy to take this philosophically, though: Cluny had undertaken to be here. And having told the story to the Old Man, who'd taken it seriously . . . 'Beer, please. But Franco –'

'Has gone Belo Horizonte – two hundred, two-fifty kilometres. Take his wife to her mother. Father is mine manager – some accident, gone hospital, old woman on this telephone scream blue murder.' He'd pointed at it – telephone on the wall behind the bar. 'Blue murder, that how you say it?' Smiling, putting the beer glass and half-empty bottle on the bar in front of him, Andy delving for *dinheiro* – the equivalent of about a shilling, which at home would have got you two pints.

'When d'you expect him back?'

'Tomorrow.' Hand raised, fingers crossed. Pale, soft-looking hand. 'If is possible.'

'*This* time tomorrow, I suppose.'.

'*Si*. But maybe – *maybe* – Wednesday? Excuse me . . .'

The place wasn't crowded, but he was being kept busy, single-handed. Spotting some new arrival now, waving over people's heads with one hand while dispensing cachaca with the other: 'Oi, Mario!'

Mendoza: limping this way. In uniform, removing his cap and tucking it under his left arm; look of surprise as he spotted Andy. 'My young frien' from the *PollyAnna*!' Tapping his forehead for memory: 'I say to you come Manolo's, uh?'

'Came last night, Captain.' Shaking hands and reminding him, 'Holt, third mate. Buy you a beer, sir?'

One 'sir' would last out the next few minutes. The little guy *was* about twice his age, and master's rank. Too old one might think to be sliding an arm round the even littler waitress – Manuela, her name was, and she could easily have been his daughter – and asking her if she'd missed him; she was saying yes in Portuguese, and he kissed her, nodded now to Andy: 'Beer, yes, very nice . . .'

One beer would be his lot too, Andy thought, signalling the order to Manolo. Neither Cluny nor the tall girl being here, and anyway needing to save a few cruzeiros for his birthday. Cluny's absence hit him again then: if he didn't get back before Wednesday, and the *Glauchau* was to shove off between now and then, taking her secret with her . . . ? The Old Man would get a signal off to the RN in that case, surely – deep-laden Hun motor vessel, possibly acting as support-ship to a raider: in any case a Hun, eligible for attention – whether or not port regulations or the Hague Convention permitted the use of W/T in a neutral harbour – wouldn't he? Andy thought of asking Mendoza about this, but decided it might be better not to: it was skipper's business – most certainly not any third mate's – and the Old Man most likely knew all about it; meanwhile, best neither to be informed of prohibitions if they existed nor to mention that any such notion might be in the wind.

If it was. Josh Thornhill wasn't a man to go off the deep end or do anything in a rush.

Mendoza had seized his arm, wanted to move to a table that had just been vacated by some Frenchmen. Andy paid for the beer, then followed him to where Manuela was clearing away glasses and cheroot ends. She was wearing a provocatively musky scent, he noticed. Mendoza commenting – having seen him enjoying a close look at her – 'Girls very nice, eh?'

'One in particular – saw her last night, not in here, outside, but she might have been in here – tall, long dark hair, really *beautiful* –'

'You speak with her?'

'No. She was with a commander or lieutenant-commander. Man about your size – *could* have been her husband, but –'

'Capitao de Fregato is commander.' Three fingers on his shoulder indicating the rank stripes on shoulder-boards. 'Capitao de Corveta is more junior commander,

or is also Capitao Tenente' – two stripes – 'how you say it
– lieutenant-commander?'

'The middle one, I'd guess. Junior commander. Man
about your height.'

'Da Sousa. Captain of minelayer *Cabedelo.*' Wave of a
hand roughly in the direction of Sao Joao; the minelayer
was berthed just this side of it, of course. Mendoza smiling:
'She not his wife. Wife live Rio de Janeiro. This one name
Arabella. Ah, yes, beautiful, I loving her. Many, many loving
her.'

'Well – I'm not surprised . . .'

'You like meet Arabella?'

'Ah – yeah, some time. But –'

'Tell Tonio. He fix.'

'Just like that? Well . . . But listen –'

'You like drink cachaca?'

'In a minute maybe. But –'

'Better now. Soon maybe get –' hand movements
meaning the place might get full suddenly. 'Manuela!'

She brought them the cachacas. Mendoza had been
saying that he'd piloted the French ore ship in this evening,
berthed her on the south side of the river, a berth still
under construction, Cais Atalaia. 'Not so good. Railway
line completed OK but for loading use ship's gear and the
– what you say –'

'Buckets?'

'Buckets.' Indicating the size of them – huge, nothing
like buckets in any conventional sense. Nodding. 'Slow,
eh? Not like where is *PollyAnna.* You going good, eh?'

In fact they'd finished number five hold's first instal-
ment and had moved the ship in mid-afternoon to make
a start on four. Holds weren't to be filled completely one
by one; numbers five, four, three and two would be filled
to about one-third of their eventual content, then number
one half-filled; two, three and four then filled to capacity,
and after that numbers five and one topped-up – so as to
finish with the right trim and draft but without imposing
undue stresses at earlier stages. And at this rate – with luck,

including no breakdown of machinery – it looked as if loading might be completed some time on Saturday. Mendoza was pleased to hear this: Saturday, then, he'd be piloting her out. An afternoon job, he guessed; subject of course to tides, which was the crucial factor. Tomorrow, for instance, he'd be taking out the *Volcao*, but if she wasn't ready to sail by about midday she'd have to wait until the tide turned at 1900.

'Where's she bound?'

'Cayenne. French Guiana.'

'And what about the German?'

'Huh?'

He hadn't meant to ask anything about the *Glauchau* – to mention her at all. But the question had tumbled out more or less naturally – this ship arriving, that one sailing . . . Anyway, he'd asked it now, and it seemed to have brought Mendoza up short; Andy adding – in for a penny, in for a pound – 'Still waiting for engine spares, is she?'

Brown eyes on his and as alert as they'd ever been. A shrug, then: 'I guess must be. But how I know?'

'Only thought you might. You bring 'em in and take 'em out. And frankly, that awful damn music –'

'I think is from Berlin. March music – Third Reich marching – yes? I don't like, *you* don't like – uh?'

'Could do without it, sure.' He picked up his glass. 'Anyway, here's how.' High-proof cane spirit: and memories of the old *Burntisland*, whose junior engineer had brought a few bottles on board in Rio to celebrate his birthday, and Cadet Holt then aged seventeen had found himself still pie-eyed next day, which fortunately had been a Sunday.

Didn't like the smell of it much. Rum, of course, although colourless, but by no means of the finest. 'Cheers, Captain.' Grimacing then: 'Ugh . . .' Mendoza began telling him, leaning closer after throwing a quick glance around, 'We have ask him – *Glauchau* captain – please to switch out. *Off*, to switch. This is before departure of Capitao da Tovar.'

'Port Captain?'

A nod. 'Go Montevideo.'

'And what happened?'

'One hour, switch off. One hour. Capitao da Tovar departing'– Mendoza miming the flipping-up of a switch – 'again, boom-boom-boom!'

'Like now. Ever since.'

'*Si*. All days, all nights.'

'No one else tried telling them to shut up?'

'Port Captain not here, so –'

'How about Caetano?'

Surprise again: 'You know Mario Caetano?'

'Met him here last night. Introduced himself as Acting Port Captain. He was with his wife and someone called Ferras.'

'Mario Caetano – you see, port enlargement, for make new berths, roads also, soon bridges –'

'Engineer?'

'What he is doing – yes, engineer. Now Port Captain not here, sure, he's boss. Ferras is work for Capitao da Tovar, but he and Caetano very – like *this*.' Two fingers entwined.

'Buddies.'

'Buddies. Yes.' Mendoza leant closer. 'I give you secret. Caetano is Nazi. I think also Ferras. You see?'

'When might Captain da Tovar get back?'

A shrug, shoulders rising almost to his ears. 'I not know.'

'*He's* not a Nazi?'

'Not! Good man, he! Very small number Nazis here. In *Brazil* only small number.' Silent, wide-eyed, thinking about that. Then: 'You like cachaca?'

'Thanks, but wouldn't want more than this.'

'Like meet Arabella?'

'Yes – *yes*, but not tonight . . .'

'Morrow?'

'Maybe Wednesday?'

On gangway watch were AB Parlance and OS Clover: two men on the job so one could stay put and the other take messages or whatever. Andy asked them how they liked the Germans' music, and Parlance said he liked it fine, he'd been practising the goose-step. Clover, he added, had tried but made a hash of it, on account of his legs being so short.

'Low centre of gravity might yet stand you in good stead, Clover. Old Man turned in, I suppose?'

They reckoned he had. But there was a light burning in the day cabin, and he'd asked to be informed of developments *vis-à-vis* Cluny, certainly should be told about Caetano being a Nazi. Andy went up, knocked, found the master sitting in his vest and underpants writing letters.

'Come in. Shut the door. See your South African, did you?'

'Afraid not, sir.' He told him about Cluny having to go up-country, to the mining district where maybe their ore came from, and not being expected back before earliest tomorrow evening, possibly not until Wednesday.

'If I had to bet, I'd say Wednesday.'

'Looking on the dark side?'

He shook his head. 'Two-fifty kilometres each way, Manolo said. And Cluny's ma-in-law's in a state, apparently. He won't get away *that* easy.'

'You've been learning the facts of life, Holt.'

'Learnt one other thing, sir. Our pilot, Mendoza, was there, we had a drink together and he said the so-called Acting Port Captain – Caetano – is a Nazi. His real job is the engineering works, port development. And the one who was with him last night, name Ferras, is an assistant to the real Port Captain, name of da Tovar. I asked when he was due back, Mendoza didn't know. He thinks Ferras is a Nazi too.'

'Place seems thick with 'em.'

'But when the second mate and I went ashore last night, sir, they were clapping us in the street – on account of the *Graf Spee*, apparently.'

'Mendoza have anything to say about the *Glauchau*?'

'Only he'd no idea how long she'll be here. Or whether

128

she really is waiting for spare parts. I asked him – on account of the brass bands, that we wouldn't mind some peace and quiet – and he just didn't know. Doesn't like Huns or Nazis, I'm sure of that, but he'd have to be a bit cautious, I suppose.'

'With Nazis running the port, dare say he would.' Frowning, fingering an unlit pipe. Then nodding. 'Right. Find Mr Halloran, ask him to step up here. You get your head down. For your private information, though – since it was you started this – we'll keep a dark-hours watch on the Hun. One man, monkey island'd be the place, dusk to dawn, maybe two-hour watches, to let me know if she looks like weighing. Torches on the foc'sl, sort of thing. If she did, I'd put a message out, pronto. Otherwise, we'll wait for your man to deliver whatever it is he's got.'

Andy nodded. A third mate didn't comment on his skipper's decisions – not unless the skipper asked him to. Skipper adding, 'To square *your* yardarm, Holt, I'll tell Mr Halloran you have a contact ashore, you're pursuing it on my authority and meanwhile I've told you mum's the word.'

Halloran asked him – Tuesday morning – 'Some person the Old Man says you're in touch with – that the girl you were on about?'

'Wasn't exactly "on about". Answered your question, was all. But no – no connection.'

Halloran would most likely have resented Andy's having gone to the Old Man with his story, of course, would have maintained that he should have passed it through *him*. On the other hand, the Old Man had approved his having gone to him directly: it was that sort of business – master's business – as he'd have made plain to the mate last night.

No mail. None yesterday and none today. Martensen came on board on Dundas Gore business in mid-forenoon, when the chute had been hard at work on numbers four and three holds, filling the warm air with choking grit as well as deafening everyone within a hundred yards of it, and he'd have brought mail if there'd been any. None came later in the day either, which left only Wednesday itself. In fact it wasn't bothering him now: letters would have been written, would be in the care of GPO London somewhere or other, would eventually turn up, while on the Northern Patrol and at Helensburgh glasses would undoubtedly be raised to him. Letters might be at the bottom of the sea, of course; but they still existed or *had* existed, one required no proof of it, and in any case they were no more than tokens of the bonds of affection that existed between the four of them.

It might have come to matter less, he realised, through the *Glauchau* business taking up so much of one's thinking. The ship herself still lying out there with her black-and-grey, orange-spotted reflection shimmering in the river's moving mirror-surface; deserted-looking, except for an occasional sighting of groups of men promenading on her upper deck, sometimes individuals trotting round, taking exercise. They were never at it for long: one only heard that such phenomena had been spotted; otherwise the ship's inert appearance was discounted only by the noise reasserting itself when the chute was stopped for a breather, and for longer than that in early afternoon when the *PollyAnna*'s gangway was slung up clear of the quay, her breast ropes and wire springs shifted under Batt Collins' eagle eye, while the tug that had annoyed Mendoza nudged her astern in readiness for the loading of the next hold.

Loading wasn't going badly at all. Elevator roaring and clattering, leaking steam, chute's body shaking like a dinosaur with palsy, its spout clanging and convulsing. Fisher shouted – on the poop, where the gunlayer and trainer, ABs Bakewell and Timms, were doing a mainte-nance routine on the gun, greasing and polishing – 'Hope the Germans like the concert *we're* giving *them*, eh?'

Couldn't see the *Glauchau* from here, since *PollyAnna*'s superstructure blocked the line of sight. Had only to go for'ard or up to bridge level, though, and there was the Hun quartermaster on his chair as ever, starboard side amidships. Nothing any different, except that an hour ago it had been noticed that there was no boat at the foot of the Jacob's ladder. Captain gone ashore, maybe, or a party landed for fresh stores – such items as milk, fruit, eggs, fish.

Hun skipper visiting Caetano, maybe.

Andy yelled in Fisher's ear, 'You don't mind taking the duty again tonight?'

'No, that's OK. Be ashore late, will you?'

A shrug. 'No later than I can help.'

Cluny wasn't there. Nor was anyone else he knew – except for Manolo. Whose name was *not* Manolo, Mendoza had informed him last night. Tonio had taken over the business from a fellow Spaniard called Manolo some years ago and retained the name for the sake of continuity; was quite happy that a lot of his customers thought it was his own.

'*Oi*, Tonio.' Andy had learnt this too from Mendoza; having heard the little waitress, Manuela, calling '*Oi!*' to new arrivals, he'd asked him why she did it and had been told it meant 'hello'.

He put the obvious question: 'No Franco?'

Shake of the head. Seeing Tonio from certain angles and when he wasn't smiling, one realised he had to be pushing fifty. He was opening a bottle that was either champagne or dressed up as such: passing it across the bar to Manuela – who a moment ago had blown Andy a kiss – and moving along this way now. 'He return tomorrow evening. Was on telephone. Want beer?'

'Cachaca, please.'

'You learn our ways, eh?'

'From Captain Mendoza. But just one, and I'll be off.'

'Cachaca, one.' Bottle's neck clinking on the small, thick tumbler. 'You should try some time Caipirinchas.'

'Say it again?'

'Cachaca with lime juice, sugar, ice.' Pointing with his head at a tall glass in a woman's hand. 'Tomorrow, uh? Want table reservation – your birthday, uh?'

'Did I tell you that?'

'You tell Franco. I think he tell me. Or I hear you tell him.' He scooped Andy's money off the counter's glass top. 'Thank you, senhor.'

'I'm called Andy.'

'Good.' He tried it for pronunciation: nodded, finding it easy. 'Want reserve table, Andy?'

'I don't think so. Don't know what time or how many 'll come, anyway. It'll be Dutch, by the way – not *my* party, all paying their rounds. And no food – sorry, but we'll have had supper on board. You sure Franco'll be here?'

'*Si.* Sure. He swear it, he *want* be here. Excuse me . . .'

Manuela joined him then. She might have been waiting until her boss had moved away. '*Oi*, big boy.'

'*Oi*, Manuela!'

'How long you stay Vitoria?'

'Just a few days. Come out with me one evening?'

She'd taken his free hand in both of hers, was kneading it. Dark eyes troubled, gazing up at him: 'Somebody saying you like Arabella.'

'Never met her. And I hadn't met *you* the one time I did set eyes on her. Anyway –'

'She very beautiful, eh?'

'But you're – you're *sensational*, Manuela.'

'Oh, you – you *say* –'

'I mean it. Truly. You're more than just attractive, you're –'

'What I?'

'Just plain scrumptious!'

'Scrumpuss nice to be?'

'Why, certainly –'

'Saturday I work here lunchtime, evening I am free. You like – Saturday – go ozzer place?'

'I'd love it, but I don't know I'll still be here. It's likely to be the day we'll finish.'

'Friday, finish here eleven.'

'*Well.*' She was facing him, arms round his waist, leaning back to look up at him, moving to the music's beat. He said, 'I could take all-night leave –'

132

'Sure.'

'How much?'

'Huh?'

'*Quanto?*' Another of the half-dozen words he'd learnt. She glanced back over her shoulder, calling a snappy-sounding reply in Portuguese to some people who were clamouring for attention. Back to him then: 'Not to ask *quanto* in this place, *por favor.*' A husky laugh. 'Only bring plenty.'

Wednesday 20 December – a date which for a long time had seemed a distant prospect but had now suddenly arrived. Twenty-one years since he'd come crapping and howling into the light of day. Actually he'd been born in the afternoon, so wasn't *quite* there yet. Manuela though, Friday night: in the early light in his cabin she was smiling at him as she had been in Manolo's, when it had occurred to him that he could just about have had her there and then. Would anyone have noticed? Yes – the bunch at that table who'd been getting ratty, demanding service – *they* would have. Given them food for thought, if nothing else. Manolo – Tonio, rather – had said to him *sotto voce* across the bar some minutes later – Andy having told him he'd be making tracks now – 'Mario Mendoza is saying last night maybe you like fix up with Arabella. Most beautiful young lady in Brazil, uh? But two night now we not seeing her, I guess she plenty busy. Maybe tomorrow, but –'

'Doesn't matter. Truly doesn't, Tonio. In fact I'd sooner you didn't say anything if she does come in.'

Tonio had shown surprise. Andy actually surprising himself, too. Turning down that vision, that raving beauty – even if she *were* to be available? Tonio shrugging his thick shoulders: 'OK. OK . . .' Andy explaining to himself that having settled for Manuela he didn't want to hurt *her* feelings; and that in any case, a bird in the hand – or virtually in hand . . .

Friday, he thought, turning out, realising that he *had* been looking forward to this birthday, was now more keenly anticipating Friday night. Liking her, as well as – all the rest of it . . . Shaving then, and showering, speculating as to how things might have gone by the time Friday came. No doubt at all they'd still be here – and for a day or more after that, since loading wasn't likely to be completed before Saturday noon – afternoon, maybe – whereas the German might up-anchor at any time. That was one factor – inescapable, and nothing one could do about it if it happened – and the other was what Cluny had to tell him. The skipper was taking it seriously enough now – enough to have waited up for his return from shore last night. Andy had found him smoking a pipe on the gallery outside his cabin, leaning on the rail and gazing across the shine of dark water to where the *Glauchau* was virtually stern-on to them, her riding lights seemingly close together because of that angle, the nearer of them slightly to the right and lower than the one on her foremast. Lower by fifteen feet, for sure, in compliance with international regulations for a ship of her length lying at anchor: Messrs Janner and Gorst could have told one that – rattled a whole chapter of it off by heart.

'Skipper, sir?'

'Holt? Your man turn up?'

'No, sir –'

'*Damn!*'

'He'd telephoned, though, and his boss is certain he'll be there this time tomorrow.'

'Then you will be too, I take it.'

'Certainly will, sir.'

'Reasonably sober even though it is your birthday. Reminds me – a drink in the day cabin at twelve noon. I'm inviting Halloran and the chief to join us.'

'Thank you very much, sir.' A nod towards the German's dark shape. 'I was thinking, Hun crew must be going loco. No shore-leave, and that racket –'

'Our lads wouldn't put up with it, that's for sure.'

Over breakfast, with the chute's noise already at full blast, everyone was wishing him a happy birthday or many happy returns. *Glauchau* still there: tide flooding, so no view of either her watch on deck or the motorboat. Fisher said over his eggs and bacon – very small Brazilian eggs, you needed three or four of them – 'This should be your lucky day for mail from home.'

'Time we had a mail in any case.'

'Say that again.' Dewar, the senior wireless man – still pale and flabby-looking – 'Last I heard, my sister was expecting a happy event. Imminent, mother said. That was five or six weeks ago!'

'*Is* a war on, Bill.'

'Take a chance on it, call him *Uncle* Bill.'

He liked that: chuckling, jowls wobbling. 'Like to know what it was – *is* – that's all.'

'And how *she* is, you're supposed to ask.'

'Well, it's her third, she'll be all right.' Glancing up as his number two, Starkadder, arrived. Circling the table, patting Andy on the shoulder: 'Congratulations. I mean –'

'I know what you mean, Frank. Thanks.'

'Kind of dramatic news just came in, though.'

'Well?'

'The *Graf Spee*'s captain – Langsdorff – shot himself last night.'

'Oh, Christ . . .'

'In Buenos Aires. Wrapped himself in a German ensign, then – *pow* . . .' He stooped to the pantry hatch: 'Four eggs please, Jackson.'

Andy reported to the skipper in his day cabin at noon precisely and had a glass of gin and water in his hand by the time Halloran and the chief engineer arrived at a minute past the hour. The skipper poured more gins and proposed, loudly enough to be heard over the surrounding noise, Third Mate Andrew Holt's long life, happiness and success; they all drank to it, wished him luck and so on. There was some talk then about the non-arrival of mail from home, and various theories to account for it – misdirection, enemy action, GPO making sure of their getting it by sending it to await the *PollyAnna*'s arrival at her next port of call.

'Do we know where that'll be, sir?' Halloran, chancing his arm.

Hibbert observed, 'Hun's got his ensign at half-mast, I see.'

'Has indeed.' The skipper raised his glass. 'No one else is obliged to drink this one, but – to that poor devil's immortal soul.'

They all drank to it. Skipper than asking his engineer, 'The *Glauchau*'s a motor vessel, diesel, twin screw I'd say, a smidgin bigger 'n *PollyAnna* – six-five GRT, say, deadweight nine-five. What speed would you reckon?'

The big man ran a hand around his jaw. Small shrug. 'Fifteen?'

'All right. You won't have heard about this, Chief, but these two have. If or when that bugger sails, I'll be letting the powers that be know about her. Don't know what ships the RN still have on this coast, and it's anyone's guess what course she'll set, but guessing her speed near enough, they might catch her with a Vignot curve of search – uh?'

Halloran had nodded. 'But I'd say fourteen knots – if I was asked.'

'Know what a Vignot curve of search is, Holt?'

'Heard of it, sir. Read of it, somewhere. Relies on the ship being hunted maintaining a straight course, though, doesn't it?'

A nod. 'As she would – at least for the first day or two, putting distance behind her. Least, *I* would. Then you might try to confuse the issue . . . Well – for a birthday treat, explain to the chief how a Vignot curve works?'

He'd done that and had a second gin, and that was it. Long day ahead, paperwork to be attended to, also inspection of the crew's quarters aft, which for some reason was a third mate's responsibility, although Halloran as first mate was required to visit every part of the ship every single day. Bosun and donkeyman in any case made damn sure those quarters – still known to their denizens as 'the foc'sl', although they were actually in the poop, mess room/recreation space entered directly from the well-deck; bunk-rooms below that at 'tween-deck level, washplace/heads right aft – were kept clean and in reasonably good order. But of course, if they'd not been up to their jobs . . .

Six p.m.: invited to join the rest of them in the saloon, to eat some of the cake which the cook, Will Bloom, had baked for him. Twenty-one candles on it, and to wash it down, cachaca provided by Halloran, who'd also arranged for the bosun to be present, Batt asking him after a series of toasts and a couple of slices of the cake whether he'd be so good as to visit the mess room, where a few of the lads would like to drink his health. Said lads being, it turned out, ABs Martin, Crown, Harkness, Shuttleworth, Parlance, Edmonds, Ingram and Bakewell, OSs Brooks, Morton, Sholl, Huggins, Cox and Gardner, and – backing up Batt Collins – the carpenter, Postlethwaite, and – late arrival, representing the Black Gang – Donkeyman Mick Smart. A flatteringly large turnout; Andy guessed that some of them might simply have been caught there in the mess room and stuck around because of the provision – source unknown – of yet more cachaca. The bosun must have organised it, maybe had a whip round, but there'd certainly been none in sight when he'd made his inspection earlier in the day. They offered him their good wishes, sang, 'For he's a jolly good fellow' and clapped him, after which he made a somewhat slurry speech beginning, 'Slightly *pissed* fellow', and thanking them for their goodwill and the booze.

Supper was cottage pie, and he needed it as blotting-paper. Had meant to follow the skipper's advice more assiduously and lay off the hard stuff, but couldn't be that stand-offish with chaps who were genuinely trying to be friendly – even though the cachaca did creep up on one.

Take it easy ashore tonight, for God's sake. Drink in Manuela's smiles, in place of more raw spirit. Watch it with her, too – knowing how one could be in that department after a few too many. An hour's sleep wouldn't have done him any harm, but he might well have *over*slept. He stood for a long time under a cold shower, therefore, then put on civvies and headed for the gangway, where Ingram asked him, 'You all right, sir?'

'Don't I look all right?'

'Well – look fine – considerin' –'

'G'night, then.' Making it down to the quayside with some degree of care. He'd told the others – or some of them – that he'd see them there, at Manolo's. Some might have gone ahead, others might have their heads down, having thought better of it. It hadn't been an invitation, only a suggestion: he wouldn't care if none of them showed up – make it easier in fact, sorting things out with Cluny.

'Hey, Andy!'

Hurrying, half-running footsteps, then a hand clamping on his arm, and Don Fisher breathing hard, grinning at him. 'Stealing a march on us, eh?'

Instinct told him that Ingram might well have sent his winger, Brooks, to suggest the third mate might be standing into danger. Bloody cheek, if so. Still – 'Good to have your company, Don.'

'The rest'll be with us shortly. Thought you'd've got your head down.'

'Might not have got it up again. Who else is coming?'

'The cadets are certain starters. So are Shaw and Starkadder. I think Tom McAlan. Maybe others.'

'Bless 'em. Bless 'em.'

'You're walking better now, anyway. *Were* weaving a bit. I expect it was the fresh air hit you. Shouldn't have much more, though, if I were you –'

'My twenty-first, God's sake. Hard a-port now . . .'

Cluny was there, all right. From halfway up the room Andy waved to him and got an answering salute. Reached the bar then, with Fisher hissing into his right ear, 'They have a soft drink they call Suco –'

'And a better one called cachaca. *Oi*, Frank!'

'*Oi*, to you.' Quick grin. 'With you in two shakes.' They were busy: a lot of people, a lot of noise, twanging strings and a woman's wailing, slightly Arab tones. Looking around: Manuela was there, either hadn't seen him yet or was being run off her pretty little feet. But *there* . . . 'Oh, Lord.'

'What or who –'

'That short-arse commander – in civvies tonight, but he was the one had Arabella in tow out there. Sunday night – that tall, *lovely* girl?'

'The one you were going ape about. Andy, why more cachaca, why not –'

'Randy little sod's waiting for her. Maybe she's stood him up. *Oi*, Manuela!'

'*Oi*, big boy!'

He put his arm round her. 'Don, this is Manuela.'

'We met, I think – Sunday night?'

'*Oi*, Don.'

'She's the love of my life, you can forget that other one.'

'Ozzer come soon, big boy, see you *can* forgetting her!'

'Watch me. Just watch me!'

'Sooner have a fast word, man.' Frank Cluny. 'While we can?'

He nodded, releasing Manuela. 'Sooner the better. How's your father-in-law?'

'What do you care? Oh. Well – he'll live. Here – tell you about the trip.' To Fisher, 'Excuse us, one minute?' Then to Manuela in a sharper tone, 'Didn't you notice, this is a hungry, thirsty crowd. Andy – sorry I had to duck out on you, Monday. Name is Andy, isn't it? Damn, there's bloody Ferras now . . .'

The Nazi, stopping to talk to the minelayer's skipper, Arabella's half-pint-sized suitor. Ferras with his back this way, fortunately. Cluny checked that he and Andy had space around them, and began talking fast. 'Listen. About the *Glauchau*. Other guy isn't here – the guy who told me. He's sort of a runner for a joint called Casa Colorada – brothel, worth steering clear of, girls there've been known to have the clap. Ferras sent him out to the *Glauchau* reckoning they'd like to have whores visit – what with no shore-leave being granted. Well, Gomez saw with his own eyes – and *heard* – where the guards sit now, after starboard corner of number three – small hatchway with a grating there, looks like a ventilator but it's a hatch down into the 'tween-decks. They got prisoners in there – Merchant Navy guys. Now for Christ's sake don't let on you heard it from me; I got to live here, man – accent on *live* – OK?'

Turning away to rejoin Tonio, who was making it plain he needed help. Andy near-stunned – *sober* – seeing Arabella come sweeping in and the little commander jumping up; Ferras too, opening his arms to her. She was truly something out of this world – but as far as Andy was concerned a long way out of it, remote from anything that mattered now. To his surprise Cluny had turned back, grabbed his arm: 'They paid Gomez to keep his mouth shut, and Ferras threatened him – *Know what's good for you, bastard, don't want to wind up drowned – you and them?*'

'*Them* meaning the prisoners –'

'Like kill *him* and destroy the evidence.'

'But he still told you –'

'I know. Funny. Except he does tell me his troubles. Drinks like a fish and queer as a fucking coot but we get on, some reason. What d'you want – cachaca?'

10

The Old Man had Halloran with him and the cabin door standing open; Andy didn't have to knock.

'C'mon in, birthday boy . . .'

'Surprised he's still on his feet.' Comment from Halloran: Andy looking at him, thinking that maybe he should warn him he might have picked up a little something he wouldn't exactly relish, in the establishment he'd been patronising. Telling the Old Man instead, 'I saw Cluny, sir – got the works. It's – well, *Christ* –'

'Sit down, help yourself to coffee.'

There was an enamelled pot of it on the table and a punctured tin of condensed milk, also an unused mug. He sat, reached for it.

'Weren't ashore long, then.'

'No, sir. Just heard what he had to say and –' Shaking his head, pouring coffee. At Manolo's he'd given Fisher a handful of cruzeiros, asked him to stand the others a round when they got there and apologise for the fact he couldn't stay; then on the street corner he'd met Janner and Gorst – told them to go on in, report to the second mate – and on the quayside had been waylaid by McAlan, Shaw and Starkadder, who'd tried physically to detain him.

Drinking his coffee black. It wasn't as hot as it might have been, but he could feel it doing him good. Thoughts wandering a little, assessing the general situation: including the fact he'd need to draw another advance against pay before Friday night; recalling that *Bring plenty* . . . He put down the empty mug. 'Thanks for that, sir.'

'Let's hear it now.'

A deep breath. Then: 'The *Glauchau* has British Merchant Navy men as prisoners on board. Where the watch on deck sits all day and night they've taken out one hatchboard, got a sort of mock-up ventilator over it, plus a grating as on a fiddley, and a ladder down to where they're holding 'em in the 'tween-decks. Explains why the guard's rooted to that spot, and the loudspeaker – cover any row they might kick up.'

'Be damned . . .'

Old Man looking as stunned as Andy had felt when he'd heard it. Glaring at Halloran then: 'Us sitting around like dummies, and our fellows – hell, in spitting distance . . .' To Andy then: 'Did he know what ship or ships they're from?'

'No.'

'Boarding party, sir?' Halloran stubbed out a cigarette. 'I'd be glad to take a bunch of the lads and—'

'You'd be a damn fool, then.' Jerk of the grey head. 'We're four miles from the sea, stuck here, they'd be prepared for trouble and they have the backing of these local Nazis. Also that minelayer might be disposed to interfere. I'll give it a lot more thought, but what I'd reckon on is getting a message out, alert the RN and the diplomats. RN blockade out there, diplomats negotiate our chaps' release. Any idea how many?'

'No, sir. Couple of other things, though.'

'Well?'

'Cluny got all this from a pimp by name of Gomez. Gomez was sent out to the *Glauchau* by a port official I mentioned – Nazi called Ferras'– he was explaining this to Halloran – 'assistant to the absent Port Captain – to see whether they'd like to be visited on board by whores from a knocking-shop called the Casa Colorada. Whores incidentally with the reputation of being unsafe, health-wise. And he – Gomez – somehow got to see the hatchway and

142

heard the prisoners. The guard on duty must have slipped up somehow – maybe turned the speaker off to hear what he was saying. Anyway, the Huns paid him to keep his mouth shut, and Ferras threatened him, told him if he said a word he *and the prisoners* could end up dead. The way Cluny explained that was kill *him* and destroy the evidence.'

'Charming.'

'Do it outside, I suppose.' Halloran gesturing down-river. 'Hardly get away with it here in the port. They'd shove off and –'

'No doubt. No doubt.' The Old Man grim-faced, maybe picturing it. Andy remembering the boatload of corpses he'd had the job of inspecting. Some solution of this kind to *that* macabre puzzle, maybe? Old Man nodding: 'Does happen to be a violation of international law to retain prisoners on board in a neutral port – that's why the *Graf Spee* had to land *her* prisoners in Monte. Didn't hear about that? She did, anyway. But this South African – did it seem to you he was taking the threat as more than bullshit?'

'Definitely. Scared for his own sake too, if they got to know he'd passed this on. Does seem to me, sir – if I may suggest it – well, if we were to go on the air they'd pick it up, sure as eggs they'll be on listening watch, and being cats on hot bricks, as I'd guess they must be –'

'Back to Cluny. If it puts him in such danger, why tell you? He volunteered the info, didn't he? First time you showed your face?'

'We're the first Red Ensign ship that's come in since the Hun. First English customer he'd had since then. He's a decent sort of guy, told me on Sunday he'd thought of going back to SA and joining up, only he'd be worried for his family here. And disliking Nazis like we all do –'

'And how come the pimp risked telling *him*?'

'Pimp's a drunk, also queer. Cluny said he couldn't explain it but they get on well and Gomez does tend to cry on his shoulder. Trusts him, I suppose – urge to tell someone – and maybe told him *because* he's scared.'

Halloran had lit another cigarette: looking impatient, angry. The Old Man noticing, challenging him: 'Well, Mister?'

Shake of the head. 'Bloody frustrating, sir – put it mildly. Our own people over there, fucking Huns keeping 'em in God knows what conditions –'

'Still thinking of a boarding party.' A nod. 'Shut you up a bit quick, didn't I, but' – shake of the grey head – 'that's not thinking, Mister, it's going off half-cock. Well, as reactions go, mine's the same – get over there, get 'em out, apply blunt instruments to square heads – eh? *But* – neutral port, neutral country, smart little warship less than a mile away, machine-guns all over her – what's more she'd have the legal right to use 'em – uh? Fancy the thought of getting the *Anna* arrested, all of us interned?'

'There's another thing I should have said.' Andy, cutting in. 'The minelayer's skipper's a friend of Ferras. They were together in Manolo's tonight – as it happens I'd seen him before Mendoza told me who he was. Junior Commander, Capitao de frigate or corvette, wife in Rio and a tart here about twice his height. Struck me then – as long as the real Port Captain's absent and Caetano's in charge –'

'Sir' – Halloran, butting back in – 'what I'd propose wouldn't get seen from anywhere. A dozen men, say, in our motorboat – send a couple up that Jacob's ladder, taking another ladder with 'em and chucking it over, all up then and rush the guard. Any luck we'd catch 'em on the hop – choose a flood tide so their lookout's that side, I'd bring the boat in close under her counter from this blind side, they'd have no sight of us!'

'Sight *and* sound, like as not. That boat's not quiet at the best of times – and you'd be heading into a three- or four-knot tide. Coming up for Springs, aren't we. Then again – fact they've a watch on deck starboard side for one special purpose – as we know now – doesn't mean there's no proper, all-round lookout.' He raised a hand: 'All right – they might *not* hear the boat's engine, with that other shindy. Fact remains, unless they're bloody stupid they'd be – as Holt put it – cats on hot bricks. And you'd be taking a dozen against a crew of, let's say, fifty?'

'Well.' Shake of the head, expelling a lungful of breath, black eyes liquid-looking in their sockets.' You're the Master –'

'Happens I am.' He said it quickly and firmly, his expression cold enough to emphasise that he and Halloran were by no means blood brothers. Adding, 'And first thing tomorrow I'll go see our consul. Take it from there, then. Meanwhile, keep our mouths shut – eh?'

Thursday 21 December: waking into his twenty-second year with a fairly major hangover. Last night the shock of Cluny's information had had the effect of sobering him, but the raw spirit had still been in there, drying out his liver or whatever it was cane spirit did to you.

Tomorrow evening, no cachaca. Or maybe try the diluted, sweetened drink recommended by Tonio. And certainly not a drop tonight. He'd have the duty on board tonight in any case; and by then, with the Old Man visiting the consul this morning, touch wood there'd have been developments.

Have to be. Old Man's right, playing it softly-softly, but one thing we can be sure he won't do is leave those poor bastards where they are.

In the saloon he told Jackson through the pantry hatch, 'Eggs and bacon please, two eggs,' and McAlan said with his mouth full but otherwise straight-faced, 'I'd have thought a pint or two of black coffee'd have sufficed.'

'You'd have thought wrong then.'

'Right as rain, are you?'

Fisher acknowledged, 'Must say you bore up pretty well.'

'Got on all right without me, did you?'

'We managed. Didn't stay all that late.'

'Maybe *some* didn'a. I'll say one thing, Holt, that's a wee smasher of a waitress, that Manuela, eh?'

'Yeah. I like her.' Sitting down with his eggs; Janner pushed the coffee jug along. 'Like her very much.'

'But yon tall lass, now –'

'Arabella?'

Fisher broke in: 'Her little commander left even before I did. Left her with the Nazi.'

'Well, what d'you know . . .'

The chute clattered and roared into action out there: loading was in progress on number two now, Andy remembered. Thinking of the *Glauchau*'s number three then: wondering how many and – as Halloran had said – under what conditions they'd be living. Shut up in that noise – no air, no exercise . . .

Halloran banged in, banged the door shut behind him, shouted, 'Only coffee, Jackson!' He'd already have had breakfast, probably, would have been up there seeing things were in order for the start of loading – the timber partitioning and dunnage in that hold, and probably elsewhere as well – and would now have left it to the bosun.

Slopping coffee into a mug, asking Andy, 'How's the head?'

'Expect I'll live.'

'What you said about the Casa whatsit – that the honest truth?'

'It's what I was told, that's all.'

'When?'

'Last night. It came in reference to the bloke who spilt the beans.'

'Well, well.'

'Hope you *stay* well. He wasn't saying they all have it – or even that any of 'em do now, only that it had been known.'

'But warning you off, was he?'

'Well – maybe . . .'

'Hm.' Coffee mug in one hand, the other holding up crossed fingers.

The Old Man went ashore at nine-thirty; he'd told Halloran he'd be calling first at the agent's office, then visiting the consul. If he wasn't back when the time came to shift her again, Halloran was to see to it.

Martensen told him where he'd find the consulate, which was also apparently a trading company; he had an idea Bruce Partridge was still away, but if it was only some routine matter, his wife, who worked as his secretary and assistant, would probably take care of it.

'Away where, d'you know?'

'Montevideo – like so many, including our Port Captain. Should be back soon, I imagine, now that show's all over. Is there some way *I* can help?'

Shake of the head. 'Port Captain also back soon, d'you think?'

'At the weekend, was what I heard. Frankly it doesn't concern any of us very much, his job here is something of a sinecure. He has a marine assistant by name of Ferras who knows what he's about, while the figurehead in da Tovar's absence is a landsman – actually a civil engineer – by name of Mario Caetano. He is always most helpful.'

'Glad to hear it . . .'

He didn't trust this fellow. Had asked him a couple of days ago about getting the Germans to shut off their noise, and the Dane's advice had been to put up with it: the port authorities after all were tolerating it, Anglo-German sensitivities or disputes weren't much of their concern, and confrontations of any kind were very much to be avoided; the martial music might seem to be a form of challenge or self-assertion – offensive maybe, to British ears – but look, if the port authorities demanded that it should cease and it did not, it would put *them* in an invidious position. Trade was trade, was what a port was for, was vital to Brazil and to all her people, who were entirely and *strictly* neutral . . .

Josh had remarked on that occasion, 'Of course your country's neutral, too. Last thing you'd want is to provoke the bastards.'

'To an extent perhaps that's true . . .'

'Even when employed as agent for British ships – wouldn't want to upset 'em by insisting they turn their bloody wireless down?'

'Oh, well.' Superior smile. 'I hardly think such action would result in the Germans marching into Denmark, Captain. But it *is* essential I remain on good terms with the port authority.'

On this occasion Martensen offered him a cigar, which the skipper refused. The Dane asking him then as he showed him out, 'Do you still expect to complete loading on Saturday?'

'Yes. So clearance Saturday forenoon, pilot provisionally early afternoon – two p.m., say. Be able to see to that, will you?'

'Well.' Same smile, accompanied by raised eyebrows. Wasn't going to let *himself* be provoked either, by this uncouth master mariner. 'Best thing might be if I visit you tomorrow afternoon for confirmation.' A nod: 'If it's all right with you, I'll do that.'

The consulate was a private house with some of its ground floor converted to offices, with a separate entrance and a notice in English and Portuguese labelling it as the Consulate of Great Britain; also head office of Partridge Import Export, General Traders. A fat, fair-haired woman of about thirty answered the doorbell and told him that unfortunately Mr Partridge was away.

'In Montevideo?'

She had a nice smile. 'He was there for all the excitement, but on his way back he's stopping off in Rio – for consultations at the embassy, as it happens. So – Sunday, I *hope* . . .'

'You're Mrs Partridge?'

'Oh, indeed!'

'English by marriage therefore, but –'

'Dutch. It sounds like it too, doesn't it? And you are?'

'Josh Thornhill, Master of the SS *PollyAnna*, in the port here loading iron ore.'

She'd opened the door wider and stepped back: she was wearing a cotton housecoat and bedroom slippers. 'Come in, please . . .'

'Would it be possible to get your husband on the phone?'

'Is it a matter of much urgency?'

'It is. Also highly confidential. One of the problems, I may say, is the absence of the Port Captain. I mean the real one – forget his name, but –'

'Jaoa da Tovar. He and his wife play bridge with us, we're friends. Whereas that beastly little man Caetano –'

'Haven't met him, personally, but he's one of the niggers in the woodpile.' A sigh, shake of the head. 'I'd sooner not go into it here and now –'

'But if we got through to the embassy you'd have to, wouldn't you? Otherwise what –'

'Bothers me, too. But – the way things are –'

'Nothing else for it, is what you are saying. Yes – well . . . If I find I can get through, and if he happened to be there just at this time – that's of course a long shot – but you'd like me to try?'

'Yes, but – new thought you've given me there – if you're able to get through, might persuade the ambassador – rather than your husband – to speak to me?'

'I could *try* –'

'Because – looking at it squarely now – without offence to your husband, Mrs Partridge –'

'None at all – if it's such a major issue, my husband could only refer it to the ambassador, or even to some member of his staff. Yes – very well, I'll try. You take a seat now. Would you like some coffee?'

Halloran moved the ship astern by a few more yards shortly before noon. The tide was flooding, so that the tug's job was less to move her than to hold her against the force of it while ropes and wires were shifted and re-secured. Loading had resumed when the Old Man returned and sent for Halloran and Andy to join him in his cabin. He told them, his voice pitched high to beat the racket from the chute, 'I've a telephone call booked for five p.m. to our ambassador in Rio. Got through to the embassy half an hour ago and he wasn't available; they told this consul's wife to try again at five o'clock when he would be. Sounds like easy hours the bugger works. Consul's away, but he'd be no use anyway – visa applications, passports, be about the extent of it. Wife's all right though, very helpful.'

The *Glauchau*'s music was inaudible, thanks to the chute, the thunder of incoming ore. The German was lying stern-on in this tide, so there was no view from *PollyAnna* of the watch on deck; but mental imagery, as one looked at her and her Nazi ensign barely stirring in the breeze, of incarcerated British seamen. You could guess at this being in the skipper's mind as he turned back to them from the scuttle.

'Time being, then, that's it. Never spoke with an ambassador before, but if he comes up to scratch . . . Well, bloody *got* to . . .'

Didn't, though. He went ashore in good time for the five o'clock call, and returning on board at about seven – stevedores having knocked off at six, the noise all coming from the *Glauchau* now – the Old Man hauling himself up the gangway which this soon after high water *was* a steepish haul – and gloweringly telling Halloran, who'd been alerted by the gangway watch and had come hurriedly to meet him, 'Ambassador's on his holidays. Whoever it was said he'd be there didn't know he and his missus were leaving by air this afternoon for La Paz – Bolivia. How's that for a waste of time and money?'

'Leaves us on our own too, doesn't it . . .'

Thinking of his boarding party again. Old Man glancing at him, seeing that and shaking his head. 'I'll tell you, Mister. Mrs Partridge come up trumps, called the da Tovars' private house – da Tovar's Port Captain, right? Social call, they're friends – asked when would her husband be back in town, and the good news is she's expecting him tomorrow, train from Rio getting in at noon. And *he*'s the best answer to this whole bag of tricks. She left a message – Mrs Partridge did – personal and confidential – soon as he's back, to call her. So I'll be at the consulate by midday – get her to call them again if they don't come through.' Switch of subject: 'You on board tonight?'

'Think I will stay on board, sir.'

'Holt has the duty, has he?'

'Yes. Does Mrs Partridge know what it's about?'

'No. Accepts it's urgent because I told her so. Got her head screwed on, that woman. But see, if da Tovar was to take a search party out to the Hun –'

'Would they release the prisoners to us, d'you reckon?'

A shrug. 'Sensible thing, wouldn't it. Wouldn't want 'em on *their* hands. And arrest the *Glauchau*, I'd imagine. That's my hope. What should've happened days ago. A lot better than us shouting our heads off on W/T, alerting those buggers and having 'em push off during the dark hours. Specially as—'

He'd checked. 'We'll talk this over later – eight or thereabouts, in my cabin. Bring Hibbert with you – and Fisher, no reason to leave him out of it.'

To hang on, taking a chance on da Tovar, did make sense, they all agreed. The Old Man had wanted a breadth of view on it, this being a highly unusual and potentially explosive situation, men's lives quite possibly depending on how you handled it. One did remember, vividly enough, that swamped lifeboat, floating knacker's yard. It had been a very bad moment for him when Mrs Partridge had told him about the cock-up in the Rio embassy: he'd thought then of trying to get through to Todhunter in Uruguay, asking him to get in touch with the British minister there, man by the name of something-Drake, who Todhunter had said was so well thought of. But Todhunter had also mentioned that the telephone lines around Monte and from there to the ambassador in Buenos Aires were highly insecure; also the existence of a Nazi party in Monte – who'd like as not be in cahoots with their brethren here, Caetano's lot – and the thought of shouting all this stuff over a long-distance line, in sufficient detail and clarity for Todhunter then to approach the British Minister with it, gave him the jitters: possible outcome being the *Glauchau* weighing anchor in a hurry and clearing out. He'd been wrestling with this and asking himself, Christ's sake, *what* then? when Mrs Partridge – 'Right off her own bat, bless her little Dutch heart' – had phoned Capitao da Tovar and struck gold.

Chief Hibbert had agreed that going on the air, in plain language at that, could blow it absolutely. 'You're seamen and I'm supposed not to be, but my guess is the *Glauchau* could get away at any damn state of the tide. Not pinned against any wall, is she. And being twin-screw she can turn easy enough without any tug. Turn on her cable – eh? Diesel too, don't need the time we do getting steam up. Well, Christ . . . Another thing, Josh – where'd the Royal Navy be starting from if you did put a signal out? Monte? Don't know, do we, but that's a distance of – what?'

Fisher told him, 'Thousand miles. Could be anywhere on that stretch of coast, though.'

'Or *nowhere* on it – by this time?'

The Old Man had nodded. 'All right. Conference concluded. Don't anyone forget to say his prayers.'

Friday. The chute was at work on number five, probability was they'd be topping up number four in mid- or late forenoon, move the ship then for the last time and spend the rest of the day on number one. It would leave a couple of hours' work for tomorrow, Saturday, full completion by noon in any case. Then goodbye Vitoria.

But tonight, *oi* Manuela!

Must draw cash . . .

'Hear that, Holt?'

Halloran had been telling Fisher something on the other side of the saloon table, but Andy with Manuela in mind hadn't been tuned in. The mate repeated it now: 'The Old Man'll be shifting her, by and by, then visiting the consul's missus once again – you know what for – and he's reckoning on buying coffee to take home. Consul runs a business that handles it – wholesale, see, good price. Any of you want some, and has the cruzeiros –'

'Not me. Need to draw some, in fact.'

'Shore again tonight?'

He glanced at him, shrugged. 'Thought I might.'

Ask the skipper for all-night leave, too . . .

Janner asked Fisher, 'What'll we be on, this morning?' He was asking what subject they'd be studying in their instructional period.

Fisher told him and Gorst, 'Winter and summer loadlines, tonnage of cargo embarked, effect of depletion of bunkers on passage from summer zone to winter zone. Touched on it once before, if you remember. It's simple enough, but you both threw fits.'

Gorst put his coffee mug down carefully, told Janner, 'I can feel one coming on right this minute.'

Having moved the ship – on a flood tide again, same routine, letting the river do the hard work, tug only taking her weight while it did so – the skipper went ashore, made his way up to the consulate and found Mrs Partridge stifling tears: telling him as he walked in, 'Only this *minute* she telephoned –'

'And?'

'To tell me that her husband had telephoned her and the soonest he can be back is tomorrow evening! Some naval function he can't get out of – oh, isn't it *damnable*!'

It was. In fact more than damnable. The shock of it froze his mind. Muttering that he'd think of something, go about it some other way, don't worry my dear, certainly not *your* fault . . .

Todhunter?

No. Take bloody hours, and then he wouldn't be there: or if he was you might be talking into Nazi ears as well as his.

Wireless had to be the answer. Bull by the horns, last resort, just bloody *do* it; last resort was exactly what it was!

'Mrs Partridge – I owe you a bit on that last call. Then for the coffee beans you so kindly offered –'

'I'd like to make you a present of them. In the circumstances –'

'Most kind, but no. You've already been more than helpful. Hours on the damn blower. Here, now – that's what I owe: and here's for two tins of the coffee . . .'

None of his officers had wanted any or had money for it, apparently. It was as good as you'd get anywhere in the world, and dirt cheap. He liked to take a few surprise packages home to his sister and brother-in-law when he could – being a widower and living with them, feeling a bit like an old cuckoo sometimes in their little house – and would be more than ever now with food-rationing starting up. Wouldn't be many weeks before every damn thing was on the ration, just as it had been last time.

He left Mrs Partridge smiling through incipient tears, set off with his coffee in two hessian-wrapped tins and the full bloody awfulness of the past two days racking his mind. Nothing for it but to go on the air. Risk to those poor sods' lives, maybe, but – face it, what else, what other hope did they have? Draft the message now and work on it, make it as concise as possible, have Dewar tap it out tomorrow on their way down-river. If there *were* any RN ships within – please God – a few hours' steaming distance, the *Glauchau* would have had it; but in any case you'd have fingered her – naval squadrons or patrols all over would be on the lookout for her.

Emerging on to the dockside road and crossing it diagonally towards the quays, he was already hearing the racket of the chute, and a minute later had *PollyAnna*'s forepart in sight, and the iron ore dust-cloud overhanging it. Giving that cloud a wide berth on his way to the gangway, the head of which now rested abaft the central 'island', a fair distance from the activity around the chute. Holt was there, he saw, and moving aft, away from the noise and dust-cloud, were Halloran and the second mate and – oh, the pilot who'd brought them in on Sunday. Name of – Mendoza – and recognisable by his limp. Fisher had turned at that moment and spotted him: all three stopping then, looking this way, the pilot giving him a long-range salute. The Old Man shifted one parcel so both were under his

154

left arm, responded with a wave then pointed up at his own cabin, indicating that he'd meet him up there. He was in the cabin himself half a minute before Halloran appeared in the doorway with him.

'Good day, sir!'

'Pilot. Captain Mendoza. Good to see you.'

'Want me to stay, sir?'

'Might as well, Mister. What can we do for you, Pilot?'

'Me do for *you*, I think. A message coming from Senhor Martensen that you wish depart tomorrow two o'clock p.m.?'

'Told him that yesterday, he's supposed to be coming this afternoon for confirmation. But – yes, two p.m. 'd suit us. Glad it's to be you again. Mind you, senhor, you're not overworked, exactly?'

It was intended as friendly ribbing, and Mendoza accepted it as such. Shrugging, 'This week, not. Only my French frien' there – and the *Volcao* who depart; now however coming two more British – and tomorrow, five o'clock the morning, depart that *Glauchau*. Finish music, eh?'

'Five, you say?'

A glance at Halloran.

'High water five-forty, eh? From anchor needing the flood only for passing Sao Joao. My colleague José Ybarra take her out five sharp. He speak German a little, is why he, but also he bring in British SS *Thelma Vale*, berth where was *Volcao*. All before your departure two p.m. Flood tide for you then – low water half-hour before noon, OK?'

The Old Man had nodded. Glancing at Halloran again. '*Glauchau*'ll be weighing at first light, then.'

'Ah, yes.' Mendoza mimed sleep: eyes shut, face on his hands, snoring. 'For me, five o'clock not good. For José Ybarra not so bad, maybe. Uh?' Laughing again.

Halloran asking him quickly, causally, 'Where's she bound, the German?'

'Where bound?' Hands spread and a vacant look. 'I not knowing. Not ask. Clear for German port, maybe. You like I ask?'

The Old Man told him – before Halloran could say yes please – 'No skin off *our* nose. But what about the spare parts she was waiting for?'

That high shrug again: 'Maybe has come?'

The Old Man told them – Halloran, Hibbert, Fisher and Andy – 'Port Captain da Tovar won't be back before tomorrow evening. He telephoned his wife and she called Mrs Partridge.'

Halloran snorted: 'So *that*'s scuppered.'

'On top of which we just heard from our pilot, Mendoza, that the *Glauchau*'ll be weighing at five a.m. A German-speaking pilot's boarding her at that time. Mendoza's booked to take *us* out at fourteen hundred. So she'll be nine hours ahead of us, route and destination unknown. Mendoza offered to find out, but hell, she could clear for Timbuktu and aim to sneak through to Bremen. And I still wouldn't want to display much interest. What we don't know that really matters is what RN ships, if any, may still be on or anywhere near this coast. As it looks now, we'll be sitting here watching that bloody Hun steam out with our own people locked up inside her.'

Hibbert stirred. 'Wouldn't feel too comfy doing that.'

'No.' The skipper agreed. 'Nor'd I. And if the sod sails at five – that's it, she's gone, *they've* gone. Well, I'll make that signal – have to – but unless there *are* ships damn near this hole—'

Hibbert cut in again, 'Hundred to one against it?'

'Dunno. Maybe. But we'd have let our folk know what she is – prisoners on board, and maybe a *Graf Spee* support-ship – and where she's starting from, estimated speed say fifteen knots . . . I wouldn't put a lot of weight on the threat to murder 'em, but they're still gone, aren't they – and you could say we'd deserted 'em. *I'd* say it – we *would* have. Well – the W/T problem we've gone into, in the short term doesn't help, telephones not secure – and no bugger on the other end at that – no consul here, no port captain, no legitimate authority whatsoever. Other words, we're on our tod. Any argument with that?'

'Argument for a boarding party then?'

'Not as you proposed, no. Whatever we do has got to bloody *work*. A few lads shinning up Jacob's ladders – won't wash, Mister. And if what we do don't pay off, result might be – I said it before – *PollyAnna* arrested and us interned.' He looked at Hibbert. 'Any ideas, Chief?'

'*You* have, haven't you?'

'Of a sort. Of a sort, yes. *Hellish* chancy, but . . .' Thinking about it: all eyes on him, and his own round blue ones moving from face to face. They were quite unusually round, Andy realised, as the pale-blue gaze left him, settled on Fisher.

'When's moonrise tonight, Second?'

Fisher went into his brain-racking state: face blank, eyes blinking not fast but very regularly. Holding it long enough for some others present to glance at each other, thinking, how long, oh Lord, how long?, but getting there just before the questioner might snap, '*Well?*' He nodded: told the Old Man, 'Shortly before 0400, sir. 0350, maybe. Except this overcast may thicken – could even be rain –'

'Be out of the river by four, any road.' Skipper's hand running around his jawline. 'High water here 0540, Mendoza was saying, so 0200 it's flooding, and no moon. I'll want steam for 0200, Chief. And no sign we're raising it, certainly not before dark. Nothing happening anywhere as might look fishy. After dark, cover and secure number one hold. We'll leave tomorrow's ore behind us. Owners'll scream like stuck pigs, but – never mind, *my* lookout, no one else's. Trim won't be as perfect as we'd want – just can't be helped. Cover of dark, Mister, prepare the ship for sea – nice and quiet and showing no lights as wasn't showing last night.'

'No shore-leave, then?'

'No. And no bloody arguments. Anyone has arrangements made, forget it. *She*'ll get over it.' She will too, Andy thought, but tonight she'll be spitting mad. He felt distinctly sad about it himself – more than disappointed, a better word might be *deprived* – and Halloran had thrown him an amused glance. The skipper was saying there was a lot of detail to be settled, most of it between himself and the mate. And that later he'd address the whole crew in the mess room.

'You, Second, will have your work cut out getting us down-river in the dark with no pilot.'

Andy, thinking about that passage, wondered what the minelayer might be doing by that time. Whether in fact – intriguing thought – the answer might depend at least to some extent on Arabella – whether the little skipper might be preoccupied with her . . . Maybe not, though: Fisher had said the little squirt had left her with that Nazi. Fisher asking the Old Man now, 'What about Customs clearance, sir?'

'Forget it. *Can't* clear. Not a word, any of you, to the agent, either – he may be along, by and by. Or to Mendoza if he happens along again. Far as either of them's concerned, we're sailing fourteen hundred tomorrow, getting clearance during the forenoon. Fact of it is we'll be breaking every rule in the book – can't bloody help it.' Looking round again for reactions: 'Any useful comments, suggestions or alternatives?'

Hibbert shifted his massive fame. 'Alternatives to *what*, Josh?'

11

The Old Man bawled to his chief engineer – on their own in the day cabin now – 'Tell me how *else*?'

He'd said he wouldn't be comfy doing nothing, but wasn't happy with the action as the skipper had outlined it, either. The racket outside went into decline before he'd had time to answer: elevator coming to a halt in a roar of released steam, the last of this day's intake of ore crashing down through the trunking's ringing steel and thudding into the foremost hold, and what had seemed for a moment like blessed silence was at once invaded by the Germanic oompa-oompa. Hibbert now able to *say* instead of shout, 'Heck of a thing to be taking on, Josh. Even if the lads were trained for such malarkey – or *you* were . . .'

'Bugger training. Not going to be a naval battle, Dick – just a bloody rough-house. All right, if I make a bollocks of it –'

'Disaster all round. And even if it comes off – without casualties, would you expect? Even loss of life?'

'Say our prayers and take our chances, is all.' Thumbing shag tobacco into his pipe. 'Have to, no bloody option. All right – *I* have to. You reckon if we behaved like proper little non-combatants we'd arrive home with a clean bill of health?'

A nod. 'To all intents and purposes . . .'

'Those are *our* people, Dick. The sort I'd soonest not be judged and found wanting by. Sooner not let down – uh?'

Flare of the skipper's storm lighter. Hibbert shrugging, half in agreement, but scared of consequences. 'You'll be chancing your own crew's lives and freedom. How about *their* judgement?'

'I'll be putting it to 'em fair and square.' He had his pipe going. 'Ask 'em are they game for it, or –'

'And if they say no, the terms of their engagements –'

'Last thing they'll do. Long and short of it is there's a bunch of their own kind over there, locked up and destined for bloody Germany. What if it was us, and we heard another Red Ensign ship had known about it and done bugger all?'

'The lads'll vote to have a go, I'm sure. But it's *your* head on the block if it goes wrong – as you and I know very well it could.'

'And that's what I should be thinking of? Safeguarding yours truly? That how you'd see it if you were Master?'

The engineer wagged his head. 'Maybe not, but –'

'There you are, then.' Sucking on the pipe. 'There you are.' He checked the time. 'Have your crowd told no shore-leave, will you?'

Halloran told Batt Collins, 'No shore-leave, Bosun.'

Shock in the bony, hard-eyed face. 'Last night in – no leave, sir?'

'Captain's orders. You'll hear why soon enough, he'll be addressing all hands in the mess, later. But put it around right away – any of 'em try nipping ashore between now and then, it'll be Wilful Disobedience.'

For which the statutory penalty that could be awarded by a magistrate's or naval court was imprisonment for up to four weeks, with or without hard labour, as well as loss of pay.

Batt's eyes still held the mate's. He'd have preferred to know the reason now, *before* he passed on the edict. 'Reason that'll satisfy 'em, is it?'

'If you don't think so when you hear it, Bosun, you can call me a liar.'

'Well.' A shrug. 'There's some won't be overjoyed.'

'If you like, tell 'em Mr Holt had a heavy date tonight, and he's not even allowed ashore to tell her he can't make it.'

The chute trunking was clear of the ship now, and the hands who'd been waiting had gone down into the hold – number one – to square things off. Halloran left the rest of it to Collins and went up to see the Old Man, arriving just as Hibbert left – skipper telling him quietly, 'Chief – steam for 0130, let's say, kick-off 0145.'

'Can do.' Seeing the mate arriving then: 'Can do, sir.'

'Come in, Mister.' Waiting, puffing at his pipe until the door was shut. Then: 'Got it worked out, after a fashion. See what holes you can pick in it. What it comes down to in numbers is one party of twelve and two of eight, total twenty-eight – I'd hope all volunteers.'

'I lead 'em into the Hun, do I?'

'No.' Pointing at a chair. 'No, we'll give Holt that job. You've a bigger one. See here . . .'

He'd sketched it on the back of an old chart: two hull shapes alongside each other, *PollyAnna* with her starboard-side forepart impinging on the German's port side amidships, that point of contact – or impact – marked 'A'. Explaining quietly, 'At "A", the group of twelve, Holt leading 'em. Straight over, rush the guard and any others that may be there, and – up to Holt, this, depends on how he finds it – down into that hatch to the 'tween-decks, smash in there, bring the prisoners up out of it and over into the *Anna*. You're there at our rail with the first party of eight – who'll have secured us alongside after he's gone over – standing by to receive the prisoners. If it's all gone nice and smooth, mind you – otherwise you send 'em to support Holt's lot, if they're in need of it. Same applies to the other eight – who might best be further aft here.' Port side, abreast number three hatch. 'There again, Mister, only send 'em into the scrap if or when they're needed. How I'd *hope* it might go is the first rush goes over, Holt with as many as he needs gets down inside, rest of 'em keeping that deck-space clear of Huns until he's back up with the prisoners. Then double-quick back on board – some rearguard action no doubt, your reserves lending a hand or staying put at the ship's side – your judgement, what's needed. *Then*, Mister, you count 'em all back, signal me by whistle that we've got 'em all, and – cast off, we're away.'

Looking at him. 'Well?'

'Could be awkward, the disengaging.'

A nod. 'It could. Principle'd be to get the prisoners over first while our lot lay into the Huns and drive 'em back. But also stick together, no heroes getting cut off on their own.'

'Right.'

'Why this has to be your job, see. Holt's is to break in, get 'em, break out again, get 'em across to the Hun's port side and over. He doesn't have to think what else is happening. That's what *you* do – see he gets the support he needs and none of 'em gets left behind. I'll be trying to hold her alongside, but in that tideway – well, what d'you say to a few fathoms of four or four and a half inch Manila, at points A and B? You there, bosun here, a couple of hands at each point going over behind Holt's team to make lines fast. Lines with eyes in 'em, so securing's quick an' easy?'

A nod. 'Cadets could do with splicing work, I'll put 'em on to it. How about the start of it – 0145, you were saying?'

'Tide'll be flooding. Low water's 2320, 2330. Step one, rig a steel-wire rope – four-inch, maybe – from the foc'sl to a bollard well up ahead of us. 0115, say, do that. Don't want to attract attention, mind, no torches. Then when we're set, bosun nips ashore with two or three hands, casts off breasts and springs, back on board and brings in the gangway. There again, no torches, and we'll show no lights. Ship's weight in the tide's now all on the wire out for'ard: soon as I have her moving off the quay and there's slack in it, let it go from inboard. So we leave the port of Vitoria one steel-wire rope for a Christmas present. Alternative might be if we had a wire long enough to pass around the bollard and bring back inboard, but I doubt we have, eh?'

'Sure we haven't, sir. But' – he'd had two fingers crossed, uncrossed them now – 'weapons for the boarding parties. Have Postlethwaite knock up some battens, shall I?'

A nod. 'Good thinking. Whatever timber he's got that's right for it. Two by two maybe. Say twenty-four inches long, and chisel the corners off one end for a hand-grip.'

'Twenty-eight of 'em. Better say thirty. If he's got that much that's suitable.'

'If he hasn't, use something else. Lengths of hawser – or rigging-wire. Best get a move on, hadn't he? But listen now – question of holding us alongside. Might turn out to be not only the flood tide – which we'll be stemming, obviously, three or four knots for that – but if the Hun's wide awake he could be working his engines to separate us. In his shoes that's what I'd do – aiming to trap our blokes on board – eh?'

'If Holt can do *his* stunt like greased lightning –'

'Then no problem.' The skipper touched wood – not for the first time. 'But we don't know what he'll be up against. And if he gets stuck in there – or can't get through to the prisoners – well, see to it his front-runners have an axe, cold chisel, fourteen-pound hammer maybe, crowbar . . . Best have a torch too, hadn't he.'

In the mess room, where the evening meal hadn't yet been cleared away, the skipper, backed by a gaggle of his officers including Andy, faced close on fifty intensely interested deck and engine room hands, and began by telling them, 'Before we get into detail, here's the issue in a nutshell. That German out there – motor vessel *Glauchau* – is holding British merchant seamen prisoners in her 'tween-decks.'

Like letting a bomb off. Shocked, startled faces, then growing anger, a swelling growl of it, which he silenced with a raised hand.

'We don't know how many or from what ship or ships.

163

All we know is they're in that *Glauchau* and she's due to sail at 0500 – pilot's booked for that hour. To sneak home to bloody Germany, you might guess. Another guess is she may have been going to act as a support-ship for the *Graf Spee* – she holed-up here the day after the *Spee* got into Monte – awaiting fresh orders is my guess; *her* story is she's been waiting for engine spares – and she's got away with it this far because the Port Captain's away and his deputies are bloody Nazis. That's fact, not fancy, could be why she picked this place or it was picked for her.'

The donkeyman – Barnes, senior engine room rating – was on his feet. A Welshman of average height but unusual width, he was said to have once lifted a full-sized trimmer under his left arm and a greaser under the other and banged their heads together.

'Cap'n, sir –'

'Yes, Barnes?'

'Reckoning on boarding and breaking 'em out, sir?'

'You wouldn't be opposed to some such action, eh?'

'By God *no*!'

Nor would any of them, by the sound of it. The skipper quietened them again.

'You'll see why I couldn't grant shore leave tonight. We'll have steam up by one-thirty, cast off one forty-five, and I'll lay *PollyAnna* alongside the Hun shortly before two. First mate and I've worked out a way of handling it from there on; I'll just tell you some of the background to this state of affairs, then he'll take over. Anyway, as even the ship's cat's aware, we're non-combatants: boarding and bashing Huns is *not* our business. Just happens I don't believe we've any option. I've looked for other ways of going about it – after Mr Holt, who'd had suspicions of his own, had it confirmed by a shoreside barman, I might mention. I tried the British consul, but he's away, couldn't have done much anyway; telephoned the embassy in Rio and damn me if the ambassador's not gone walkabout as well. Well, we could go on the air, get the Andrew on the job, but point one, Huns'd pick it up on their wireless and run like riggers; two, the cruisers as were on this coast might by now be days away. And right here, the Port Captain who's said to be a good 'un was due back noon today and I was hoping to do business with him, but he's been held up in Rio. What I'm telling you, see, is I've tried and got bloody nowhere, so – no choice, uh?'

Andy told his team of twelve, aft on the upper deck, 'Battens and fists. No knives. Skipper's orders, that.'

AB Parlance asked him, 'Brass knuckles allowed, sir?'

'Well, it's not Be Kind To Huns Night, is it?' That drew some chuckles. He added, 'But we don't want to leave knife wounds behind us.'

'What if they got pistols?'

'Skipper thinks not likely. But he has a Colt revolver and Cadet Gorst's a practised pistol-shot – he'll be on the bridge-wing with it and any gunmen do appear they'll be his target.'

That had been decided in the saloon half an hour ago, skipper having mentioned that he had this old six-shooter, couldn't hit a barn door with it point-blank, and Gorst had come up with the fact he'd been in his training ship's pistol-shooting team, didn't profess to be any dead-eyed Dick, but had been known to hit targets smaller than barn doors.

The other cadet, Janner, was to be Halloran's 'doggy', running messages or errands as required.

Andy went on, 'Draw battens from the carpenter. If he runs out of timber he'll provide lengths of hawser or standing rigging-wire. Near the same weight, I'd guess, might even be handier. The wire'd be fairly lethal. Now listen – Ingram here's my back-up: if I get clobbered he takes over. And if *he's* done in, Edmonds.'

'What if *I* buy it then, sir?'

'We'd be in trouble.' He shook his head. 'But none of us is going to buy it – please God. Anyway, my job's to get in and down to the 'tween-decks and bring up the prisoners. Inside the hatch there must be a vertical ladder as in a fiddley, at least as far as the 'tween-decks where the prisoners are. May have some of it partitioned off, boarded-up, whatever: that's what the axe is for, and the crow-bar – Parlance with the axe, Edmonds with the bar. You two come in behind me, then Ingram and Crown. That should be as many as we'll need inside; the rest of you keep the hatchway area clear of Huns so we can bring the prisoners up and across to *PollyAnna*. Distance of maybe forty feet – her beam must be about the same as ours, fifty or fifty-five, say. The other two teams of eight'll join in if Mr Halloran sees we need it. He won't send more than are needed – all got to be brought out of it when we finish; fewer the better really. For the same reason, stick together, support each other – right?'

He wondered whether the Germans might not have guns – on the bridge-wings, for instance – machine-guns, even. If this was – or had been – a *Graf Spee* support-ship – as she almost certainly was. The skipper had revealed only this afternoon that among War Intelligence Reports he'd received in recent days was one to the effect that the *Spee's* well-known support-ship, the MV *Altmark*, had made what was believed to have been her final rendezvous with the battleship on 27 November in the vicinity of Tristan da Cunha, and had been ordered back to Germany on 7 December; the signal recalling her had been intercepted and deciphered, and she was now being hunted over a wide area. *Glauchau* might well have been sent south as her replacement. A secondary point the skipper had made was that 27 November, date of the *Spee's* last fuelling from the *Altmark*, had been the day *PollyAnna* had come across the boatload of corpses – also within spitting distance of Tristan da Cunha. The *Anna's* second escape by a mere whisker, therefore.

Now 0140, or near as dammit. Creak of a derrick as the gangway was swung inboard and set down with only the faintest of thuds. Batt and his wingers had rigged the forward-leading wire and then taken the other ropes and wires off her quickly and quietly – rubber-soled shoes and whispers instead of the usual shindy – and Andy now had his team here on the port side for'ard, squatting behind the cover (from the Germans' angle of sight, if any of them were looking) of numbers one and two hatch coamings, and dressed more or less as he'd advised – dark-coloured trousers and sweaters, or boiler-suits. Most of them would have had a couple of hours' kip – as he'd had himself. Had in fact considered writing a letter to his father, but sleep was really a more sensible use of the time; and letters written before action had certain implications, whether or not one was writing them in that spirit – which he would not have been.

(Hadn't the least notion where or when any such letter would be posted, either. Or when they'd get any. Non-arrival of mail was beginning to rankle slightly.)

Thrum of the engine. Steam up and – yes, big old screw churning, *PollyAnna* on the move, deep-laden with her bellyful of ore. Fisher was up there with the skipper, AB Shuttleworth on the wheel, Harkness manning the telegraph, and spare hands – odd-job men or errand-boys – OS Curtis and galley-boy Starling.

Moving. And the rasp of the steel-wire rope as the foc'sl party knocked a slip off and the wire slid willingly away. Ship now clear of the quay with the flood tide's force helping to turn her bow out into it: and still no lights moving or changing out there in the anchorage, no lights at all that the Germans hadn't shown every night this week. A dimly lit patch on the south bank of the river were illuminations on and around the Frenchman. If the Huns didn't see you coming, they wouldn't hear you either, with that dirge blaring away as usual. Skipper on the bridge would have his glasses on her: if the bastards *did* see, hear or otherwise suspect, might get a sudden flood of light and noise other than music; on the other hand, if they'd been drilled to it you might not – orders might be passed quietly, upper deck filled silently with Huns standing by to repel boarders.

With guns in their hands. Guns against sticks. He thought it *was* distinctly possible. Skipper dismissive of it because there'd be nothing he could do about it – it was part of the risk he was having to take.

Halloran coming aft now, bosun with him. Through the darkness Halloran tallish, bosun like a medium-small ape bounding bow-legged at his heels. Andy stood up, identifying himself; the *Anna* by this time twenty feet clear of the quay and gathering way, vibration building as revs gradually increased. The skipper had said he'd try to get her out there speedily enough to have a fair chance of not being seen, since once she was under way every minute of exposure added to that risk. All portholes and weather doors had been shut and she wasn't showing navigation or steaming lights; to the Germans she'd been a darkish mass on that quayside for the past six nights, and with luck that was all they'd be seeing now.

'Holt. All right?'

'All set.'

'I'll join you, starboard side, as you go over. Or on impact, say. Second team will move into your place here, then join me.'

'Aye aye.'

They'd been over it all about forty times, for God's sake. Mention of 'impact', though – at this speed, maybe eight knots through the water, meaning four or five made good, there *would* be impact. Bloody great crash, in other words. He'd warned this lot, 'Get there and crouch, hold on, hope to God we stay in contact – or jumping distance anyway.' There'd been discussion of that potential source of very unpleasant casualties – jumping when you shouldn't – or clumsily – falling between two ships each of about 9,000 tons deadweight which might then close in again.

Still no movement and no visible disturbance. Music steadily gaining strength. A lot of them would have their heads down, saving their energies for the 0500 departure. Time now – no, couldn't read it. Not much short of 0200, in any case. And revs *de*creasing: you could feel it in her steel. He said quietly, 'Won't be long now. On your marks . . .'

Slower still. You heard the river, saw *PollyAnna* in your mind's eye as if from the *Glauchau*: black shape almost bow-on, looming closer every second and surely visible to anyone with eyes who as much as glanced this way. *PollyAnna* in, say, quarter-silhouette against the soft radiance of the town?

Manuela grinding her teeth? Or just her hips? Some lucky sod . . .

Engine slowed. Keeping way on her, not much else he guessed, revs calculated just to get her there, against the tide. *Glauchau*'s riding lights vivid white, superstructure and funnel clear-cut against the stars. Frothing of the tide visible too now under and around her stern.

And – *impact*.

A lot bigger than he'd expected after that reduction. Old Man should have reduced sooner, maybe. Long, iron-scraping, rail-bending side-swipe, and the German actually rocking away from it. They'd remained crouched through those few seconds – as well they had, would have been knocked flying if they hadn't – but were up now and running, over number two hatch and between it and the derricks; *PollyAnna*'s forward way still holding her along-side, nuzzling the German. Andy was over, others with him, into a glow of light that lit the forefront of the *Glauchau*'s superstructure and one white-shirted German on his feet – had been down, knocked over by the impact, was now up and another of them coming, shouting and stumbling out of the weather door at that corner.

First time I ever hit a Hun . . .

Hun on his knees again, Ingram kicking him in the face and two others taking on the second one. Andy had shouted, 'Keep 'em from coming out that door,' seen one German bounce off the top of the starboard-side rail and go cart-wheeling, bellowing; didn't hear the splash because he was in the shelter to the hatchway, 'tween-deck entrance, the shelter from any distance looking like a squat ventilator.

Now had the grating open – a hinged hatch replacing a hatchboard that had been removed – glow of light from below, didn't need the torch as he'd thought he might – was on the ladder, less climbing down than free-falling with his palms slapping the iron rungs, and other men's feet and legs coming down on top of him. The source of light from below was a bulb in a cage above a timber door with a grille in its upper part, from the other side of which he had an impression of men shouting – as far as he could make out, over the racket from above, it could have been wishful imagining – and – glory to God, two large, ordinary bolts, one at the top, one near the bottom. Jerking the top one back and then stooping to the other he realised he was standing on a hatch: get back on the ladder and pull up that lid, you'd find ladder-rungs continuing into the lower hold – from which even with the hatch shut there was an odour that told him fairly plainly what the access might be for. He pulled back the lower bolt, put his shoulder to the door and shoved – Parlance at his side – and a few feet back from the door as it banged open a dozen or more faces: glaring eyes, snarling mouths, bearded or part-bearded faces distorted by alarm or anger or both, but – extraordinarily – silent . . .

'You British? How many?'

'*Christ* – he's – you're –'

All in full cry suddenly: he had a job to make himself heard. 'Come on – up and out! *Quick*, before the Huns've got 'emselves together – OK? How many of you?'

He'd heard – *thought* he'd heard, in a bedlam of other shouts plus music still thumping overhead – 'Seventeen,' then a clearer voice correcting that with, 'Sixteen and the lass.'

'Parlance – get 'em moving, come up with the last of 'em, try to make 'em understand what's wanted.' Shouting upwards then: 'Go on up – clear the way – Ingram, all of you!' Grabbing an iron rung, one foot on another until those above gave him room, Parlance telling the prisoners – *ex*-prisoners – 'On deck, chums, our lads'll beat the Huns back, get you lot port side an' into the *Anna*. Comprendo?'

'What's the *Anna*, then?'

'SS *PollyAnna*. Blood Line, out o' Glasgow. Wanna get you aboard sharpish, see? Then –'

Then sound as well as smell fading below him as the music strengthened: he was at the top, crawling out of the shelter covering it and on his feet then in patchy, moving light and darkness and a crowd of struggling, cursing men – Ingram, Edmonds, Crown, Hughes the cook – and others, defending and widening the deck-space against encroaching Germans, some of whom were armed with bottles. Brooks and McCandle still blocking the weather door, although they – Huns – would have other exits they could use. Edmonds with his crow-bar was the most effective, others using fists as well as battens.

Andy yelled to Smythe – a trimmer – and firemen Sams and O'Keefe – the latter's face streaming blood – 'Prisoners coming up, look after 'em!' The first of them were already out, a huddle of three, four, as unkempt and scrawny as Pathans. Andy's eye caught then by a knife in the hand of a German who was going for Cox: he charged him, fists up but kicking him in the crotch – right on target – the German doubling-up and Andy in close then with fists swinging, Cox back in it using *his* boots too, knife skidding away towards the starboard scuppers. Broken bottles were as bad as knives, though, were being used as missiles too, and there was a lot of blood around. One bearded ex-prisoner had acquired a batten: might have got it from Edmonds, who didn't need that as well as his crow-bar, from which the Germans truly *were* keeping their distance. That one and others in a tight group had O'Keefe and Smythe hustling them over towards the *Anna*, while Germans advancing across number three to intercept them had themselves been taken in the rear by the first reserves Halloran must have sent – the bosun with gunlayer Bakewell and trainer Timms, bosun wielding a two-foot section of steel-wire rope, Clover and Priestman ditto –

and Bennet; a lot of those had gone for the rigging-wire. Huns scattering now – one unwisely backing into range of O'Shea's batten then encountering Smythe's fists and boots, finishing up crouched on the hatch with his arms covering his head. Andy dodging a flying bottle – had already been hit by one that had gashed his neck behind the ear – and charging the little squirt of a man who'd hurled this other one, kicking his heels from under him then slinging him at some of his friends.

Germans were tending to stand back now, and the first of the former prisoners had reached the ship's side, were clambering over, Janner and others helping. Halloran was there: and there *had* been movement between the ships' hulls – see-sawing with the gap between them opening and closing – as the skipper had predicted. Andy was back at the 'tween-deck access with Ingram and the others, and what must have been the last of the prisoners were emerging now into their protection; Parlance was with them, so those *had* to be the last. Parlance was king-pin, with his battleaxe which the Germans seemed disinclined to face. Several had been hauled away by their friends after close encounters with Edmonds' crow-bar, but the axe *really* frightened them. Weren't showing a lot of fight in any case, acting more like hyenas milling around at a safe distance while watching for chances and now and again taking one, the *Anna*'s men still having to dodge an occasional flying bottle. Half the prisoners must have been over in the *Anna* by this time, and of that last group out, now halfway across, one of middle-age – bald with grey in his beard – had an arm protectively round the shoulders of a smaller, much slighter one who was shrouded in an oilskin, and behind them another young one seemingly sheltering them both, at close quarters with Andy for a moment, yelling at him out of a darkly unshaven face, 'Blooming miraculous, sir!' It needed some explaining, but the slim one – beardless, with bright, scared eyes – was a *girl*, for Pete's sake . . . He remembered that answer to his question in the 'tween-decks three or four minutes ago – *Sixteen and the lass* . . .

He shouted to his own group – primarily to Ingram – 'Stay with these now!' Because the job seemed to be damn near done, all over bar the shouting, although progress was slow at the ship's side – ex-prisoners in a bunch, some hold-up there. Wasn't quite finished, though: a large, bulbous German in a singlet and shorts lurching out of the screen door, the door with his weight behind it catching McCandle off-balance, sending him staggering, and the German lunging with a knife – kitchen-type, he'd be a cook maybe – breasts like a woman's bulging the singlet, huge biceps, shaven head. Andy had started forward but Parlance was ahead of him, axe swinging up ready to split the gleaming skull – all it needed, man-mountain stopping dead, dropping the knife and lifting its great arms in surrender. Meanwhile, those last three were making better progress – the girl with the older man, and the lad protecting them. They had Ingram, Hughes, Edmonds and Crown flanking them; Brooks and McCandle back here between them and the weather door, other *Polly Anna*s here and there: the action was all on the port side now – and the ships *were* moving in relation to each other, Andy realised, might have accounted for the hold-up. He yelled to McCandle and Brooks, jerking a thumb, 'OK, you two!' – meaning job done here, shove off – but swivelling to face a Hun rushing at him, whirling a length of chain; an officer, no less, epaulettes on his shoulders. Andy stopped him by jabbing the batten into his yellowish-looking face, was in close then, inside the scope of the chain, landing a good straight left followed by a right cross, which didn't connect as the man tripped backwards, went sprawling across the hatch-cover. No purpose in following up: his own orders to the lads had been to keep Huns at a distance but not on any account get in among them. Looking to the ship's side again now: the girl and the older man were climbing the German rail, Janner courteously rendering assistance from *PollyAnna*'s. The Germans weren't trying now, only pretending to, fifteen or twenty of them in an ostensibly threatening half-circle, as if to give the impression they'd forced this withdrawal. Halloran and the bosun were summoning men back over: Andy with Ingram, Parlance, Edmonds, Crown and Hughes were going to be the last: facing the Huns still, guessing that turning their backs on them might give them ideas. But you couldn't stand around for ever: he shouted to Ingram, Crown and Hughes, 'Go on, you three. Bloody good job you've done.' Keeping Parlance the axeman and Edmonds the crow-bar man because they were the best Hun-frighteners. Despite which, a few Huns, seeing this bunch thin out, *had* begun edging forward – hesitantly, though, looking round at others for support. Halloran bellowed through a megaphone, 'Holt – finish, pack up!'

'Give me the axe, Parlance. Off you go. You too, Edmonds.'

Holding the axe up and clearly visible, letting them know there could still be skulls split if they insisted, while giving those two time to get over. There was a lot of to-and-fro movement on the ships, grinding of hulls and lurches from time to time as the securing lines came up bar-taut. Should by rights have parted – and might yet. But OK now, maybe. Keeping the axe in view while backing to the rail – then on it – on the German's rail and over it, heels on the iron coaming outboard of the scuppers. There was a gap between the ships' hulls of about two feet and it was widening – very good reason *not* to wait for ever. Had to let go of the rail behind him – the *Glauchau*'s – and jump from his heels while grabbing for the *Anna*'s. The gap was now more like three feet and *still* – well, Christ . . .

Over. While Halloran, grabbing at his arm, had been slashed in the face by glass from a bottle shattering against a kingpost. Reeling back, hands to his face: there was a lot of glass and blood about. Two blasts on a whistle then – Halloran's – telling the skipper all hands re-embarked: the bosun was on his knees sawing through this tether of Manila rope. They'd already cast off the other, which would have accounted for that sudden widening of the gap.

174

Halloran, holding a wad of cotton-waste to his torn fore-head, snarling at Andy, 'Took your fucking time, didn't you?' Then – surprisingly – 'Done a nice job, for all that.'

Anna Homebound . . .

12

The anchorage at Halifax, Nova Scotia, a vast expanse of water called the Bedford Basin, protected then by a boom and anti-submarine net across its entrance, was full of ships – forty-six at this stage but with more to come in the next few days. *PollyAnna* had got in yesterday – a Sunday, 14 January – and the fifty-odd steamers already there, or at least enough of them to sound like fifty, had welcomed her with shrieking and tooting steam-whistles. Andy had told Julia when he'd come down from the bridge and found her at the rail with her friend Mark Finney, 'All that hullabaloo in *your* honour, d' you realise?'

'More likely in yours for rescuing us, I'd say.'

Smiling a little, and speaking quietly in her pleasantly low-pitched way. Her uncle had been master of the refrigerated cargo-vessel MV *Cheviot Hills*, was one of a considerable majority who had *not* survived. But as to that noisy welcome, the *PollyAnna*s were all celebrities now, especially in the eyes of Merchant Navy men: the name *PollyAnna* was almost on a par with those of the cruisers who'd nobbled the *Spee*, and Josh Thornhill was to be awarded the OBE. Informed of this by signal a week ago his comment to Chief Wireless Officer Dewar had been, 'Go on, pull the other one . . .' He himself having set the ball rolling in the early hours of 23 December with a signal informing the Admiralty and any nearby naval forces that the German MV *Glauchau* had been scheduled to depart

179

Vitoria 0500/23, destination unknown but as likely as not attempting to return to Germany, best speed estimated as fifteen or sixteen knots; sailing might be delayed beyond 0500 as he, Thornhill, Master of the SS *PollyAnna*, had been able to lay alongside her at 0200 in the roadstead at Vitoria and extract British Merchant Navy prisoners whom the Germans had been holding in their 'tween-decks and were survivors from MV *Cheviot Hills*, sunk by gunfire from a U-boat two weeks earlier, 300 miles southwest of the Azores when on passage from Christchurch New Zealand to London via Panama. Heavy casualties had been sustained in attempting to fight off the U-boat and survivors numbered only seventeen, including a passenger, Miss Julia Carr, niece of the master, Harry Carr, who'd gone down with his ship. Other survivors were Chief Engineer Ron Dixon, First Mate Sam Cornish, Apprentice Mark Finney, Steward Mervyn Benson, ABs T Raikes, W Rogerson, J Smith, P Taylor and A Willis, OSs H Ellis, J McAndrew, L Thomas, Greasers K Sawyer, T Small and A Rahman, Chinese Laundryman Ah Nong. The *Glauchau* had stored and bunkered in Lisbon and had been on passage to R/V with *Graf Spee* when informed by signal from the U-boat of the position of the sinking and that there had been some twenty-four survivors in the only boat that had been launched. In fact there had been twenty-two, and five had died of wounds during the four and a half days before the *Glauchau* had hove into sight flying the Red Duster.

Julia had told Andy, 'That was an awful let-down – when we realised they were Germans. Why'd they have flown false colours? We couldn't have got away, or done anything . . .'

'Save 'emselves any trouble getting you aboard, I suppose. At least they did search and pick you up. Odds'd have been heavily against finding you, incidentally. *Terrific* luck that they did, in fact – after a four-day interval, especially.'

'In some ways it was worse on board the *Glauchau* than in the boat. Except for those poor men dying – and not knowing who else, how *long* –'

'Don't talk about it, love.' The *Cheviot Hills'* chief engineer, Dixon – who'd been acting as guardian to her. He was a man of fifty, same age as Harry Carr had been, tallish and thin, slightly stopped, had a wife in Whitley Bay and two sons at sea. 'Try not to think about it, love.'

'Difficult to think of anything much else, I'd guess.' Andy looked from her to the engineer. This had been in the saloon, somewhere between Vitoria and St Lucia, probably only a day or so out of Vitoria. Andy with the back of his neck a fearful sight, where Halloran had sewn him up. There'd been quite a lot of such rough-and-ready repairs for the mate to attend to, after their guests had received some similar attentions and been settled down. Christmas Day maybe, this conversation might have been, when the *Anna* had been off Salvador – Maceio – or Boxing Day, when she'd been passing Recife and Natal. He'd added, aiming to rationalise the thinking, depersonalise it – if that was possible, which he didn't know, but out of sympathy for her was a natural inclination – 'It's surprising they'd have been so keen to pick you up. Obviously must have taken them off-course; and as they'd have known, ten to one against finding you. Unless they'd time to kill before the scheduled rendezvous, of course.'

'Concerned to save lives, surely.' Dixon again. 'Give credit where credit's due, I'd say. U-boat wouldn't have had room for prisoners, must have known the *Glauchau's* route south from Lisbon – would have, wouldn't they? They'd be kept informed so as not to attack one of their own ships. So *Glauchau* obliges, and pulls it off – maybe to their own surprise – and being stuck with us then, not giving two hoots, mind, for our comfort or –'

'Not *one*. You can believe it.' She muttered – for Andy's information, but not looking at him – 'An oil-drum in the lower hold, winched it up at night and emptied it, and – that was *all* . . .'

'And no fresh air. Or exercise, I suppose. And that music –'

'The days in harbour – yes. Like having plugs in your

ears – deaf as well as blindfold. How it felt, I mean.' Shaking her head. 'No, no fresh air at all. Except the first few hours – kept us on deck to start with while they cleared stuff out of the store-rooms that had been built in there – where you found us.' A glance at the engineer: 'Ronnie, I'm sorry, I *shouldn't* go on – I know I shouldn't . . . Funny thing is that what one remembers as the worst is the *last* thing – I mean, when there's sort of a series of awful things – so maybe it *does* fade, in fact the earlier part *has*, to some extent; it gets to be something like – you know, something you heard or read about?' Shaking her head again. 'Not making much sense, am I. But Charlie Knox, for instance . . .'

He'd never heard of any Charlie Knox, and didn't ask because Dixon had frowned, shaken his head warningly, but was told later by the apprentice, Finney, to whom it was still a nightmare, that Knox had been an apprentice too, his chum, both of them aged seventeen – and had died in the boat in Julia's arms, with a shrapnel wound in his head and one foot blown off. Finney himself near weeping when he described it, and Andy with a longing to take Julia in his arms and hug her, comfort her, but not able to, either in front of others or when they were alone – as they were on occasion, briefly – even though his motives would have been entirely decent and honourable. He'd mentioned this in a letter he'd written and posted in St Lucia to his sister, Annabel, adding self-deprecatingly and for her entertainment, *Well, all right, tell* that *to the Marines!*, but finding he had then to add, *Although it does happen to be true.* Really getting old? But Julia did have virtually constant companionship: old Dixon for one, and Finney for another. It was Finney who'd called out, 'Blooming miraculous, sir!' on the *Glauchau*'s deck; he was never far from the girl's side, and quite often they sat or stood, holding hands. She did clearly need contact, comfort, companionship, which those two must have realised long before *he* did. She was about his own age, he'd gathered, and was very attractive, with an oval face, light-brown hair and pale-brown eyes that were very quick and sensitive, reacting to whatever she was hearing – or thinking, he supposed. Not, he thought – in fact was sure of it – not consciously sorry for herself or fishing for compassion so much as shocked, scared, bewildered, at times barely able to believe that any of it had happened, really *having* to think about it, face it, talk about it – mostly talking rationally enough, saying for instance at a later stage, in that conversation or another one, that she was astonished the U-boat had bothered to signal their whereabouts to the *Glauchau*. It definitely *had*: the survivors had been told this by a German galley-boy who spoke some English and as often as not brought their food down to them; he'd answered the men's questions quite freely – about the ship's last port of call having been Lisbon, that her home port was Bremerhaven, and so forth, for which no doubt he'd have been in trouble with his superiors if they'd known of it. Julia's surprise, though, was that the U-boat commander had bothered to make any move towards having them picked up after treating them and their ship with the utmost savagery, blasting her with shell after shell, also machine-gun fire, in the course of it killing three-quarters of her company. Theirs had been the only boat that had got away, hadn't been smashed by shellfire or machine-gun fire in its davits – as others had, with or without men in them. She'd told Andy this, concluding, 'Go to such brutal lengths, then as it were toss us a lifeline?'

He'd suggested, 'Would've done better to have made a signal giving the position in plain English, if he'd had lifelines in mind.'

'Of *course* he would. But why even what he *did* –'

'I'll tell you, love.' Ron Dixon, slowly, choosing his words carefully: 'See – got his dander up good an' proper, as I'd see it.' Tangentially then to Andy: 'This young lady's uncle, Harry Carr – well, if you'd allow it as fair comment, Julia, love – strong-headed feller, weren't he? Giving the Hun as good as he got – least, aiming to – keeping stern-on to the

U-boat no matter what it tried, keeping that stern gun bearing – not *hitting*, more's the pity; you might say our gun's crew never got the practice they should've, but then again, could've struck lucky any moment, one direct hit, Hun would've have had his chips. *Had* to smash us up, didn't he – an' quick, or *he*'d've had it.'

Finney had put in, 'Could have finished us with a torpedo, couldn't he? Let us abandon ship first?'

'Except, lad, he opened up with his gun – which he'd've reckoned on being enough to send us to the boats, maybe – and from then on a gun-fight's what it was. Any case, how many torpedoes might a U-boat carry? What if he'd used 'em all – or needed to hang on to what he had?'

Julia had persisted, 'But then to signal to the *Glauchau* –'

'Cooled down, maybe. Had time to think it over – the state he'd left us in. Thought better of it, like.'

What state *PollyAnna* had left the *Glauchau* in was something else. Slightly dented maybe: rails bent, hull scraped to bare shiny iron; some straightening-out then yet more chipping and red-leading might be necessary. On *PollyAnna* too; she'd run alongside much more heavily than the skipper had intended, heavily enough that on her way down-river the carpenter, Postlethwaite, had busied himself dipping every tank and hold in case there might have been more serious damage. That possibility hadn't occurred to anyone else, but it happened to be a ship's carpenter's job – had been since ships were all made of wood – so he did it, and thankfully found all compartments dry, as he reported soon afterwards to Halloran. They'd have left a few fractured German skulls behind, and had some injured men themselves – Andy with his gashed neck for one. The worst of that from Andy's point of view had been Halloran's first washing out the wound with Milton then pressing its edges together between finger and thumb of the left hand while driving what felt like a skewer through, with a leather sailmaker's 'palm' cushioning the palm of the other. No cushioning of the back of the neck and no anaesthetic, just plain bloody agony. The mate's own face had had some small craters in it, but after picking out the glass he'd doused them in disinfectant and sealed them up with plaster: hadn't been able to shave since then, looked like a haphazardly clipped poodle walking around on its hind legs. Some of the rescued had needed attention to similarly minor injuries, but considering the rough handling they'd been given, had mostly come through in surprisingly good shape. Exceptions were the *Cheviot Hills*' first mate, Cornish, who had broken ribs and a leg wound of a kind the *Ship Captain's Medical Guide* had no advice that could be acted on in present circumstances, the Old Man therefore deciding to land him to hospital at St Lucia, together with OS Ellis and greasers Small and Rahman, who were also in need of more professional care than could be provided on board.

The Old Man had given Julia his sleeping cabin and had a cot put in the day cabin for himself. The sleeping cabin was only cupboard-sized, but at least she had it to herself, with ablutionary facilities close by. The injured Sam Cornish was installed in the spare berth in Halloran's room, Chief Engineer Dixon moved in with Hibbert, and the apprentice, Finney, was given the spare upper berth in Fisher's cabin. Andy, whose cabin was smaller and contained only the one berth, offered to change with Fisher, allowing the more senior man to remain in sole occupancy, but Fisher decided it wasn't worth the upheaval. The rest of them were accommodated aft, as directed by Batt Collins and the donkeyman, while the steward – Benson, a short, dumpy man – had volunteered to help out, easing the overload imposed on galley, saloon and mess-hall.

PollyAnna plugging northward and northwestward then, making for St Lucia in the Windward Isles, where she'd be bunkering and watering and where Julia hoped to buy some clothes. She was living meanwhile in the rags she'd been wearing since the sinking – although they'd been washed and ironed by Ah Nong within a matter of hours – and some items of borrowed gear – striped pyjamas presented by Gorst, for instance, Gorst's legs being about the same length as hers. All the survivors were in need of clothing – light stuff for now, but cold-weather gear as well, since after St Lucia they'd be heading north – for the ice, eventually – and for these and other purposes cash advances were to be made available by the *Cheviot Hills'* former owners, Messrs A & J Hills Ltd of Tynemouth, through their agents in Castries, St Lucia.

Cash assistance to Julia would be paid against credit due to her uncle. The owners had been in touch both with his widow and with Julia's mother – who had sent her a cable which Julia received when they docked at Castries. Half an hour after that a khaki-painted van brought to the gangway a bulging sack of the mail they hadn't received at Vitoria; Andy had a long letter from his father, two from his mother and one from his sister, all written well before his birthday. He guessed this lot might have just missed them at Montevideo and been forwarded to St Lucia in case of just missing them again at Vitoria.

Halloran had three letters: two in Leila's handwriting on that same violet-tinted stationery, and one more nonde-script – addressed in a rounded, childish hand, and grubby, as if it might have been kept for a long time in a dirty pocket. Andy was in the saloon, had picked up his own mail and in so doing cast a swift eye over Halloran's, when the latter arrived in his customary rush and snatched his up – waving Leila's for everyone to see and calling, 'Better late than never, uh?' The scruffy letter he'd only glanced at then pushed into a pocket of his shorts, was obviously less thrilling to him. Julia, arriving in the saloon with young Finney – they'd been up in the skipper's day cabin dealing with Messrs A & J Hills' agent – had had to stand aside as Halloran hurried out again, and murmured as she and the boy joined Andy, '*He* looked as if he'd had good news?'

'Two letters from his wife. Her name's Leila and she writes on funny-coloured paper – can't miss it.'

'I suppose you get to know all about each others' fami-lies and whatnot.'

'Not really. Some. But he rather goes on about his wife. Odd bloke, some ways. Did you get your business fixed up?'

She nodded. 'Shan't be looking like a down-and-out much longer, touch wood. Just waiting for Ronnie, then we're off to the shops. Oh, but I had a lovely cable from my mother. She wants me home *at once*!'

'She would, wouldn't she. And you will be – soon as we can get you there.'

'That's what I've said, more or less. But I'm keeping you. You want to read your letters and answer them, don't you – get answers off before we sail?'

'I suppose so. Try to.' He hadn't opened any of them yet, only checked them for weight and thickness and the smudged dates in postmarks. 'Anyway, good luck with the shopping.' He put a hand on Finney's shoulder, warned, 'Don't let her go mad, now.'

The agents, both *PollyAnna*'s and Messrs Hills', were still up there with the Old Man, who, when he'd finished his business with them – which would include changing all the Brazilian cruzeiros he'd been stuck with into either sterling or Canadian dollars – would be landing to pay calls on the Sea Transport Officer and – by signalled request – the office of NOIC, Naval Officer In Charge. One of the things about which the Navy and HM Government would be wanting to know more than it had been possible to convey in plain-language wireless messages was the Nazi element in Vitoria. Holding prisoners on board in a neutral port had been a clear breach of the Hague Convention; if it could be proved that the shore authorities had connived in it, the skipper had pointed out, they could stuff any complaints they might have against SS *PollyAnna* – such as her having sailed without clearance or a pilot.

Poor old Mendoza should be in the clear – as long as Capitao Whatsit was back and asserting his authority over Caetano and Ferras – but one other who *might* get it in the neck was the skipper of the minelayer. When *PollyAnna* had been steaming out past her, working up to half-speed and nosing into the narrows off Sao Joao, there'd been activity of sorts on and around the little warship, most alarmingly a searchlight flaring out from the vicinity of her bridge, sweeping across the water to lick at the *Anna*'s stern before losing her, the headland of Sao Joao intervening. Fisher, who'd admitted to having been already on tenterhooks, facing the hazards of getting her out in darkness through four miles of narrow river, dreading in particular the possibility of all the navigational lights on buoys and shore-marks suddenly being extinguished, sweating again as he told Andy, 'Really did think she was coming after us. On the flood tide she *could* have –'

'I'd guess *would* have, if her skipper'd been on board.'

'Reason to think he wasn't?'

'*Some* reason to suspect it. Why else didn't the bugger chase us?'

If not Arabella, he thought, what about Manuela, who'd have been at something of a loose end?

At Halifax now, *PollyAnna* having steamed virtually due north for a week, Andy had another letter from his father – a single-sheet Air Letter Form mostly congratulating him on having taken part in the rescue operation, news of which must just have reached him when he wrote. He wanted answers to various questions, most of which Andy had already supplied in the letter he'd sent from St Lucia: he'd had very good reason to write, since the old man's letter which had reached him there had had a birthday cheque for £50 in it. A huge amount of money – plus a tenner from his mother, so sixty in all, the largest sum he'd ever possessed at any one time in his life. There seemed little point in cashing or depositing the cheques, seeing as he'd be able to do so in England in a few weeks' time, and especially as he had enough left over for immediate needs in any case – former cruzeiros that he would have splurged on Manuela but which had now been changed back into pounds, shillings and pence.

Might get ashore tomorrow or Wednesday, he thought: see the town, have a few beers and a meal. He'd have liked to take Julia with him – she was ashore now as it happened, with Dixon and Finney, looking for clothes again; but those two were the problem – she barely moved a yard without them, and if he'd suggested it he might have found himself lumbered with them as well. They'd gone ashore today at the skipper's invitation in a launch that had been sent to bring the skipper and the masters of some other recently arrived ships to Admiralty House to discuss the HX (Halifax homeward) convoy of which they'd be a part. Departure was set for Friday, final and full-scale convoy conference Thursday, but for *PollyAnna*, who hadn't sailed in convoy before, and her master, who hadn't since 1918, a lengthier and more leisurely introduction was essential. There was a mass of detail to go into: formation, routeing, station-keeping, emergency procedures including tactics if or when attacked by surface raider, U-boats, and – closer to home – aircraft. Plus convoy routines, signals, navigational cooperation, etc. At the final conference, involving masters and navigators of about sixty merchant ships, plus the convoy's Commodore and Escort Commander, all under RN chairmanship and packing out a very large room or hall, you wouldn't want to be asking too many daft questions.

Foul weather was predicted. There were no broadcast or published weather forecasts now – they'd been stopped on the first day of the war as being helpful to the enemy – but a rough passage was to be expected, apparently. The prognosis of gale and storm conditions must have been mentioned in some signal, or in the welter of official bumf delivered on board soon after *PollyAnna* had dropped her hook and the cacophony of sirens and steam-whistles had petered out; in any case, Halloran and the skipper had been discussing it in the saloon last evening – a virtual certainty of storm-force winds out there in the middle, easterlies at that, both unseasonable and unwelcome, would surely slow them down – and preparations to be made before departure – details such as extra lashings on boats and hatch-covers. A jollier note had been struck by the skipper telling them he'd had a letter from the owners absolving him of blame for 'what might in other circumstances have been seen as somewhat rash or intemperate actions in Vitoria, or for the minor damage incurred.' He'd read the letter's final paragraph then: 'The chairman and his fellow directors indeed congratulate you and your officers and crew on having contributed significantly to the good repute of our Company.'

He'd glanced round the faces at the table. 'So there you are – we're good lads, all of us. Mind you, no mention of the ore we left on the quayside. May not have rumbled that yet.'

Julia and her escorts returned on board in the afternoon with sackfuls of winter-weather gear. By this time the bent stanchions had been removed, straightened and replaced, and the ship's side was being attended to by men working on slung staging. Andy, meanwhile, with Janner's and Gorst's assistance, had been sorting the contents of the flag-locker, at the after end of the bridge deck. In convoy there'd be numerous flag-hoists called for, and if any International Code flags or pendants were missing this was the time to replace them. In peace-time tramping one didn't use all that many flags, so some might well have gone astray: in fact none had, but they did need sorting, and it wasn't a bad thing for himself and the cadets to familiarise themselves with individual flags and the system generally.

Julia came on board fairly glowing from the cold. Even for the time of year and latitude 45 degrees north it was exceptional. She loved Halifax, she told him, meeting him on the ladderway en route to her cabin, he coming back up to the bridge deck.

'Meaning you had a whale of a time shopping?'

'It *was* fun, yes. Marvellous to have found everything one wanted. And the people are so friendly!'

'You ever find anyone *un*friendly?'

'What d'you mean?'

He'd held back on it. Might have blurted out something to the effect that looking as she did, being as she was, no one in his senses could ever be less than – 'friendly'. But Finney was with her, carrying parcels, and one didn't want to overdo it, maybe put her on the defensive, spoil what was an enjoyable but necessarily cool relationship.

Why *necessarily*?

Partly because she was still in the process of recovery from the ordeal of recent weeks, and Finney and Dixon were the supports she needed, had been through it with her. He was an outsider: an admiring one who'd do best to keep his admiration under tight control.

Write again to Liza, he thought suddenly. Actually he more or less did have to, having promised he would when he knew he was on the way.

Julia had dumped her purchases, came to join them at the back end of the bridge, asking Gorst, 'What's this one?'

'Flag "Z". "Z" for Zebra.'

'Pretty.' A shrug: 'Bright, I mean.' Black, yellow, blue and red, four contiguous triangles with their apexes in the centre. 'Oh, but it's torn, look – here . . .'

'Not much of a tear—'

Janner cut in with, 'But if you did happen to have a needle and cotton –'

'I *do* have!' As if the prospect of making herself useful delighted her. 'Some of the things I bought in St Lucia I've got to alter, so I invested in what you might call a repair kit. And look there!'

'Answering pendant. Gets more use than any of 'em.' Andy nodded. 'If you really wouldn't mind?'

He was having second thoughts now about writing to Liza. She probably wouldn't have left home yet in any case; an even better reason was that he didn't have all that much to say to her. No more than he'd have to say to any of the others – Sheila Gilchrist, for instance, or Paula – Paula

West – or Susan Shea, whose father was an Aintree vet. He'd seen a lot of her, first when he'd been finishing at *Conway* and then again when he'd been down there on Merseyside sitting for his second mate's ticket. A consideration in having told Liza that he *would* be in touch was that after this fairly long time at sea one would have quite a bit of leave due. They'd upped it recently: an officer got two and a half days for every month he was away. Supposing *PollyAnna* made it home the first week in February, having sailed from Cardiff last 6 August, he'd be entitled to – oh, fifteen days. Long time to sit around doing nothing, *might* get around a bit . . .

He'd stay on in *PollyAnna* if he could. Would have to sign off when she docked – because at the end of a voyage one had to – but could sign on again immediately, if the Old Man was agreeable.

The Old Man came back from shore in late afternoon – light already fading, grey drizzle driving in from the sea, wind like serrated knife-blades – with his old attaché case stuffed full of paperwork on all aspects of sailing in convoy, all of it to be studied and complied with by watchkeeping officers. There were a number of jobs to be seen to immediately, ranging from an overhaul of lifeboat equipment to checking out the zigzag clock which had been installed in Calcutta, checked then but never used; and tomorrow *PollyAnna* would be moving into the dockyard for bunkers, fresh water and 12-pounder ammunition, and while alongside embarking various extra stores that would be ready for them: additional lifebelts, and flares of two kinds, one variety to be carried in the boats – ditched, they floated and burnt brilliant orange, theoretically visible for miles – and the other for launching as distress rockets. Also smoke-cannisters, which in the event of surface attack would be dropped over the stern – on the orders of the Commodore or Escort Commander – to create a smoke-screen. The Commodore being a retired rear-admiral, who'd be embarking with his own staff of signalmen in the MV *Empire*

Quest – lying at the far end of this anchorage, not visible at present from this berth – and the convoy's escort was to be the armed merchant cruiser *Kilindini*.

Andy, Halloran and Fisher had waited to hear what other escorts they might be getting. Old Man pausing in his extemporary and sketchy briefing, glancing round at them: might already have told them more than he'd have thought necessary at this stage, having started naturally enough on the ship's immediate programme when they'd met him on deck at the ladder-head, and continued on the way up here to his day-cabin. They were outside it now, on the flat where one ladder ended and another continued upward to the bridge. It seemed that was all they were getting on the subject of convoy escorts, anyway, but having pushed the cabin door open and stumped in, he gestured to them to follow; dumping the attaché case, explaining further: 'The AMC – *Kilindini* – is protection against surface attack. Won't be any submarine attack this side of fifteen or twenty west. These last few weeks there's been damn-all U-boat activity around the UK, even. Except minelaying, apparently.'

Halloran queried, 'Saying there *is* U-boat activity now, sir?'

'Seems so. Started up again. But before fifteen west we'll be met by escorts out of UK ports.' Lifting a hand and tapping his forehead: 'Reminds me. In the dockyard tomorrow forenoon they'll be mounting machine-guns in the bridge wings. A double mounting in each, things called Marlins. It's all they've got spare, machine-guns being in short supply, it seems. They're for use against U-boats at close range, or low-flying aircraft. Belt-fed, American-made, not as modern as they might be, but better than nothing, eh?'

'Never saw a Marlin.'

'Nor did I, Mister. Any road – guys who fit 'em'll be staying on board to show us how to use 'em.' Pointing: 'Out there.' Meaning, in the open sea; and adding to Fisher, 'Might get a few rounds off from the twelve-pounder, Second. Long time since we did, eh?'

Fisher agreed. 'For want of shells, mostly.'

'By tomorrow you'll have plenty. The Marlins, by the way, are more reliable than Lewis guns. A Lewis tends to jam, and these don't – or not so often. So I'm told. Snag is they don't have much range. Any luck we'll have no use for them and get something better when we're home.'

'Any timing on that, sir?'

'No. Routeing won't be discussed until the conference, Thursday. It'll be an eleven-knot convoy, though; we'll have a knot and a half in hand.' Shake of the grey head: 'Eleven depending on the weather we meet, mind.'

'And – sixty ships?'

'Looks like it. Ten columns of six. Thousand yards between columns, six hundred between ships in column. Means four and a half miles wide, one and a half deep. That's if we all keep a nice, tight formation, which in foul weather, as is expected –'

'None too easy –'

'– fog, too. Not as you'd expect it, this time o' year and the winds we're told we should expect. Reminds me again, though – Postlethwaite's to make us a fog-buoy. I've a sketch here of one.' Snapping the attaché case open. 'With all the rest of your homework. This lot here.' Looking up again: 'Another thing – visits for those who want it to a doctor – includes you, Holt, get some o' that cordage out of your neck? Tomorrow when we're in there, there'll be an ambulance alongside. Make us a list of who else, Mister . . .'

13

Friday, 19 January 3 p.m. *PollyAnna* two miles offshore
with her engine thumping at slow ahead, pitching to
a northeasterly swell as she closed up in column four –
fourth column from the right, becoming number three
in that column and therefore flying in one flag-hoist the
numeral pendants four and three. Four-two, on which she
was closing up, was a French motor vessel by name of
Soissons. With the Old Man's permission Andy had Julia
and Finney with him on monkey island; hearing now the
clang of the telegraph as the helmsman or spare hand
rang down for dead slow ahead – only just enough revs
to keep steerage-way on her, and to hold her at about this
distance astern of her next-ahead. He told Julia, 'That's
us in station on the frog – or near enough.' Pointing out
on the port quarter then: 'Tankers coming up. Four of
'em. We'll have one abeam to port here and two beyond
that – meaning columns five, six and seven – and the
fourth astern of the one in column six. Standard pro-
cedure, I'm told, hiding 'em as it were in the middle of
the herd.'

'*Is* like a herd, isn't it. Getting more so every minute.'
Lifting her head: 'Moo! Moo!'

Finney said, 'Because tankers are the U-boats' prime
targets, I suppose.'

'But' – Julia, quickly – 'no U-boats anywhere near –'

'No.' Andy assured her, 'Won't be for about three weeks,

195

either. Longitude twenty west or even fifteen west's about their limit. So we're told.'

'How far from here?'

'Couple of thousand miles. You warm enough?'

She nodded. Wearing a duffle-coat with its hood up and a wool scarf wound round inside, loosely covering her mouth. And sheepskin gloves. They'd weighed anchor and left the Basin in a sleet shower; it was clear again now except for a murky area to starboard obscuring the horizon, but bitterly cold. Exceptionally low temperatures were prevailing in mid-Atlantic, according to the notes Fisher had made yesterday at the conference, to which as navigator he'd accompanied the Old Man, taking with him his notebook and a rolled up chart 4009, *North Atlantic Ocean, northern portion*. Storm-force winds had been predicted – as the Old Man had mentioned, and at that northeasterly, which was itself exceptional – and on top of this, what was called 'evasive routeing' – evasion of U-boat concentrations – might take them as high as sixty north, out there in the middle: sixty north being the latitude of Cape Farewell on Greenland. It wasn't going to be any pleasure cruise. Not that anyone was making much of it in Julia's hearing – Andy telling her instead, 'One good thing about foul weather – if we get it – is if it extends east of fifteen or twenty west we may well not see hair nor hide of 'em. U-boats, I'm talking about. They can't operate in really rough conditions, apparently. Night attacks on convoys are made on the surface, storm or gale-force would make that impossible, and in daylight a periscope can't see over the big ones – big seas, that is. Submarines can't keep their trim near enough the surface even to *use* a periscope. I'm quoting what was said at the conference – courtesy of Don Fisher – the RN team included a submariner, who gave 'em a talk. What it boils down to is the best thing for us would be storm-force all the way to Loch Ewe – *and* on around the top.'

Loch Ewe in northwest Scotland – Ross and Cromarty – being the initial destination, convoy there dividing into

196

sections for west- or east-coast ports, *PollyAnna* being bound for London continuing up around Cape Wrath and through the Pentland Firth, then south into regions where convoys frequently came under air attack, these days; Julia ignoring that – if she knew of it, which she might not – only insisting, 'I'll be so sick I won't *care* about damn U-boats!'

'You'll have found your sea-legs long before that. A few days is all it takes.'

'I'm feeling it *now*!'

'Sooner it starts, sooner you'll be over it. Same applies to a lot of us. Haven't had any really rough stuff in months, have to get used to it again. Off South Africa – the Wild Coast as they call it – it was a *little* bumpy, but –'

'A little's more than I need.'

'Well – tight belt, don't drink more than you have to – dry biscuits –'

'Mind if we don't talk about it?'

'Won't last long, anyway.' Pointing: 'That's our Commodore. Lead ship in column six, cargo-liner *Empire Quest*. And the empty billet this side of him – column five – is where the AMC'll be parking itself. HMS *Kilindini*. Time being, she'll be wandering around somewhere back there, chivvying the others up. I tell you, I never saw this many ships all in one place!'

'From the way you talk, I thought you knew all about it.'

'I know how it's *supposed* to be, because we've had it all on paper, and Don was at the conference.' He told Finney, 'It's to be a ten-knot convoy, by the way.'

'Thought they said eleven.'

'One or two masters or their engineers had doubts of maintaining more than ten. In fact, if the weather's going to be as bloody as they say –'

'May not even manage that.'

'And station-keeping's no fun at all. If a ship's going to straggle through lack of power she'll still straggle, no matter what the rest of us are making good. Because we'll

197

all be doing our level best, and if some bests aren't as good as others – see what I mean?' They were on their way down now, Julia having had enough of the icy wind. Restless, threatening wind, Andy thought – muttering to itself, gusts now and then like snorts. Getting set to run amok? Finney asked him, 'Subject of station-keeping, how do we know when we're six hundred yards astern of our next-ahead?'

'Sextant angle on her masthead. Having all masthead heights – as we do, they're all listed – we'll check by sextant angle until we know well enough what six hundred yards looks like, then put the sextant away and judge it by eye.'

'Right.'

'RN ships are better off, they're used to steaming in close company – flotillas and squadrons, so forth – and they have distance-metres, pocket rangefinders. Maybe we'll get 'em, one day. You know my watches are eight to twelve a.m. and p.m., I suppose?'

A nod. 'I'll try to make myself useful.'

'Don't worry. You *will*.' Finney was going to stand watches as Andy's dogsbody, as Gorst and Janner did with Fisher and Halloran. Andy added, 'And Julia'll be all right on her own.' He raised his voice: 'Long as she's got a bucket in there.'

'I think you're hateful!'

Laughing . . . But she'd lost her other guardian; Ronnie Dixon had been appropriated by the *Caradoc Castle*, whose own chief engineer had been landed with appendicitis. Some of the *Cheviot*'s ratings had also transferred to other short-handed ships: three of the ABs, and the one remaining greaser. But she'd miss old Dixon, he guessed.

He hadn't been ashore – except for visiting a naval hospital when they'd taken *PollyAnna* in this last Tuesday to top up bunkers and fresh-water tanks, embark fifty rounds of 12-pounder ammunition, and for ordnance arti-ficers to fit the two twin Marlins. These had been tried out at sea against floating crates, later in the day, and Fisher's gun's crew had engaged a similar target at ranges of between 2,000 and 4,000 yards and not done badly. It had been dark when they'd re-entered the Bedford Basin, groping their way in between the dozens of other steamers tugging at their cables, riding-lights bright above low-lying drifts of fog; a launch had come out to return the artificers to the dockyard, where next morning they'd be going through the same process with some later arrival. Everything at breakneck speed, to get the convoy away on schedule. He'd thought again about spending an evening ashore, but in fact had plenty to keep him busy on board – on top of routine duties, absorbing 'homework' on half a dozen different subjects, each section of it starting with Halloran, who'd read and then initial it, passing it to Fisher, Fisher then to Andy, who'd also been working up his knowledge of flag signals, memorising the dozen or more which the Commodore and/or the Escort Commander would be likely to make most often. The groups were all listed, and he was having the lists copied out by Gorst so that the skipper and his watchkeeping officers and the cadets would each have a copy; but as signals were his job he wanted to be able to recognise them at first sight, not have to look them up. The ones likely to be seen most often were 'Keep better station', 'Stay closed up', 'Make less smoke'; but also orders for emergency turns or adjustments to the convoy's speed. Or 'Enemy in sight bearing . . .' followed perhaps by 'Make smoke' – drop smoke-floats. General signals would be made by flags, those to individual ships by Aldis lamp. The Commodore had a staff of RN signalmen, and as professional seamen – a damn sight more professional than a lot of those could be, at this stage anyway – one didn't want to turn in a second-rate performance.

Among items already mentioned such as smoke-floats, flares, etc., they'd been supplied with red sails for the lifeboats. Reason for this being that a red sail showed up much better, to ships or aircraft searching for survivors, than white ones which in an even slightly disturbed sea were hardly visible at all, from any distance. There was a certain amount of rerigging involved: the bosun had put a couple of ABs on to it on the Wednesday forenoon, and the display of red canvas had caught Julia's eye; she'd asked

Andy, who'd happened to be nearby, 'Red sails now?'

His explanation had left her silent, pensive. Back in her memories, he'd guessed. Perhaps of – what was his name – Finney's fellow apprentice: Knox, Charlie Knox, with his head-wound, head in her lap when he'd died. In his imagination Andy could see it – see them, *her* . . . He broke into her silence with, 'Doesn't mean *we*'ll be going sailing. In fact you can be ninety-five per cent sure we won't.'

He saw her thoughts shift to another tack then. Eyes on his, and that quick, slightly quivery smile . . .

'Know that song "Red Sails in the Sunset"?'

'Hardly help but know it!'

'Danced to it a few times?'

'Of late, done very little dancing. As it happens. You do much?'

'Not *much*, no. But in Newcastle they have weekend thrashes at what's called the Assembly Rooms. So – now and then . . . Well, when my cousins are home especially –'

'Your uncle's sons. Both second mates, you said.'

'Garry and Dick – yes. But "Red Sails" – I was trying to remember the words –'

He managed a line or two, and she joined in with him for the next verse. Laughing . . . She had a sweet voice, he thought. Nodding, brown eyes on his: 'You thought I might be having a fit of the horrors, didn't you? Lifeboats, etcetera.'

'It'd hardly be surprising . . .'

'Uh-huh.' A quick head-shake. 'I'm not letting it last for ever. Down in the dumps occasionally maybe – even bad dreams, but –'

'I don't know whether you're more attractive in profile or full-face. Either way you're – really *something*, Julia. Shouldn't be saying this, I know – no intention of – you know, what they call *taking advantage* of you in any way, but –'

'You wouldn't be. Don't worry, Andy, I'm not walking wounded – I dare say I *was*, but –'

'What you *are*, Julia, is bloody marvellous.'

*   *   *

Dusk. Convoy formed – more or less – with the AMC – drab-looking former passenger liner of about 17,000 tons with two tall funnels and several 6-inch gun mountings, and flying the White Ensign – in the lead of column five, 1,000 yards on the commodore's starboard beam. Commodore having hoisted flag K and numerals one-zero, meaning 'Speed ten knots': all ships in convoy flying that now, as well as their positions *in* convoy, such as *PollyAnna*'s four-three. Commodore setting the pace, the AMC keeping station on him – on the *Empire Quest* flying the Commodore's flag, a blue St George's Cross, its blueness fading in the dying light. That front rank – as much as one could see of it beyond others in the darkening mass and from this angle of sight – still looked ragged. Basic problem in station-keeping being the ships' widely differing characteristics: half speed ahead in the MV *Empire Quest*, for instance, not by any means matching half ahead in the SS *PollyAnna*. Or even between more similar types of ship – *PollyAnna* and other single-screw tramps of between 6,000 and 6,500 tons gross register, 9,000 or 10,000 tons deadweight, say. Differing size and pitch of screw, depth of screw beneath the surface, hull shape, sail-like wind-catching upperworks, for instance. You'd settle down to it, acquire the skills and judgement as time went by – and revise it later when you hit foul weather – but for now it was makey-learn, pretty well hit or miss. Preferably, miss. With the light going, sound-signals were being used – predominantly one short blast meaning *I am directing my course to starboard*, two for *I am directing my course to port*, three for *My engines are going full speed astern* – which with so many ships in company could be overdone, lead more to confusion than to safety, when several gave tongue simultaneously. Speed adjustments, meanwhile, could only be made by whistling down the tube to the engine room and requesting, 'Up two' or 'Down four', meaning two, four or however many revolutions more or less per minute. There was no rev-counter in the bridge, and the number of revs per minute didn't need to be memorised; the decision had only to be whether to speed up a little or slow down. For larger changes one had the telegraph on which to ring down for dead slow, slow, half or full ahead – or astern – or in really drastic situations *double* full ahead – give her all there is. But if when you ordered 'Up four' and at the same time your next-ahead realised he was getting too close to *his* next-ahead and came down four, you could find yourself having to put your helm over to avoid running up his backside, then maybe steaming abeam of him for a while; and getting out of that embarrassing situation could be tricky – especially if your own next-astern had meanwhile seen fit to close up to where you had been.

The only lights being shown were stern lights – white, half-strength and visible over an arc of only 135 degrees, or 67½ degrees on each quarter. Which was fine, as long as there was no confusion as to which ship's stern light this one or that might be – if, for instance, your next-ahead found it necessary to haul out of line. The *Soissons* wasn't doing at all badly, though. And to starboard the *St Benedict* – a tramp smaller than *PollyAnna* – was holding her own. All of them pitching more than rolling. Steering to pass clear to the north of Sable Island – on a course of 080 degrees, which meant plugging just about directly into wind and sea. Wind of the lacerating, streaming-eyes variety, and in the frequent sleet showers binocular-plastering: you wiped the front lenses, got maybe half a minute's clearer vision before they plastered up again. Staying in the shelter of the wheelhouse was no answer, as its windows fogged-up *and* plastered-up. It had already been pitch-dark when Andy had taken over the watch from Halloran, and for this first hour or so he'd found it hard-going – aware from the first minute that it simply wasn't possible to keep a truly efficient lookout, and of the hazards implicit in that. OK, so that was how it was, what you had to cope with. The Old Man was up there with him – had been there through most of Halloran's watch too though, wasn't present only on account of his third mate's comparative lack of experience – and Finney, whose main value lay in maintaining contact with the bridge-wing lookouts and in contributing to the (naked-eye) all-round looking-out, as well as later being sent down to the galley to bring up pannikins of tea. The Old Man standing hunched mostly in a fore corner of the wheelhouse, although when the sleet did obscure its windows he usually moved outside. There were windows you could open but usually going outside was better. However blinding (as well as freezing) it was, you could usually see a length or more ahead out there, as long as you wiped the binocs often enough. Skipper'd be out there on the starboard side mostly, Andy port side – less distant from the voicepipe – and the only conversation they'd exchanged in an hour had been Andy commenting – having heard the Old Man cursing to himself – 'Moonrise near ten should improve things, sir,' and an answering growl of, 'Hell it will . . .'

He was right, too. The overcast was heavier and more solidly continuous than Andy had realised. Just after ten he thought he saw moon-flush on the beam for about half a minute, then it vanished. Sleet driving hard – and more motion on the ship, he thought; by that stage must have whistled for increases and reductions in revs forty or fifty times, he guessed. And had not had to say a word to the helmsman about his steering. When at about ten-thirty AB Timms reported that he'd been relieved at the helm – helmsmen were standing two-hour watches, and changed over at the half-hour – he was glad to acknowledge with, 'Couldn't've done better, Timms.' Having held her for two hours within about 2 degrees either side of 080 – despite her having wind and sea smack on the bow – and at the same time kept a wary eye on the Frenchman's stern light, ready to sing out if it began going noticeably astray. Anyone who saw that as easy, Andy thought, should try it.

It was livening up when he handed over to Fisher at midnight, and gale-force by the time he was up for morning stars; turning out and getting himself up there despite the sound and feel of it because one had often found it wasn't as hopeless as you'd guessed it would be. It was, though: not a chance of any kind of sight, only blacker-than-black storm clouds racing from the east, howl of the wind, morass of tumbling sea. No less cold, but no sleet or snow either, which was something. In the slow leaking-away of darkness, the *Soissons* was plunging along ahead of *PollyAnna* at about the right distance, a mound of white-streaming foam with black protuberances – stem or stern alternatively, masts and the midships superstructure leaning hard this way and that – the *St Benedict* too – never less than half-buried in it – slightly abaft *PollyAnna*'s beam to starboard, tanker *British Stream* abeam to port, maybe a cable's length closer than she should have been, while astern, the *Eileen Harper*, an engines-aft grain carrier out of London and more recently from the Plate, seemingly pretty well in station, her bow-on appearance in this sea-state not unlike a broad-beamed submarine's. *PollyAnna*'s own forepart lifting to the oncoming, white-plumed ridges like – he thought, imaginatively – a short stretch of macadam: that length and breadth and blackness rising as each ridge came racing – the biggest for some time lifting her now – up, up – then faltering, listing away to port, slamming down into a boil of ocean piling all round, bursting across the foc's'l-head and flooding aft, feet-deep over the hatch-covers. Stern rising then, forepart burying itself, multi-ton loads of North Atlantic exploding against this central island's lower levels – where the skipper had wisely retired an hour ago, would now have his head down on the cot which he'd have somehow jammed or lashed in place, while on the other side of the thin dividing bulkhead Julia would no doubt be braced between it and her bunk's leeboard.

Old Man snoring, he guessed; Julia most likely awake. Like bracing herself against being flung around in a tin drum, sick and maybe scared. She'd be all right if she remained horizontal, poor kid. In a couple of days, or three or four, when this lot had blown itself out. Or even if it hadn't. If the predictions had been right it wouldn't

– not that soon. She'd be OK, though. She had the sea in her blood in any case – as she'd probably agree, something to live up to. Her father, William Carr, skipper of his own trawler working out of Blyth in Northumberland, had drowned in 1923 when she'd been four – trawler lost with all hands in hurricane conditions somewhere off Alesund. Her uncle Harry, then – recently master of the *Cheviot Hills* – thirty-five years at sea mostly in tramp steamers, and both his sons now second mates.

Her uncle George in New Zealand to whom she'd been on a visit – last chance, they'd all agreed, before the balloon went up, and it had gone up a few months too soon – had given up the sea when he'd still been young, emigrated to New Zealand in 1922, married a Scots girl and become a farmer. And her grandfather, who'd spent his early years at sea as AB and ship's carpenter but then set up a boat-building business at Gateshead, which when he'd died in 1921 had been sold very well and the proceeds divided between his children, buying William his trawler, starting George off in New Zealand, providing Harry with the security which in those hard times when he was working his way up through third, second and first mate to Master Mariner he'd needed as allegedly he'd used to say 'for ballast', and – later, after Julia's father's drowning – allowing her mother to go into partnership with a friend in a dress-making business in Newcastle. (Which had been reasonably successful but was now facing the rationing of clothes and materials, apparently. They'd learn how to cope, or try to, but at present saw it as a looming state of emergency.)

Andy had had all that from Mark Finney. Finney was no relation or connection of the Carrs, had only happened to have had indentures bought for him a year ago in Messrs A and J Hills of Tynemouth, and to have hit it off pretty well with Julia when they'd met on board the *Cheviot Hills*. Then in the long, long hours first in the lifeboat and afterwards in the *Glauchau*'s 'tween-decks, needing other things in their heads than what was actually happening around them, they'd learnt just about everything there was to learn about each other. He'd even enjoyed talking *about* her, to Andy, who'd come to realise that he – Finney – was entirely smitten with her. Which was all right, he'd concluded, Mark being just seventeen, and Julia having had her twenty-first this last October. She thought of Mark, Andy had decided earlier, when Dixon had been around, as she might of a younger brother.

At 0800 – second day out, 20th – in greyish early light the Commodore hauled down his K.10 hoist and ran up in its place K.8, a two-knot reduction in the nominal speed of advance to make it easier for the convoy to reform. There were gaps from which ships had strayed or straggled, and this would give them a chance to regain station. Wind and sea might have eased a little, might even be nearer force seven than eight now. This anyway was Andy's impression while taking over from Halloran, who'd already whistled down for the cut in revs; it had been Janner apparently, now on his way below, who'd seen that signal drop from the *Empire Quest*'s port yardarm and the other go whipping up in its place. Another impression though was that this section around *PollyAnna* had become the convoy's nucleus – *PollyAnna* herself about the right distance astern of the Frenchman, the four tankers bunched more or less where they'd been last evening, the *St Benedict* admittedly nearer the *Anna*'s quarter than her beam – but she'd put that right now, easily enough – and the *Eileen Harper* if anything rather too close astern. So no great problems here, although the rest of it was a shambles, the port-side columns being in particularly bad order, columns seven, eight and nine for instance seeming to have no leaders.

Halloran's comment, with the glasses at his eyes, was, 'Amateur night all round. Dunno where they found the buggers.'

'Commodore's flashing.'

Aldis lamp – flashing As, calling-up one of the ships in that port-column mess. Halloran watching the dots and dashes for a moment – the addressee evidently being slow in answering – then handing Andy the glasses. 'Course still oh-eight-oh, revs for eight knots. Shouldn't think we've been making-good more than eight all night.' Looking all around, and at *PollyAnna*'s own plunging forepart, 'Eased a fraction in the last hour – eh?'

'I was thinking the same.'

'Old Man's gone down to his breakfast. He'd put a DR on – you see it?'

'Forty miles northeast of Sable Island.' Andy put the glasses up, adjusted their focus slightly on the *British Stream*. He'd left Finney at the chart first to extend their track and DR's to midday, then to see that the lookouts in the wings were wide awake and taking notice. Andy added, with the glasses at his eyes, 'Should be home by Easter, at this rate.' Then: 'Think Easter eggs'll be on the ration?' From British newspapers received in Halifax one had gleaned that butter, sugar, bacon and ham were now rationed – as from just after New Year, and for the first time since 1918. A glance at Halloran: 'All right, I got her.' Glasses down again, to clean their lenses, and – as Halloran withdrew – nodding a good morning to Ingram at the helm. Since the schemozzle in Vitoria he'd come closer – or felt he had – to his fellow members of the boarding party. Not that he'd ever been all that remote from them: only that having shared those few minutes of action – above all, *successful* action – the experience was a bond you all had in common.

PollyAnna bow-down, butting into it, the white stuff rising like boiling milk, flooding over and aft; over hatch-covers and leaping around foremast, ventilators and lashed-down derricks, streaming and flying on the wind over the gun'ls and via scuppers on the lower side, which-ever way she happened to be rolling. It *was* easier than it had been during the night, though, and the small reduc-tion in revs was making it easier still.

Little doubt, for all that – remembering the convoy-conference forecast, the note of certainty about it as recorded by Fisher – that worse *was* to come.

Not that it mattered. Except that it was bound to slow them down – as even last night's blow already had. Julia, he guessed, might enjoy a spell of really wild weather – might find it exhilarating, once she got over her present indisposition . . . Glasses up again, checking on the neighbours. On the *St Benedict* who was moving up into her proper station, then – well, the gap between *PollyAnna* and the *Soissons* had become more like 400 than 600 yards. He hauled himself over to the pipe, unplugged it and blew down it, heard the whistle from its lower end followed by a yell of 'Aye?' – which would have come either from McAlan or Howie – and shouted into it, 'Down four!' *This* whistle went back into this top end, like a stopper. Glasses on the *Soissons* again then – and *St Benedict* briefly, then back to the frog – but thinking again of Julia – as one tended to, off and on – and of the *Cheviot Hills'* steward, Benson, who now that most of his former shipmates had moved elsewhere was working mainly in the saloon, also tending to Julia's needs, and had told Andy and Finney during their hurried breakfast half an hour ago that she was a game 'un, wouldn't let a bit of a blow confine her to her cabin much longer. He'd tapped on her door, apparently, asked her was there anything she'd like – black tea and toast, he'd recommended – but she hadn't wanted anything, had thanked him and said, 'Maybe later. Sooner get this over, be done with it.' No mention of the bucket – presumably she was taking care of that herself. Benson wagging his head as he gave Andy a plate of beans and thick, rather greasy bacon: 'Game 'un, to be sure.' At midday he was going to take her some dry toast and beef tea – without asking her, just take it along – querying this with Finney, who'd approved it: 'Just the thing. We'll soon have her on her feet.'

It was the same syndrome, Andy realised, thinking back on it and on his own much lesser business of the boarding party: Julia and company had been through hell together, in a sense *belonged* to each other through the shared experience. While he himself was and could only remain an outsider, not of that ilk, irrespective of having feelings for her of a kind he'd never had before.

At noon the Commodore ordered a return to ten knots; by this time the convoy was more or less rectangular again, with previously empty spaces reoccupied. There'd been excessive smoke emissions from old coal-burners fighting their way back into station, and commodorial attention had been paid to them. As indeed it should have been: that old boy's job was to enforce certain basic disciplines in all such matters, to have an orderly, *manageable* mob, at least by the time he led it into U-boat territory. In *PollyAnna*, Andy still had the watch, and ordered the increase in speed; Fisher was with the skipper at the chart table, deciding between them what latitude and longitude to hoist as their reckoning of the noon position. Every ship in the convoy was required to show its own hand on this within a few minutes of midday, having by then in normal circumstances, i.e. halfway decent weather, worked out a meridian altitude; there was a competitive element in it, to be first (or at least not last) as well as navigationally correct, but since there'd been no glimpse of sun, moon or stars since leaving Halifax, one could only offer an EP – Estimated Position – which was obtained from the DR – Dead Reckoning – position calculated from the course steered and distance covered as recorded by the log, this DR then adjusted by an estimate of the effects of wind and tide, which in present circumstances had to contain an element of guesswork.

Gorst and Janner were hovering around the flag-locker at the after end of the bridge deck, hanging on to stanchions and other solid fittings to hold themselves in place while waiting to be told which flags to hoist; Andy had sent Finney to help them. It would require two separate hoists, one for latitude and one for longitude, each with five flags in it. The halyards were turned-up back there, ran through blocks in a wire stay linking foremast to funnel-top. Fisher coming from the chart-table conference now with the magic figures in his notebook, calling them to the cadets as he pushed out into the wing and around the back end of the wheelhouse – to what Gorst had grandiloquently referred as the 'flag deck'. Flag-hoists were already climbing above the bridges and fore-decks of several other ships. Andy, watching the distance shorten between *PollyAnna* and the *Soissons* – *PollyAnna* for some reason responding more quickly to speed changes than the Frenchman did – excessive propeller-slip in the frog's case, presumably – heard Fisher's yell of 'Forty-four thirty north, fifty-eight ten west!' and stepped out into the wing to see the two hoists rising simultaneously. They'd got them right, too – thank God – given their neighbours no grounds for ridicule. But *Soissons* was definitely too close: he lurched back inside, whistled down to Howie and bawled, 'Down four!' Skipper coming from the chart now, on his way out to the wing to see how his guesswork compared with others' – with the tankers', for instance, and of course the Commodore's.

He'd stuck his head back inside. 'Too close to that bloody frog, Holt!'

'Just came down four, sir.'

'None too soon – eh?'

'Sir . . .'

Shuttleworth, who'd been on the wheel since ten-thirty, had only half an hour to go, was grinning to himself as he watched the compass card and the lubber's line; Adam's apple wobbling like a turkey's, long thin legs braced against the roll. Strange-looking fellow, with that striped woollen hat covering his bald dome, but as prime a seaman as you'd find. *PollyAnna* was rolling more than she had been, he realised: wind most likely shifted a point or so, veered to something like east by south. Checking that by the way the spray flew off waves' crests . . . She wasn't pitching any less either, come to think of it. Looking back over his shoulder as the starboard-side door opened and slammed shut again, admitting Fisher. 'Our lads did all right, you'll be glad to hear!'

'It's the quality of the instruction they've been getting.' Pointing at the clock, the one fitted with the zigzag apparatus, electrical contacts collar-like around its dial. It was well after noon. 'Don't feel like taking over, do you, by any chance?'

14

Course 050 degrees, revs for eight knots; 26th now, one week out of Halifax. They'd been on this course and speed since noon on the 23rd, the day (actually early evening) that Julia had emerged from hibernation, made her way unsteadily down to the saloon and forced herself to eat whatever it was the galley had laid on for high-tea that day. Pale and shaky, and *PollyAnna* pitching as hard as ever, if not harder, jolting and battering and rolling like a barrel, the change of course having put the obstinately unseasonable wind and sea 30 degrees on her bow: so you could say – as Julia did, charitably, at that first meal – that it wasn't poor *PollyAnna*'s fault.

'But why such a big change of course suddenly?'

Finney had told her, 'They call it evasive routeing.' Cocking an eye at Andy for confirmation. He – Finney – had been under the weather himself for a couple of days, staying on his feet but making frequent use of buckets on the bridge and elsewhere. 'Evasive routeing – that right?'

'Has to be. Held on like this, we'd fetch up in the Faeroes – so you can count on it we'll be altering again in a day or two.'

For Julia's sake he hadn't wanted to go on about the U-boats that were assumed to be deployed out there and might already be getting long-range direction-finding bearings of an eastbound convoy and planning later interception, the convoy (or Admiralty wirelessing rerouteing instructions) doing what it could to outwit the bastards. Maybe shift them northwards, while praying that they'd be getting weather at least as bad as this.

As *this* now – on the 26th. Estimated noon position 52 degrees north, 33 30 west. Heavy cloud-cover persisting, no sextant observations possible in the course of the past week, wind between 25 and 30 degrees on the bow, gusting force nine, convoy surprisingly enough still more or less intact but – Andy guessed, and had overheard an exchange between the Old Man and Halloran in which the same doubts had been expressed – might well not be able to maintain even this rate of progress, unless conditions improved substantially. Not that the rate of progress would be making the Commodore all that happy even now. Revs for eight knots didn't give you eight knots when you were slamming into a force nine. Lucky to be making-good even five. On the other hand, if conditions did improve, they'd improve for the bloody U-boats, too.

Other ships had taken it harder than *PollyAnna* had in any case, three of the fifty-eight having dropped out now. Fifty-eight, not sixty, because although they hadn't known it at the time, there'd been two non-starters – for reasons best known to themselves and presumably the Commodore – each of the two outer columns starting one ship shorter than the others.

Julia said – this was lunchtime, with the saloon table's fiddles raised and a wet cloth on it as a further stabilising measure – 'At least we didn't run into the fog you were expecting on the Newfoundland Bank.' Brown eyes flickering to Andy: 'Or did we, after I'd keeled over?'

'Couldn't have, in that blow.' Halloran cutting in, turning his black snake's eyes on her. 'You can have wind and fog together sometimes, but when it gets up to that extent – see, what makes fog is the cooling of damp air – and OK, *slight* increase in wind can create it, by mixing air of different temperatures –'

'What it is to have studied for a master's ticket.' Chief Hibbert, drily, forking up corned-beef hash. A shake of the head then: 'Sorry, Halloran. Didn't intend that to sound as it did.'

There was some general surprise – emphasised by a silence around the table – CEO Hibbert being such a quiet-spoken, good-hearted character – you wouldn't think ever likely to be gratuitously rude. Halloran could be a dead bore, though: had been lecturing during a recent meal on Cyclonic Depressions and Irregular Disturbances – which no one had asked for. Hibbert smiling – repeating, 'Sorry.'

Crash . . .

An exceptionally big one she'd slammed into. You could hear the rush and roar of it pounding aft, the ship shaking herself like a dog as it drained away, shakes all through her as her forepart rose and she leaned hard to port – stem now pointing slantwise at the sky, stern deep, engulfed in white: in your mind's eye you saw pretty well exactly how it would be out there – how you'd been seeing it for days, only now suddenly worse. Hibbert said to Julia, with a smile that might have been intended to reassure her, 'Excuse me. Take a look below.' Steward Benson, who'd been circling the table, pulled his chair back for him, pausing there as she rolled the other way and Hibbert made it to the door in two long strides, Benson staying where he was for a few seconds, using the chair-back for support and, as it happened, holding Halloran's black glare across the table: the mate demanding, 'Something the matter, Benson?'

Shake of the head. Short, tubby man in what a few minutes ago had been a clean white sweater that was now patched with tomato ketchup. 'Nothing at all, sir. Caught us on the wrong foot like, is all.' He'd been able to let go of the chair now. 'Minute back, though – since you ask, sir – speaking of fog as you were, I was thinking of them two days we was in it, on the old *Grant Stuart*?'

'Hell, *were*n't we just.' The mate's tone was affable enough. 'Couldn't see as far as you could spit. Two whole days and nights, wasn't it. *And* bloody ice all around us.' But he was on his way too now – on his feet, a hand flat on the bulkhead for support while she stood on her ear again and a few more tons of ocean thumped down on her fore-deck. Pushing off then – with a sardonic smile and a bow in Julia's direction – mimicry of course of Hibbert – 'Excuse *me*, Miss Carr . . .'

Gone. That had been a hell of a sea they'd shipped, and he'd be thinking of the hatch-covers. In a sea like this they did tend to come to mind. While the chief engineer's concern would be for the morale and wellbeing of his team in the engine room and stoke-hold; also for the effects of the propeller racing in air or at least nothing more than foam, as it had been in those moments – bow digging deep, stern soaring, racing screw, danger of shaft-bearings over-heating.

The answer would be to slow down. Skipper might have cut the revs already; or Tom McAlan, second engineer, currently on watch down there, might have done so off his own bat if he'd thought the need was urgent. *PollyAnna* was a tough old bird, but there had to be a bloody limit. Fortunately, Josh Thornhill OBE was also a tough old bird, Andy thought – on his feet, to take a look up top as well. Might be wanted, might as well *be* there. Hatch-covers, and boats too: they were secured in their davits still, davits not turned out as they would be later when attack by U-boats would have to be anticipated, but – well, Christ, seas of that size could smash lifeboats no matter how well they were secured. He nodded to Benson: 'You and Mr Halloran were shipmates at some time, then.'

'Was indeed.' Reminiscent smile, cocking his round head. 'In the *Grant Stuart*. Cargo-liner, Grant Line?'

'Tartan funnels.'

'Shortbread tins, we used to call 'em.'

Finney was looking up, mutely querying whether Andy might require his company up top: Andy shook his head, indicating Julia – look after *her*.

The Old Man had decided to hold on, anyway. It was a fact – you'd get a rogue wave like that occasionally, it wasn't by any means unheard of, didn't necessarily mean there'd be others like it. The Commodore hadn't ordered any reduction, nor was the screw racing now: Chief Hibbert, after his inspection of the nether regions, had reported that the shaft bearings were a degree or two warmer than he'd have liked, but the old girl had been at it hammer and tongs for the past week. As of this moment, anyway, no problem. If it got any worse, mind you –

'All right. Thank you, Chief.'

Fisher had put the weather down in the deck-log as force nine, the Beaufort Scale measurement for 'Strong Gale'. *PollyAnna* was not fitted with an anemometer, which left this kind of assessment as a matter for one's own judgement – or for one's skipper's. Force nine meant a windspeed of between forty-one and forty-seven knots, and the next step up – ten, or 'Whole Gale' – covered speeds of forty-eight to fifty-five. Above that you had force eleven, which meant 'Storm' – fifty-six to sixty-five knots – or force twelve, anything over sixty-five, qualifying as a hurricane.

Meanwhile, revs for eight knots, the Old Man reckoned, wouldn't be giving her more than four. Might come down to revs for six – obviously would if His Nibs so ordered; might have to anyway. At anything less than that, though, you'd be just about stemming wind and sea – making no forward progress at all. You'd turn her head into it then, just ride it out.

Andy had thought the Old Man might want an inspection made of hatch-covers. In this sea-state it wouldn't be much fun, risking your neck down there, but since damage to any of the hatches could lead to that hold flooding and – not to put too fine a point on it – sink the ship, it might have to be done, and Third Mate Holt being young and fit might be the man to do it – along with old Batt, maybe. All right, so a hatch smashed in was a hatch smashed in and the ship immediately *in extremis* – especially when her cargo was iron ore – but such damage could possibly be averted – stitch in time stuff – by hammering in any of the wedges that might have been loosened; alternatively – if physically possible, in these conditions – by lashing an additional tarpaulin over any that had been ripped or looked like carrying away. There were three thicknesses of tarpaulin on each hatch at present. As far as could be seen – looking down from the wheelhouse and bridge-wings, the Old Man and Fisher with binoculars – they looked all right: under continual, heavy assault, but so far standing up to it. Under the stretched tarpaulins were hatchboards – rectangular sections of thick timber – resting on iron beams running both fore-and-aft and athwartships. The boards' edges butted against flanges on those beams – which were removable for purposes of loading and discharging, were then replaced and bolted down. Had last been bolted down in Vitoria, of course. And holding the tarpaulins down tightly on the boards were battens which passed through cleats surrounding each hatch and were held tightly in the cleats by timber wedges driven in above them. These wedges could – theoretically – be loosened or even driven right out by heavy seas, and were therefore what you'd check on first.

To check hatch-coverings would have been Halloran's immediate reaction too, after that huge impact. Whatever else he might be, he was a seaman, knew his business: as soon as he'd begun to move, one had known what would be in his mind. But after conferring with the skipper, the decision must have been to leave well alone – not to risk men's lives down there when you didn't have to.

Fair enough. Although even with binoculars one's view from up here was limited by the angle of sight as well as distance. Anyway – it was one-thirty now. Fisher had this watch, Halloran would take over from him at four, and in the absence of any more of those huge tonnages of sea dropping on them – which touch wood *might* have marked the height of this storm, it might conceivably have hit its peak and be moderating again now – well, get the head down, he thought, prepare for what might well be strenuous dark hours ahead. Surely would be. Dark-hours watch-keeping in convoy and this kind of weather was, he'd discovered, *extremely* hard work. Cold work, too; even in the middle of the day it was freezing cold up there. Looking into the saloon first, though, he found Julia and Finney still there. Julia had tried a cigarette, she told him, and it had tasted awful: she was thinking she might take the opportunity of giving up smoking altogether. 'But listen, Andy – how stewards and galley-boys can make it across that after well-deck with food and drink for the mess-hall – how *anyone* can, for that matter – well, beats me!'

'Judge the right moment, then move quick, that's all. They all have to – going on and off watch. And there *are* lifelines rigged.' Batt Collins had set them up before departure from Halifax, two stretches of steel-wire rope from the poop along the ship's-side edges of number four and five to the after end of this central island and access to engine-spaces.

Should have lifelines for'ard as well, he thought – for purposes of hatch-inspection. Julia of course hadn't got as far as considering that possible requirement. He sat down across the table from her and Finney. 'Imagine how it'd be if crews still lived for'ard – which they would be doing if the old girl hadn't been redesigned when she was actually on the stocks – crew accommodation under the poop being the new thing then, and Dundas Gore pretty well obliged to conform. They'd bought her half-built from some foreigner who'd gone bust. Bargain-basement price, no doubt. That's how she has the modern bunk-rooms and mess-hall arrangement, only stores and so forth in the foc'sl-head, but still looks a bit old-fashioned – I mean, externally. As you'd know, I'm sure, foc'sl life was always hellish – thundering racket, leaks, either ice-cold or suffo-cating hot, rats by the hundred – and my *God*, the sani-tary arrangements –'

'I've been told.'

'How it *was*. Still is, here and there. Certainly was in the ship I spent two years in as a cadet, Blood Line steamer *Burntisland*. And she's still in harness – last I heard, she was. Must be a lot of old tubs working that shouldn't be.'

Pausing while *PollyAnna* dug her snout deep in the trough then reared slowly with the shakes again, hung for a few moments before slamming down and then toppling almost on to her beam-ends, hanging there – taking more thumping, deafeningly loud punishment before slowly righting herself. And now again – bow *down* . . . Julia pushing her chair back, telling him and Finney, her voice a touch unsteady, 'Think I'll get some shut-eye.'

It wasn't moderating. Definitely was *not*. Taking over his watch at eight that evening – revs unchanged, course the same, weather on the bow near enough where it had been for days now – having looked around for a minute, he yelled at Halloran, 'More like force ten than nine, isn't it?'

'I'm calling it ten.'

Turning away, en route to the chart table to complete the log for the past four hours. The wind was a shrieking roar, *PollyAnna* pitching as savagely as ever, and rolling harder – her rolling less regular than the pitching, at times hanging over for so long and so far you could begin to think she wasn't going to bother rolling back, was as it were trapped under the weight of water already on her: whitened sea pouring over and flying up virtually solid, smashing across this bridge, let alone heavier impacts on the island's lower levels; if you hadn't convinced yourself she *would* always recover, you could have thought more than once, *Christ, here's come-uppance finally* . . . And – *should* cut the bloody revs . . . The Old Man was on the bridge, though, nearly all the time – meaning all night, as he was *every* night, no doubt would be as long as this lasted. Keeping himself to himself, letting officers of the watch get on with it, present only because conditions were as they were and if he should be needed – well, here he was, short, stocky figure, most of the time with its glasses up. *He*'d order a reduction in revs if he considered it essential: and the screw *was* racing, in longer and steeper bow-down periods, the helmsman using every ounce of his skill and strength – needing plenty of both – to hold her on or even near the course, or get her back on to it when she'd yawed away or the sea drove her off it and the rudder hadn't enough solid water to grip on or for the screw *not* to race.

Keeping station, for all that. The Frenchman, *Soissons*, with her stern light only a pinpoint in a patch of white expanding and contracting in the black heave of darkness out ahead; the *St Benedict* similar – except no light visible and with differing variations of shape – more or less on the beam to starboard; the tanker *British Stream* out to port and often invisible – that low freeboard completely engulfed, so showing only the bridge and accommodation structure aft. The nub of it was that you followed the frog, assuming he was where he should be; as some check on that, you also had the stern lights of the ships each side of him, which by an effort of somewhat inessential memory you knew to be the *Maida Vale* (astern of the *Kilindini*) and the *Empire John* – number two in column three – being as you were inside the 135-degree arcs of their stern lights.

'All right, Edmonds?'

A bark of either acknowledgement or mirth – wrenching the wheel over to counter a slide away to port. Stem crashing down, and the whiteness soaring . . . '*Gotter* be, ain't she!' He'd added something to that but Andy hadn't heard it over the surrounding racket of wind and sea. *PollyAnna* bow-down still and the stuff still flying, whitening-out any forward view; searching alternatively for the *St Benedict* then, and not finding her either – being deep in this trough, wave-tops higher all round: but on her way up now – at last . . .

At ten-thirty the gunlayer, Bakewell, took over the wheel from Edmonds. Edmonds reporting to Andy, 'Helmsman relieved, sir, course oh-five-oh.'

'Well done.'

Edmonds had had his thirtieth birthday at sea between Cape Town and Montevideo, Andy remembered. Finney lurching in then to report that the bridge-wing lookouts had changed over. 'Brooks and Curtis on now.'

'All right. Half an hour, you can get us some tea.'

'Be glad to!'

In the dim glow from the binnacle, as much of the boy's face as was exposed to view – between the pulled-down woollen hat and a towel wrapped around inside the neck of his oilskin – looked blue with cold. Andy said, 'Wishing we'd left you safe and sound in the *Glauchau*, I dare say.' He put his glasses back on the *Soissons* – finding her well to starboard of where he'd expected her to be, consequently shouting to Bakewell, 'Ship's head now?'

'Oh-three-nine. Sorry, sir, she's –'

Eleven degrees off-course: not the *Soissons* way off *her* station.

'– getting her back now. Sort of heavy for'ard, sir.'

'Heavy?'

Big one, then: *very* big, a wall of it rearing over the foc's'l-head – but more on the bow, starboard side, catching her with that bow exposed through still being something like 10 degress off course, shrieking wind and hammering sea nearer 50 degrees on the bow than 30 – this *mountain* towering with its streaming-white upper fringes curling like claws, poised and still swelling, gathering strength and weight as if set on finishing her this time – and dropping – thundering black mass shot with white and boiling ten feet deep, pouring aft, but its potential for damage nothing like expended yet, the noise like close, heavy and continuous gunfire deafening as it hit this island and rocketed, the bridge structure itself feeling unsafe from such tremendous impact – and a crash from back there somewhere – timber smashing? Andy's fast, shocked mental image being then of the hatch-cover on number four stove in; then, *no, closer than that, one of the boats* – damn near the whole ship for some moments virtually submerged, weighed-down and struggling, vibration enough to shake rivets loose. Lessening now, recovering, and the Old Man who'd been hanging on through that half-minute to whatever he'd had in reach of his short, thick arms, stocky figure in its oilskins and sou'wester hauling itself this way as the avalanche's thunder reduced enough for a human voice pitched high to be heard: 'Holt – see what that was – starboard side amidships. Boat, likely. Bakewell – feels heavy for'ard, you said. Like water in her?'

Andy would remember later having thought – on being ordered below to establish what that virtual explosion had been – *Be down there when the next one comes – well, goodbye girls, just your rotten luck!* But goodbye Julia, too – and *that* wasn't funny, really wasn't; it was a revelation to him how *un*funny . . . As it turned out he didn't have to go down anyway, was stopped at the top of the ladder since someone else was coming up – guessing it might be Halloran, and proved right, Halloran bawling at the skipper that both starboard-side boats had gone, bosun and others down there clearing away wreckage. The motorboat had been smashed completely, its engine dropped clean out through its bottom; and he, Halloran, while down there with the bosun had made a quick check on the hatch-covers of numbers four and five and found them absolutely sound. Old Man bellowing, 'May not be the same story for'ard, but don't go checking, not you nor no one else, Mister!' He'd just blown down the tube to the engine room, Bakewell having answered his question with, 'Wouldn't be surprised, sir' – meaning yes, *could* be water in her. Andy thinking, a hatch-cover gone, or leaking: couldn't be a *small* leak either – as through ripped tarpaulins, for instance – not if the weight inside her was already significant enough to affect the rudder's influence on her. He had his glasses up again, searching for the *Soissons'* stern light; *PollyAnna* with her stem pointing at the invisible racing clouds, stern deep, shuddering, Old Man shouting into the tube to reduce to revs for five knots – which must have been queried by the engineer on watch, as he'd now had to repeat it. Halloran lurching up beside Andy, asking him, 'What's up?'

'Helmsman – Bakewell – reckons she's heavy for'ard, could have water in her.'

It would feel something like having an anchor out

for'ard: as if when putting the helm over you were turning her stern around that kind of pivot. Although it wasn't stopping her from chucking herself around. Halloran hadn't commented – thinking it over, no doubt – but the skipper had yelled to Bakewell, 'Bring her easy to zero-seven-oh!'

'Oh-seven-oh, sir . . .'

To stem the weather, at revs reduced by almost half. Should make it easier for her – which if she'd been shipping water for'ard was obviously essential. Although stemming wind and sea was *all* she'd be doing; might even be driven backward. Convoy bashing on, *PollyAnna* straggling, solo, with an unknown quantity of water in her and two of her four boats gone. Would be found missing when daylight came, as others had been earlier. Since wireless silence had to be total – well, no signal, no way for her skipper to explain her absence or condition. Might have passed a brief report of the situation by Aldis lamp – he, Andy, could have done, if called upon to do it; alternatively Dewar or Starkadder if summoned from the W/T office where they spent all their time in headphones, eavesdropping on this and that but did not on any account transmit. But there again, the Commodore had insisted he didn't want Aldis lamps flashing all over the shop at night – 'Any chat that's necessary, let's do it in daylight – uh?' Fisher had made a note of that. But in weather such as this no explanation was really necessary in any case: it was odds-on there'd be others besides *PollyAnna* falling-out tonight. The thing *now* was the method of slipping out of the formation reasonably safely, when there'd be say six or eight ships back there she might run foul of, once out of her proper station. The Old Man had her now anyway: having passed helm and speed orders directly, usurping the function of his officer of the watch. Andy with his glasses up, a mere spectator, focusing on what he assumed to be the *Eileen Harper*, a white mound – or *disturbance* more than mound – overhauling *PollyAnna* to port; and the skipper shouting to

Bakewell to bring her back to 050 degrees. Made sense – having moved out to roughly midway between columns, resuming the convoy course to stay middled while those on her quarters drew ahead. Two to come on each quarter – if they were still there and in station you'd have them passing at roughly 300 yards on each side. Andy yelled into Finney's ear, 'Tell wing lookouts ships from astern'll be passing close, long as they're not inside a cable's length abeam, no worry.'

'Right . . .'

Skipper's shout then: 'Finney – wait!'

'Sir?'

'Do that, then find the Chief Engineer, tell him I'd like a word.'

Andy had an idea of what Finney's next task after that might be. *Should* be. Also asking himself what he'd do now or next if he was in the Old Man's boots. Well – one, get her clear of the rest of them – as he was doing – and two, back on to a course of 070 or 075, her nose into the weather, and three, find out where the flooding was. It would be the carpenter's job to sound round – i.e. to dip all tanks and bilges.

Please God let it be a tank and not a hold.

'Ship passing close to port, sir!'

Three-quarter buried in foam, battling through it. Column four, number five or six, that would be. While a binocular sweep to starboard found nothing. Meanwhile, back to that last thought – *PollyAnna* with her stem in deep, shipping it solid over that bow and as far aft as number three – that vision of Postlethwaite sounding the forward holds . . .

Scary. Fore-peak or the deep-tank was one thing, a hold very much another: but anyway, in this sea-state no more feasible than it would be to check the for'ard hatch-covers. Simply could not get there to take his soundings.

'Wanted to see me – sir?' Hibbert – staggering colossus steadying itself with a hand up to the deckhead. 'Revs for five knots now – had that passed to me, but –'

'May be taking in water somewhere for'ard, Chief. Feeling it in the steering. Any ideas?'

'Only to have Postlethwaite sound round.'

'Bloody hell, man, *look*!'

PollyAnna obliging with a demonstration of her corkscrew roll: sea swamping over on the weather bow, piling deep and white over and around the hatch-covers, flooding aft still deep – solid white – until she'd lifted and begun to roll the other way. If Postlethwaite had been down there with his sounding-rods he wouldn't be there *now*. Hibbert standing back, clear of the wheel and binnacle. 'See what you mean.' She was shipping it in quantity over the other gunwale then: Andy thinking, maybe she *was* hanging bow-down longer than she should have. Could be imagination, though. Bakewell's imagination, even? But wasn't that wishful thinking . . . Old Man shouting at his engineer, 'Easier when her head's into it. Postlethwaite's last soundings showed tanks empty for'ard, did they? Fore-peak dry?'

'If they hadn't, we'd've pumped!'

'So try now with the pumps, see what you get.'

'Aye . . .'

Pumps – one main one and one auxiliary – with lines to all tanks and bilges, were in the engine room. Controlled from there anyway. You got suction on this or that bilge by opening valves on certain lines, shutting others. Postlethwaite's daily soundings were recorded on a black-board on one of the gratings at the top of the engine-space; like the bosun he was primarily responsible to the mate, but with pumps being engineers' business, the responsibilities overlapped.

Hibbert had gone down. Andy had in his glasses the plunging profile of a steamer whose name he remembered as the *Muriel Sykes*. Shouting over the din, 'Last of column three overhauling starboard, sir!'

'That the lot?'

'*Should* be –'

'Come to oh-seven-five, Bakewell!'

'Oh-seven-five, sir . . .'

The weather-stemming course.

'Still feel heavy?'

'Yessir. No worse, I'd say, but –' Grunting, as he wound starboard rudder on her. *PollyAnna* leaning hard to port and the *Muriel Sykes'* stern light glittering through flying suds closer than Andy had thought she was. Bakewell finishing with '– answers so *slow*, seems.'

'More'n just a few gallons in the peak, then.'

'I'd say so, sir.'

Meaning *guess* so. Imagination did play its part – that and what you either feared or hoped for as the answer. Andy telling himself that if her head could be held dead into wind and weather, at these revs she might – *might* – ride it out, ride *most* of it out, not have any but those real bastards rearing up and smashing down on hatch-covers that might already have been weakened to the extent of letting the stuff in. Then one might – after watching for a while to be sure how she was weathering it – chance taking a look down there. Himself and Batt Collins maybe, and Postlethwaite with them. Well, say a team of half a dozen – and while at it, rig lifelines.

Not that it would be up to him. But if there was any general discussion . . .

At first light, maybe. Eight hours' time, say. If *PollyAnna*'d stick it that long. Depending on how much water she had in her already, and the rate of intake and how well the pumps might cope with that. Face it, that *was* the situation: you were on a ship that might bloody founder, might *not* have eight hours – or six – or four.

Or ten minutes.

'Course oh-seven-five, sir.'

'Try her on oh-eight-oh now.'

'Oh-eight-oh, sir . . .'

'Riding better, Holt, wouldn't you say?'

'Yessir. But – suggestion, sir –'

'Uh?'

'If you're handling her, I'm assistant OOW, we don't need Finney; he might best see Miss Carr's all right?'

15

They had a pump sucking on the bilge of number two hold, Hibbert had been up to tell the Old Man. They'd tried the fore-peak and the deep-tank and got nothing out of either, then number one hold – which was also dry – and after finding water in number two – a real gusher, Hibbert had called it – had tried number three and were able to confirm that *that* was dry. So now you knew where it was: but not how deep it was or whether the pump could cope with it, extract more than was getting in there. When Hibbert had come up it had been running for about ten minutes, and that had been a quarter of an hour ago.

Another question currently unanswerable was whether, if the pump could *not* beat the inflow, the ship would float when that hold was full. Andy didn't think she would, and the Old Man's silence on the subject made it fairly obvious that he didn't either. Ten minutes to midnight now. Andy had taken over as OOW again before Hibbert had come back up, Old Man retiring to his corner and lighting his pipe; scent of shag now filling the wheelhouse. If you could call it *scent*. Finney hadn't returned, which was fine, what Andy had intended – for Julia to have help at hand if she should need it, and meanwhile have her mind taken off whatever fears she might have. If Finney was up to that – which he would be, surely, the pair of them having been close companions for a long time now – long, arduous time, and they'd come through all that, so . . .

So fingers crossed, and God be with them. With us all, for Christ's sake. Glasses up meanwhile: concentrating on the wilderness out there. Looking out was still important – always was, naturally, always would be, but specifically here and now because the effect of having been in convoy was to make you feel you were now entirely alone, whereas there might well be other drop-outs around, none of them likely to be showing lights.

As to the rest of it – well, she was certainly rolling less. *Would* be, head to sea. Pitching less violently too, he thought: attributing this to a combination of (a) lower revs, and (b) weight of water in her forepart. This was his own opinion – assumption – based on observation and the *feel* of her. Had not discussed it with the Old Man, hadn't exchanged a word about it since that optimistic, 'Riding better, Holt?' an hour ago. But her bow *was* lower in the sea, he thought. There'd been no more of the hurricane-sized waves since the one that had smashed the boats – although that didn't mean you'd seen the last of them – and in any case there were still big ones crashing in over the foc's'l-head several times a minute; you still had it boiling over the for'ard hatch-covers really *most* of the time. She wasn't rising to the oncoming seas as she had been, which could undoubtedly be put down to the weight in number two: she was driving into them, whereas before she'd been soaring and then slamming down on them.

It had become more evident during the past hour – through most of which they'd had the pump running.

'Bearing up, are we?'

Fisher, arriving to take over. Lifejacket on over his oilskin. Skipper's orders – men on watch to wear them, those below to have them within reach at all times. Turning to the skipper: 'It's Fisher, sir.'

'Before you take over, Second, have a look at the DR I've put on. Guesswork mostly. But' – voice clearer as he took the pipe out of his mouth – 'steering oh-eight-oh since then, like as not standing still.'

Gorst, who'd come up with him, also lifejacketed, had

gone to the chart anyway. Fisher yelled – to Andy – 'Water in number two, I hear. Spoke with McAlan. Pump's running a bit hot, he says.'

'Put the auxiliary on it then, couldn't they? Turn and turn about maybe?'

'I'm sure. Anyway – still afloat, that's the main thing.' A chuckle. 'And come daylight, see to the hatch-cover, any luck.' Peering down at a sea flooding over deep enough for foam to be flying in white streamers from more than halfway up the kingposts. As much as ten feet deep on deck, that meant. Fisher adding, 'But not in *that* we won't, will we. Well, Christ . . .' Turning away: 'Hang on. Dekko at the chart.' Over his shoulder then: 'Finney there, is he?'

'Didn't need him. Skipper'd taken over for a while, I sent him down.'

Odd that he'd thought Finney might be up here – or in fact why he'd have cared whether he was or wasn't. But they were sharing a cabin, and as a matter of routine Fisher would have looked into the saloon – the pantry, anyway – for a mug of tea before coming up.

Only left one place he *could* be.

Well. Glasses up again. Why *not*? What he'd sent him down for, after all. And they would *not* – well, bet your life they wouldn't – either of them, but certainly not *her*.

Big one coming. Towering black wall, white-topped – the kind that curled before it fell on you, smashed down on hatch-covers, boats in davits, battered at the super-structure and made decks unusable . . .

Hatch-covers could stand that, they'd stand anything. Low in the sea as she was, it did virtually drown her. Bakewell cursing, battling with the helm . . . This midships accommodation block was often referred to as an island – *PollyAnna* as a three-island ship: foc's'l, bridge structure and poop – and for something like a minute the bridge and upper bridge – monkey island – *were* effectively an island: you were looking out and down on nothing but a murderous rising pile of ocean and not finding it easy to trust in the staying-power of steel plates and rivets, iron beams, the ship's ability to withstand, survive . . . Foc's'l-head and the ventilators' intakes – ventilators abreast the foremast – suddenly – surprisingly – out and clear of it, and the heavy whiteness thinning, dividing, streaming, howling away down-storm, *PollyAnna* fighting her way up out of it, even the darker rectangular shapes of hatch-covers visible to binoculars now. She wasn't bow-up: would have been if she'd been in anything like proper trim, but –

Wasn't. Nothing like.

'All right, Bakewell?'

'All right now, sir. Was twenty degree off, but –'

Gorst blundered in from the wing: 'Boats are still there, sir.'

'Makes a change to have *good* news.' The Old Man – grabbing for fresh support, having moved from where he had been. Andy telling himself there could be more of those to come. Why shouldn't there be? The Old Man bawling to Fisher, 'What d'you make of it, Second?'

The charted DR position. Fisher was coming from the canvas-curtained chart alcove, telling him, 'I'm sure your DR's as good as it could be, sir, but don't you think if we made the course oh-seven-five rather than oh-eight-oh –'

'Head to this muck is oh-eight-oh. Time being we'll stay as we are.'

'Aye aye, sir.'

Andy handed him the binoculars: 'Revs for five knots, course you know –'

'And they're pumping on number two. All right. Sleep well.'

It had been a long four hours. He *would* sleep well. She'd been banging around like this for days now, one's system was tuned to it. Not exactly music to the slumbering soul, but – hell, apart from those huge ones, which *might* disturb one . . . Might wake with nightmarish pictures in mind – of number one going as number two had, another of those great avalanches smashing through number one's hatch-cover, for instance. If that happened you wouldn't have many minutes, perhaps not even one. Or if the bulkhead split between one and two – same thing, similar effect – if you woke at all you'd wake drowning.

Better to sleep than *think*, was what that amounted to. And here and now, better maybe not to bother about tea. Because Julia and Finney *might* be in the saloon. If she'd not been able to sleep and the boy was keeping her company? Well – Christ, he *should* be . . . But if you didn't look in there you could tell yourself that was where they must have been, that Fisher might have gone straight up to the bridge from his cabin – might have, and you could leave that question unasked too . . . While another view of it was as he'd thought earlier – more or less – who cared, in all these circumstances who gave a damn?

Well – he, Andy Holt, did. For some reason. And if he stayed out of the saloon now it would be primarily for his own peace of mind. Shielding himself from any discomforture on that score – from knowing they could only have been in her cabin.

Did want a hot drink, though . . .

They were sitting at the pantry end of the table, and she was playing patience – one-handed, the other curled round a leg of the table, holding herself in place – as if that came naturally, was simply what one *did* – the cards laid out in columns alternating red and black, and Finney watching the game – or watching *her* – both of them glancing round as Andy came in and pushed the door shut behind him. Julia saying to Finney, '*Told* you . . .'

Their two lifejackets were on a chair between them. His own was slung over his shoulder.

'Told him what?'

'That you'd be along for some tea when you came off watch.'

'Exactly what I'm here for.' Heading for the pantry – and thankful that he'd come. 'Either of you want some, while I'm at it?'

'We've got it coming out of our ears, thanks all the same. But thank you for sending Mark down to hold my hand.'

'That what he's been doing?'

The galley fire was out, but there was hot water in the cistern. *Fairly* hot. He made himself a mug of tea and went back to them. 'Holding hands, indeed!'

'That was a colossal one a few minutes ago, wasn't it?'

'Biggish. But she's riding it quite well now.'

Julia asked, 'Going to be all right then, are we?'

'Of course we are. Not making much headway at the moment, but as soon as it eases off –'

'Think it will?'

He smiled at her. 'Ever hear of a storm that went on for ever?'

'Can go on for weeks, can't they? Especially this time of year?'

'No reason this should. Four days is average, as it happens. I'm not saying we'll get a flat calm, exactly –'

'But if the cover of *another* hatch gave way –'

'You know about that, then.'

'I've got ears, Andy – and no one's keeping it exactly secret.' Patting the lifejackets. 'Stone the crows, what might these be for?'

'We're pumping on that bilge, she's holding up well, and when it does ease – as believe me it *will* –'

'This one's going to come out, I think.' Talking about the game of patience. 'It doesn't often.' Shaking her head: 'You don't have to worry about me, anyway. I know the spot we're in, but – got through it once, get through it again. Mark thinks I'm bluffing, I'm supposed to crack up or something. Damn.' Throwing the cards down: '*Not* coming out. *Stupid* game. It's true, though – came tapping on my door shaking like a leaf; I had to have him on the bunk with me, hold him tight. You needn't look like that – I've been sleeping in my clothes, and all he took off was his oilskin and woolly hat – drew the line at *them* . . .

He was asleep before one a.m. and awake again just after six, having slept like them – fully dressed – and not been disturbed even once by the still violent motion or the noise of it. No point in any early visit to the bridge for stars – knowing there wouldn't be any. Black sky and angry sea was all: although – on his bunk still, listening to it and comparing the ship's motion to what it *had* been – might be a little quieter?

The fact she was still afloat with her engine pounding was the main thing. Last night there'd been no guarantee of it. Could have taken in more water during the night and given up the ghost, just slipped under: he'd been very much aware of it, and so he thought had Julia. Finney too, probably. Julia by some kind of instinct or intuition maybe, or reading it in others' eyes – including one's own – and Finney as much as anything because he was scared for *her*.

Which made two of them.

When she'd gone up last night, leaving them on their own while Andy finished his lukewarm tea, he'd said to Finney, 'That business in her cabin – cuddles on her bunk –'

'I know. Shouldn't have.'

'Innocent, I know, but someone might get the wrong idea, and – for instance, someone like our first mate?'

'I take *that* point. And it won't happen again. I didn't know what to do – she might have been lying there scared stiff – whatever she says, *might* have been . . . Isn't she terrific?'

'Quite a girl. Truly is.'

Finney smiling – a touch self-consciously, Andy had thought. As if taking that as a compliment to himself – seeing himself and her as one entity, even? Love's young dream, he'd thought, when he was turning in. Calf-love, though, little brother love: and no harm in that, absolutely none – as long as Finney came to recognise it, in due course. But as for himself – well, for one thing he wondered whether he should have said even as much as he had about the shared bunk. If Finney had sneaked back up to her cabin, stayed with her through a night in the course of which they *might* all have drowned, (a) could one have blamed either him or her, and (b) what business was it of Andy Holt's?

Fair enough to warn him about Halloran, though. And interesting that the warning had seemed not to surprise him.

Fisher arrived for breakfast soon after Andy had settled down to it, told him his own midnight to four watch had been uneventful, with none of those huge ones which truly did make you feel the end was nigh, but that he doubted whether it would be possible to inspect number two hatch-cover with conditions as they still were. 'Feel it, can't you – that's how it *is* . . .' Get a better notion of it in daylight, obviously. He thought she was deeper for'ard than she'd been at midnight: every wave that came now did swamp over and come lumping down from the foc'sl-head on to the hatch-covers. There'd been some discussion of it between Halloran and the Old Man when the watch had been changing over at 0400; Halloran had been putting his view that number two should be sounded at the first opportunity – *and* the hatch-cover attended to – Old Man maintaining stolidly, 'We'll see how she is, come daylight.'

The pump – *a* pump – was still running, Third Engineer Shaw told them. They'd switched several times between the main one and the auxiliary; those pumps did tend to run hot when overworked. Another danger was of the intake choking up – getting choked with fragments of dunnage, for instance.

'But' – a closing of the eyes, and rapping the table – 'so far, so good.'

'If the intake did choke up, that'd fix both pumps and not a damn thing anyone could do to clear it – right?'

'Right. But there's a thought Tom McAlan and I was having – if anyone'd care to hear it.'

Andy nodded. 'Sure we all would.'

'If it's decent.' Starkadder, that was, between slurps of porridge. Others listening were Clowes, the junior Marconi boy, Fourth Engineer Howie, and Willy Gorst.

'It's like this.' Shaw's Lancashire tones resuming. 'Suppose it's not the hatch-cover – suppose when we rammed the German – *Glauchau* – we started a few rivets

234

like – only loosened a couple, I mean, nothing as showed up on the way north, but now the seven, eight days' bashing around's *really* done it?'

Fisher shook his head. 'We hit the *Glauchau* a bit of a tonk, but I wouldn't say *rammed* her.'

'Slammed into her, then. Jesus, how it sounded to us down below there, I'll tell you.'

'Everything does though, doesn't it.'

'Eh?'

'Like banging on a drum? The motion now, for instance, ain't *that* –'

'Not all that bad. Louder here, *this* level. What I'm saying, stuff we've been through these last days – hell, could've done more 'n knock a few loose rivets out – if there *was* some – could've opened a seam, broken her bloody back even!'

Fisher said, frowning, 'Could have, but wouldn't necessarily have started with bumping into the Hun.'

'Carpenter went round sounding tanks and bilges, didn't he? On the way down-river?'

Andy put in, 'Conscientious guy, Postlethwaite. Sounded all round – on his own initiative – and didn't find an egg-cupful. I'd say that if there *is* hull damage, that tells us there's no connection.'

'Don't prove there *is*, but if there was only rivets loosened then – we had an easy passage north, remember –'

'I agree with Holt.' Fisher, Andy had realised from the start of this, didn't want the Old Man accused of ramming anything. If there was any such damage, perhaps it *could* have started there, but at present there was no reason to look further than the hatch-cover. He put in – as Finney arrived, but no Julia with him, she no doubt making up for the late night she'd had – to her great credit, if she *could* sleep soundly – 'May get a proper look at the hatch-cover some time today.' To Shaw then, 'If you'd been up there when those dirty great bastards were coming down on us – hell, you wouldn't *believe* the size of 'em. Big enough to break the *Queen Mary*'s back, let alone this old steamer's.'

Looking round at the pantry hatch: 'Any more coffee there, Watkins?'

Except that her forepart definitely was lower in the water, so that as Fisher had said, every roller as she dug into it was coming greenish over the foc's'l-head and/or gunwales and filling the well-deck with a white flood covering the hatch-covers several feet deep – so if there were leaks in number two the topping-up process would be more or less continuous – there wasn't much difference from how he remembered it at midnight. Except that then of course one hadn't been able to see anything but the whiteness, and now it was startling to see how little freeboard she had for'ard there. He guessed the hold might well be full – in which case the pumps were wasting their time and effort, sucking out less than was coming in, achieving damn-all. On the other hand, the Old Man was clearly right: you couldn't make that assumption and have them stopped – perhaps have the hold fill up *then* and sink her.

The hatch-cover *looked* OK – in moments when it was in clear sight, tarpaulin gleaming blackly in the early light. But it was more likely to be the cause of flooding than Tommy Shaw's allegedly loosened rivets. Secondary danger: if the hold *was* full, or even half-full – was of the holds' dividing bulkheads giving way to the pressure of that mass of water being slung constantly to and fro with the still violent motion of the ship, the frightening but inescapable truth being that if they or even one of them gave way, the flooding would instantly spread right through and she'd be on her way to the bottom, finish the century on a bed of sand 9,000 feet down. Pitch darkness, white crabs, no ocean movement in that deep silence, *PollyAnna* resting easy while the crabs clawed into whatever they found that took their fancy, and over the years rust consumed the rest.

Shaking his head. Something of that sort *might* come about – at some later stage, some other voyage. But not

236

this time. *This* time you were going to get her and her cargo home.

Cargo and passenger.

'All right, Holt?'

Halloran back from the chart where he'd been conferring with the skipper. They'd come back together, skipper into his usual corner, beyond Axe-man Parlance who was on the wheel now and for the next half-hour. Crazy-looking, with that squint – no wonder the Huns had tended to keep their distance. Eight o'clock now – course still 080, revs the same, DR position on the chart the same as yesterday and the day before that, only a matter of rubbing out the previous date and substituting today's – 27th. Assuming, with no certainty and no way of checking, that to all intents and purposes you'd been standing still.

He'd nodded to Halloran. 'Got her.'

Forepart buried. Vibration from aft was from the racing screw. Skipper bawling – an afterthought to the discussion they'd been having – 'We'll also think about flooding the deep-tank aft, Mister!' Halloran moved away in the Old Man's direction and Andy turned back to his looking-out. They knew a lot more about it than he did, but he suspected the decision might still be a tricky one. Deep-tanks were essentially trimming tanks, filled for instance when the ship was in ballast, although they could also be used as cargo-space, were empty now because the iron ore had her down to her winter North Atlantic marks; flooding the after one would trim her stern down, thereby level her to some extent and increase the working depth of the rudder and propeller. By the same token, though, you'd be increasing her already excessive weight and draught: with the hold flooded she'd already be below her marks.

Decision for those who knew. And a biggish sea coming now: mound of dark-green, white-fringed water higher than the foc'sl-head, *PollyAnna* dipping her bow deep in the trough preceding it as it came towering, drawing itself up as they always seemed to – *bridge*-height, that streaming crest – and *on* her now – smothering her forepart, foc's'l-head buried, green sea piling over, drowning not only hatches but ventilators, winches, lashed-down derricks, thundering around this bridge structure, spray sheeting and rattling like bullets. Old Man bellowing at Halloran as the bulk of it flooded aft and overside, 'Care to've been down there *then*, would you?'

Bark of what might have been a laugh. Then – 'But this past half-hour – and maybe the next again –'

'We'll see how it goes, Mister.'

Halloran must have been arguing in favour of inspecting the hatch-cover and sounding the depth in that hold. Skipper obviously not in favour: his flat tone had indicated decision reached, no further argument. And another of that kind coming now, Andy saw – likely to confound Halloran's theory and reinforce that decision. He yelled, 'Another coming!' Halloran moving swiftly to the ladder and the Old Man crooking an arm round the stanchion that carried the engine room telegraph, watching how Parlance handled her through this new thundering maelstrom. Then, as it subsided – *PollyAnna* shuddering, but holding her own despite the weight in her – telling Andy, 'Going down for a spell, Holt. Any problems, *whistle*, don't fuck around – all right?'

By 'don't fuck around' he'd meant not to dither over interrupting his captain's forty winks, but in fact there'd been no reason to until in mid-forenoon he realised the wind was backing, was on the bow to port, the ship beginning to roll as well as pitch. In accordance with Master's Standing Orders this did need to be reported, and he'd been on the point of doing so when the Old Man reappeared of his own accord after only a couple of hours below – his full ration of sleep out of the past twenty-four, and some of that time he'd have been eating, one might guess . . . Arriving back up then he'd spent a few seconds sniffing the wind and watching the sea before telling Andy, 'Try her on oh-seven-oh.'

'Aye aye, sir.' He looked at Ingram, who was on the wheel now, and having heard the skipper's shout was waiting for Andy to formalise the order with, 'Steer oh-seven-oh.'

Acknowledgement, and wheel over. And Finney getting something to do at last – entering the alteration and the time of it in the log. *PollyAnna*'s fore-deck was still under water most of the time, but there'd been no more giant ones. In fact you'd have said force ten rather than force eleven now. Wouldn't count on any lasting improvement, though – not yet. There'd been false hopes raised more than once in the last few days.

'Course oh-seven-oh, sir.' Ingram's grey mop of hair showing under his tam-o'-shanter. Deepset eyes, jutting brows, hooked nose. He was from somewhere in Argyll, had mentioned that he'd been a lifeboatman at one time. His chief distinction in *PollyAnna* now was that he'd been one of the stalwarts of the boarding operation. *PollyAnna* was coming round to the new course readily enough, despite the weight for'ard and the stern-up angle which one would expect to be reducing the rudder's effectiveness. The wind might have helped: was on her nose now, but having backed by about a point before that had maybe helped nudge her afterpart around.

Confused sea, you'd call this. Heavy enough, but less regular.

'How long since it began to shift?'

The Old Man, at his side. *PollyAnna* scooping a load of green over her bow, port side, flinging it back across and out to starboard. Andy told him, 'Only minutes, sir. I was making sure of it before calling you.'

'Backing this quick, may end up where it should be this time of year.' Wave of a hand westward. 'Won't make it any warmer, eh?'

Meaning – Andy guessed – that in passing through north-west it would be coming from the ice. He put his glasses up again. It *had* been brass-monkey cold these last days. Gales all the way from Spitzbergen, maybe. Greenland, a shade west of north, was of course a good deal closer. He asked – chancing his arm, third mates weren't expected to engage their skippers in conversation when on watch, but the Old Man seemed to be in a chatty mood – 'Will you flood the after deep-tank, sir?'

'If we get the blow astern of us – not like it has been, mind – least, pray God it won't' – pausing, with his round blue eyes on Andy's – 'we'd bloody *need* to – uh?'

'To trim her so she'll answer her helm better?'

'And the screw in deeper, and less chance she'd drive under, maybe.'

Meaning that with the wind astern and enough revs to push her along a bit, the bow-down angle plus excessive weight for'ard, might – *might* – cause her to drive herself under. And levelling her even slightly should make that less likely.

He nodded. 'Thank you, sir.'

'Try her on oh-six-oh.'

Fisher came up shortly before noon, to take over his twelve to four, and Halloran also reappeared. Andy had sent Finney down to keep Julia company, the Old Man had also allowed himself another break, and Gorst had come up as usual with Fisher; so there were three officers and one cadet on the bridge, with Ingram still on the wheel.

Andy told Fisher, 'Still pumping on number two, course is oh-three-oh, revs unchanged, wind's been backing steadily over the past two hours, sea's all over the place.' Meaning erratic, having problems making its mind up. *PollyAnna* dipping into it, though, as a standard-size wave came rolling in fine on the bow, swamping over and smashing itself into lather on and around the steam windlass, sluicing down to swirl three or four feet deep in the well-deck then. With her pretty well constant bow-down angle she wasn't getting rid of it as fast as she would have even four hours ago.

He thought the hold might have filled in that time.

Halloran shouted, 'That as big as they're coming now?'

'Well-deck's awash three-quarters of the time.' He added, in case the mate hadn't heard what he'd told Fisher, 'Wind's down a notch and backing.'

'Old Man got his head down?'

Fisher had a comment overlapping that: 'She's got damn little freeboard for'ard there!'

'I know. Not good, is it.'

Fisher was looking shocked, and was probably right to be. It was the shape she was in, though, nothing you could do about it. He supposed that actually it wasn't far off a disaster scenario: for some time now, had not been far off it. Nodded to Halloran, his question about the Old Man. 'Or he's getting an early meal. Said he'd be back up inside the hour.' Checking the time. 'Gives him twenty minutes.' Back to Fisher then: 'So – all right?'

'Can't say I'm exactly *happy* with her.'

'Orders are to keep her head to wind. Speaking of which –' He shouted to Ingram, 'Bring her to oh-two-five!'

'Oh-two-five, sir . . .'

'How's she feel, Ingram?'

A quick glance in Halloran's direction, while holding rudder on her, eyes then back on the compass. 'Heavy, sir. Not much different, though.' To Andy then: 'Course oh-two-five, sir.'

'All right, I'll take her.' Fisher's hand out for the glasses; Halloran indicated that he was staying put, guessed the Old Man would agree they might take a look at number two now. Nodding down towards what was more a big swell than a wave as she drove into it – or you might say it enveloped her, whereas in normal conditions she'd have ridden over it. At higher revs she could do that and drive herself under, Andy thought. Asking Halloran – 'If he agrees to that, d'you want me with you?'

'No. Me, bosun and Postlethwaite. Postlethwaite can take his soundings – then we'll know if the pumping's doing any good. If there's, say, six or ten feet in there, it's doing its job; if she's full up it's a waste of time – unless we can fix the hatch-cover.'

241

'Shaw has a theory it could be hull damage. Loosened rivets.'

'If we find the cover's intact, he could be right.'

He told Julia in the saloon what was happening weather-wise and what Halloran hoped would be happening in regard to the flooded hold if the Old Man went along with it. Telling Julia and Finney, but also as it happened McAlan, Howie, Janner and young Mervyn Clowes. All of them with lifejackets handy. He slung his own over the back of a chair: 'Damn thing.'

'Why say that?'

'Because I've been wearing it on the bridge, and the tape that goes over one's head gets in the way of this and makes it sore.' Touching the back of his neck. He was still wearing the dressing the Canadian doctor had put on it in Halifax, securing it with sticking-plaster; it had seemed desirable to keep it covered, where the removal of stitches had left it raw, and nothing that Halloran might have produced out of the medicine chest was likely to measure up to that doctor's effort. He remembered the doc warning him, 'This may hurt some,' and while snipping the mate's stitches out asking him, 'What kinda pain-killer'd he give you when he put 'em in?' Andy had told him, truthfully, 'Large tot of whisky,' and he'd demanded, 'No morphine in your ship's stores?'

'Do have morphine tablets. Didn't think of it, though. All in a rush, and didn't expect it to hurt all that much.'

'Huh. What Nelson might have said when they cut his arm off. Hold on now . . .'

Actually, he and Halloran had thought of the morphine tablets, but there hadn't been so many of them in the jar, and the *Cheviot*'s first mate – Sam Cornish, whom later they'd landed to hospital in St Lucia – with his broken ribs and a leg wound that looked like turning gangrenous, had had greater need of them. Halloran had in fact done a good job on Andy's neck, but not a neat one. Julia, when she'd helped with re-winding the bandage – somewhere

242

off the north-east coast of Brazil – had murmured, 'Crikey. Regular dog's dinner . . .' and he'd thought of suggesting, 'Kiss it better?' She might have, if he had proposed it – knowing her better now than he had then. But even at that stage, two or three days out of Vitoria, he'd begun to think she was something special. Asking him now – after he'd groused about the lifejacket – whether he'd like her to change the dressing. 'If I asked Mr Halloran –'

'No. Thanks a lot, but – only an irritation, doesn't hurt.'

The mate's scars must have healed, too. Although he hadn't shaved since Vitoria, only clipped his beard with scissors.

PollyAnna was rolling a bit. Fisher should be bringing her another 5 degrees to port, maybe. Slamming thud followed by the after-shake of digging into a head sea then . . . Behind him, Steward Benson telling Dewar, who'd just walked in and wanted to know what they were getting for lunch, 'Corned dog and mash today, sir.'

'Again?'

'First time this week, sir!'

'Well.' Pulling back a chair and dumping his lifejacket on the deck beside it. 'If you say so.' Looking round the faces: 'Anyone interested, mate's about to inspect the cover of number two. Taking Collins and Postlethwaite for'ard with him. I just met 'em.' A nod to McAlan: 'We're cutting revs while they do it.'

Finney got up – reaching for support and leaning against the motion. 'Want to see this.'

'From monkey island then. Skipper won't want the bridge cluttered.'

'Right –'

'Finney.' Andy pointing: 'Lifejacket . . .'

It was tempting to go up and see the show, but having spent the last four hours up there Andy opted to keep Julia company instead. In any case, the Old Man wouldn't want spectators getting in the way.

Julia asked him, 'Going out on that fore-deck? Sea washing over it all the time?'

'Not seas like we *have* had. The Old Man'll have been watching, must reckon it's OK. We do need to know what's happening in that hold.'

'Where the water's getting in.'

'And how much – and if possible seal it up. We've been just stemming wind and sea – as you know – only know very roughly where we are – but if we're going to have a westerly behind us now –'

'Make tracks for home?'

'Exactly. Next stop Newcastle. Here comes your lunch.'

He heard afterwards how it had gone. The bare facts of it went round the ship within minutes; he had fuller accounts of it after that from eye-witnesses Fisher and young Finney, close-up detail later from Batt Collins.

The three of them had judged their moment and gone trotting for'ard when there was a slight up-angle on her and no more than a foot or so of water left from the last inundation, hatch-covers and other gear thus in plain sight. Halloran leading, then the bosun, then Postlethwaite with his haversack containing the sounding-rod slung over one shoulder. Access to the sounding pipe for number two was immediately for'ard of its hatch, between it and the fore-mast and laterally between two cargo winches; he had a special tool for unscrewing the brass cap that covered it, and he'd be concentrating on that job while the other two looked for damage to the cover and/or wedges that might have been loosened. Each of the three had a fathom and a half of hemp line secured in a bowline around his waist, tail-end to be hitched to some solid fitting, and when he moved, shifted to another. Gear to which they could attach themselves included the winches and the cargo derricks, two of which were lashed horizontally above the hatch-cover, between the foremast and the kingposts.

PollyAnna was rolling as well as pitching because the wind was more variable than it had been, the helmsman – Harkness, under the skipper's close and watchful eyes – holding her as near as possible bow-on to it but not always closer than 5 or even 10 degrees. She was shipping plenty, despite having reduced to revs for three knots: at anything less than that you'd have risked losing steerage-way, and then – broaching-to, broadside-on to it, say, and in her state of trim – well, God forbid . . . Although these weren't the great swamping seas she'd been running into earlier; the ropes' ends would be needed for sure, but as long as they were used intelligently – when shifted, for instance, shifted quickly . . .

Halloran threw the end of his line over the starboard-side derrick's boom, securing it there with a round turn and two half-hitches; any experienced seaman would be able to do this one-handed in the space of about three seconds. He and the bosun each had on his belt a seven-pound hammer for driving in loose wedges; they'd share the hatch's after (thwartship) coaming, then move for'ard each on his own side – looking for loose wedges, rips in the tarpaulins etc., – while Postlethwaite crouched at the hatch's for'ard end between the two winches, to either of which he could secure his lifeline while he was sounding the hold. The 'rod' was in fact a flexible chain of flat metal plates, each six inches long and half an inch wide, with point-line spliced to one end so the rod could be lowered down the pipe to the striking-plate in the bilge. But he didn't need to go that far or anything like it: it took him less than half a minute to discover that the hold was full. While neither Halloran nor the bosun found any damage to the hatch-cover.

Batt Collins, later: 'A wedge 'ere and there – maybe five or six in all – was half loose, needed a whack in, like. Nothin' adrift noplace else. I were up by the winch, port for'ard corner, like – Possie'd begun his sounding an' packed it in – packed up his gear and begun looking for wedges as might be loose up that end – found a couple, come up off of his knees wanting a 'ammer which he didn't 'ave, see, and Mr Halloran passed him his one. Well, Possie let go of his pack – reachin' over for the 'ammer – and a sea comes over, takes charge of it like, washes it over Mr

245

16

He'd not been wearing a lifejacket. The Old Man had of course seen this when they'd come into his sight running forward, had looked (Fisher said) at first incredulous then furious, focusing his glasses on them. Questioned about it, the bosun said he'd asked the mate whether he shouldn't have had one on – he and Postlethwaite had been wearing theirs, naturally – and Halloran had replied, 'No bloody point, Bosun. Oh, skipper's orders, sure – but not for *this* lark . . . Get on with it, shall us?'

Andy had to agree that there'd been a certain logic behind that 'No bloody point.' Wrong entirely in putting his own interpretation on captain's orders, setting such an example of indiscipline, but as Postlethwaite had remarked, 'If you was going over the side in a sea such as that, what'd you want to float around for? Bloody vanish, don't you – 'ad your fuckin' lot!' A shake of the narrow, balding head: 'Sooner have it done with, like.'

But on top of that to have cast off his lifeline – not shifted it further along but simply cast it off, for no better purpose than recovering the sounding-rod assembly, which of course had gone with him in that same sudden, overwhelming rush of sea – and right there under the skipper's eyes, was typical of Halloran's show-off arrogance. As Batt Collins put it – to Andy and Fisher, in an admiring tone – 'Never give a toss for no one, that bugger didn't.'

The immediate problem was still that of keeping the

ship afloat, but with the advantage now of knowing that (a) the flooding was from submerged hull damage, and (b) the hold was full, so its effect could hardly get worse, *unless* – barely thinkable, true and total disaster scenario – by its extension from number two into one or three through the collapse or splitting of either bulkhead. That possibility obviously did exist, could happen in the next minute, hour or day: might in fact be put crucially to the test when she was turned across the wind, getting her round on to an easterly course with wind and sea behind her.

'Morning'll be soon enough for that. Long as it goes on easing as well as backing. Say our prayers for that, Holt. Eight o'clock maybe. If it looks like we'd get away with it, I'll aim to put her on oh-seven-five about then. That's accepting the DR we got on now. Sooner than that maybe if it shifts quicker. And revs then according to how it looks. Uh?'

Asking not for his third mate's concurrence, but whether he'd hoisted that in. Andy had nodded – shoulder to shoulder with the Old Man at the chart, Finney up front meanwhile, maintaining lookout, and Timms on the wheel. Andy had the navigator's job now, and Fisher had been elevated to acting mate. The Old Man was going to stand the watches that had been Andy's, eight to twelve a.m. and p.m., with Janner in support; Andy would take over the twelve to fours with Finney, and Fisher with Gorst would have Halloran's four to eights. Three p.m. now, so this watch was Andy's; *PollyAnna* meanwhile on a course of 015 degrees, sluggishly stemming a force seven.

There were to be no obsequies for Halloran. This happened to be a Sunday, and soon after daylight the Old Man had had him – Andy – pass the word that since he didn't intend leaving the vicinity of the bridge there'd be no Divine Service aft; and to lay on anything of the sort for him now – well, lay on *what*? Not a 'burial at sea' service: you could say he'd already conducted that, single-handed, and the fact was that it had been an utterly stupid thing he'd done, as well as a direct contravention of orders regarding lifejackets. The Old Man being a forthright, plain-speaking, as well as God-fearing man wouldn't have found it easy either to gloss over that or to speak ill of the dead; and in the situation they were in, and thanks to that idiocy having only two junior officers to back him up, he'd told Fisher, who'd asked him about it, 'First things first, no bloody folderols . . .'

The Old Man had gone down for an hour's kip, but resurfaced at four when Fisher had come up to take over the watch; the skipper first checking the state of things then asking Fisher whether he was happy to remain in the cabin he was now sharing with Finney. The point being that in taking over the mate's job, Fisher could really have laid claim to that guest-room cabin – which in fact he did not, saying he'd as soon stay where he was.

'Job for you then, Holt. Get Mr Halloran's gear together, pack it out of the way, have that room cleaned out and ask Miss Carr if she'd care to move into it. Make sure she does. Then have my little hole swept out and the cot returned to store.'

'Aye, sir. Mate's cash and personal correspondence, though –'

'Personal correspondence can go with the rest of it. Cash and accounts, ship or company business – on the desk in my day cabin, please.'

The lovely Leila's portrait, too, with a package of violet-shaded letters, would go with the rest of the former mate's gear in two suitcases he'd had stowed for'ard. Batt Collins dug them out – incidentally crossing the fore-deck to get them – and sent them up by hand of the Chinaman, Ah Nong, who was to take care of laundry requirements. Glancing at Leila's letters, though, Andy's eye was caught by a faded postmark: London SE3. Whereas she was supposed to reside in Greenock, in some rented house, which the mate had complained had been costing him 'an arm and a leg'. On the brothel evening in Calcutta he'd groused about it: about the Grant Line having done him down, all that. The Greenock address – 11 Merriwell Way

– was on other papers – things the Old Man wanted. To make sure of it, though – or out of plain curiosity – fiddling the flimsy sheets out of their still slightly scented London postmarked envelope, taking care not to focus on any of the text, only looking at the top right-hand corner of the first page, he was surprised to find no address, only the words: *You know where.*

Of course he'd have known where – seeing that he was paying the rent. There was an allotment form among his papers – none of Andy's business and he wasn't prying, but the stuff had to be looked through, sorted. The Old Man would know of this one anyway; in dealing with advances against pay, he'd have to. It was a surprisingly large allotment, something like three-quarters of the mate's pay that was being remitted directly to Mrs Halloran by the owners. He himself presumably making do with funds arising from whatever other source – legacy or somesuch, he'd referred to it as a bit of luck he'd had, some wind-fall that had saved him from disaster when Grant Line had declined to renew his contract. Andy imagining some old aunt's or granny's life savings permitting young Dave to patronise Queeny's in Calcutta and the Casa Colorada in Vitoria – to name but two of them – while still doing the right thing by Leila.

Which undoubtedly he had, financially.

There were some other items, though, which might have surprised her, when she came to sort through the contents of these cases. Might, but then again might not: Leila did have a racy look about her. Part of her attraction. Anyhow – best do the decent thing, take charge of these oneself.

He found Julia in the washplace laundering underwear. Presumably not entrusting such a personal chore to Ah Nong.

'Sorry to intrude. Old Man wanted me to ask if you'd mind moving to a larger room.'

'You mean to Mr Halloran's?'

'Right. It and the one Chief Hibbert has were intended

for the owners or their valued customers. It's roomy, you'll be more comfortable, and the Old Man'd get his own bunk back. D'you mind?'

'Course not. It's been very kind of him to let me have it. He *is* a kind man, isn't he. Of course I'll move.'

'Fine. I've been packing Halloran's gear away, and Benson's doing the room out now. Clean sheets, so forth. Give him half an hour, then it's all yours.'

'All right. But, Andy, how could a man like him – experienced, Master Mariner for God's sake – how he'd be so *crazy* –'

'Perhaps he *was* slightly nuts. Had a tendency to show off, anyway. Odd chap, in some ways.'

'Married, wasn't he?'

'Was indeed. The one who wrote to him on that violet paper?'

'Oh, yes. But – tragic, anyway. Stupid – such a *waste* . . . Will your owners notify the wife?'

'In due course, I suppose. When *they* get to hear about it. We won't be breaking wireless silence just for this, though.'

'No – of course.'

'Wind's slowly dropping, anyway. Notice the difference?'

'Still plenty of bumping around. But – yes, I suppose . . .'

'We're adjusting course all the time, keeping her head into it. Once it's round to the west or northwest we'll be turning for home and cracking on a bit. With that hold full as we now know it is – she's managing all right, and it can't get any worse –'

'Can't?'

'Can't get any fuller. And the Old Man reckons by morning we'll be steering east with wind and sea astern.'

'How long then before we're in U-boat waters?'

'Can't say exactly. Don't know where we are, for one thing. Just guessing, though – say, two or three days. To latitude twenty west, that'd be – mightn't be any that far west anyway.'

Might indeed not, if U-boats didn't like foul weather.

Dewar produced a BBC report later that evening to the effect that in the past week Britain had been subjected to the worst storm of the century, with an accompanying cold front that had frozen the Thames for the first time since 1888. Part and parcel of the rough stuff *PollyAnna* had been through – and since the BBC had been allowed to mention it one might assume it had blown itself out, which if the U-boats had been off-station, might now bring them back. There was a lot of unidentifiable chatter on the airwaves, Dewar said, all in cipher, some of it maybe of Hun origin. He'd shrugged: 'We'll learn to know it when we hear it, by and by. Right now being new to it we're guessing.'

'Can't tell where it's from – how far or which direction?'

Jock Howie had asked that. Earlier the talk around the table had been mostly of Halloran, but they'd been avoiding that subject after Steward Benson had chipped in, moaning that he thought Mr Halloran might have been allowed a prayer or two; it had been McAlan who'd shut him up. Dewar's jowls wobbling now as he shook his head, 'Strength of signal isn't necessarily –'

'Sooner not know, anyway.' Julia, eyes down on a game of Pelmanism she was having with Finney, Andy and Willy Gorst. 'Sooner be like the three wise monkeys.'

'Hardly be like all three of 'em.' Finney. 'But with that whole convoy to go after, why bother with little old us?' Scooping up a pair of Jacks and asking Andy, 'Sea's quite a *bit* down, wouldn't you say?'

'Feels easier, doesn't it? What other news on BBC, Bill?'

'Russians versus Finns, mostly. Russians launching new attacks through Karelia, Finns holding firm, reckon they've killed fifty thousand of them. Russians all at sixes and sevens, apparently.'

The weather was still easing during Andy's midnight to four watch. Wind down to about force five but variable in direction, shifting frequently between north by east and north by west, sea confused and *PollyAnna* corkscrewing, scooping up the solid black and tossing it back streaming white. The Old Man feeling the roll in her motion came up twice, both times went back down to his regained bunk, muttering, 'Give it until daylight.' Andy had her on due north when Fisher took over at four: sunrise would be at about seven-thirty and it made sense, he thought, to wait for daylight. It might be tricky, making that alteration; as well to be able to see immediately how she reacted to the new conditions. Stemming the weather, OK, she was holding up, but when you put wind and sea astern and increased revs, she'd be as it were in new surroundings, all bets off. Simple truth being that she wasn't in any natural state to be afloat: and the vision of her suddenly sliding under was a background to all the rest of it – including the fact you had only two boats for more than fifty men and a girl.

Not that boats were likely to come into it. If she was going to slide under, that was what she'd do. Wouldn't give advance notice. You could be on watch on the bridge or asleep in your bunk, and next minute – *whoosh*, hello Davy Jones.

Nobody'd ever know. One or two of the ships in convoy might have seen her dropping out and recognised her as the *PollyAnna* of Vitoria fame, but that would have been the last anyone would hear of her.

He was in the bridge soon after six-thirty. Had slept and dreamt of Manuela, woken in surprise, and resolved that with the thought *Horses for courses* . . . Next surprise being the amount of roll on the ship. Steering *across* the weather now? Thoughts of navigation following: sunrise according to the *Nautical Almanac* being due at 0729; and a possibility of broken cloud, stars or the odd planet visible maybe. He'd prepared a notebook for use as a Sight Book – which all navigators (and most deck officers) kept, recording every sun, moon and star-sight they took, all in neatly pencilled figures and capitals. Don Fisher's was a model of neatness and clarity. Andy had started one for himself on his first voyage as third mate, but it had got a bit messy and he'd scrapped it; now in the capacity of navigator he had to start again.

Arriving in the wheelhouse he yelled to Fisher, 'Come up in the hope of stars.'

'*No* hope. But it's practically a millpond – eh?'

Some millpond. Heavy swell from – he checked the compass, grunting a good morning to Edmonds – eight- or ten-foot swells rolling at and under her from a point or two north of west. *PollyAnna* being on due north still was consequently rolling like a drunk.

Black overhead. Certainly no chance of stars. Ice in the wind.

'Skipper know we're steaming across this swell?'

'No, he did not!'

Speak of the devil: the Old Man himself. Fisher quick to explain, 'Your orders were hang on until first light, sir – not far to go for that, and you wouldn't want us steaming *west*, so –'

'How long like this?'

'Very rapid change, sir. Less than an hour. Still backing.'

'Should've called me.'

'I thought you'd feel it, sir, and if you didn't – well, with first light about seven –'

The Old Man had grunted, turned away: looking all round, assessing sea-state, wind, sky, *PollyAnna*'s motion and the amount of ocean she was shipping over her frighteningly low freeboard. Wind was from west-nor'west, say; Andy thinking she wouldn't be any *less* comfortable on an easterly course, as long as these swells didn't overwhelm her from astern. The Old Man turning to him then, having apparently reached a similar conclusion: 'From the DR we have, what course to clear Bloody Foreland?'

'I'll check, sir, but near enough oh-eight-oh.'

'Check it. Second – warn the engine room I'll be calling for revs for ten knots.'

After days and nights at these low revs, just as well to warn them. Trimmers and firemen having had a comparatively easy time of it through several days of fairly minimal coal consumption would be having to put their backs into it again. Poor sods. Except it was the life they'd chosen – presumably . . . At the chart, Andy laid the parallel ruler from the three-day-old DR to clear Bloody Foreland – northwest corner of Ireland, which one had heard from gossip in the Liberty Inn canteen in Montevideo was an area much frequented now by U-boats – and the course to clear it by, say, twenty miles. He ran the ruler to the compass rose, and lo and behold – 080 degrees. He went back and told the Old Man.

'Second – revs for ten knots.'

Waiting. Wanting to have a bit more way on her before putting the wheel over, bringing her stern around. Voice-pipe whistle: Fisher answered it and McAlan confirmed the increase. But although the engine would be providing that number of revs per minute, propeller 'slip' meant she'd still take a few minutes to reach the desired speed through the water. Old Man still waiting, therefore, although you could feel the increased vibration.

'Gorst – ask Mr Hibbert please to come up.'

'Aye, sir . . .'

'All right, Edmonds. No more than ten degrees of rudder, bring her to starboard to oh-eight-oh.'

Nursing her round. *PollyAnna* rolling heavily, her deep-sunk forepart wallowing in the swell. She was answering all right. At this stage, broadside-on to it, shipping it more or less continually – forepart submerged, swells simply rolling over. One had foreseen this as a hazardous manoeuvre and of course it was: if she shipped enough ocean at any one time, a weight of it six or ten feet deep over the full length of the well-deck from bridge structure to foc's'l-head – weighing her down even further while the screw's thrust drove her already down-angled bow into the troughs and the rising slopes beyond them . . .

Cut revs until she's round?

He didn't suggest it. Third mates kept their mouths shut and their misjudgements to themselves. *Was* a misjudgement too: she needed that much engine-power to *get* her round.

'Chief engineer's on his way, sir.' Gorst: of whom no one took the least bit of notice.

PollyAnna leaning her shoulder into the depths of a trough: *would* drag herself up out of it, please God – please, *PollyAnna* . . .

Was doing so – laboriously enough. Into corkscrewing again, swells racing in on her quarter, lifting her stern, forepart slumping while listing hard enough to send you staggering if you'd not been holding on. With that huge weight in her – in terms of which at an earlier stage he'd guessed that if the hold filled she *wouldn't* float. The swells were driving in from directly astern now: angle of approach would be just a few degrees on her quarter when she was on her new course.

Course for *home*. Although distant, and the odds fairly heavily against her getting there. Doing her damn best, was all . . .

'Hibbert here – sir.'

Huge figure detaching itself cautiously from the ladder. Old Man telling him, 'Hang on, Chief,' while leaning across to check where her head was at this moment, Edmonds putting reverse rudder on to meet and check the turn as her bow rose slowly, well-deck's scuppers near as dammit level with the frothing surface. Edmonds intoning, 'Course oh-eight-oh, sir.'

'How's she feel?'

'Awkward, sir.'

'Think flooding the after deep-tank'd help?'

'Reckon it might, an' all.'

'So we'll risk it, Chief. Not shipping all that much for'ard now, are we.' He had his glasses focused on her bow, was seeing more of it than Hibbert could, Hibbert therefore not commenting, only waiting for his old friend to make his bloody mind up: aware of the dangers but also that the only way to be sure it was the right thing to do was to do it and see what happened. A mound of ocean ran in under her counter, lifting her and powering on, *PollyAnna* riding the tail-end of it like a goose landing clumsily in heavy surf, forepart risen at first but then – as it finished with her and ran on – falling, *sagging*, even the foc'sl-head awash. It was the broken sea you saw, the whiteness as it engulfed her and closed over, seemingly held her down while you wondered, *Coming up out of that, or going on down?* Hearing close to his ear Fisher's involuntary, '*Christ* . . .' and the Old Man's bellowed repetition of, 'Not all that much, are we . . .' and then Hibbert's contribution, the engineer finally expressing *his* view, 'I'd say she'd go easier with that deep-tank flooded, Josh.' By 'go easier', Andy interpreted to himself, meaning something more like *be less likely to founder than she looks to be right now . . .*

He told them in the saloon, 'We're flooding the after deep-tank.' Amplifying that to Julia then: 'Get the stern down deeper, level her a bit. Because' – restraining himself from resting his palms on her shoulders for a moment as he passed behind her chair – 'we have wind and a biggish swell astern, are now – believe it or not – on course for home.'

'Sure of that?'

'Hah.' Moving on past her and Finney to pull back a vacant chair. 'Good question.' A wink at Finney. 'Smart cookie, eh?'

'Say *that* again.'

'Should have said heading *more or less* homeward. Course to be adjusted when we get a sight of the sun or stars. Must get a clear patch some time.' Nodding to the assistant steward: 'Morning, Watkins. Porridge, please. Sleep well, Julia?'

'Oh, yes.' Crunching toast. 'In my stateroom – did indeed. *Very* well. How about you?'

'Had a couple of hours. Get a couple more during the forenoon, touch wood. Had to be up top early in case of stars.'

Tommy Shaw – who to his credit hadn't mentioned having been proved partially right in his theory about hull damage – asked him, 'What revs on now?'

'For ten knots.'

'Did you say they *had* flooded the after tank?'

'Probably doing it right now. Your boss went down to see to it just before I left the bridge.'

A shrug: 'Still plenty of movement on her.'

'Flooding that tank won't stop it, either.'

Julia asked, 'Are seas still breaking over us, where poor Mr Halloran –'

'No. Flooding over when she digs her snout in – over the whole length of that deck – but not *breaking* over. Swells about ten feet high running up from astern are what's rocking us about.' Feeling the downward lurch then: 'There – like that.'

She asked him later, when they were to all intents and purposes – audially at any rate – on their own, 'Would you say we're out of danger now? I mean, apart from U-boats?'

'Well . . .'

'Whole truth and nothing but, please?'

'Fact is, there still *are* problems – that hold's still flooded, obviously – but we're coping – the Old Man is – and, OK, it's by no means an ideal situation, if she was badly handled, could be quite nasty. As it is, weather's improving, Old Man's got it all in hand, and – long as nothing *else* goes wrong –'

'Such as?'

'Well, nothing, really, just –'

'Andy –'

He took a breath, shook his head. 'If the damage was to spread, for instance. Whatever it is – just rivets loosened, or – see, this is a different motion now, on the face of it less violent – but – not knowing what new stresses might be set up, such as water-pressure in there cracking the bulkhead into number one or three.' Looking into the lively, obviously concerned but seemingly unfrightened eyes: maybe for his benefit determinedly not showing fright, or maybe just her own natural, built-in self-control. Either way, to be admired . . . Telling her, 'You want the whole truth and nothing but – and that's it. More or less enough, I'd have thought.'

'We just keep our fingers crossed.'

'Put it that way, if you like. What I was going to ask *you*, though – d'you live right *in* Newcastle?'

'Just outside. Short bus ride or brisk walk. Why?'

'May I visit you there some time?'

A silence – not of the ship around them, but between them. Flickery light-brown eyes questioning, and lips not moving but for a second or two with that almost imperceptible tremble, as if in search of words – such as yes, no, better not, or something scornful like *what for?* Another second – then quietly, 'I think I'd like that.'

'You *would*?'

'*Think* I would. Forget it until we're on *terra firma* somewhere?'

All-over cloud again meant no meridian altitude, which Andy'd hoped he might have got if it had been really breaking up. The cloud was high and grey instead of low and black, but it still wasn't letting any sun through. He'd had his bread-and-cheese lunch early so as to take advantage of any such clearance and still be on time in relieving the Old Man, consequently was up there at ten minutes to the hour, explaining, 'Had false hopes of a mer. alt., sir.' Looking around – nodding to Helmsman Bakewell – 'Force four, about?'

'Four gusting five. We've revs on for twelve knots. Came up just gone eleven. It's noted in the log.' Glancing skyward again: 'Stars tonight, maybe. All well, below?'

'Much as usual, sir.'

'Miss Carr happy with her quarters?'

'And grateful for having had the loan of yours, sir.'

A grunt: nodding towards the foc'sl-head, the heavy rise and fall, protracted virtual immersion and slow recovery about twice a minute; and even then the fore-deck still awash, foam flying ahead down-wind. Old Man growling over the racket of her jolting, slamming progress, 'Taking these revs well enough. Needs watching, though.'

That 'needs watching' was a give-away, belying the calm

tone. It wasn't news that the flooded forepart needed watching, or conceivable that watching it was going to save her if or when she gave up the struggle, allowed it to drag her down.

There were no stars visible at dusk, no moon either – at this stage the moon was keeping daylight hours – but around 0300 – 29th now – the cloud began to break up and at 0650 in the starboard wing, with Gorst noting down the times for him, he got a planet and two stars, which when he'd worked them out put *PollyAnna* sixty-five miles SSE of the extended dead-reckoning position. The Old Man's instruction to Fisher had been that if Holt got even a half-decent observed position he should reshape the course – to clear Bloody Foreland and Malin Head by a safe margin – and course was therefore altered from 080 to 068 without disturbing him. Position then, at 0700/29th, 51 degrees 12 minutes north, 28 degrees 21 west; distance to cross longitude 20 west, supposed limit of U-boat operations, 330 miles. At 9.8 knots, which was what she'd been making since that last increase, say thirty-four hours, arrival in the U-boat zone therefore tomorrow evening.

Tuesday, 0700/30th – good stars again, and as daylight hardened you could see she was comparatively dry for'ard. Wind and swell had been decreasing during the middle watch, the frightening swooping motion easing significantly, and although when he'd gone down at four the well-deck for'ard had still been intermittently awash, hatch-covers had been mostly clear of it. Now – better still: and the stars for which he'd come up at six-thirty had confirmed that despite her handicap she'd been making-good ten and a half knots.

The Old Man was lingering at the chart, tapping a pencil against tobacco-stained front teeth. He looked better for having had a few hours' rest – and had better feelings, probably, about his ship's chances. Threat still present, obviously: you couldn't expect those bulkheads to hold out for ever, and there wasn't a soul on board who didn't know it, but at least the weather was giving her *some* chance now.

Decision-time, therefore: a nod to his own thoughts, and a clearing of the throat . . . 'We'll make for the Clyde, Holt. Londonderry's nearer, but – Clyde facilities, dry-dock essentially . . . Last night I was thinking Londonderry, but – hundred miles more, is all. They'll tranship the ore – or rail it.' A glance round: 'Get Fisher, will you.'

Leaving the forefront to Gorst, Fisher came back with Andy, and the Old Man told him about making for the Clyde.

'All for it, sir.'

'Three days – if she holds up and the bloody U-boats leave her in peace. See here – I'd guess our convoy'll have held on north of Rockall, then around the Butt into North Minch. If that's the case, U-boats might've been drawn up there too.'

'Leaving the run through to North Passage clear for us.'

A sniff. 'Be nice, wouldn't it. But –' Pencil-tip on their track, 065, a 3-degree alteration resulting from the 0700 star-sights, to where it intersected longitude 20 west. 'Midnight – any time then, might have 'em at us. And two boats is too few – even if we got 'em both safe in the water. Call it fifteen men to a boat, still leaves twenty – say four rafts.' Jerk of the grey head: 'Dry down there now – we'll take a chance it *stays* dry, use hatchboards from number two. Alternate ones, not adjacent – and planks across the gaps before lashing-down again. Or whatever they got. Rafts with rope strops all round for swimmers, and coir between 'em when they're launched. Rafts and boats too – always best to stay in company. All right, Second? Collins and Postlethwaite and however many hands they need – I want it done and the rafts secured on deck before sundown. Two for'ard and two aft – eh?'

Fisher was also to allocate men to boats and rafts. Miss Carr to a boat, of course, with young Finney to look after her. Better have an abandon-ship drill then, all hands to know where to go and what to do.

'Another thing's lifejackets. Eight slabs of cork in a canvas weskit – same as they give us last time, and same applies – jump in from a height, fair chance it'll break your neck. So tell 'em – jump with it under your arm and dog-paddle while you put it on. Got to be jumpers, see, with rafts – rafts over the side, lads jump in and swim to 'em. Which side the rafts go over depending where the damage is.'

'Otherwise lee side.'

A glance at Fisher, shrugging at such a statement of the obvious.

Late in the forenoon Andy met Julia on the railed walkway outside her cabin, starboard side. He'd been checking the state of the flag-locker and its contents and the halyards there, after the spell of bad weather, was on his way down for an early pre-watch snack. Julia was out there in her duffel-coat with its hood up, enjoying the brilliant seascape and some lungfuls of fresh though knife-like air. *PollyAnna* pitching a little, rolling a little: heavy, waterlogged, nothing you could be sure of yet. But the sun was getting through now and again and she'd had her face raised to it.

'Isn't this marvellous, Andy?'

'Think so?'

'Certainly do – after how it's been. I was wondering if I'd ever see that thing again!'

'*Might* never have, too.' Pausing beside her: and *not* putting an arm around her. 'You've been aware of that, I suspect.'

'Well – I'm not a *complete* idiot –'

'Ask me – I know, I said it before – you're a bloody marvel.'

'Mark and I will be in number two boat, we're told.'

'*If* the worst came to the worst –'

'Where'll you be?'

'On a raft, for sure. Won't come to that, though. Heck, only three days to go –'

'I'm not worrying unduly. We've had this conversation

262

before, haven't we – more or less. It's kind of you to worry *for* me, but –'

'Kind?' He moved the edge of the hood aside by a few inches so he could look in there and see her better. 'It's not just *kindness*!'

A frown: small shake of the shrouded head. 'Mark is quite a sensitive soul, Andy.'

'But you're just – close friends – companions –'

'We've been through a bit together. As you know. And as I say, he's – well, he *may* think it's something more than that.' Brown eyes quiet, serious. 'I'm very fond of him – and *he's* been marvellous; I can tell you there were times I couldn't have done without him. What I'm saying is I certainly wouldn't want him hurt.'

PollyAnna crossed 20 degrees west longitude that evening. Sunset had been at eight minutes past five and he'd had another good set of stars. The rafts had been completed and lashed down on the hatch-covers of numbers three and four holds, two on each, and Fisher had presided over lifeboat drill in mid-afternoon. Julia had taken part, mustering with Finney and others abreast their boat; Andy had been on watch, but was told by Fisher that if/when it was for real he was to take charge of the two rafts for'ard, getting them over the side and the men down on to them.

Wednesday, now. The Old Man recorded in the log when Andy took over from him at midday: *Jan 31 noon position 54 05' N., 15 30' W. Sea moderate, wind W. force 3, vis. poor.* Except for the restricted visibility, conditions would be favourable for U-boats, too; and *PollyAnna* was now entering water more likely to have U-boats in it than those she'd been in for the past eighteen hours. Lookouts had been doubled and the two boats turned out – davits turned out, boats still bowsed in against the griping spars, but even that would save a few minutes in the process of lowering them, minutes having importance in terms of lives and deaths, getting away or not getting away. Julia understood it all, and on the day after the drill – first day of February, days and nights tending to run together now – when the skipper invited her to visit the bridge at midday and questioned her on the subject, she'd impressed him, apparently. He'd shown her the chart as well, with the new noon position marked on it by that time; Andy meanwhile in the wheelhouse, quartermaster Parlance altering course to due east, Malin Head at that stage bearing about 115 degrees, distance fifty-five miles and Bloody Foreland only thirty miles away, but in this damp haze not a shadow of land visible, not even through Fisher's telescope from monkey island. Skipper telling Julia as they came back from the chart, 'Five hours to dusk now, see. Be off Malin Head by then – in what they're calling the War Channel – kept clear of mines by sweepers out of Londonderry. It's U-boats been laying mines – them and aircraft too, so they tell us.'

Parlance growling, 'Course oh-nine-oh'; Andy grunting acknowledgement, glasses up to probe the haze – which was thickening, might by evening qualify as fog – in which U-boats wouldn't be able to see much either. The skipper had pointed this out to Julia, adding, 'No reason any of 'em'd be sitting off Malin Head waiting for us, mind. *Or* between there and the Mull. You've only to keep your fingers crossed one more night and day, Miss Carr.'

She said afterwards – at supper, after Andy's taking of evening stars – 'He's a nice man, isn't he? *Does* look tired, though.'

'Keeping regular watches *and* tabs on everything else between whiles. No chicken, either.'

'How old is he?'

'Pushing sixty. Fifty-nine, I think.'

'And how old did you say your father is?'

'He's – forty-six.'

'Just a nipper. Second in command of a cruiser, you said?'

'Of an AMC. Armed merchant cruiser. Like the *Kilindini* in our convoy. He's RNR – a commander.'

'You sound proud of him.'

'Do I . . . Well, dare say I am. He's a great guy. Only

thing gets between us is he'd like me to have switched to RNR like him.'

'You won't though – will you?'

'No.' Smiling at her: liking that assumption. 'No, I won't.'

Off Malin Head at sunset they altered to starboard to 100 degrees, and when Andy took over at midnight were approaching Rathlin Island. The supposedly mine-free War Channel here wasn't much more than a mile wide, and the haze *had* thickened into fog; anything you sighted would be close enough to spit at. The natural and proper thing, conforming to Rule of the Road, was to stick to the channel's southern edge, the Rathlin side; stay as close to it as one could be without risk of straying into unswept water. Any westbound traffic should similarly be holding to starboard, the channel's northern side.

Might not, though. Not having been warned by the routeing officer of any rogue straggler coming this way, might be tempted to cut the corner.

'Finney?'

'Yessir.' He'd just come back in from the starboard wing. The Old Man – who understandably had stayed up and still had the ship, although Andy had been ready to take over from him half an hour ago – asking him whether he knew which switches controlled the navigation and steaming lights; Finney confirming that he did, and Andy appreciating that the Old Man had in mind lighting the ship up if necessary, in any sudden close confrontation with another ship or ships.

Not having taken over the watch, he – Andy – had put himself in the wheelhouse's starboard fore corner, with that window lowered – for the sake of visibility, not wanting misted glass in the way as well as fog, but also to listen out for the fog gun at Altacarry on Rathlin Island. The thick glass window dropped like those on the doors of railway carriages, on a leather strap: turned the wheelhouse into an ice-house, but –

There – the signal gun's double crack. And welcome. You knew where you were, within, say, 1,000 yards, but when some feature failed to come up when it should have done, in this case a double *boom* as from a cannon somewhere out there to starboard – where there was no horizon, no difference at all between sea and moonless sky – moon having set at about ten-forty – well, you felt a need of that confirmation, a touch of anxiety until you got it. He was moving to the door out into the wing, to get some notion of Altacarry's bearing next time it went off, when Finney burst in from the other side, howling, 'Small vessel three and a half points to port, sir!'

The Old Man had lurched out – sending Finney staggering – and Andy was back at his open window, putting glasses up. Wouldn't have needed them, though – dark shape steering to pass extremely close: small, stubby, single funnel, high foc's'l that would have a gun on it. Armed trawler. Couldn't have seen *PollyAnna*, extraordinarily enough: other things having their attention, no doubt. Fair turn of speed, though: if it had been 40 degrees on the bow when Finney had reported it, and already coming up abeam – passing – then out of sight from here, although the skipper in the wing might still have his glasses on it . . .

Now a much larger shape out there, though – Andy reporting it while wiping his glasses' front lenses and putting them up again – this new one finer on the bow and well clear, closer to mid-channel. Tall funnel, and a wide gap between it and the bridge/accommodation island. Steamer about the size of this one. One of the old Clan ships, could be. Biggish, but he wouldn't have picked her up without the glasses at that distance in the fog-thickened dark.

Looking for others ahead now – if this was a convoy you were running into . . .

Nothing anywhere close ahead at this moment. That one – Clan McWhatsit – had been about two points on the bow. Broader now, of course: two and a half maybe . . . Swinging back and sweeping to starboard – not that you'd expect to find anything outside the channel, in water that couldn't be guaranteed clear of mines; but if *PollyAnna* wasn't as near the channel's edge as he'd reckoned – which might account for how close that trawler had been –

Christ!

Low, small – *very* small – and as distinctive as— He'd jumped past Ingram to the port wing doorway, yelled, 'U-boat fine on the bow to starboard!' Back out of the way of the Old Man, charging in and slamming *that* window down, glasses up in his other hand . . .

'Starboard wheel and ram, sir?'

Aware then that he might be hanged for making that suggestion: but ahead, fine to port, the night flared up in yellow flame, a vertical leap of it that first died down then grew again, expanding laterally – and a second later the thud of the explosion – torpedo hit, but interior explosion right after it. At least, how it had seemed . . . Glasses back on the U-boat by then: still there, surfaced, in profile or semi-profile, still ignorant of *PollyAnna*'s existence, watching the approach of *west*bound ships, and now in the light of that burning freighter – cargoliner, stopped and burning – and the U-boat with a white feather lengthening at its stem, on the move from right to left . . .

'Steer to ram the bastard, lad.' Captain to helmsman, in a surprisingly calm tone of voice, one hand on Ingram's shoulder and the other pointing in case he hadn't seen it – which he *had* – captain now ringing down for full ahead and repeating it – *double* full ahead . . . By the flames' light you didn't need glasses – Ingram didn't – putting on rudder but not a lot of it – not needing much, even with the handicap of the heavy forepart, had only to bring her round by about 10 degrees – and the submarine well illuminated, Andy's own concept being of maybe two or three Huns in that conning-tower, maybe part-blinded by the firework display as well as looking for a new target and no reason to expect intervention from *this* direction. Bloody fool Huns, if so . . . But thinking also – the thought having struck initially within a second of rashly blurting out that suggestion – which he knew damn well would *not* be what had galvanised the Old Man into doing this, *risking* this – *PollyAnna* by no means needing any new damage for'ard . . . *Happening*, though, committed to it, Ingram grunting with the effort of reversing helm to check the swing that had taken a while to start and would now take some stopping. It would have been at about this stage they saw her coming – by the flames' light and almost but not quite bow-on, aiming-off by a few degrees, and to the Huns close enough to be like something out of a nightmare, their only hope being to crash-dive, get their craft down under her fore-foot's reach probably faster than they'd ever dived before. Like a whale spouting, only from several vents, spray pluming, glittering in the rush of high-pressure air from ballast tanks, sound like ripping canvas. You were *that* close. Old Man bellowing to Ingram, 'As she goes, lad, hold her as she goes!' The U-boat's forward way noticeably reduced in the act of diving, but its forepart already dipping under, conning-tower and periscope standards aslant and most of the hull submerged when *PollyAnna*'s deep-sunk forefoot struck, carved into it, heavy jolting impact jarring through her and the clang of the telegraph ordering 'stop'. Having done the job – beyond doubt destroyed that *thing* – but not wanting to tear one's own bow off if that could be avoided – which most likely it could not. Hun done for, for sure, but *PollyAnna* too? Hun going first, was all – filling and dragging clear, down into – what, not much more than fifty fathoms here?

'Finney – carpenter to sound bilges, tell Mr Fisher all hands stand by boats and rafts. Then stay with Miss Carr, send Janner up here.'

'Aye, sir!'

On his way. And that steamer on *her* way, sea dowsing the fires in her as she settled by the stern, raked bow lifting. There were boats in the water, a roar of escaping steam, and punctuating that the bark of the Altacarry fog gun. Old Man bawling to him, 'Get out the Aldis, Holt, look for swimmers. No – have the wing lookout do that. You go down, see that they know they're mustering, not abandoning. May get away with it – else she'd be on her way by now. Tell Fisher see Postlethwaite gets a wriggle on – and Dewar, I want *him* –'

'Postlethwaite's got no sounding-rod, sir.'

'Damn it, so he hasn't. Well – tell Fisher if there's Hun swimmers, embark 'em for'ard, toss 'em a line and haul 'em in; don't want boats launched unless we're going down. Then see the chief, tell him if there's water in the peak or deep-tank – or number one – get his pump on it, but if she's dry we'll be underway soon as I know it.'

'Aye aye, sir. But' – pointing – 'armed trawler, sir –'

Where the boats were. Trawler nosing in towards the boats with a searchlight, or maybe it was an Aldis poking around, its beam ultra-brilliant in the fog. Looking for swimmers, obviously. German survivors, if any, *PollyAnna* would look after. More than they deserved – who did *they* ever look after? The flames were dying – had died – and the fog had the upper hand again: you could barely make out detail even with glasses, except what the trawler's light lit up; but the main feature was the cargo-liner vertical in the water, huge-looking, heart-stopping in her isolation – that was the last he'd seen, was rattling down the central ladder and the two below it, out on to the fore-deck, looking for Fisher and wondering whether that trawler was the one that had passed them earlier, or another. The whole business having taken only about twelve minutes, and here was *PollyAnna* lying stopped – surprisingly, as of this moment still afloat – and the trawler and the torpedoed ship's boats 1,000 or 1,500 yards away, fog wreathing the surface between here and there in whorls and drifts, and again, distantly, the double-barrelled blast from Altacarry.

17

From the vicinity of Rathlin, where they'd hauled three half-drowned U-boat men out of the water, the run to clear Kintyre by a safe margin was thirty miles on ESE, with visibility no better but a fog signal bleating from the Mull, and, after covering about half the distance, the company of an armed trawler which came up from astern showing its steaming lights and took station on the beam to port. A signal, one of many, had informed the Old Man that this escort would be joining them – either out of Londonderry, or one they'd encountered westbound off Rathlin Island; that apparently blind one, maybe, and there was no relaxation of the lookout. Andy's watch ended at about this time, but as navigator and in close proximity to land he'd stayed on the bridge; in fact had manned the Aldis when the trawler had called them up and flashed: '*See the conquering hero comes*', replying to it with the Old Man's rather lame: '*Glad to have your company.*'

There'd been a whole succession of wireless signals, after the *Anna* had woken them all up with a report to Clyde Naval Control. That she was still afloat and getting home under her own power would have been welcome news, but on top of that to have sunk a U-boat – they might have wondered whether they were having their legs pulled. Congratulatory signals were still coming in: from Naval Control, and Admiralty, and most recently from the owners, informing the Old Man that the chairman, Sir Alec

Dundas, would be on the dockside to greet him. Dry dock in Port Glasgow, this would be, but there was a stop before that; in greying light – no fog now, but sleet showers and low cloud – a rendezvous off Brodick on Arran, where they were met by another trawler and a tug, a Clyde pilot on the tug and in the trawler a party of Royal Marines to take charge of the prisoners – the U-boat's captain, a junior lieutenant and some kind of petty officer. They'd been accommodated in the bosun's cordage store in the foc's'l-head, and had looked somewhat resentful as well as the worse for wear, but they'd been (a) pumped out, and (b) given tea, biscuits and blankets; really had very little to complain about. Off Arran they were induced to transfer to the trawler, which sped off with them, and the *Anna* had got underway again with the pilot conning her and the tug in company. The armed trawler, her job done, had turned back south.

North by east then, four miles up-Firth to enter the narrows between Garroch Head and Little Cumbrae; Great Cumbrae then, and Rothesay off to port. Lazy man's sailoring, with the pilot doing all the work – and very welcome, being tired and hungry, having had no sleep except for a doze last evening before midnight, and no breakfast yet, but still reluctant to go below even for ten minutes, miss any of this homecoming: Skelmorlie there, for instance, and Wemyss Point, Ardgowan; then the Cloch – where the boom gate was standing open for them and the Old Man remarked to Chief Hibbert as the pilot guided them through a crowd of ships at anchor in the Tail of the Bank – ships mainly in ballast, no doubt awaiting convoy westward – 'Must be scared if they held us up a minute we'd bloody sink,' and Hibbert shrugging: 'Still might, at that'; adding, 'Red carpet treatment, though, is what it is. You're a hero all over again, Josh. Knighthood this time, shouldn't wonder.' Suppressed mirth from Ingram, who was on the wheel: and to starboard, Gourock coming up, Andy using Fisher's telescope to spot the Bay Hotel – where by golly there'd been high jinks from time to time. Between Gourock and Kilcreggan now: and as the woods on Roseneath Point slid away out of the line of sight – there was Helensburgh. Home – the house itself not visible, but where by the end of what was certain to be an exhausting day he was counting on ending up in a soft bed between clean sheets – well fed, at that – and come to think of it, when the time came you wouldn't want to turn in all that soon, even if you *were* half dead on your feet.

Here and now, anyway – back to the other side, the starboard bridge-wing, for a better view of the southern bank through more driving sleet. This was Kempock Point to starboard, and Greenock with its pier coming next: you were out of the Firth, in the river itself now, with Port Glasgow up ahead.

Hibbert hadn't been far wrong about red carpet treatment. There was quite a bit of a crowd cheering and clapping the old *Anna* as she slid her half-sunk forepart into the dock, the tug with a line on her stern to middle her until wire ropes were out and secured both sides, stern line then cast off so the dock gate could be shut and pumps started to drain the dock down, eventually settle her on the blocks. Andy was on the stern end of all that – since the Old Man hadn't needed him on the bridge, and Fisher as acting mate had to be up for'ard – while a brow with handrails was being lowered into position by a crane, and the chairman of Dundas Gore, Sir Alec Dundas, was the first to cross it, along with his marine superintendent – Captain Straughan – and a middle-aged civilian by name of Colley, Blood Line's office manager, and two younger men, clerks, whom an hour or so later – an hour of fairly thorough-going chaos – this Colley person would leave to do the rest of the donkey-work after he, Colley, had been ordered by Sir Alec to visit Mrs Halloran, impart to her the sad news of her husband's death – which Messrs Dundas Gore hadn't known about until now – and convey to her his own and his fellow directors' deepest sympathy. Colley, of course, had no option but to comply, but asked to be accompanied by someone – a deck officer, presumably – who'd actually *known* Halloran.

Which of course came down to Andy: on the Old Man's orders, relayed to him by Fisher.

Colley, at the wheel of his Morris Twelve, trundling westward along the river through continuing rain and sleet, was a red-faced man of about fifty: dark blue suit, macintosh and bowler hat. He and Andy had loaded the former mate's gear, suitcases and his sextant, into the back of the car, were taking it as well as the chairman's condolences to Leila at 11 Merriwell Way, Greenock.

'What sort of fellow was he, then?'

'Oh. A good first mate. The men liked him. Stood no nonsense, but – fair, you know.'

'Pierhead jump, wasn't it, the way he joined us. Replacement for Harve Brown when he got took ill. Consequence of which we don't know much about him – except he was on tankers, then did a stint with Grants. Know anything about the wife, do you – the widow, I should say?'

Andy shook his head. Windscreen wipers squeaking monotonously and the car jolting in and out of potholes. He said, 'Only that she's pretty and quite a bit younger than him. He had a portrait of her in his cabin.'

'Hm.' Frowning at the downpour. 'Not a nice task, this. I can see Sir Alec really had no option but to send me, but – well, I'm glad to have you along, seeing as you knew him.'

'As well as anyone did, I suppose. Can't say we were close friends, exactly – first mate and third, after all. But we went ashore together once or twice.'

Once. 'Once or twice' sounded better, somehow.

Even without having been detailed for this by the Old Man, he'd have volunteered. After the months of sneaky glances at Leila's portrait, and envy of Halloran – who'd sensed it and seemed perversely to have taken pleasure in it. But to show willing in any case – feeling that at least one of the man's brother officers should pay respects, offer sympathy. Fisher hadn't been volunteering – in fact had given Andy a funny look when he'd accepted the instruction so readily. While the Old Man certainly couldn't have taken it on, even if he'd had any such inclination; he'd had his hands more than full enough already, entertaining the chairman – who, incidentally, had offered to take Julia in his Daimler to the Central Hotel, where her mother, who was on her way from Newcastle, had said she'd meet her – and coping with the Marine Super, answering or maybe stone-walling fussy questions about the flooded hold – as well as the routine arrival tasks such as Customs entry, cargo documents, health regulations and – most time-consuming of all – paying off the hands. A lot of it would be dealt with by Fisher and Colley's clerks, but that still left plenty needing the master's personal attention. On top of which there was a trio of shore-based naval officers taking up his time, or waiting to do so, primarily on the subject of the U-boat, but also the *Glauchau* business; there was to be a press release covering all of that, even a photographer standing by.

The Old Man had had no sleep last night, either. At his age, would be feeling at least as rough as Andy, who had his head back and eyes shut when Colley asked him, 'What's your future now, Holt? Signed off from the *PollyAnna*, have you?'

'Not yet. Old Man being up to his eyes in it at this stage. When we get back I'll try to see him. If they're going to mend her good and quick – well, might take a couple of weeks' leave. Happen to be rather well-off at the moment – had my twenty-first when we were in Brazil, so –'

'They'll waste no time mending her. Ships aren't being left idle these days. I'd guess he'd be glad to have you sign on again. We'll be asking him to stand by her, I'd imagine. Might install Harve Brown, come to that – seeing he knows her inside-out. You live at Helensburgh, that right?' He didn't wait for an answer, instead began to brake – pulling over to the right then. 'Here'll do us, now. I'll ask 'em where Merriwell Way might be.' He'd stopped in front of a newsagent, was out of the car and hurrying across wet pavement, hunched and turning up the collar of his mac. Andy, hungry as well as tired, reflecting that he might have gone along too, found something like a bar of chocolate – depending on what was rationed or available or not in this wartime Scotland in which one was virtually a stranger. But Colley was already on his way back, telling him as he got in, 'Easy enough by the sound of it. Straight ahead then a left and second right. Merriwell Close, Merriwell Walk, *then* Merriwell Way . . . *What* grand weather you've come to, eh?'

'You had it worse a week or two ago, we heard.'

'You're right, we did. Some o' the same lot you was in yourselves, I dare say. And *that* couldn't 've been much fun – eh? But now where the dickens . . .'

'There?'

Number 11 Merriwell Way was one half of a cube of yellow brick. One window downstairs, with flouncy curtains in it, and two on the floor above; in front, a few square yards of mud and weeds bisected by a concrete path. If this had been costing Halloran an arm and a leg, they must have seen him coming. Or seen Leila coming – he'd said proudly that *she'd* found it, Andy remembered. Colley switched off the wiper and then the engine: 'Best make sure she's at home before we haul his stuff out – eh?'

'I'll do that.'

A vision in mind then – unsought, unexpected, maybe prompted by Colley's reference to foul weather – as he approached the blue-painted door. Mind and memory back in that Atlantic storm, its incredible ferocity, the *Anna* three-quarters buried in it, battling to remain afloat, and the doubt in all minds that she'd be able to; whether any of them – including most prominently in his own thoughts, Julia – would be alive by evening or morning, whatever . . . How many days and nights, facing that? And having by some miracle come through it – what, sniffing around Halloran's leavings now?

All right. Motives as stated. But some of which he wouldn't have tried to explain to Julia.

He'd hardly taken his finger off the bell-push when the door jerked open.

Blond girl. Well – woman. Thirty-ish. Not unattractive, in an obvious sort of way, but nothing at all like Leila. Her figure – well, neither the skirt nor the sweater were doing much to hide it. She turned to look behind her, snapping, 'Won't you belt up now, Billy?' Welsh accent: and the scowl changing to a smile as she swung back and looked up at him – he'd edged in slightly, out of the weather, removing his uniform cap. He'd have shifted into civvies before coming ashore but there hadn't been time – Colley wanting to get away, have it done with and get back again . . . The girl asked purringly – as a toddler squeezed up beside her, clinging to her – 'What can I do *you* for, then?'

'Does Mrs Halloran—'

'When she's in the mood, she does, but—'

She'd checked that, the giggle faltering and smile fading as she saw the car and Colley climbing out of it. 'What *is* this, then?'

He'd been about to ask did Mrs Halloran live here – because the blonde might have been a relation of some kind – but that facetious answer had suggested she *was* Mrs Halloran. Although even if she'd dyed her hair . . . Hell, *couldn't* be. She was gazing up at him suspiciously, while the child clung to her leg and slobbered around the dummy in its mouth. He told her, 'My name's Holt – third mate of the SS *PollyAnna*. Are you Mrs Leila Halloran?'

Jerk of the head, tossing back yellow hair. 'Name's Lucy, not Leila. Is Dave in some kind of—'

Checking again, watching Colley struggle with one of the suitcases. 'You and your friend coming to stay, is that it?'

'Bringing your husband's gear, Mrs Halloran. I'm terribly sorry. Excuse me though, just one moment –'

'Sorry for *what*?'

'Give us a minute?'

Jamming his cap on, hurrying to join Colley at the car; taking that heavy case from him and the other from inside,

276

leaving the sextant in its brass-handled box for the older man to bring, muttering to him, 'It's her, but not the one in the portrait, and her name's Lucy, not Leila, says she never heard of Leila, and – see . . .' The child had tottered out into wind and rain, she'd sprung after it and caught it, called as she dragged it back inside, 'You'd best come on in. But' – dumping the child and turning back – 'bringing his gear, you say – where's *he*?'

'This is Mr Colley, office manager of Dundas Gore, the *PollyAnna*'s owners. Mrs Halloran, I'm dreadfully sorry to bring such news – as I said, my name's Holt –'

'Something happened to him?'

'Yes.' A glance at Colley – who was resolutely leaving this to him. Back to the girl . . . 'He drowned, Mrs Halloran. Swept overboard in terrible weather four days ago. We docked this morning in Port Glasgow. Captain Thornhill asked me to tell you how sorry he is, and the same goes for all the rest of us. We were in really huge seas, had one hold flooded – tell you the truth, we were in danger of foundering. Your husband took two men for'ard to check for damage; they had lifelines but for some reason his didn't hold – big sea hit us and – well, he didn't stand a chance, he just – *went*.'

She was still gazing at him. Wide-eyed – still *dry*-eyed – mouth slightly open. Hadn't sunk in yet, he guessed, wasn't real for her yet. Colley put his oar in then: 'As Mr Holt mentioned, Mrs Halloran, I'm with the owners, and our chairman, Sir Alec Dundas –'

She'd stooped to the child. 'Gentlemen come to say you've no daddy now, Billy-boy. Have to find you a new one, won't we . . .' She'd kissed him, straightened now with one hand resting in his curls, refocused on Colley. 'Excuse me – you were saying –'

'My chairman – Sir Alec – asked me to express his sympathy in your tragic loss, Mrs Halloran. He himself was only apprised of it this morning. I must add that – well, turning to practicalities such as money that may be due to him – and now of course to you – you've been receiving a monthly allotment, I know that, but whether there may be any balance due –'

Andy said, 'I'll wait in the car.'

'All right. Mrs Halloran, I'll sort it out in the next day or two, and we'll be writing to you. Meanwhile however . . .'

She'd find the violet-coloured letters when she went through the cases, Andy realised. Would see then why he'd thought her name was Leila: and from the portrait in the leather frame would get to see what Leila looked like. Might even know her? Probably not, though. Probably wouldn't have an address – not if Leila had been consistent with that *You know where* dodge.

What the dodge had been for, perhaps?

Colley came hurrying, wrenched his door open. 'Phew . . .'

He'd been meaning to telephone home before returning to the ship, but Colley didn't want to stop, and on the way back he decided it might anyway be sensible to leave it until he had a better idea of what was happening, one way and another.

The dock had been pumped out, *PollyAnna*'s keel rested on the central blocks with a forest of timber props out on both sides all down her length to hold her upright; engineers and dockyard mateys were moving around under her dripping forepart. It felt like a dizzy height he was looking down from, crossing the swaying brow to the fore-deck, after end of number three. Colley had been right – they certainly weren't wasting any time. On board, Fisher told them she was quite badly holed, that it looked as if she might have struck some underwater object – which was possible: at the height of it all she might have come down on some submerged or semi-submerged – well, God knew *what*, but it could have happened without anyone being aware of it, when things had been at their worst. Damage couldn't be assessed from inside yet; cranes were being brought up to start unloading the ore from all five holds, and floodlighting would allow that to go on all night and round the clock until they'd emptied her.

Fisher asked him, 'How did it go with Mrs Halloran?'

'She took it surprisingly well. But – that sudden, out of the blue – well, by *this* time –'

'Yeah. Sink in later, maybe . . . Like her picture, is she?'

'Surprisingly, not at all. For one thing, she's a blonde.'

'Peroxide, or –'

'Not that girl at all. And there's a child, about two years old.'

'Good God!'

Chief Hibbert and Tom McAlan were still on board, apparently – or in the vicinity, the dock bottom maybe – but most of the officers and crew had left, including the *Cheviot Hills* survivors – Benson, Ah Nong and company – who'd been taken to the station by some individual from A and J Hills' Glasgow agency. Finney had gone with them, en route first to his family in London but then – so he'd told Fisher – to a berth Messrs Hills had for him in some ship sailing from Liverpool in a week or ten days' time. And Julia had gone. Andy had guessed she might have, having seen that the chairman's Daimler was no longer on the quayside. Her absence left him feeling – well, lonely. Actually, sort of cut off at the knees. That she'd have left without a word – message – anything at all. Admittedly he'd left *her*, when he'd dashed off with Colley; simply hadn't envisaged her not being here when they got back. Although she could hardly *not* have gone, he realised, when the great man had been ready to hit the road and she'd already accepted his offer of a lift.

From home, he thought, get her number from directory enquiries. First thing in the morning.

Fisher told him – in the saloon, Andy gulping stale bread and mousetrap cheese which he'd foraged from the pantry, Fisher at the table working through a stack of paperwork that would have been for Halloran to deal with – 'The Old Man went with 'em. Chairman was dropping him off at the St Enoch's Hotel, which now houses Naval

Headquarters, apparently. He'll be back by and by. Expects you to sign on again – what *you* want, isn't it?'

'Except that right away I'd like to take some leave.'

'He knows that. He wants a break, too. So do I. *PollyAnna*'ll be in dock a week or so, any case. Here and now I'd stick around, if I were you . . . By the way, Julia left a farewell note – did you see it? In your cabin?'

He pushed his chair back. 'No –'

'Must be there somewhere. Unless she changed her mind or they didn't give her time. She *said* she was going to –'

'I'll be back to finish this.'

His cabin looked as if a bomb had gone off in it. He'd been sorting gear ready for packing, and it was scattered around in heaps. He'd looked in here briefly on his way to the saloon, hadn't seen any note: wouldn't have, without specifically searching for one . . . But there it was – brown envelope with ANDY pencilled on it, and inside that – ripping it open – a half-sheet of paper with what looked like a telephone number at the top and below it:

Andy dear. Have to run without saying goodbye. Going to the Central Hotel, where my mother's arriving soon or may have already. I don't know if we'll be staying the night or going straight back to Newcastle – it probably depends on trains – but anyway here's our home telephone number, and if you still want to pay us a visit, just ring and say you're coming.

I very much hope you will. Meanwhile, thank you for everything – you really have been an absolute darling. Even if you find you can't make it this time, some time please do get in touch?

All my love – J.

He'd muttered aloud, 'Oh, crikey. Oh, *Julia* . . .' And read it through again before going back to finish his bread and cheese.

POSTSCRIPT

I would like to thank Captain Iain Irving FNI, a former Merchant Navy shipmaster of wide seagoing experience, for his kindness in having read the script of this story and put me right on several points of detail.

The wartime Merchant Navy, it seems to me, has not had anything like its fair share of literary attention, especially considering the huge importance of its role and the extent of losses in ships and men. Figures for loss of life in the services, for instance, have been estimated as Army 6%, RAF 9%, RN 9.3%, Merchant Navy 17%. On that basis it might be said that the seas were a lot more cruel to those 'non-combatants' than they were to the rest of us.

A.F.